# A CRUCIBLE WITCH

*Spellcasters Spy Academy, Crucible Year*

## A MAGIC OF ARCANA UNIVERSE SERIES

## ASHLEY MCLEO

Meraki Press

# BEST READING ORDER FOR THE SPELLCASTERS SPY ACADEMY SERIES:

A Legacy Witch, Culling-year

A Marked Witch, Internship (Eva's POV)

A Rebel Witch, Grind-year

A Crucible Witch, Crucible-year

*I* stirred the cauldron with bated breath, waiting for the moment that Morgan assured me was coming.

"Any second now," my ancestor repeated, her twinkling eyes glued on the potion. The scent of bitter nettles and mushrooms wafted off the boiling liquid, herbaceous and earthy.

"Three, two, . . . Stir a little slower, Odette. You're going too fast." Diana paused, her lips parting in rapt anticipation.

Behind her, I caught a flash of motion, and dragged my gaze from the brew. Hunter had snuck back inside and was poking his head into the room. He caught my gaze, and with a trickster wink, pointed at Diana's back and pressed his finger to his lips.

I smothered a laugh. It was official, a week in such close quarters was too long. Hunter never would have dared to screw with Diana back home—in the future—where we lived in an expansive magical academy most of the year. But after three days of monsoon-like rains and being stuck inside a tiny cottage, it appeared that Hunter couldn't help but cause a bit of mischief.

"Almoooost," Diana cooed, her blue eyes locked on the bubbling, yellow liquid. "It's going to change n—"

"Now!" Hunter leapt into the room at the exact instant that the potion turned neon green.

Diana let out a strangled screech, and purple magic shot from her fingers as she whipped around.

"Dammit, Wardwell!" She batted at his shoulder as if he was a gross spider, which only made Hunter laugh harder. "I nearly jinxed you!"

"You should have," he replied, wiggling his fingers at her and shaking his hips in a way that made me snort out a laugh. "I need to practice my counter-jinxes."

"That can be arranged." A man with a long, brown beard shot through with white strode into the kitchen, his arms full of herbs.

A beaming Eva trailed behind him, her copper hair damp and arms laden with bits and pieces of artifacts she'd picked up. The relics were from a nearby Roman site that she'd been begging Merlin to show her since he'd mentioned it two days ago. The girl looked like she'd won the lottery.

"It's been far too long since I jinxed anyone." Merlin twisted to face Hunter. "Morgan can practice too. She always came up with the best, most original jinxes. She's so clever."

"I have a few untested ones." Morgan's cheeks had pinked at her paramour's flattery, making the freckles that smattered the bridge of her nose stand out more. Usually, she appeared goddess-like and wise, but in that moment she was just a girl enjoying the praise of her loved one.

Hunter paled, and I wrapped my arms around my stomach and dissolved into full blown laughter.

"Not what you meant, my boy?" Alex's ancestor arched a bushy eyebrow.

"He can't handle you or Morgan," Eva teased.

For once, her beau didn't provide a snappy rebuttal.

Merlin's bright blue eyes ran up and down Hunter. "Not now, but perhaps one day he will be able to."

I stopped laughing and straightened to stand. Eva and Hunter blinked, stunned. The compliment was huge—even if it was a 'perhaps'. We were talking about *the* Merlin and *the* Morgan Le Fay, two of the most legendary witches in history. The witches who would eventually seal the Hell-gate that I had unwittingly split wide open.

The room stilled for a second, before Morgan broke the quiet, scooping a ladle of potion into a mug. "What do you lot say we get this to Alex? After that, we'll start lessons. The day is clearing up, and we should use the light while we have it."

"I'll take it to him." I held out my hand, and Morgan passed me the cup.

As I left the room, conversation began to flow again, and

my lips quirked up. No matter what happened, how shocked or out of place we were in this era, M&M's cottage never stayed quiet for long.

I stepped outside and covered my head with my arm only to find that the springtime drizzle I'd expected had ceased. Morgan had called it.

A smile bloomed on my face as I approached the small outbuilding, excited to see my man for a moment. The main cottage was where we hung out and ate our meals with M&M. Like most homes of its time, the dwelling was basically one room with a small section partitioned for sleeping. The older witches stayed in the cottage while the rest of us shared the shack that the legends had built after Merlin experienced a vision of us arriving.

Our quarters were about the size of a large backyard shed. A tight fit, but preferable to squeezing all seven of us in the cottage. And since it was too dangerous for us to rent rooms in the nearby village, we made it work.

I knocked on the door. "Alex? Are you awake?"

"Yeah." His tone was lower than usual.

I repressed a sigh. He'd been grumpy since we arrived in the past, and understandably so. He was stuck in a room that reeked of hay and too many bodies packed in tight. All I could do was try to be a bright spot in his day.

"Hey." I pressed the door open. Alex was still reclined in our bed of hay, a blanket draped over him, and a candle lighting the dark room. "What are you reading?"

"A healing text." He grinned, one of the first smiles I'd

seen from him since he'd woken up four days ago. "I'm learning all about the humors and bloodletting."

"How interesting. Perhaps for your next birthday, you'll get a bag of leeches."

"That's love." He gestured to the cup in my hand. "Is that for me?"

"Yup. Morgan has been doing a lot of research on non-spirit walkers moving through the ghost realm. This will help to ground you in our world faster." I handed over the cup of liquid.

Understandably, Alex hated feeling as if he'd float away at any second. But according to M&M, traveling through the ghost realm often made people who weren't spirit walkers feel weightless, ill, and lethargic. Especially those who were totally unprepared. Which Alex had been when a demon-possessed ghost kidnapped him from Spellcasters and transported him through the spirit world so that he could arrive in London in mere minutes.

Add in timewalking through centuries shortly after traveling through the ghost realm and Alex was a total mess.

For now, the poor guy was allowed only one walk per day for exercise. During that walk, we had to watch after him and keep him grounded—literally. He couldn't even relieve himself unaccompanied; perhaps selfishly, I was thankful that task fell to Hunter. Until the sensation that he'd float away at any moment disappeared, Alex was stuck here.

"Bottoms up." He chugged the potion, then wrinkled

his nose as he handed the empty mug back to me. "That was awful."

"You don't want to know what we put in it," I admitted.

"If dragon piss will make me better faster, I'd drink it all day." He glanced at the healing books Merlin had given him. "I'm trying to remain upbeat, but I'm missing out on so much. Especially now that your lessons are starting."

My heart broke for him. Being bedbound when there were two legendary witches around to learn from was torture for Alex. It didn't help that we'd barely had any time alone in a week.

My hand slid over his. "I know, babe. But if anyone knows how to make a potion that will help, it's Morgan. I'm sure you'll be up and running in no time." I bent down and kissed him. "In the meantime, I'll tell you about everything I learn. That way, you have something meaty to chew on."

"I can't wait to hear all about it," Alex replied with a smile that almost hid the sourness in his tone.

The door to the main cottage slammed shut, and voices grew louder as everyone stomped outside.

"Odie!" Eva called out. "We gotta go!"

"Guess that's my cue."

I felt terrible leaving him after such a brief visit, but I was also undeniably excited to get started. Although it had only been a week of resting and allowing our magic to acclimate after timewalking had screwed us all up, it had felt like a year. Not to mention, Morgan had something important she wanted to discuss with Eva and me. We'd been on pins and needles for days, wondering what it might be.

Alex tried to sit up to kiss me. I laid my hand on his chest and forced him to lie down again before pressing my lips to his.

"Get some rest, babe."

A sigh dripping with resignation left him. "Have fun." He reached for his book and cracked it open again.

Trying not to take his mood personally, I kissed him on the forehead and left to join the others.

# CHAPTER TWO

My feet ached in the small boots Morgan had lent me for tromping through the muddy woods. "How much farther?" I asked, hoping it wouldn't be long, and I'd be able to take the damn things off.

"A moment more," Morgan sang back, her long, red braid swaying from side to side like a snake.

"She said that ten minutes ago," Eva muttered.

"Right?"

"You kids are consumed by how quickly things happen," Morgan replied without looking back. "Is this what everyone in your time is like? It's a very unappealing trait."

I pressed my lips together and stayed silent. If it were anyone else, I'd have retorted that they didn't understand how painful walking in ill-fitting shoes could be, but that wouldn't fly with Morgan. She would just suggest I take them off and walk barefoot. Like her.

My ancestor was an all-natural goddess who rarely wore shoes, and *never* in the woods around her home. Pine needles, stones, and sharp twigs didn't deter her from trekking miles barefoot. Or even climbing trees with her little monkey feet.

My modern, shoe-conditioned feet couldn't handle such things, but the tennis shoes I'd worn when I traveled into the past were soaked from our earlier adventure—searching the nearby swamp for potion ingredients. They'd take days to dry.

"Here we are!" Morgan called out, jostling me from a daydream involving dry, warm, well-fitted shoes and the fluffiest socks imaginable. "Hurry, loves!"

When we caught up, we found ourselves in a clearing that looked like the others we'd passed on the way, with one notable exception.

Gray stones, still damp from the last rain, formed a circle within the clearing. At hip height, they weren't even close to the size of the huge monoliths of Stonehenge, but they gave off that important, ancient vibe all the same. I was sure they'd be incredibly heavy. It must have required a great deal of effort to get them here—the middle of nowhere.

"What is all this?" Eva asked. "Is it fae in origin?"

Morgan twirled her hand in the air dismissively. "Why would I bother you with fae nonsense? No, girls, this is something bigger. Much more special—and necessary, if I'm to test you."

A shiver of anticipation sprinted down my spine. "What are you testing us for exactly?"

"Now that your magic has settled after timewalking, I think it prudent to examine your demon-touched marks. However, we need to be in a safe place to do so—a godswood."

Goosebumps pebbled my skin as I looked around, seeing the verdant, dewy clearing ringed with stones with fresh eyes.

*A godswood.*

There used to be many godswoods. Although, in the era I hoped to return to, few remained. The old gods who ruled over magicals and humans alike had been long forgotten— at least by the humans.

And perhaps for an excellent reason. The legends rarely painted them in a good light. They were largely cruel, and demanded *all* humans and magicals worshipped them.

"A godswood," Eva murmured. "A place where the old gods used to congregate?"

"Precisely." Morgan looked pleased that Eva understood the significance of this place. "But godswoods weren't only meeting places for the gods. They were sanctuaries too."

"Sanctuaries?" I asked. "What could a god need sanctuary from? Weren't they made of pure aether and nearly indestructible?"

"And yet, they've disappeared from our lives." Morgan arched her eyebrows. "Everyone requires a safe place. Had the gods used theirs more effectively, they might still be with us. Never underestimate the power or necessity of a sanctuary." She waved us inside the circle.

I joined her, and a surprising wave of pleasant warmth rolled through me. My shoulders loosened. It felt like I'd just received a massage, I was so relaxed. Not at all the reaction that I'd been expecting considering that I was demon-touched, but perhaps that was a good thing. Maybe it meant that the light in me greatly out-weighed the dark.

"So what did they do here?" Eva asked, walking around the outskirts of the circle, occasionally placing her hand on one of the stones. She didn't seem negatively affected either.

"They hid from the royals of Hell—their greatest adversaries. Their own kind, turned dark." Morgan made a gesture to encompass the circle. "But within the stones, demons, even the royals, cannot pass."

"Interesting . . ." Eva said. "So why are *we* here?"

Morgan stayed quiet for a second longer than normal, and suddenly, I understood.

"You said you wanted to test our demon-touched mark . . . Like you want to see if Ishtar will come here? Will we be safe in this circle?"

A tinkle of laughter left Morgan's ruby red lips. "No, we won't be calling any demons today. However, we will be investigating demon magic. For that reason, I wish to be here so that the godswood can cloak you."

Eva and I exchanged long, confused glances. When she shrugged, I turned back to Morgan. "Okay, we bite. What are you talking about?"

"You two went to Hell, correct?"

We nodded.

"No one who has gone to Hell has ever returned unchanged. And though I cannot provide evidence that someone who is demon-touched might also have absorbed demon magic, I sense that this has happened to you. Or rather, the dark magic within you has now been activated." Her eyes landed on Eva. "I can sense it in you both, but particularly in you, Eva. However, I will need to study your scar closely to know."

Eva's hands flew up to cover her mouth.

"What?" I asked, nervous.

"The night we fought the demons," Eva whispered. "Something happened that night to my magic. I didn't understand it at the time, but the color was off—a darker, murky kind of yellow." She shot a glance to one of the stones and shook her head. "I thought it was because of the stressful situation. That I was manipulating my powers in a new way—like how some people can make their magic colorless . . ."

Morgan nodded. "A reasonable assumption. Did you experience something similar, Odette?"

"Not that I can remember, but I was pretty occupied at the time."

I was trying to sound level, non-judgmental, although inside, I was a little upset that Eva hadn't mentioned her magic acting strangely. We'd already gone over a lot about that night since arriving in the past. Had she kept it a secret because she was ashamed? Because she hadn't understood what had happened? Or did she not not want *me* to know?

"What are we going to do if we have demon magic?" Eva asked slowly, as if still unable to believe this was a possibility.

Morgan perched on a stone. "Learn to use it. I have a strong intuition that demon magic could be the thing you need to fight the royals on even ground."

My lips parted. Until now, I hadn't had a clue what I was going to do to best Ishtar, who was a thousand times more powerful than me.

"Dark magic is simply the demons' magic, gifted to a witch—or other type of magical, as you saw for yourself with the shifter pack," Morgan continued. "Most black witches who have made deals with the royal demons do not have their magic inside them. They carry it within trinkets, like the stones you mentioned."

She paused, and her gaze leveled both of us. "But you're not black witches. You're demon-touched. You have the royal's magic *inside* you. If you learn to control it properly, that makes you much more powerful. Why couldn't you use it to fight Ishtar or Lucifer? Perhaps even protect your-self from possession?"

Fear coiled in my stomach. Possession by a royal was one of my greatest fears. Morgan's totem had helped me fend off the possession before, but more than anything, I wanted to be able to defend myself. After all, my totem might be ripped from my neck at any second.

"I want to learn," I said firmly.

"Me too," Eva agreed.

"Then discovering what dark power you have, and teaching Odette to timewalk accurately, will be our primary goals." Morgan rubbed her hands together, whether from excitement or to fend off the chill, I wasn't sure. "Luckily, they go together. While Merlin and I will do our best to help you practice, we can't do it all. We will seek teachers throughout time who know more about the dark side than us. Those who would understand how black witches might manipulate Hell-born magics. Then you will use that knowledge to bring down the very creatures who gave them those powers."

I blinked. "Are you saying that we're going to travel through time and look for black witches? Like, starting now?"

"Today, I'd simply like to see if I'm right. Perhaps try to coax the darkness out of you. That's why we're here. Anything that happens in this circle is invisible to the creatures of Hell. If you try to access your demon magic, and it works, they'll never know."

My stomach churned. Black magic was forbidden because to possess it, the witch had to make a deal with a royal demon. A barter for their soul. Or they had to be touched, often in malice, like Eva and me.

As much as I didn't like the idea, there was no denying that dark magic was powerful. More powerful than even M&M. We might be training with legends in the witching community, but individually none of us had any hope of becoming as strong as the fallen gods who ruled Hell.

Unless we beat them at their own game.

"Let's try it."

I hoped I wouldn't regret agreeing. So far, my demon mark had brought only pain, but if there was even the slightest chance that it was hiding something to help us defeat the demons in our time, it would be worth it.

Morgan stood. "Show me your mark again, Odette."

I lifted my pant leg. My mentor squatted down and began examining the mark that Ishtar had left. It didn't feel like anything, only like someone touching my ankle, but I knew it wasn't. Her power, bright fuchsia like mine, was pouring out of her as she analyzed the scar.

I held my breath, watching and waiting, as Morgan's eyebrows pulled together.

After a couple of minutes, she let out a long "Hmmmm."

I felt ready to jump out of my skin in anticipation. "Did you feel anything . . . dark?"

Instead of answering, she stood and gestured for Eva to join us. When she did, Morgan turned to me. "Place your hands on Eva's scar."

I gave Eva a look, asking for permission. She nodded, and I gently placed my fingertips on her cheekbone.

The scar tissue was cool to the touch, just like my demon-touched mark. Usually, I only felt it when I was in the presence of demons or those who called them their masters. When that happened, the scar seared hot.

"Close your eyes," my mentor instructed.

I did so, well aware of the benefits of depriving myself

of one sense so that the others—in this case, my magical senses, might become more sensitive.

"Think of a time when you've seen Ishtar . . . even better if she was with Lucifer."

My mind traveled back to the night Alex was kidnapped and taken to Hell, before the eve of the Spy Games' third trial. After we'd emerged from Hell, the Hellgate had broken open, spilling hundreds, if not thousands, of demons into the modern world.

It was the only night I'd seen Lucifer, king of the demons. Even in the dark of night, his burning red skin had contrasted starkly with Ishtar's blue coloring. He'd had horns, wings that spanned at least ten feet, and a tail that flicked with pride.

Ishtar was much easier for me to envision. I'd seen her up close and personal, and she sometimes haunted my dreams. In my mind, I placed them side-by-side and shuddered. Even in my vision their eyes glowed with hate and malice.

I nodded. "I see them both."

"Now, focus on Eva's scar while you think of them."

I did as Morgan instructed, concentrating harder than ever. When my heart began to thunder, and my mind wanted to stray away from the devils, I pulled it back. Though it broke my heart to do so, I even ignored the trembling of my best friend beneath my fingertips.

If I could access this power, it might change everything. And if a little discomfort on both our parts was necessary, then so be it.

After what could've been hours, but was probably no longer than five minutes, a spark ignited at the end of my middle finger.

I gasped and nearly pulled my finger away.

"Hone in on that," Morgan directed, her tone low.

I did and clenched my eyes shut. The spark grew and seeped into my fingers. A sensation that I could only describe as thick, artery-clogging, and corrosive ran through my bloodstream. It brought with it a darkness, something that made my body vibrate, and my jaw tighten. The foul sensation continued to trickle through me and the urge to retract my hand grew with it.

"Keep it there," Morgan instructed.

I complied, the sensation growing more intolerable by the second, until finally, it bloomed into something terrible and unstoppable, as if a freight train were tunneling through me. Like an alarm, my scar burned like I'd pressed an iron to it.

I wrenched my hand away with a yelp.

Eva's eyes were already open, full of terror and watching me. "What was it? What's inside me?"

"The same thing that's inside Odette," Morgan replied. "Yours is simply a little stronger, easier to find."

"Why?" my best friend asked, her chin trembling. "Why would my demon-touched mark be stronger? It's not like Lucifer is more powerful than Ishtar, or vice versa. They're equals, both terrible."

I understood why she said that. And yet, the idea that

she wanted my dark power to be as strong as hers stung a little.

"Yes, they are equals." Morgan spoke more softly in response to Eva's fear. "Yours is only stronger because you actually took in part of Lucifer's blood. When that succubus attacked you, and her acidic magic entered your bloodstream, you imbibed the *actual* blood of Lucifer." Morgan's eyes turned to me. "I don't think you carry Ishtar's blood. Only her intent to bend you to her will, and the magic that seeped into your skin when she tried to make that a reality."

Morgan released a sigh. "Both are horrible, but they're what you will need to rid your world of the demons, and free yourselves from Lucifer and Ishtar." Her expression hardened. "That is . . . if you're willing to unleash the darkness within you."

# CHAPTER THREE

*E*va and I agreed to try to access our black magic. And we did, a dozen times. But by the time we left the godswood, we were no closer to uncovering our demon magic than before.

Eva seemed confused by our lack of success, which made sense if she really had uncovered her dark power before.

Personally, I was both relieved and disappointed. The sooner I could figure this out and learn how to timewalk by myself, the sooner we could get back to our time.

Then again, knowing I had demon magic *terrified* me.

Was I ready for such power? Did I want it? If I let it loose, would it change me?

I was still ruminating hours later, as my crew walked the narrow village lane to the tavern. M&M allowed Alex only a single stint of exercise daily, and he usually used it to get as far away from our little shack as possible.

Whatever he wanted, the rest of us indulged. No one wanted a grumpy Alex on their hands.

Plus, the tavern was fun, and one of the few places Morgan and Merlin would let us go unaccompanied. This was largely because they owned it, and as their guests, we were protected. Especially after they made it clear that anyone who bugged us at the tavern would risk dire repercussions. So far, no one had stepped a toe out of line.

In the time it took us to arrive at the tavern, Diana, Hunter, and Alex had noticed that Eva and I were strangely quiet. And they'd started to ask questions.

Although I didn't want to admit that I had dark magic, even to myself, I finally broke down after a rosy-cheeked maiden brought us a round of ales.

"Morgan suspected that Eva and I have demon magic. Today, she tested us for it." I took a huge swig of the ale and winced.

If people thought cheap beer in the present sucked, they didn't know anything about ale in the past. It was disgusting, but considering my current state of mind, necessary.

"Are you freaking kidding me?" Hunter said loudly, earning him a few strange looks from other patrons.

*Thank the universe we chose the back table.*

No matter how hard we tried, or how on point the clothes M&M lent us were, we stood out in the past.

Hunter twisted to Eva. "Sugar, why didn't you tell me earlier?"

Eva shrugged. "I'm still processing. And Odie didn't mention anything either, so I figured she wasn't ready."

The others quieted, obviously not sure if they should push it, but Eva's words had a different effect on me. Her admission that she had been waiting for me to feel ready took the sting out of her keeping quiet about her possible use of black magic in London.

Even though we were besties, bonded by being demon-touched, and shared practically everything, she was right. Sometimes, people just weren't quite ready to share, even over-sharers like Eva. I needed to remember that. And cut her some major slack.

"Will you tell us the rest?" Diana asked, cutting through the careful silence.

Eva's hand traveled to her scar. "Apparently, the magic seeped in when the demons touched us, but was activated after we went to Hell. I have no idea how Morgan knew that. I suspect that she's been studying up on Hell. You know, to close the Hellgate at one point or another."

Alex's blue eyes had grown wider and wider as I spoke. "So if you hadn't saved me, you wouldn't have dark magic?"

"Don't blame yourself," I insisted. "There's no way we'd have let you rot in Hell. We were always going to come get you." I took another gulp of ale and set the heavy mug down with a *thunk*. "Actually, Morgan thinks this might be a good thing."

"How so?" Diana leaned forward. Out of all of us, she was the only one who seemed calm about this information.

"Because if we can harness demon magic, then we can fight the royals with power that rivals their own."

"Will Morgan and Merlin teach you?" Hunter asked.

Eva shifted uncomfortably, and I gulped, sure this next part wouldn't go over well.

I leaned in closer. We might be a fair distance from other patrons, and they were definitely a little intimidated by us, but they were also a curious crowd. We didn't need any eavesdroppers listening in on this conversation.

"We have to timewalk again," I said barely above a whisper. "To a period when a black witch who mastered demon magic might have lived."

Alex's spine stiffened. "That's dangerous. Foolish, even. Black witches *report* to demons."

I bit my lip. There was no denying that truth. If a witch had acquired black magic, they'd only done so by making a deal with a royal demon. What would stop them from turning us in to their demon master?

"It's our best shot," Eva argued. "Not only will it even the playing field, there's a chance that mastering black magic will keep the royals from possessing us."

"It's an interesting idea . . ." Diana hummed. "I'll be honest, it almost makes me wish that I was demon-touched."

"Don't say that," I retorted, annoyed by the flippant remark.

"I'm serious. You two are embarrassed and ashamed right now, but you have an actual shot at ending this." Diana shrugged. "Call me power-hungry or whatever you want, but after what the demons and the Dark Court have done, I want a hand in ending them. Just like they've stolen the lives from so many others." Her eyes dimmed a little.

Suddenly, I realized that while Diana might *seem* like she wanted glory and recognition, her true motivation went deeper. Her best friend had been one of our classmates killed by the devils.

While I hadn't thought about Tabitha Goode in a while, Diana probably remembered her every day.

"You're right," I conceded."We didn't ask for this, and shouldn't be ashamed. Especially when this magic has the potential to help." I sucked in a breath, knowing that Alex was going to hate this next part. "Which is why Morgan and I are leaving tomorrow. We're not sure for how long. She wants me to practice timewalking before we take Eva. Maybe we'll even find a black witch willing to help on one of these trips."

"Tomorrow?" Predictably, Alex's jaw tightened. If he didn't cool it, he'd probably crack his teeth.

I placed a hand over his. "Yes, tomorrow. And there's no logical reason I wouldn't go, or for anyone else to go with us. So now that everyone is filled in, what do you say we stop talking shop, and make the most of tonight?"

gripped the side of my head and groaned as I rose from the bed of hay that I shared with Alex. No one could argue that we hadn't made the most of last night. After Eva and I told the others about our demon magic, I'd joined my friends in ordering ale after ale. The drink helped dim our worry and temporarily allowed us to lose ourselves in the moment.

Now, however, it just made me feel like crap, especially because its stench permeated the shack. My stomach heaved a little, and I wrinkled my nose.

*Get it together, Dane. Today's a big day.*

Although Diana had put a positive spin on our power, I was still nervous. Terrified, even. And not just over the idea of harnessing black magic.

I'd timewalked once, practically by mistake. I hadn't known what the heck I was doing. Even though I knew Morgan would be at my side today, holding my hand every step of the way, timewalking was dangerous. People had sustained serious injuries after poorly executed warping and timewalking experiences. Loss of limbs being some of the most severe.

Still, I couldn't claim that I wasn't going to practice because I was hungover and scared. No matter what, I had to be the one to timewalk my friends and myself back to the present. Morgan couldn't because as my ancestor, we couldn't occupy the same space in time in what would be her future. It sucked that timewalking could only work one way where family lines were concerned.

Glad that Diana, Hunter, and Eva had already left the shack, I got dressed quickly. Once I was done, I leaned over Alex and laid a gentle hand on his shoulder.

"Hey, babe, I'm leaving."

His eyes blinked open, and his hand found mine, gripping it tight.

"Do you need anything before I go?" There was no need to add that I wasn't sure when I'd be back. He already knew that it was hard to predict the exact moment a timewalker would arrive in the future or past.

I shuddered. What if I never got good at timewalking and we returned to the present to find that a decade had passed? What sort of dystopia would our loved ones be living in?

"I don't need anything," Alex murmured and rose onto his elbows. "Be careful. Listen to Morgan. Let her help you."

"*Excuse* me. I'm not the prideful one in this relationship."

He breathed out a laugh. "I just want to make sure I'm not rubbing off on you."

I kissed him, and savored the heat between us. We hadn't had much alone time since arriving in the seventh century, and we were both missing it. A lot.

"You are rubbing off on me," I replied as we broke apart. "In a good way."

"I love you, sweets."

"Love you too." I squeezed his hand and kissed him one more time before leaving.

"About time." A voice cut through me as I shut the shack's door, making me jump. "I was thinking I'd have to send the chickens in to get you out of bed."

I turned to find Morgan, her red hair glinting in the morning sun and blue eyes twinkling. Not for the first time, it struck me how much she looked more like Eva than me. Then as my gaze traveled over her, I noticed something else. She was dressed differently than usual, in a drapey, white dress that reminded me of a Greek goddess.

"One, the sun just came up, it can't be that late. And two," I gestured to the outfit, "what on Earth are you wearing?"

"You like it?" Morgan beamed. "I got it on one of my recent timewalking trips. It's all the rage in Rome."

*Rome* . . . My mouth dried up. "Is that where we're going?"

"I think it's a good start. Traveling back a couple more

centuries will test your limits—see how far you can stretch into the past. Rome has the added benefit of being home to many great witches. Perhaps we can interview some with darker proclivities."

I'd been hoping to try timewalking into the future, but Morgan knew best. I would do anything she said if it got me closer to my goals.

"Okay. Do you have an extra one of those dresses?" I asked.

Currently, I was wearing a loose, brown dress with a shawl wrapped around my shoulders to fend off the early morning chill. It wasn't extravagant, so I suspected that it wouldn't necessarily stand out where we were going, but it also didn't look a thing like Morgan's attire.

My ancestor's lips curled up. "Of course. It's lucky that these outfits are roomy. They'll easily accommodate your height. If we were traveling to a period with more fitted fashion, you'd have to make do with what you're wearing until we picked something else up."

She led me into the sleeping space she shared with Merlin. It was the first time I'd been in their private area, which was little more than a bed on the ground and a pile of clothing.

But oh, what clothing they had.

It was clear that Morgan had been on many timewalking trips. She had everything from Greek-goddess-style dresses, to a gown I was sure would have fit in at Louis the XIV's court at Versailles. Each fabulous find only made me miss my closet and all the beauties within it more.

"How do you get all these?" I held up a sassy flapper gown with an eight-inch long fringe that I'd love to try on.

"You mean how do I pay for them?"

I nodded. M&M weren't poor, but judging by the styles of dress, she'd have needed dozens of different currencies from different times to pay for them all.

"I conjure something up and sell it." Morgan shrugged. "Once you know what people want, it's easy to get what you need to blend in. At this point, I've been timewalking for long enough that I have a collection of items from my favorite periods, so I can usually show up already in character."

"Wow," I breathed, unable to believe that I hadn't even considered this aspect of my power.

Morgan's eyes twinkled at me. "Perhaps when this demon debacle is behind you, you can use your new skill for a little fun." She handed me a dress almost identical to hers.

"Here's hoping." I stripped and put on the new outfit.

Once everything was in place, Morgan appraised me. "Perfect. Now, let's go outside."

"Am I going to get to say goodbye to the others?"

She cocked her head. "Goodbye? Why would you need to do that?"

I gulped. "What if we're gone for a long time?"

She released a musical laugh. "Oh, don't worry about that, dear. I'll make sure we return within a few hours."

I blinked. Morgan was a talented timewalker, but to be able to land somewhere with such precision was almost unheard of. Top timewalkers could land within a day or two of when they desired. Less able ones might be weeks or months off. As a newbie, I'd likely be closer to the latter, something I didn't really want to think about at the moment.

*Hopefully, I can learn to be accurate like her.*

She led me away from the cottage, to the outskirts of the woods that surrounded her home. I didn't spot my other friends or Merlin.

"Here we are." Morgan gestured down to a spot on the ground.

A white powder, salt, had been laid on the earth to form a perfect circle.

"What's this for?"

"A protection circle. A precaution in case we get split up. If you leave this circle, you'll still be tied to it, and will be able to reappear here more easily than if you timewalked without it. Step inside."

I did as she said, and she joined me.

I was familiar with protection circles. At Spellcasters we sparred inside them. Those circles were mostly used to keep those *outside* the circle safe from stray weapons or spells. As a result they generally felt a little stuffy and constricting. This one, however, felt different.

"Why is it so warm and cozy in here?"

"I designed it suited to your preferences, or as best I could from what I know of you."

Damn. Morgan was a badass with a capital "B". I needed to soak up her experience and teachings.

"Will you show me how to do that later? After the time-walking?"

She beamed at me. "Of course. But for now, let's focus on our main goal. You know of the Colosseum, yes?"

"I've been there," I replied, remembering the amazing family trip I'd taken with my parents before my senior year of high school. We'd traveled all around Italy, and even taken a private tour of the old gladiator ring.

"That's lucky, because that's where we're going. Envision it."

*Easy peasy.*

In my mind, I called up a memory of the iconic arena. It was so vivid, I could smell the dirt on the ground, and sense the warm, Roman sun on my skin as I walked in the ring.

"Now, open a warphole."

This was familiar to me too, and I did it without issue.

"Very good," Morgan breathed softly. "Now take that image and place yourself back in time. When you see the strands of time forming around you, grab the one I point out."

"I didn't have to do that before. Threads of time just spun around me, and we moved through the warphole."

Morgan smiled and tapped my totem with her finger. "That's because I was guiding you. You brought time into being around you, and I claimed the proper strand. Otherwise, who knew where you'd end up?"

I chewed on the inside of my cheek. I hadn't thought about that so deeply. When we'd first arrived here, we'd all been so happy to be safe and away from the demons, details were forgotten. But now that I considered it, her explanation made so much sense. I hadn't even gone through the warphole first, my friends had. So yes, *obviously*, someone other than me had to have chosen the era we landed in, and they'd done so very purposely.

"Thank you. I'm sorry I didn't say that sooner."

Morgan smiled. "It was my pleasure. Now, envision the Colosseum."

I nodded, and closed my eyes. I imagined myself in the ring, wearing this dress, and staring up at a crowd of cheering Romans. Someone resembling a leader—a caesar, I supposed—waved. The air around us grew hotter than it normally did when I made warpholes.

"Odette, open your eyes."

I did as she said and gasped. All around us, strands of time spun. Sounds came from them, mostly cheering. Although I heard a couple guttural screams too.

"That one," Morgan said after squinting at a specific strand for a few seconds longer than the others. "Take that one. As soon as you latch on, pull your warphole toward us."

I blinked, unsure how she knew which strand to grab. They were all colored differently and measured various lengths, but gave no indication as to the era they led to. Still, I trusted her, so I did as she said.

My arm stretched out of the protective circle. I plucked the short bright yellow strand of time out of the air.

I was immediately hit with the sensation of oil being

poured over my body, and then dirt being blown over top of the oil coating me.

*Gross.*

"Pull the warphole into the protective circle," Morgan whispered, bringing me back to the task at hand.

Calling the portal to me, I did as she said, allowing its inky darkness to slip over my head, and the heat, followed by a snowstorm of cold, to wash over me.

Both being veteran warpers, we slipped through the warphole naturally. I grinned, barely daring to believe that timewalking could be this effortless.

Suddenly, the strand of time dissolved, taking with it the icky sensation of oil and dirt on my skin.

"Wow," I breathed as a beam of sunlight blinded me at the same time our feet touched the ground.

I closed my eyes, waiting for the spots to vanish and relishing the heat on my skin. Dust filled my nostrils, alongside a tangy scent that I couldn't quite place. The sounds of a cheering crowd hit my ear.

My heart rate kicked up a notch. We'd made it.

"How did you know what strand to pull?" I asked.

A chuckle left her lips. "It's part of your natural magic. Once you become more comfortable slipping through time, they'll start to call to you. You'll figure it—" She stopped speaking and her hand tightened around my arm. "Odette, back up slowly."

I blinked my eyes open and shielded them with my hand. Morgan's face came into focus against the stark sunlight. Her eyes were wide as she guided me backward.

"What? Why?" I blinked again, and the rest of the world came into focus.

I had timewalked us to Rome, into the Colosseum. The dead center of the Colosseum—complete with gladiators brandishing weapons, and beasts prowling all around.

And a few feet away, a lion, thin but with a bushy orange mane stared us down as he crouched to pounce.

# CHAPTER FIVE

My blood pounded in my ears as we eased our way backward. With every step we took, the lion responded by creeping closer, his amber eyes trained on us.

"What are we going to do?" I hissed.

I glanced around the stadium. We'd drawn attention. Romans were screaming and pointing, some even looked to be cheering for us—or maybe the lion, there was no telling. The gladiators we were in the ring with didn't seem to have noticed our appearance, but they were fighting their own beasts.

"I'm going to try something. Don't run or cry out," Morgan whispered seconds before the dirt around us kicked up as if we were in the middle of a sandstorm.

I choked on the whirlwind of sand and closed my eyes to protect them. The predator tracking us growled, presumably because the dirt was irritating him too. I was about to ask Morgan what she was doing, when her hand landed on mine, handing me something.

*A blade. She's a damn genius.* She'd wanted to hide overt conjuring from the humans in the stands. Now they'd probably assume that we had them on our hips, or in the folds of our dresses, all along. In regards to magic, humans usually saw what they wanted to see.

The dirt and sand fell to the ground, and I wiped my eyes clean to locate the lion. Morgan stood by my side, an even larger sword in her hand.

She kept her gaze firmly on the big cat as she spoke. "We can't use much magic, certainly not for fighting. If we do, the crowd will go crazy. Even the dirt cloud was risky, but you need time to figure out how to survive. This sort of thing can happen when you timewalk. So how are you going to get us out of it?"

I gawked. "Me?" I had been about to ask why she hadn't already created a warphole for us to slip through.

"This is a prime lesson. If you can't work under pressure and get yourself out of trouble that you've stepped into by timewalking, you don't deserve to wield the power. Get us back home—quickly."

Did I think Morgan was a badass earlier? I actually meant crazy. Totally batshit crazy.

The lion roared and took two more steps forward.

I gripped my sword tighter. "What about the time strands? I don't know which one to pick."

Out of the corner of my eye, I caught her nod. "When you can get that far, I will choose one. But I won't call time for you." Her blue eyes darted to me for a second. "Don't make this timewalking excursion your last."

The lion leapt, and Morgan and I twirled apart, screams ripping from both of our throats.

"Work fast, Odette! And only use magic to make the warphole and call time." Her hand gestured to the crowd. "Or they might drag us out of the arena and burn us alive."

I gulped. Morgan was right. Being a witch may not always be a desirable prospect in the world I came from, but historically? It was deadly. Just like the lion we were up against.

Morgan charged the beast. She swiped at its face, and the big cat flinched backward and batted at her with his paws. Morgan moved again, this time coming at it from the side and pushing the creature back.

I took advantage of the space, lowering my sword and getting to work. The visualization was easy enough. I knew where I wanted to go . . . to the salt circle. The warphole was easy too.

As a blackhole ringed with fuchsia spun into existence, screams and cries of astonishment flew up from the stands. One glance up told me that we had the arena's attention. I had to work fast.

I pushed harder, searching for the threads of time.

Men yelled close by, and I twisted my neck to find three gladiators running toward me, swords extended and scowls on their faces. *Shit!* Were they coming to help? Or because of the magic they'd seen? Something told me it was the latter.

My warphole dissipated.

I darted to Morgan's side. "We have company." I gestured to the gladiators.

She swore beneath her breath. "Start working again. As soon as you have the strands up, I'll assist, but not a moment sooner."

I complied, straining through my fear to reopen the warphole and call strands of time into existence. Out of the corner of my eye, I watched the lion swipe, his claws coming close to Morgan's arm. My terror surged, and the threads of time flitted away. Tears sprang to my eyes as I pushed again, and again, and again.

Finally, after what felt like a decade, a single orange strand of time popped into existence.

"Is that it?"

Morgan gave it a glance. "Keep trying."

I shot a look back to where the men had been, and saw to my relief that another big cat, a lioness, had stopped their progress, buying me a few seconds.

I pushed harder.

Silver, pink, green, blue, and white strands popped into existence one after another. My eyes scanned them, not seeing any discernible difference. And because it was so loud in our immediate surroundings, I couldn't hear anything coming from them, either.

My teeth gnashed together. "Morgan! Look!"

She swiped at the lion, forcing him to back up. Once she had a little space, her attention snapped to me. "It's not there. Dig deeper. Or those men will end us."

Another glance over my shoulder revealed that one of the gladiators had just slammed his sword into the side of the lioness. Her golden body dropped to the dirt, and they spared her a single victory cry before turning once more to me and Morgan. Their swords lifted and their eyes glinted as they stalked our way.

My fists clenched so hard that my fingernails drew blood from my palms. I closed my eyes and pushed my magic harder than ever.

Although I couldn't see them, I could feel more strands of time popping into existence. There was a faint difference between their energy and that of the warphole. And then, as sure as I was that the sky was blue, the right one popped into existence. I opened my eyes and saw it shining, a deep green that reminded me of Hunter's magic.

"I have it! Morgan, I think I have it!"

Again she swiped at the lion with her sword, and then twisted to look my way. A smile bloomed on her face. "So you do. I'll be right there."

A few more strokes of her weapon kept the predator at bay while she backed up. Once she was close enough, she grabbed my hand.

The beast crouched, ready to pounce.

"Grab the strand and pull the warphole our way!" Morgan commanded.

I grasped onto the hunter green strand of time and yanked the warphole over our heads just as the lion leapt through the air, his paws reaching out for us.

# CHAPTER SIX

The scent of damp leaves and mud filled my nose as a chill rippled across the bare skin of my arms.

*We made it.*

I collapsed onto the ground. Salt dug painfully into my forearms, and then the shaking began.

My entire body trembled like I was buried in snow. My teeth chattered so hard, I feared they might crack. Even my ribs shook.

"It's okay, love." Morgan's hands landed on my arms. She rubbed me gently from shoulder to elbow, trying to calm the tremors that wracked my body. "We're back. We're safe. You did marvelously."

I couldn't respond. Words wouldn't form, my limbs were out of control. My brain was barely functioning. All I could do was replay what had happened. The gladiator ring, the men coming for us, the goddamn *lion* that had nearly swiped my head off.

How could Morgan say that I'd done well? I had timewalked us into the middle of a gladiator event. We'd almost died.

Realizing that I wasn't able to speak, she helped me up and assisted me into a cottage. When she opened the doors, everyone else was at the table. Bowls of hearty stew, sprinkled liberally with fragrant thyme and rosemary, and accompanied by a loaf of fresh baked bread, sat before them. The savory aromas made my mouth water, and suddenly, through the tremors, I became aware that my stomach was aching.

When the others caught sight of us, they leapt up, and taking in my expression, Eva and Alex sprinted toward me.

"Odie! What happened!" Alex asked. "Are you—cold?"

"What's going on?" Eva squeaked, her hands over her mouth. "What's wrong with her?"

"She's in shock. She needs to sit, and eat to replenish her energy. The food will help ground her." Morgan gestured for them to move aside.

Alex's lips flattened, but he listened, going to the table and pulling out a chair for me.

"Is this just from timewalking?" Diana asked, examining me from afar like I was some sort of scared animal.

"She traveled into the past. That in itself is enough to throw someone for a loop," Morgan agreed. "In fact, the further you stray from your period of origin, the more time messes with you. And then . . . we saw some unusual activities in our travels."

"A lion!" I blurted. My voice was unnaturally loud and embarrassingly wobbly. "We went back to the Roman Colosseum! We fought surrounded by gladiators! And lions!"

"We only came up against one lion," Morgan said. "And like I said, love, you did well. Most people who timewalk vomit or pass out on their first few times. You clearly have the stomach for it, *and* you remained cognizant. And mostly kept a cool head when those gladiators came after us."

"Gladiators came *after you*?!" Alex sucked in a long inhale. "You need to start from the beginning."

Morgan told the entire story, giving me what I felt was a bit too much credit. When she finished, my friends were staring at her, blinking.

Her partner, however, burst into laughter. "Morgan, you must be easier on the girl. Why not timewalk back to a pleasant field, or somewhere nice? Stroll through a peaceful village? Or even take her to a celebration? Why did you need to take her to the Colosseum of all places?"

My ancestor shrugged. "To be fair, I assumed she would deposit us in the stands. Once again, I was reminded to assume nothing. However, it was a good moment of instruction. These things *will* happen when she timewalks. And when they do, she needs to know how to work under pressure. If she can timewalk with gladiators at her back and a lion about to rip her face off, she can face the demons. And anything else." There was a tone of pride in her voice.

Even though I didn't feel like I deserved it, what Morgan said was true. I *had* timewalked. I'd gotten us there *and* back. No doubt Morgan could do it more quickly and smoothly, but she hadn't needed to.

I turned to look at my mentor hovering over my shoulder. "People saw us use magic. Humans. Are we going to show up in history books?"

Again, Merlin laughed and his blue eyes crinkled at the corners into familiar lines. "If everything that supernaturals did showed up in history books, there wouldn't be any pages left for what the humans themselves accomplish."

"Still . . ." I trailed off, nervous about the idea.

He waved a weathered hand. "More likely than not, nothing will come of it. But, since much in the future is weighing on your abilities, I'll send word to a friend of mine. She's a powerful mind witch—capable of modifying memories. When she can stop by, Morgan will take a trip back to Rome." He winked at his paramour. "In fact, maybe we'll all go."

A girlish laugh tinkled from Morgan. "I'm going to hold you to that." She took a seat next to Merlin.

Hunter waved to Eva, beckoning her back to the table. She glanced at me, as if afraid that if she left my side, I'd fall apart.

"I'm okay," I assured her. My trembling had lessened substantially, and my breath was coming easier. "Finish your meal. I'm going to eat too." My stomach gave an audible growl, as if supporting that choice.

Alex moved only to get me a bowl of stew and come sit

at my side. When we were both settled, he eyed me. "It was clearly traumatizing, but how do you feel about time traveling all by yourself?"

"Proud, but not ready to go that far again yet." I spoke loud enough so Morgan would hear.

In response, my ancestor chuckled. "Duly noted. However, you know better than anyone that there's no time to waste, love. We're going to get you some rest and try again tomorrow." Her hand fluttered to land on Merlin's arm as her eyes pierced me. "But yes, next time we'll travel to a safer era. We'll practice *only* timewalking for the next few days, making sure we cover as many variables as we can."

The legendary witch paused, her gaze shifting between Eva and me. "And when you're ready, we'll take a much more important trip."

# CHAPTER SEVEN

Over the next five days, I practiced timewalking to a dozen periods in human history. Ultimately, none of the others were as terrifying or jarring as our trip to ancient Rome—thank the universe for that. But safe? I think not. Safer, *maybe*, but not safe.

Morgan and I had walked the streets of Paris right before the French Revolution broke out. The tension in the air had been undeniable, and resentment and dissent burned in the eyes of everyone I passed.

In another era, we popped in and out of shops where everyone was gossiping about an invention by a man named Gutenberg. Some hated the printing press that would revolutionize the world, and were vocal about it. Others saw only opportunity.

During my favorite trip, we visited England under the reign of Queen Elizabeth I. While there, we snacked on the candied violets the queen loved, and rubbed shoulders with the likes of Shakespeare, Sir Walter Raleigh, and, to my great delight, the renown witch and seer Ursula Shipton.

Along the way, we picked up outfits that would fit Eva's petite frame, in case we returned. Additionally, everywhere we went, Morgan searched for a black witch, and once, we actually found one. Unfortunately, she wasn't very powerful, which was a letdown.

After speaking with Mother Shipton, who suggested a few strong black witches she'd seen in her visions, we arrived back at M&M's cottage to drop off the outfits we'd purchased.

We stayed the night, and I soaked up every moment with my friends, telling them of my journeys, while Morgan conferred with Merlin as to where we should go next. Everyone went to bed that night with a belly full of stew, happy to be together. But when I woke the next day, my timewalking mentor had disappeared.

"Where's Morgan?" I asked Merlin, who sat at the table, poring over a book with Alex. The famed wizard had recently deemed my boyfriend strong enough to leave our group shack. Alex was taking full advantage of the privilege, rising early and soaking up every ounce of knowledge from Merlin.

"My love awoke at dawn and said only that she was going exploring," Merlin replied, looking totally unbothered.

"Exploring . . . here? Or elsewhere?"

Merlin chuckled. "You have the measure of her. I expect she's timewalking alone."

"Oh . . . okay." I tried to keep the dejection from my tone and failed.

Merlin's face softened. "Morgan is not the most patient of witches. Truth be told, it is one of her few flaws. If I had to guess, I'd say that she went alone so that she might find a black witch to train you sooner."

My lips twisted. While that should have made me happy because it indicated that she understood how important it was that I left soon, her taking matters into her own hands stung.

Had I been slowing her down? I still wasn't a pro at distinguishing the strands of time, but I was getting better. Or so I'd thought. Maybe she just wanted to get rid of us? Have her life and cottage back?

"Don't take it personally, sweets," Alex said, reading my mind. "Morgan knows that others are depending on us. She wants to help, and there are a lot of black witches throughout history to appraise."

"That's no joke," Diana said as she breezed into the room. "My mother used to be obsessed with researching black witches. She said it helped her understand the enemy better."

They were both right. I was being too prideful, which, considering everything we'd be up against soon, wasn't just dumb, it was dangerous.

"I hope she returns soon," I said finally.

Alex patted the seat next to him, and I joined the guys at the table. My eyes landed on the tome laid out on the scarred and weathered wood.

The book was new, the leather scent strong. The handwriting on the pages was fresh, and the painted illustrations, bright with natural pigments. All of M&M's books—whether from the past, their time, or the future—were works of art. Many were also, usually, extremely hard to read. Personally, I'd take typed text any day. Diana and Alex, however, seemed to enjoy and even have a knack for reading the older texts with archaic, loopy scripts.

"What are you studying?"

"This is an old book of spells," Morgan's paramour replied. "Some of which I plan on teaching you lot today."

I peered at the page. "Do we know any of them already?"

"None that I've come across," Alex said excitedly. "Merlin asked me to review them with him and pick ones I thought would be beneficial against the demons. So far, I've found at least a dozen that could be helpful."

"Hmmm," I hummed. "But we have a few spells that work against demons. *Nex* for lesser demons. *Morsultimus* for greater demons and royals. Why do we need more?"

"Not everyone will be able to command a sacred enchantment like *Morsultimus*," Merlin reminded me. "Of course, they might not be able to use these spells, either, but you should not assume that. Give them the tools to try. Pass on this knowledge, spread it to those who fight with you."

That made sense.

Diana glanced at the page. "The words look so strange. Certainly not Latin-based, like most of the spells we know. What culture are they from?"

"These are from the druids. Translated, this means 'to seal wings'." He pointed to another that I could barely read because of the script. "This is to freeze, and the last one is to dissolve acid," Merlin explained.

Dissolve acid? That would be useful against succubi, who spewed the stuff.

Merlin smiled at me as if he knew what I was thinking. "Each is helpful in their own way. And yes, they are tailored to specific demons, as druids fought them often. It's said that their spells are passed down from the old gods. They're powerful, and so ancient and forgotten that your enemy will not anticipate them."

"Are they aether-based?" Diana asked.

"No," Merlin replied. "These are for witches. Not rare fae, or godlings. Even in this time godlings are rare and as the devils hunt them viciously, they grow more rare by the day." His eyes dimmed a little at the idea of a hunted magical race. I didn't want to tell him that in my timeline godlings were long extinct. "The old gods could be cruel, but when they gifted knowledge they were sensible."

My spine straightened. I'd never thought much about the old gods. Here, however, they seemed to pop up in conversation often.

"The druids were like the old gods' priests and priestesses, right?" I asked.

"In a way," Merlin answered. "They were the priests and priestesses in this area. Other parts of the world had spiritual leaders that went by different names—many existed before the druids."

"When did the old gods live . . . or whatever you would call their existence," I qualified, unsure whether something made of aether, the fifth and most powerful element, could truly 'live'. "Did they travel? You know, like spreading the word?"

Merlin's blue eyes twinkled, reminding me strongly of my man when he was talking about something he found intriguing. It seemed this was a subject of interest. "They are timeless, limitless, and boundless. They transmuted endlessly—some, as you know, into royal demons, while others became new versions of themselves. For instance, the old gods were revered in ancient Egypt, then Greece, and Rome. Often, devotees merely called the same deities different names. That trend continued as other cultures progressed. Our own magical ancestor, the line from where the first witch kings and queens originally received their power, stemmed from a magic goddess. Isis, Hekate, and many lesser known goddesses, are all one in the same."

"So someone like Odin was also Zeus?" Diana's eyebrows pulled together. I was glad I wasn't the only one who was working this out.

"Correct." Merlin smiled at her, and the corners of his eyes crinkled into his familiar smile lines, deepening them. "And after he was Zeus, his followers called him another name. And another, and another, as humans explored and settled the world."

"The god formerly known as Zeus," I joked, which earned me a confused look from our teacher, but chuckles from the other two.

"Indeed." The wizard shrugged and glanced out the window before rising from the table. "The daylight is upon us. Where are Eva and Hunter?"

"In the shack," Diana replied. "And I'm not going to get them. They were giggling and kissing when I left . . ."

I snorted. Hunter and Eva were less inhibited than me and Alex; we had only snuggled and kissed since coming here. But I knew full well they were taking advantage of their free time right now.

"Let's leave them be," Alex said wisely. "They'll come out when they're ready."

"Very well," Merlin said with a laugh. "We won't begin anything new until they arrive. Nor will we go far, just to the field on the side of the cottage. They can catch up later."

# CHAPTER EIGHT

It took two hours, but Eva and Hunter finally emerged from the tiny shack, their lips swollen, and Eva's mop of red hair an absolute mess.

I sniggered when I caught sight of them rushing up to meet us. "Please tell me you remembered to leave the door cracked open."

Eva stuck out her tongue at me. "We did. There will be no bow-chicka-wow-wow smell when you go to bed tonight."

"Bow-chicka what?" Merlin asked, his bushy eyebrows arched in amusement.

"Uhh, nothing," Eva said, her face turning red. She'd never been quiet about her and Hunter's sexcapades, but around Merlin and Morgan, she was more demure. It was like she was starstruck. "What are you all doing? Where's Morgan?"

"We think she's searching for black witches." I pointed

to the book Merlin had brought out and set in the grass. "And we're learning druid spells."

Eva's eyes lit up. "Cool. Are any of them working?"

"Errr." I shrugged.

They'd worked for Merlin, but the rest of us hadn't experienced success yet.

Merlin leapt into the conversation, explaining what he'd told us earlier, and then listing the spells we'd tried. Once he had filled them in, he tilted his head. "And now that you're here, Eva dear, I'd like to test something I've been considering. Would you mind?"

"Oh, sure," Eva said, approaching where our mentor knelt by the book.

Merlin gave her a bright smile and began flipping through the pages. When he paused, the illustration on the page caught my eye.

A creature that resembled a wraith, a lesser demon with wrinkled, gray skin and a hundred rows of shark-like teeth, stared back at me. Except, somehow, this guy was even more hideous than the wraiths I'd seen in real life. He had a serpentine tongue that protruded a foot out of his mouth, and claws as long as my hand that seemed to emit some type of magic.

"What is that?" Alex asked, his brow furrowing.

"That is one of the first forms of demons," Merlin told him. "They no longer exist in this time period. Nor in yours, I suppose. They were absolutely deadly and terrifying, a boon for the royals. Unfortunately for them, they also had the bad habit of devouring each other."

"If they don't exist, why are we looking at this illustration?" Diana prompted, ever the one to get down to business.

Merlin pointed to the page. "Do you see they possess magic?"

We all nodded.

"That's not just black magic. It's said that these demons were once witches who made deals with the royals. And once the witches had received what they wanted from the demons, this is what they became. It was ideal for the royals, because they gained a new soldier with an inherent grasp of magic—no matter how temporary their existence. However, in their new bodily form, spells had to be modified."

His blue eyes traveled to Eva's scar. "These altered spells became even more deadly—to all sorts of demons. But only those who bore a demon-touched mark or had been turned into a demon, like the one depicted here, could manage them. Since you have said that you are the only two demon-touched witches in centuries, I doubt a soul in your world remembers that spells of this nature existed." His gaze dropped to the page. "Alas, there is only a single spell in this book for witches like you. However, it seems particularly useful for defense."

"Are you saying that you want Odie and me to try out the spell?" Eva murmured.

Merlin nodded.

The simple motion tied my gut into knots. I'd known for over a week that I'd have to contend with the black magic running through me, but timewalking practice had pushed that chore to the back of my mind. I hadn't expected to have to try today.

And yet . . . if Merlin was right, and the spell concocted by the witches-turned-demons gave us more tools to fight our foes, then we needed to try. Particularly if the black witch we sought out turned on us.

Morgan was seeking out someone powerful enough to teach us how to guard our minds. If they betrayed us, we would need protection sooner than we thought. And if this spell was as old and little-known as Merlin claimed, it was ideal.

"Let's do it," I said. "Or at least try to make our black magic appear. If anything, this could give us a head start for when Morgan finds a witch to tutor us."

Eva nodded slowly, hesitation written all over her face.

Merlin nodded and picked up the book. "Very well. Let us move to the godswood. You'll be safe from alerting any nearby demons to your presence." He turned to the others. "You three come with us."

Everyone fell in line, tromping through the woods. The walk was faster this time, probably because I was dreading what I'd agreed to do.

When we arrived at the edge of the godswood, Merlin pointed to a small clearing outside the stones. "Alex, Diana, and Hunter, continue practicing the druid spells we've been working on over there. I'd suggest working with the freezing one. It's the simplest. When you get one to work, move on to the wing-sealing spell. Many demons have wings, so it could be of great use."

"When? Don't you mean *if*?" Diana muttered, clearly bitter that she hadn't nailed the druid spells yet.

"You will master them eventually," Merlin assured her. "The magic of the old gods is difficult. It deals with a more removed part of yourself, something that magicals of your time have not had to access for many generations. But they can do it still, and the more tools you have to fight the devils, the better off you will be."

Alex, Hunter, and Diana nodded and split off to work. When they were gone, we stepped into the godswood.

Unlike last time, a strange sensation rippled over my skin as I entered the sanctuary of stones. Not a chill, per se, more like cold water running slowly over my skin.

I paused and turned to face my best friend.

Eva's blue eyes were wide as they met mine. "Did you feel that too?"

"Yeah, that's new."

Merlin grinned. "You have not accessed your demon magic yet, but it appears that Morgan is right—it's been awoken by you seeking it out. That is a good sign for this experiment."

"And the godswood reacted to our demon magic?" I asked, still confused. "Shouldn't it throw us out or something?"

Merlin shrugged. "No one knows. But it didn't, and that's all that matters. For now, you're safe in here."

He faced Eva. "I'd like you to start with this." He turned

the page so we weren't looking at the illustration of the ugly demon any longer, but an almost blank page with two paragraphs on it.

His finger landed on a word. "Read this."

I joined Eva in squinting at the annoying, loopy text. "Bind a demon's power? How does that differ from the *relligo* spell?"

"It says here," Merlin pointed further down the page, "using this black magic spell will *not* bind the demon to an object, say a lamp for an ifrit. That is what *relligo* is for. This spell binds the demon's powers *within* the creature. Makes them easier to kill, I suspect."

I bit my lip. "Does this apply to the royals?"

Disarming Ishtar, Lucifer, Xaphan, and the Furies would give us a huge advantage in the fight to come.

"I'm not sure, but it's in this book for a reason," Merlin replied. "Unfortunately, we have no demon around to test it on, but that is not necessary. For right now, I simply want to see if this spell, which was cultivated for a melding of witching and demon magic, will help draw out your black powers."

Eva gulped. "Okay. I'll go first."

My best friend stepped forward to get a better look at the page. She mouthed the awkward word and then moved away, turning so that her body faced the expanse of greenery before us.

My palms began to sweat as I watched her and wondered if this would really work.

Eva held out her hands. They were trembling. Silently, I sent strong vibes to my friend.

"Imagine one of the creatures before you, my dear," Merlin prompted. "It might help draw the dark powers out. When you're ready, try the spell."

Eva's eyes narrowed. "*Itoarazicus.*" Her voice wobbled.

As it had the day before, sunshine yellow magic appeared and fizzled, doing nothing.

Eva scowled and spoke the word again, louder this time.

Once more, her yellow magic made an appearance before quickly disappearing.

She threw up her hands, already frustrated.

I pressed my lips together. It wasn't like Eva to lose her cool so quickly, but I understood why it was happening. This seemed like an accessible baby step. If we couldn't do this, would we be able to access the dark power at all?

"Let me try," I said, wanting to give my friend a moment to collect herself.

Stepping away from Merlin and Eva, I inhaled deeply.

*You can do this.*

An image of a wraith popped into my mind, but I shook it away and envisioned Ishtar. If I was going to access demon magic, might as well go big, right?

Staring into the green woods, I could practically see her standing before me, smiling a dangerous smile, her blue wings spread, and her horns glinting in the sunlight.

I shuddered, and surprisingly, my ankle began to burn. I

cocked my head. That had never happened when I'd *thought* of Ishtar before.

Digging deeper, I added detail to the vision. Spirals on her horns, claws, and even the black jewelry and crown I'd seen her wear. With each detail added, she grew more real, more ominous, and my scar burned hotter.

I extended my hands. "*Itoarazicus.*"

Fuchsia magic flew from my palms, but like Eva's magic, it fizzled out and disappeared.

I dropped my hands, and was turning to tell Eva and Merlin about my scar burning, when I noticed my best friend was clutching her face, wincing.

"What's wrong?" I asked.

"I don't know," she replied. "When you worked your magic, my scar seared. It didn't do that when I spoke the incantation."

My spine straightened, and an idea washed over me. "What demon did you envision when you cast the spell?"

Eva arched a brow. "A succubus. You know the one."

I did. The biotch who scarred my friend's beautiful face.

"You should try the incantation again," I suggested, "but this time, envision Lucifer." I paused, because I knew she wouldn't be comfortable with the next bit. "And touch my scar when you do it."

Eva jerked back as if I'd struck her. "But . . . why? What if I hurt you?"

"Then it hurts." I shrugged. "Can't be worse than when Ishtar branded me."

Merlin inched closer. "I understand what Odette is

getting at. It's a clever workaround. This would be easier for both of you if you were confronted by an actual demon, and could feel their darkness closing in. Perhaps touching the other's scar while envisioning your greatest enemy will bring the dark magic to the surface."

He turned his gaze on me. "But Eva is correct. You may well be injured—or perhaps, because you possess demon magic, the spell could work on you—bind your powers. Are you willing to take that chance?"

I hadn't considered that. "Would it only bind my demon magic? Or my witch powers too?"

"There's no way to know," Merlin replied.

I chewed on my bottom lip. Was I willing to return to a state in which my powers were useless?

Immediately, an answer presented itself: Alex had unbound me once, I was sure he could do it again. As for the pain . . . that was worth it.

*We really need this insurance against the black witch.*

I nodded. "I'm willing."

"Then you two should try," Merlin said.

Eva held my gaze for a long second. "If you're sure."

"Positive."

I hiked up my pant leg, and my friend crouched. The burning sensation had died down, but when Eva's fingers landed on my scar, it flared up again.

She gasped and glanced up at me. I was glad that I hadn't let the pain show on my face.

"I'm fine," I told her.

She gulped and held one hand out in front of her. Merlin and I waited, me holding my breath for any pain to come.

Finally, after what felt like days, Eva spoke.

"*Itoarazicus.*"

I gritted my teeth as a searing pain shot up my leg. Eva let out a yelp, and yanked her hand from my scar to cover her mark, which apparently had reacted too. But, instinctively or not, she'd kept her other hand out in front of her.

And black smoke was trickling from her fingertips.

I gasped. "Eva! Look!"

I pointed to the smoke, which wasn't going anywhere, though it certainly wouldn't have been strong enough to take on a demon.

But it was *there*, irrefutably proving that she could work with the dark magic inside of her. Command it, even.

Now I needed to learn how to do the same.

# CHAPTER NINE

After we began using our scars as launching points, our demon magic started flowing. A little. We spent the hours practicing the demon spell in the book, trying to get it to spring from our hands like our own magic.

It never happened, and by the end of the day, I was wiped. Working with demon magic was far more draining than practicing with my witch power. Merlin hypothesized that was because the demon power didn't belong to us. We'd harnessed it, yes, but we were basically using Lucifer and Ishtar's magic.

As far as I was concerned, they'd given it to us, so they'd have to suck it up.

After the dark magic drained us so much that only thin tendrils of smoke flew from our hands, we switched to practicing druid spells with the rest of our group. We trained like this for three long days before Morgan returned.

She reappeared right in the center of her home, her arms so laden with dresses that she almost toppled over. "Help, please!" she cried, and everyone jumped up from what they'd been doing.

I pulled a few of the garments off the top of the pile, revealing her smiling face.

"Pretty, aren't they?"

I glanced down at the deeply colored red and blue gowns, plush, velvety soft, and extremely intricate in their embellishments. "Beautiful. Where are these from?"

"You'll soon find out! Actually, that one's yours!" She pointed to a crimson dress, the exact same color as Alex's magic, with tiny birds embroidered on the bodice. Morgan's eyes were shining in a way that I rarely saw when we time-walked together.

Once again, a pang of hurt shot through me. We didn't timewalk for entertainment, but was I holding her back so much that she wasn't having any fun? I hoped not.

"And this one is yours!" Morgan plucked another gown from the stash and handed it to Eva. "See if it fits. If not, I have something else that might work, but it will be a wee bit out of fashion."

"Welcome back, my love." Merlin sidled up to Morgan's side, and they kissed so deeply that I was compelled to glance away.

When they were done, I broached the question burning inside me.

"So, where are we going?"

Morgan gave me a sly smile. "France. Seventeenth century. I've found the perfect black witch, horrible and powerful. Mother Shipton believed that she was demon-touched by request. After watching her for a while, I agree."

I cocked my head. I hadn't heard Mother Shipton say anything about a demon-touched witch—other than me, of course.

"She told me when you went to relieve yourself," Morgan said, reading my expression. "We didn't want to frighten you with the prospect of a demon-touched witch, rather than just a black witch. They're quite a level up, after all."

"Uhhh," Eva's mouth was agape. "Are we sure about seeking out a demon-touched witch who's loyal to the demons? They don't just communicate through things like demon stones. They have a direct connection." She pointed to her scar for emphasis.

Morgan waved a hand nonchalantly. "For the right amount of money, she'll help anyone."

"Who is she? Anyone we'd recognize?"

"Her given name is Catherine Montvoisin, but she goes by La Voisin," Morgan replied as she accepted a mug of ale from Merlin.

"You've got to be joking me," Diana barked out a laugh. "She poisoned *thousands* of people at the French court! And held black masses! Ohhhh, she *is* a baddie!"

Morgan clapped her hands together. "I know! The fact that she hid her demon-touched nature is remarkable enough. Take in the events of her life, and, well, I don't know of another witch like her."

Morgan's gaze cut to me. "Don't worry, I investigated her for a while to make sure that the royal demons weren't around. I never caught a whiff of them. I promise that La Voisin is an ideal teacher. She probably considered herself a black witch long before she asked to be touched by a royal —she knows much of the darker side of magic. Equally important, she's motivated by money, which we will supply her heartily with."

Eva and I shared a pointed look.

Someone who poisoned a court and called a royal demon master didn't seem like an ideal candidate for anything. But in this case, the pickings were never going to be good. At least now that we could use a binding spell against anyone wielding demon power, Eva and I could defend ourselves if shit hit the fan. Which, with us around, it probably would.

After a few long seconds, Eva broke our stare. "When do we leave?"

Morgan's lips curled up mischievously. "Tomorrow."

Preparing dinner that evening was a tense affair.

Since Morgan had proclaimed that Eva and I were leaving in the morning, Hunter and Alex had become *very* protective.

Other than when I needed to do my business in the

woods, Alex hadn't left me alone for more than a second. And when the group gathered for our typical supper of pheasant stew and bread, he sat so close, he was practically in my lap.

I cleared my throat and gestured to the lack of space between our butts on the bench. "Babe, I love you, but a little room, please?"

He glanced down and his cheeks reddened as he scooted over. "Sorry."

I laid a hand on his forearm. "It's okay. I realize that you're worried, but we'll be with Morgan. And we know a black spell now. We can bind the witch if we need to make a quick getaway. Everything will be fine."

"That's what Eva says too." Hunter sat across from us with two bowls of stew. Eva was just behind him, carrying her own bowl heaping high, and a basket of rolls.

If I thought we ate a lot at Spellcasters, it was nothing compared to what we consumed here. Something about being out of our own time period, in addition to practicing magic, burned a crapload of calories. The food was excellent, although it didn't make me miss cuisine from my own era any less. I'd been dreaming of Hawaiian pizza fairly routinely since we arrived here.

"We need to trust the process, but I get it, cuz," Hunter acknowledged. "It's hard to see them go."

"Exactly," Alex muttered. "I don't like being separated from any of you. Especially not by centuries."

"For sure," Hunter agreed, arching a brow. "It's not like

we can just run down the road to save you if something bad happens."

Eva scoffed. "Save us? What do we look like, damsels in distress?" She kissed Hunter's forehead to soften her words. "But Odie's right. I bet the binding spell can stop a demon-touched witch long enough for us to get out of there."

"And if Morgan is right, and La Voisin is amenable to teaching us, we'll learn even more life-changing magic," I added.

The guys fell silent, probably because they knew what I was referring to, and couldn't deny that I was right. The demon marks made me and Eva more powerful—gave us the ability to use stronger magic—but they also bound us to the royals. If they ever felt us return to the present, they could control us. Unless, of course, we figured out a way to sever, or at least muffle, that connection.

Really, seeking out a woman who was probably the most horrible witch in history was our best chance.

"Don't eat anything she gives you," Diana said, sitting down with us.

Merlin and Morgan were still in the kitchen area, flirting and chatting and watching a cauldron full of love potion bubble over the fire. Morgan wanted to bring it as an offering to La Voisin, or anyone else who might need to be bribed.

"She's rumored to have poisoned up to 2,500 people," Diana continued. "I wouldn't trust her as far as I could throw her."

"Morgan has already rented a flat near the poisoner witch's home for us to stay in," I assured her. "She says we'll get food from the market and eat at the flat. We'll only be at La Voisin's for lessons."

"Which hopefully won't take long. We need to get home." Alex let out a heavy breath. "I wonder how long we've been gone, anyway?"

I wondered that often too. Timewalking was finicky, particularly if you were a newbie who didn't have a lot of control yet. A few weeks might have passed here, but when I finally landed us back in our period of origin, it could be years in the future. The thought made my stomach churn.

"Or what's happened in our time," Diana piped up, ripping my musings off timewalking. "What's the world going to be like when we return?"

A silence fell over the table. No one could answer that question.

# CHAPTER TEN

The next day, after saying our goodbyes, Eva, Morgan, and I timewalked to Paris, 1665.

And nearly got mowed down by a horse.

"Pardon me!" the rider exclaimed as he reared the animal back, flustered by our sudden appearance. "I was distracted. My sincerest apologies!"

"No problem," I replied. When my words came out in French, I shot Morgan a grateful look.

Before we'd left the cottage, she'd gifted me and Eva with dresses appropriate for the era, as well as translation talismans. The talismans were gold rings that would allow us to understand and speak any language.

*Thank the universe,* I thought, rotating the ring on my finger as I watched people walking the streets, all of them speaking rapidly in antiquated French. My high school French would not have stood up well here.

"Where to? The apartment?" I asked Morgan.

Since she'd wanted to arrive at a very specific location and moment, she'd been the one to timewalk us here. I assumed that was because she wanted to swing by the apartment she'd pre-rented to check that everything was fine.

"Follow me," she replied, and took off down the street.

Eva and I followed.

Even though I'd have liked to consider myself cool, calm, and collected after timewalking a dozen times, I wasn't. And Eva was, understandably, worse at concealing her awe. Her mouth was hanging open so wide, I was sure a fly would soar in there at any moment. But honestly, who could blame her? There was just too much to see.

Horses were everywhere, which, me being from a city, was both strange to witness and smelly. A mix of people from all walks of life milled around, and although I didn't know too much about this period, the classes were obvious by their state of dress.

There seemed to be a lot of beggars, and just as many people trying to make a living by selling brooms they carried on their backs, or carting large buckets of water around for reasons I wasn't sure of. We passed by a woman on the other side of the street who, from her overly exposed bosom, I was sure was a prostitute trying to entice a finely dressed man in a crimson cape.

The working classes seemed to stick to brown, black, and white clothing, with perhaps a pop of color in the form of laces or embroidery. On the other hand, the higher classes stood out in bright reds and blues—like our dresses.

The men's outfits struck me as funny, billowing at the top with tights underneath.

*So unflattering.*

I was still stuck in observation mode when Morgan stopped before a door, and I nearly bowled her over.

"Do watch where you're going." She smiled in amusement.

"Sorry," I breathed and straightened my crimson skirt. "There's just . . . a lot happening."

"Thank goodness we will be here for a few days so you can see some of it." Morgan fluffed up her voluminous red mane a little. "Now, get ready. Remember, La Voisin thinks that I'm of this era, from the south of France. I'd like her to believe the same about you two—at least until I've set up the proper wards."

"We're at her place already?!" I squeaked.

*You've got this. You've got this. You've got this.*

I chanted the phrase in my head like a mantra.

"We are," Morgan replied. "Gather your wits, loves. This woman is something else."

She knocked, and footsteps sounded right away. When the door flew open, a stout, dough-faced woman was on the other side. She wore bright blue, indicating that her dress was costly.

As she took us in, her hand landed on her hip, and her thin lips curled up in a crafty smile. "I wasn't sure if you'd actually show."

I repressed a shudder at her voice, oily with darkness. In fact, the longer she stood there, the more it became obvious to me that La Voisin was unlike any other witch I'd known.

Even without placing a finger on her, I could feel the evil wafting off of her in a way that I couldn't discern on myself or Eva. I had a feeling this was because, unlike us, the poisoner had embraced her darkness. Just standing in her presence made my scar burn a little, and her voice grated like sandpaper running down my back.

*Evil to the core. We must be careful.*

"I said I would return, and here we are," Morgan responded to the witch's remark and gestured behind her. "Your pupils."

"Only if you pay half first," La Voisin said. "This is no ordinary black mass or plea for contraceptives. For this consultation, you pay half of what we discussed up front. Only then will I let you inside to negotiate specifics and discuss my additional fees."

"I would expect nothing less." Morgan reached into a bag she carried and pulled out a small gold amulet.

I squinted at it, trying to discern the details of the piece.

But La Voisin's snarky expression vanished, and she grabbed for the trinket. "It's Roman? Of Juno's cult?"

Morgan nodded. "Authentic in provenance, and imbued with magic from a powerful witch of that era."

For the first time, La Voisin looked impressed. "The woman coming here for fertility healing will eat this up. Come in. We shall discuss what you need."

I'd expected to be led into a shared hallway before

reaching an apartment, so when the witch revealed that the entire building was her home, I was impressed.

"Business must be good." I gestured to an elaborate painting as we passed.

Historically, homes were smaller than in modern day, particularly for people of lesser means. That La Voisin had so much space to herself, and was able to fill it with non-essentials like art, spoke volumes about her talents as a businesswoman.

"It's why you've come to me, isn't it?"

"Of course," I replied, reminding myself of our temporary cover.

We were young women who wished to be trained by the witch so we might start similar businesses in Lyon and Marseilles.

We arrived in a large sitting room capable of entertaining at least fifteen people. It was plush too. A space filled with furniture and decor that I would expect to see in a royal household. Not only did the notorious poisoner make a good deal of money, I suspected that she wanted her wealthier patrons to feel at home here.

Diana had informed me that much of the French court and aristocracy sought La Voisin out for spells, specialized poisons, abortions, contraceptives, and other dark deeds.

"Have a seat." The witch gestured to a couch, on which we all sat. She took the seat across from us, a design that reminded me much of a throne. "What do you wish for them to learn?"

"Many things," Morgan replied. "But first, I have a request."

La Voisin nodded.

"Do you mind if I supplement your ward with one of my own? My girls are coming to you in good faith, and I wish for them to be secure."

The famed poisoner chuckled. "You *are* more skilled than most. As long as you do not damage those enchantments I have set up, you may do as you wish."

Morgan stood and spread her hands. Fuchsia magic poured from them as easily as water from a pitcher. It flew about the living area, climbing the walls, obscuring the windows, sealing us safely in this space.

I breathed a sigh of relief. Although La Voisin was a famed witch, Morgan was certainly stronger. Whatever she'd done would ensure our safety.

"Now we can speak freely." Morgan took a seat and crossed her ankles. "My girls have come here to be taught by you, although not exactly as I have requested."

La Voisin arched a dark eyebrow.

"It's clear that you have bound your blood to darkness," Morgan's voice dropped low. "And that you're powerful enough to control yourself after making such a deal. My girls are demon-touched too. They wish to learn how to use the black magic within themselves and resist possession by the royals. Can you teach them?"

La Voisin's eyes went straight to the windows, and then the walls, trailing over everything.

Morgan chuckled. "My ward is strong. Any listening

devices the royal has put in here will not pick up my request."

"Ingenious," La Voisin muttered as she stroked her chin. She studied Morgan for a few long minutes, occasionally darting her gaze between Eva and me. "What did you say your name was again?"

"Morgan."

"No surname?"

"None that I wish to share."

"And the girls?"

Morgan gestured to me.

"I'm Claire," I said, giving my middle name just as we'd discussed. If La Voisin turned on us we didn't want her knowing Eva's and my true identities. That might make us easier to find in the future and we didn't want the demons having a leg up.

"And I'm Nora," Eva said, using the other half of her full name, Evanora.

"I'm afraid that *none* of us have surnames," Morgan added, because it was clear that La Voisin was about to pry further.

"Hmmm." The poisoner pressed her lips together until they became white. "What makes you think I have made a deal with a royal demon?"

"History assures us of it," Morgan replied smoothly. "You see, we're timewalkers. We know of what you've done, all your powers. Only someone who made a deal with a devil could perform such acts."

"Timewalkers?!" La Voisin shot up. "How should I

proceed with my life, my business? I—"

Morgan held up a finger. "I will not give you any hints as to your future. Unless you teach Claire and Nora."

The witch fell back into her seat, clearly astonished. After a moment, she began stroking her chin again.

"That information would be invaluable, but to defy a royal . . . That's the most dangerous thing one can do. For such a sacrifice, I will require *much* more than simply the tale of my future and the coin we discussed."

"Like?"

"A cloak to perform in. I have been investing in my home to attract a certain level of customer, but when I travel, I look less than appealing. I need something worthy of a queen. I wish to have it before the lessons."

"Is that all?"

La Voisin was quiet for a moment, clearly wondering how far she could push her luck.

As if trying to temper the poisoner from being too greedy, Morgan crossed her thin arms over her chest.

The black witch didn't balk, only studied Morgan more carefully. "When we're done, I will also require additional monetary compensation in the sum of a thousand livres and an act of magic from you." She pointed to Morgan.

My ancestor eyed the poisoner witch sternly as she considered the demand. "For teaching my girls, and not betraying them, you shall have it all. Your future told, the livres, the cloak, and a single act of magic. Nothing more. Nothing less."

The poisoner rubbed her hands together just as the clock

in her sitting room struck the hour. The intense glee in her face vanished, and she sprang up from her seat. "Very well. We have a deal. For now, however, you must go. I have a client stopping by—one who will not appreciate being seen here." She rolled her eyes. "It's merely a contraceptive call. As if half the ladies at court don't use it."

"When should we return? The sooner the better."

La Voisin looked taken aback, perhaps surprised that Morgan could supply what she promised quickly. "If you can get the cloak, we could start tonight. Or in two days' time. I have other . . . engagements until then. They're sure to be bloody and drawn out."

A shudder rolled through me as I recalled the black masses and sacrifices that Diana had informed me the poisoner performed.

Morgan, however, kept a cool mask and rose. She motioned for us to do the same. "We are going to get a cloak now. Do not tamper with my wards. I shall know if you do. We will return at sunset for their first lesson. You will either cancel your other appointments or schedule them around my girls' lessons. We are not paying so much just to wait around."

The poisoner considered this for a moment before nodding. "You make a valid point. I'm all yours." She gestured to the hall and walked us briskly to the door. "I shall be ready this evening."

Once we were on the street, I grabbed Morgan's arm. "You're such a badass! How did you know what to say?"

Since I'd known the legendary witch, I'd recognized her

as charming, a woman who usually got what she wanted, but I hadn't expected La Voisin to agree to our terms so easily. It was like the poisoner had said, betraying a royal demon was no joke. But by helping us learn to use their magic to protect ourselves, that was exactly what she was doing.

"When dealing with people from other times, particularly influential, powerful people, you must understand what they desire. And that stems from the world around them. When I left you in Merlin's care, I was already certain who I wanted you to learn from. I spent weeks studying La Voisin and the French court that she's entangled in. The woman wants power and recognition in her society. And those sorts of people always want one thing above all others."

"What's that?" Eva asked, her blue eyes shining with excitement.

"Control. She asked for many things, but *all* of them can be used to gain control and power. However, most of all she wishes to learn how she will meet her end. If she knows her future, she believes that she can control it too."

I tilted my head. "I thought you said we can't inform others of that. That it throws things off?"

Morgan turned to me. "We cannot tell those in our bloodline about how they will meet their ends. It is inadvisable to share that information with others too. But in this case, it will not matter. La Voisin will meet her end the same way whether I tell her how or not. Her pride will dictate it."

I let that settle as Morgan led us through the streets, pointing out shops of interest that we'd need to stop in for supplies later.

We'd walked no more than ten minutes when she paused before another door and pulled a key out of her bag.

"Welcome to your home, at least in this era. Let's get settled in. Then we will go shopping for what your teacher requires."

# CHAPTER ELEVEN

The day flew by, and soon enough, we were back at La Voisin's door, the cloak draped over my ancestor's arm.

Eva squeezed my hand as Morgan knocked. "Ready, *Claire*?"

I smiled at her reminder to use our false names. "I think so, *Nora*. Did you ever think we'd be doing something so crazy?"

Eva snorted. "You're joking, right? Pretty much every moment since our Culling-year has been one unbelievable thing after another."

"You're right. What was I thinking? Seeking lessons from a notorious murderer is mundane," I teased just before La Voisin opened the door.

Her gaze landed on Morgan's face, but quickly flitted down to the cloak. Her eyes widened, and her lips parted in awe. "That's my garment?"

Morgan handed it to her.

The cape was crimson red and embroidered with golden eagles. Easily the most luxurious piece offered in this arrondissement of the city. That had been reflected by the price of 1,500 livres. I was sure that some people lived off less per year. And yet, Morgan had insisted upon this specific cloak. She'd even already gathered the money on her last trip by performing a bit of witchcraft for one of the wealthiest mademoiselles in Paris. I suspected that if I looked in the history books, they might tell me that the poisoner possessed this specific garment.

La Voisin's hands ran over the velvet. "I must say, when you make a promise, you deliver. Please come in. We shall get started."

She led us into the same room as before, waving at the walls as she did so. "Everything is still intact. But I must ask, will your wards hinder their ability to work with black magic?"

Morgan shook her head. "I don't think so, but if we discover that they do, I will alter them."

"Very good." La Voisin gestured to a salt circle in front of the fireplace. "First things first. Which of the royals gifted you with a demon-touched mark?"

I repressed a shudder at her use of the term *gifted*. "Ishtar."

"Lucifer," Eva said, with no hint of waver in her voice.

The witch's eyes widened. The fact she was impressed told me that her mark was not from the queen or king, but one of the three Furies of Xaphan. "Very good. This will work out well. It would be harder to teach you if we were all demon-touched by the same royal. This is an ideal situation as it spreads the risk around a bit. Now, if you don't mind, please step into the circle."

"Why?" I asked.

One of the most basic rules of witchcraft was that you never stepped into someone's salt circle unless you knew what they intended to do with it. La Voisin wagged her finger in the air. "Smart girl. Remain skeptical." She motioned down to the circle. "I'm bound to Xaphan. Although Morgan's magic has, presumably, veiled you from the royals in this place, I felt it necessary to add more specific protection. The circle nulls Xaphan's reach in this home—a place where, according to our bond, he is welcome at all times."

"Why is it so small?" Eva eyed the area that couldn't have been more than three feet in diameter.

"I can't very well make it too spacious, now can I? He would feel a larger null area, and pay me a visit."

Good point.

Assured that what she said made sense and would only help to protect us, I stepped into the salt circle. Eva followed a moment later.

"We will get to the lessons, but first I need a bit more information." La Voisin positioned herself in front of us. "In addition to learning black magic, you wish to halt the influence of your lord and lady. Or perhaps hide from them in whatever era you call home. Is that true?"

We nodded.

"Very well. I have done this before, temporarily. It is not for the faint of heart. It also takes time to arrange, which is why I'm posing the question now. How familiar are you with spirit walking and talking?"

"Familiar, but we can't do it ourselves," Eva replied.

"Have you ever called a spirit?"

"Yes." The hair on my arms electrified at the memory. "But we had a spirit worker there to guide us. Nora and I didn't manage that alone."

"Well, that's how you will keep the royal demons out of your head."

"We're going to resist being possessed by banishing a ghost?" I asked, lost.

"No, girl." La Voisin looked like she wanted to roll her eyes at me and barely refrained. "By inviting a ghost—specifically, one from a mind witch—into your head for protection."

My heart began to pound. Back when Amethyst had been possessed by a ghost, I'd asked her if I was at risk too. I distinctly recalled her answer.

A ghost wouldn't want to possess me because I was naturally resistant to ghostly energies. It would be terrible for both parties involved—perhaps even kill me.

I whirled to face Morgan. "Is that safe?"

Her eyes were wide as she shook her head. "To be honest, I'm not sure. It seems rather drastic."

"Well, of course it is! This is the royal demons we're talking about here! Did you expect the solution to your problem to be easy?" La Voisin threw up her hands. "It's the only way I've found that works. And yes, it can be dangerous if a ghost possesses you, but this would not be a true possession—rather a *union*. You would *invite* the ghost of a mind witch into your body, to live life as they once did. The vibrancy of feeling alive is a lure that most spirits can't resist."

"How?" Eva asked, her voice shaky.

"I'm not sure of the specific incantation. I had to have a spirit worker perform the rite on me. But it has to do with blood." La Voisin spread her hands wide as if that was a foregone conclusion. "With ghosts, it usually does."

I nodded. When we'd banished Amethyst's ghost, he'd drunk my blood, so I could believe that.

"So all it takes is calling forth a mind witch's ghost and providing blood to create a bind?" Morgan asked. "If we learned the incantation is there any way we can do it ourselves? Not involve a spirit worker?"

It was obvious to me that Morgan didn't want to let even more people in on who we were, or our secrets. The poisoner witch was a substantial threat as it was.

La Voisin shook her head. "Absolutely not. They *need* a witch familiar with spirits to bind them. Once the spirit worker completes the binding, the mind witch's ghost will protect the girls by using the skills they had in life."

"If they're ghosts how do they do that?" Eva asked.

"Once the ghost is bound to you, it is reinvigorated by your magic. Essentially, it uses a bit of your own power and lifeforce to do what it does best. With mind witches that generally includes controlling or protecting minds." She paused, and her eyes narrowed briefly as if something frustrating had occurred to her. "Although there is one problem."

One? I could think of a dozen potential issues.

"What's that?" Morgan asked.

"I know a spirit talker who will do the deed for you. For a fee, of course. But timewalking or traveling to other realms will loosen the ghost's bind inside you. It may not last if you timewalk more than once. The further you travel through the centuries, the looser the bind. Then you'd have to start the process all over again."

I chewed on my lip. We'd totally be timewalking more than once. Of course, we knew a spirit worker who could renew the bond should it break, but she was new, our age. Would Amethyst be up for such a thing? Or maybe we could ask her parents?

Would this crazy scheme even work?

"I don't think we have much of a choice," Eva whispered to me. "We need to get home, and we need to be undetectable when we do. Particularly if we plan on using demon magic. I'm guessing that the royal we're connected to might sense someone using their power if they're in the same realm?" She looked at La Voisin.

"Yes. Which is another reason why you'll be performing what I teach you in a protective circle." The witch crossed her arms over her chest as if daring us to fight back on that.

I loosed a sigh. "It looks like we need you to get hold of that mind witch—tomorrow, if you can. Until then," I gestured down at the salt circle that I stood inside, "teach us everything about working with black magic."

# CHAPTER TWELVE

The black tendrils of magic flew from my fingers to swirl around La Voisin.

She tried to bat it away, but unlike all my previous attempts, my power stayed the course, doing my bidding.

*It only took two days.*

Since we'd arrived in seventeenth century France, La Voisin had been showing me and Eva various ways to work with our dark magic. For me, the first time I released it without a spell was the most difficult occurrence. From there, it had grown easier, although the effort still drained me a lot more than my natural magic.

From the look on her face, our teacher hadn't expected such rapid advancement. I got the sense that it actually annoyed her. Which, for some reason—probably because I knew what a terrible person she was—made me pretty happy. I grinned and bid the magic to advance on the demon-touched witch again, tickling at her arm.

"Enough," La Voisin snapped. "Clearly you're quite skilled at bidding the shadows to do as you wish." The clock on her mantle chimed the hour, and her scowl lifted slightly. "Ah! Once again, I have lost track of time. We need to move on anyhow." She waved for us to follow her.

I stepped out of the salt circle and shuddered with relief. Being inside the poisoner's protective circle was uncomfortable—prickly—but we continued to practice within its confines because it was prudent. Should the royals be lurking nearby and sense our power, they would surely come check it out. And even Morgan claimed she wouldn't be a match for any of them.

As far as I knew, she was right. Neither Morgan nor Merlin would be able to defeat a royal. If that were the case, they would have done so in their lifetimes, and I wouldn't be in this position—training for a war and risking the lives of those I loved. The best M&M could do was trap them in Hell. And that experience was in their future—after the demons forced them to split up.

"Will you be going over spells for black witches?" Morgan stood from her spot on the chaise. "We've heard of such things." She was always careful not to mention too much, like that we already knew a black spell.

"I have never come across any," La Voisin said. "And besides, after a few more days of practicing with shadows, these two won't need spells, witching or otherwise. The shadows are more potent."

As much as I wanted to argue her point, I had a feeling she was right. The shadows were scary strong, but I still liked the idea of using spells. They were more direct and less open to interpretation. The shadows, on the other hand, had strayed a couple of times, and gone farther than I intended them to once. Each instance in which they exhibited their own will, no matter how slight, worried me. I would need to be very clear in my intention when I used them.

Moving on, the poisoner pulled out a large, blue book and opened it to a page in the middle. I watched as her fingers ran down the smudged and yellowed pages of what looked like a ledger.

"So what *are* we doing?" I asked.

"This book holds the record of all the deceased witches in Paris. Or at least, those I know about. When death is a part of your business, it's good to know when people perish. From here we can choose a suitable mind witch so that the spirit worker can call their ghost to help you," the black witch replied.

"There are so many," Eva murmured eyeing the names on the page.

"Not all are mind witches, but that's to our benefit. The spirit worker I spoke with will be here at any moment to perform such a task. She will need to know who to call."

My eyes bulged. I hadn't expected that to happen today. Truth be told, I'd have been content to wait a little longer before I invited some random ghost into my head.

"Are you choosing? Or do we get to?" Eva asked warily.

La Voisin snorted. "You may choose, but as mind

witches are rare, there aren't many options." Her finger tapped three names on the yellowed page. "These deceased witches are the most trustworthy candidates and strong with mind magic. If the spirit walker I called can get two of them to come, that would be ideal."

"Tell us a little more about the mind witches. What were they like in life?" Morgan asked, probably noting the sweat trailing down my face, and wanting to calm me.

The poisoner did as she asked, relaying what she knew of the three witches, which wasn't more than the basics. One had been a baker who supplemented his income with mind magic. Another had actually lived at court as one of the queen's ladies-in-waiting. The last was a fortune teller.

My best friend and I shared a long glance as La Voisin detailed the third witch. It was clear that neither of us wanted the fortune teller in our heads. He'd not only dabbled in reading the future, but performed black masses. Even if La Voisin claimed he was trustworthy the similarities were too stark for us to trust such a ghost.

"How are we going to know if this works?" Eva asked. "It would be idiotic to call upon Lucifer or Ishtar to test it."

"By the darkness, of course it would," La Voisin spat. "If you tried that, I wouldn't dare be at your side. I work for hire, but I don't want the queen and king of darkness knowing of my involvement."

"As you've mentioned about a million times," Eva muttered.

The black witch's eyes narrowed. "Well, luckily for you, I have a plan. I'm not the only servant of a royal in Paris right now. In fact, there are two witches who serve the same masters as yourselves."

"We don't serve them," I shot back. "Obviously."

The poisoner held up her hands. "I misspoke. An honest error from a follower of darkness."

*Universe, give me strength . . .*

"Please, continue," Morgan urged, although she too looked annoyed by the witch's declaration.

"Currently, there are two black witches at court. One follows Ishtar, the other Lucifer. Both have learned to read others' minds from their masters and always carry the demon stones gifted by the royals. If you can keep them out of your mind, you should be able to do the same with Ishtar and Lucifer."

"Though I suspect that it will take more effort to keep the royals at bay?" Morgan asked.

"There's no way to know for sure." La Voisin said with a shrug. "But I believe that you're right."

I mulled that over. It wasn't an ideal situation, particularly as we'd be up against high-powered individuals in a court that respected them. Then again, nothing about this was really ideal, nor would it totally ensure our protection worked. I agreed with Morgan in that the royals would be stronger, *much* stronger. The true test would come when we faced Ishtar and Lucifer, and they tried to possess us—which was inevitable. Until then, our best hope was to trust that the vile woman in front of us was motivated by a massive payday.

A knock came at the front door.

"That must be the spirit worker now. Make your choices." La Voisin set the book down, still open to the same page, and went to get the door.

Eva and I exchanged alarmed glances at having to make such an important choice so quickly.

"Do you want the baker or the court lady?" I asked.

"The baker. Maybe he can instill some knowledge of how to make a good croissant while he's in there."

I snorted as La Voisin reentered the room with a woman trailing behind her. The newcomer wore a long, olive green dress done in a style simpler than what La Voisin wore. The shawl around the woman's shoulders was white, just like her hair, and gauzy. Most reassuringly, her blue eyes twinkled kindly as she studied us.

My shoulders loosened a little.

"Mademoiselles, this is Mélanie Citron, one of the most experienced spirit walkers and talkers in Paris. This is Nora and Claire, the two who wish to keep the royal demons from invading their heads."

"Understandably," Mélanie replied, to which La Voisin frowned, clearly in disagreement. "Catherine has informed me that binding you to the ghosts of mind witches will keep evil from possessing you. I can do such a thing—but are you young ladies amenable to such a relationship?"

Eva and I nodded.

Mélanie arched an eyebrow. "Are you sure?"

"Yes. We are." I nodded to emphasize my reply. "La Voisin told us that as long as it was mutual, the ghost wouldn't harm us. Is that right?"

"It is." Mélanie's gaze went to Eva.

"I wish there were another way, but I'm told there isn't," Eva admitted. "So yes. I'm ready."

The spirit worker gave us a small, understanding smile. "Very well then. Catherine tells me she has chosen three candidates. Who would you like me to call from the spirit realm first?"

Eva offered up the name of the baker, and Mélanie nodded.

"Excellent choice. Claude is a recently departed soul. I've actually spoken with him in life. You might call us old friends. That will make him easier to find."

I bit my lip and hoped she'd say the same about my choice.

The ghost whisperer got to work, drawing a new salt circle specific to calling spirits, and set items in the circle. The setup looked very similar to the one Amethyst had created when we banished the ghost who had possessed her against her will.

When Mélanie was ready, she invited Eva into the circle. She then pulled a small, silver dagger from her boot, and a silver bowl no larger than a half cup from the pocket of her dress.

"We must make a blood offering. Not only to attract Claude's ghost, but to bind him to you."

Her eyes ran over La Voisin, who had been standing at the edge of the room, watching intently, and then slid back to Eva. "You have been informed that this binding is not permanent, right? That the spirit may leave sooner than you wish? Particularly if you timewalk or move through realms?"

It was the first indication that Mélanie recognized we weren't from this time. It was also a reassurance that while La Voisin wasn't a good person, she had told us the truth. My shoulders relaxed a little more.

"Yes," Eva whispered. "We're hoping that they'll stick around, but we have an idea of what to do if they don't."

Holy universe, I hoped it wouldn't come to that. We would have to timewalk at least twice more. There was no getting around that. And as much confidence as I had in Amethyst and her family as spirit walkers and talkers, I only wanted to undergo this binding once.

"Very well," Mélanie said. "Remain standing right there. Cut your palm when I indicate, allow some blood to drip into the bowl, and agree to the binding when asked. Otherwise, stay silent. That is all I require of you."

Eva gulped audibly, and gave a single nod.

The spirit worker stepped up to the edge of the circle and held her hands in the air. "Spirit world, hear my plea."

I jumped as the air began crackling with electricity. Hazy violet light swirled out of Mélanie's hands, so light and bright in comparison to the dimly lit room and the dark magic we'd been working with for days.

"I request that Claude Faust return to this plane. I ask that he walk among the living once again."

Mélanie gestured to the dagger in Eva's hand. My friend sliced into her palm, and allowed blood to drip into the bowl.

"An offering is waiting for you, Claude. Come, drink. Come live once again. *Crucilarva*."

Violet magic soared all around the inside of the circle. It swirled like a vicious vortex, kicking up dust from the floor. I watched, mesmerized, as, a breath later, a diaphanous figure popped into existence in the circle, and bowed to Eva.

"May I?" He pointed to the bowl.

Eva darted a cautious gaze at Mélanie, who gave her a gentle nod. "Yes."

The ghost picked up the bowl and sniffed it as if it were a fine wine. After one sip, he sighed. "Ahhh, this is what it feels like to live again. So vibrant. So lovely."

"If you wish, you can experience it for longer. We have a barter in mind," Mélanie offered. "The young woman before you needs help keeping a royal demon out of her mind. She's sensitive to possession."

"From who?" Claude asked, curious.

"Lucifer," Mélanie replied, because Eva was keeping good on her word to remain silent save for at the appropriate moments.

The ghost's eyes widened. "I see. Well, that is rather serious. What does he mean to do to you, mademoiselle?"

Once again, Eva glanced at the spirit worker.

"Tell him," Mélanie whispered.

"He means to take over the world. This world, but centuries in the future."

Claude gasped. "No!"

"Yes," Eva whispered.

They fell silent, each gazing into the other's eyes. The ghost seemed to be thinking.

Finally, when I felt like someone had to say something or I'd burst, the ghost spoke.

"I have a son, and soon he will have a child. I have seen the babe growing in his wife's belly, though she does not know it yet." He took another sip of Eva's blood and shivered with delight. "I do not know if my family line will continue for many centuries, but if there's any chance they will, I must do what I can to help. Yes, I will assist you, protect your mind from infiltration, for as long as I'm able to resist the call back to the spirit world."

Eva breathed a sigh of relief. "Thank you."

The ghost turned to Mélanie. "I presume that you are capable of performing such a binding?"

She smiled at Claude. "Yes, old friend. Just drink your fill of blood and enjoy. I'll do the rest."

Claude did as she said, neatly setting the cup down when he was finished.

Mélanie raised her hands to the ceiling. "May two join as one until the living's work is done. May two join as one until the living's work is done. May two join as one until the living's work is done." A purple ball of light glowed in her hand, and she stretched it toward Eva. "*Capistrum*."

Claude gasped and soared toward Eva as if he was being sucked through a wind tunnel. When the ghost hit my friend, she let out a yelp and closed her eyes as she gripped her head.

A heartbeat passed in silence, two, then three. I drew in

a breath, realizing that I'd quit breathing some time ago. And still Eva didn't move, didn't speak, didn't even open her eyes.

My lips parted to ask a question, but Mélanie held up a hand, stopping me.

After seconds that stretched on like an eternity, she stepped toward Eva and placed her hand on her shoulder. "The binding is now complete."

Eva gasped and her eyes flew open. "Whoa! What was that last bit that happened?"

Mélanie nodded. "Claude was trying to find a place to settle. For an incorporeal being, it is difficult to inhabit a restrictive form again. When he found a place, he let me know. He is safe, not obtrusive, and willing to serve and protect you from the royals."

Eva's eyes shimmered with unshed tears. "Thank you."

"You're welcome, my dear. It is the least I can do. I too have family and hope my line will live through the centuries." She dropped her hand from Eva's shoulder and turned to me. "And now, it's your turn."

I switched places with Eva in the circle.

The process went exactly the same, and when my ghost, a woman named Louise, dressed in a fine gown and done up with a full face of makeup, arrived, we had a little chat.

It didn't take long before she too agreed to help. All I'd needed to mention was that she'd feel alive inside me, and Louise was ready to hop into my head.

Mélanie ran through the ritual, and I steadied myself for the moment the ghost would enter my head. When she did,

I understood why Eva had been deadly silent. It was unlike anything I'd ever experienced, as if someone was rifling through the inside of my mind, flitting about.

I could even hear Louise laughing. It was loud, and made me cringe.

After a few moments of this, unease trickled through me —like bugs walking on my arms and legs. She was taking a long time . . . much longer than Claude.

Mélanie began tapping her foot, and my instinct that Louise was taking her precious time solidified.

*Everything okay in there?* I thought, before I could even stop to question if she could hear me.

*Of course! I'm looking through your memories,* Louise called back as if what she was doing was natural. *Your gentleman friend is rather handsome, isn't he? Though his hair is quite odd. So short!*

My throat tightened. I hadn't even considered that the ghost in my head would be able to see my memories. But of course they would.

Internally, I groaned, sure she was peeking at some of my most intimate moments, things I could barely tell Eva most of the time. But I didn't want to rock the boat and risk losing her protection. That, and Louise was from a different time. Maybe people were more up in each others' business in her era?

*Oh!* Louise added a moment later. *And your name isn't Claire! It's Odette! I can see that being bound to you will be very interesting indeed!*

*Can you please not do that and settle in?* I tried to keep my cool. *Mélanie needs to finish binding us.*

*Oops! Sorry!* the ghost chirped. She ceased moving, and the feeling of spiders crawling on my skin ground to a halt.

I sighed.

"She is nosy, isn't she?" Mélanie asked, raising an eyebrow that made me wonder if she heard the bit about my name. "Are you sure about this one?"

I studied the spirit worker carefully. If Mélanie had heard Louise's comment, it didn't seem like she'd say anything around the poisoner. I moved on and contemplated her question. While I wasn't at all sure about Louise, the only other option was too much like La Voisin. I wouldn't be able to trust him at all.

"Yes."

"Very well," Mélanie said, and extended her hand to bind the ghost to me.

# CHAPTER THIRTEEN

*I* scratched the nape of my neck, trying to dispel the sense of discomfort creeping around within me. It had been hours since Mélanie bound Louise and me, but I still hadn't gotten used to the sensation of a ghost sitting inside my head.

Moving.

Chattering.

Peeking into my private memories.

I'd already come to the conclusion that Louise was a less than ideal guest.

Eva, on the other hand, appeared at ease with Claude.

*Spin it,* I told myself, and reached for something positive. *At least we have a chance at keeping the royals from controlling us.*

"Considering how much Mélanie charged for so little time, I think I might have to contemplate a new business venture." La Voisin studied me as the carriage we'd hired to take us to the Louvre Palace came to a halt. "Of course, that will be after I see how well you take to the ghost. So far, it isn't looking good." She shook her head as if she actually cared. "I don't want my clients in distress. If the experience isn't good, they won't pay."

Apparently, I wasn't hiding my unease as well as I thought.

"Yeah, you okay?" Eva placed her hand on mine.

"Fine. Just not used to her yet," I reassured my friend as I twisted to face her. "How do I look? Like someone who would stroll around court?"

"Perfect. Me?"

"Your style's on point." I winked.

We were both dressed to the nines and ready to search the Louvre Palace for the witches who called Lucifer and Ishtar master. Our plan was to nudge them into thinking we were one of them. La Voisin was sure that they would want to check for themselves by infiltrating our minds.

It still puzzled me that the royals would teach someone to do this, but I suspected it was so they'd have a presence within the powerful court—a say in what the king of France did. Truly, their motives didn't matter. As long as Eva and I could keep Monsieur Renard and Louise de La Vallière out of our minds, that was all that mattered to me.

"Remember, loves," Morgan said as the driver stepped off his platform to come open the door. "Let me and La Voisin do most of the talking. At least until we find Louise de La Vallière and Monsieur Renard. Just watch and pay attention to what's happening. If we're lucky, the witches will try to gain information on you before we even tell them who you are. Then you can practice without outing yourself."

We nodded just as the carriage door opened, and a man extended a hand. "Apologies for the rough journey, mademoiselles and mesdames. The streets are a mess."

"No apologies needed," I replied as I gave the young driver a winning smile. "Thank you."

We paid him and approached the palace. I'd been to the Louvre before, but in the era of the Sun King, what was now a world-renown museum looked different. In the future, it was hard to visualize the grandness of the palace through all the tourists, but not now.

The building itself looked brighter, cleaner. Most notably, however, was the lack of the glass pyramid that stood in front of the modern day museum. In place of the art installation people milled about an open space, gossiping and laughing, while soldiers watched dutifully.

"What are we going to do about all the guards?" I couldn't imagine that we would be allowed to simply walk around a royal palace. Particularly with King Louis XIV in residence. "Won't they stop us?"

La Voisin chuckled. "I've already made arrangements. One of my best clients, Madame Montespan, is vying to become the king's favored mistress. She lives nearby and spends much of her time at the palace as a lady-in-waiting to the queen."

"She's close to the queen and wants her husband?" Eva's blue eyes widened. "That's cold."

"Very backstabby," I agreed.

La Voisin laughed. "She will one day prevail, no doubt. The king is hardly known for his chastity. However, my client's biggest problem is not King Louis, but his favored mistress of the moment, Louise de La Vallière. She is the very witch you seek, Nora."

"Right." Eva huffed out a breath, "France really needs to come up with a new name to fall in love with . . . So many Louis and Louises!"

"So what do you do for Madame Montespan?" I asked, not wanting to get off track.

"Black masses. Poisons. Even potions." La Voisin shook her head. "The silly girl thinks after she becomes the favored mistress, she can entice His Majesty to leave the queen. A most foolish idea. My methods are powerful, but the ties that bind nations and keep the peace are much stronger." She shrugged. "I've told her such things. That she should be happy to grace the king's bed when he calls, but she won't listen. She claims every time she talks to the king, he seems just a bit more enamored with her."

The poisoner spread her hands out in front of her. "Perhaps he is. All I know is that each amulet, mass, and poison brings me more livres."

"Madame Montespan will ask about us, won't she?" Eva inquired.

La Voisin nodded. "She's loquacious and curious, but it is easy enough to distract her with talk of something new that I'm whipping up. Anytime I mention a poison or potion that could gain her the king's favor, she obsesses over it until I can provide it."

"And will she introduce us to these people who serve the demons?" Morgan asked. "Even the one she does not like?"

"She won't like leading me to Madame La Vallière, but if I tell her that the king's favorite mistress owes Mademoiselle Eva money, there will be no issue. If there's any chance to undermine Louis' prized whore, Madame Montespan will introduce us happily."

Morgan seemed placated, and we strode through the open courtyard, receiving a few surreptitious glances from a couple of the guards. I got the sense that La Voisin's reputation preceded her. However, when a young woman approached, calling out the witch's name, the guards looked relieved that they hadn't stopped us.

"Madame Montvoisin! Over here!" A curvy, golden-haired woman waved as she picked up the skirt of her heavy dress to hurry over. "I got your note that you wished to speak!"

"Indeed I do, Madame Montespan," La Voisin said once the woman reached us, reeking of rose oil so strong, it made my nose twitch. "I have a few new wares that I thought you might like to hear about."

The woman's eyes widened, and the flush on her cheeks deepened. "Indeed! Please come inside. We shall have some wine."

Madame Montespan led us through the doors to the palace and down the hallways. With her guiding us, few glanced our way. The ones who did were accommodating rather than suspicious, and asked if we needed anything.

We'd entered a more femininely decorated wing of the palace, when La Voisin's hand snaked around Madame Montespan's forearm. "Actually, Athénaïs," La Voisin switched to using her client's first name, a tactic she claimed made the woman think they were friends. "Might I ask a favor first?

"Certainly, Catherine." Athénaïs used La Voisin's first name in return as her blonde eyebrows pulled together with interest. "What can I do for you?"

"I was hoping for an introduction to two people at court. One is Monsieur Renard . . ."

She paused, swallowing for dramatic effect. La Voisin wanted Madame Montespan to believe that she felt bad about asking her to introduce us to the king's favored mistress.

She continued after a moment, "This next one, you may not like much, but my friend requires an introduction for very specific purposes. You see, Mademoiselle Nora's family," she gestured to Eva, "has been requesting money from this particular woman. She is in their debt, and Mademoiselle Nora wishes to collect."

The mistress nodded. "Who is it, then?"

"Louise de La Vallière."

For the first time, Madame Montespan's lovely face soured.

Eva stepped forward to play her part. "We would be

ever so grateful for the introduction, Madame Montespan. She does owe us quite a bit of money."

The wanna-be mistress cocked her head. "How much?"

"Five thousand livres."

Madame Montespan's hand flew to her mouth. "For shame! That is a fortune!"

"Yes," Eva said. "And she has been dodging payments for quite some time. I thought to bring it to the king—"

Athénaïs' eyes lit up as the dots connected. "Oh no! She should not be allowed to skate by. I shall make the introductions today. If things do not go your way, then I shall speak to the king *for you*. As you know, I have great influence with him."

La Voisin had figured that Madame Montespan would jump at the chance to make the other woman look bad. She had predicted correctly.

Eva performed a small curtsy. "My family would appreciate that very much."

Madame Montespan's hands fell to her side. "Well, if you'd like to get this done first, I can show you where Monsieur Renard is at this very moment."

La Voisin arched an eyebrow. "How would you know that?"

Madame Montespan frowned. "When he is not in direct service of the king, which he isn't right now," her tone soured even more, "he is always in the library, reading."

My spine straightened. If the Louvre's library was anything like a modern library, this could be perfect timing.

A quiet, untroubled space for me to test my demon powers would be ideal.

I held out hope as Madame Montespan led us through the halls of the palace. When she stopped before the door, I steeled myself. Once Monsieur Renard realized I had demon magic, he would want to investigate. I would have to be on my toes for the moment he tried to infiltrate my mind.

Louise and I would only get a few chances to silence him before he drew attention. And then we'd have to find the king's mistress so Eva could undergo the same test.

Madame Montespan opened the library door. "If you don't mind, I'll wait out here. Monsieur Renard and I do not see eye to eye, but he will not mind you introducing yourselves. He's always in the chair in the far back right corner, *always*."

La Voisin nodded and led the way through the palace library. It was a grand room, and yet, if one could look past all the gold decor and garish cherubs, the library was still just a library. It reeked of old books, and had a calming, erudite air about it.

Monsieur Renard was in the exact spot Madame Montespan had said he would be, with his nose stuck in a book. He barely glanced up as we approached, and only gave us his attention a full ten seconds after we'd stopped before him.

"Yes, mesdames and mademoiselles?" His voice was pompous, exactly how one would describe a stereotypical snooty French voice.

"Good day, Monsieur Renard," La Voisin said. "We have a few questions for you."

I readied myself. La Voisin had promised she would get to the point. The quicker we worked, the faster we could leave the palace.

"And what would they be?" he asked dully as his eyes dropped back to his book.

"We are wondering what exactly you can do with that demon stone in your pocket." La Voisin pointed to his right pocket.

The man's head snapped up from the page he'd been reading. The poisoner witch had hit a nerve.

"I don't know what you mean," he said coolly.

But my skin had already begun to prickle as Monsieur Renard called his power to him. He was going to try to read my mind, all our minds.

Knowing I needed him to attempt this only on me, I stepped forward.

"She knows, because you made it obvious," I sneered as if he couldn't disgust me more. "Gallivanting around court, giving His Majesty exactly what he wants before he even wants it. You might have bound yourself to a dark royal, but you weren't careful about it. Your rise to power was too sudden. I wonder what the king would say if we told him of our suspicions?"

The man shot up and pointed at me. "Who are you?"

"Wouldn't you like to know?" I raised a palm and allowed a few inky black tendrils of demon magic show.

Monsieur Renard's hand flew to his mouth. "Who—"

He decided against asking, and acted exactly as we'd predicted.

A presence enveloped my head, oily and sticky. Monsieur Renard was trying to break in. I allowed him to get a good grip, to believe that he would succeed, even to see who I was. Once he pulled up one of my memories of the future, I called Louise to heel.

*Get him out,* I commanded.

The mind witch yawned.

*We have an agreement,* I yelled. *Get him out, or you'll be going back to the spirit world!*

There was a heavy sigh from the ghost. *I can see this is going to be a lot more work than I believed.*

I was about to tell her she had no flipping idea how much work it would be, when Louise flew into action, and the oily, sticky sensation of Monsieur Renard trying to infiltrate my head ceased to exist.

"How dare you expel me!" he cried and crashed backward into his chair with wild eyes. "I shall call the guards—!"

La Voisin grabbed Monsieur Renard by the back of the neck, and tipped a vial into his open mouth.

The man collapsed back into the chair and began snoring.

"Wow," Eva whispered. "Did you do it?"

I nodded. "Once Louise got off her ass, it was easy. I asked her to kick him out, and she did. But before that, I felt his influence in my head. Of course, it will probably be harder with Ishtar, but still, it was so . . . easy."

La Voisin chuckled. "Do you think I went through all that work of seeking a spirit worker for nothing?"

I shrugged. She was right. There would've been no point in putting herself out there and opening her home to another witch she didn't know if this wouldn't work.

Eva gestured to the man. "How long is he going to stay like that?"

Our dark mentor's hands turned to the air lazily. "Hours. He'll wake up with a stomach ache and have forgotten all about us when he finishes shitting his pants in a few days' time."

I turned to Eva. "Let's go find your lady and see if Claude performs as well."

We made it to the door of the library, and realized something was wrong. Madame Montespan was still out there, but she was speaking with someone—no, not speaking, *yelling*.

La Voisin held out her hand to stop us. "Let me go first."

We allowed her to pass and peek through the doors. When her head popped back into the library, she was beaming from ear to ear.

"Who is it?" I asked.

La Voisin's gaze locked on Eva. "Just the person you're looking for—the king's favored mistress, fresh from his bed." The poisoner smirked, likely relishing the chaos on the other side of the door. "I'll take care of Athénaïs while you test your ghost."

～

"This is cause for celebration." Morgan opened the door to our apartment with a flourish, and twirled around with a smile.

Each of our mind witches had protected me and Eva. Not only that, but Madame Montespan had been so embarrassed that we'd caught her arguing loudly with the notorious Louise de La Vallière that she'd claimed to have an engagement that she'd forgotten. We left the palace with no one any the wiser as to what we'd done.

Once we were in the carriage and trotting away from the palace, La Voisin had admitted that she was impressed and unsure what other wisdom she could impart on us, which relieved me. We might be leaving soon.

"When you say celebration, does that mean champagne?" Eva wiggled her eyebrows.

Morgan shimmied her hips in a move that reminded me a lot of the salsa, and grinned. "There's a charming little restaurant right around the corner."

"La Voisin said that she wouldn't be able to teach us much more," I remarked. "Should we leave soon?"

"Actually, I wanted to ask you that," Morgan replied. "Do you feel ready? Because if you do, we'll pay her tomorrow morning. Then of course, I must perform whatever bit of magic she requires, and hint at her future before we can leave." Her lips turned down in a slight frown.

The monetary amount alone was staggering, but that La Voisin also required magical payment and a hint as to what her future held, gave Morgan a sour taste in her mouth.

"Thank you for being willing to do that for us," I said. "I know it's a lot."

Her hand twirled in the air. "There's no need for thanks. The money is nothing to me. And there was little doubt that she'd recognize me as the elder and more powerful witch. Her requesting a favor was bound to happen. As long as I can perform magic, and it doesn't harm anyone, I'll do it gladly."

She turned and began rummaging through the wardrobe for a new dress. Since arriving in Paris, she'd picked up a few of the latest pieces, and some trinkets for Merlin. She'd also purchased a few skimpier outfits that I was sure were for him as well.

"Get dressed, loves," Morgan said as she pulled out a beautiful red frock. "We'll begin with champagne down the street. After that, we shall see where beautiful Paris takes us."

# CHAPTER FOURTEEN

I groaned as we walked to La Voisin's home. The night before, Morgan had proclaimed we should celebrate, and celebrate we did.

So hard.

I would probably be sweating champagne from my pores for weeks to come. I couldn't wait to get home. Not only for the people, pizza, showers, and beds—but also for more moderate celebrations. The past was way too hardcore for me.

Surprisingly, Morgan seemed completely unaffected, and she'd downed at least twice as much champagne as me.

"How do you look so bright-eyed and bushy-tailed?" Eva asked, rubbing her temples.

Morgan let out a laugh. "You've seen the drinking tendencies of my time. It's part of our lifestyle."

I nodded, knowing what she meant. We'd frequented the village tavern numerous times, and seen the same people there over and over. Sometimes I wondered if they ever left.

"I was hoping it was some kind of spell or something," Eva admitted.

Morgan's spine straightened. "No, but if there's one of those in your time that does the trick, let me know. I could earn coin from that."

I snorted. "If there was, we wouldn't look like a pair of hot messes right now."

Morgan's eyebrows furrowed at the modern slang, but she decided not to question it.

When we arrived at La Voisin's home, my ancestor knocked, and the poisoner witch flung the door open with a flourish.

"I was wondering when you'd show up! Had a night out, did you?"

It was that obvious? We must look terrible.

"Indeed we did," Morgan said. "Paris is a city for cele-brating."

"So they say." La Voisin let out a bark of laughter, and waved us inside.

We followed her into the expansive sitting room where we'd taken all of our lessons. The familiar rush of Morgan's wards flitted over me as I crossed the threshold. I sighed as a warm cocoon gave some relief.

"The one for comfort. So you wouldn't let your nerves get the best of you during lessons," Morgan explained, noticing the reaction. "Apparently, you didn't need it before, but today, it probably takes the edge off."

"Thank goodness," I muttered.

La Voisin pointed to the salt circle, already drawn on the ground. "Whoever wants to practice first, hop in."

My ancestor stepped forward. "Actually, we've only come to tell you that today will be our final day in Paris. Yesterday, you said you couldn't teach the girls much more. That's our cue to move on."

La Voisin nodded, seeming unsurprised. "I thought you'd say that." She collapsed onto the chaise. "That just leaves the matter of my payment."

From the bag Morgan wore against her hip, she pulled out a small pouch of coins, then another, and another. Five sat side by side by the time she was done.

"It's all there. Count it, if you will."

La Voisin's eyes lit up like a Christmas tree as she took in the pouches of livres. "No need. I trust that *you're* honest."

My eyebrows furrowed. Her emphasis gave me pause. Did she think that Eva and I were dishonest?

"Next, the magic, and then a bit about my future before you go." La Voisin leaned forward and placed her hands on her knees. "I've thought long and hard about what I wished for most. What could you give me that I could not conjure or create for myself? It took a while before I realized what that was—the same thing that brought you to my door."

La Voisin's eyes slithered to latch on to me.

"Me?" My blood froze. "You want Morgan to give you *me*?"

La Voisin scoffed. "I already have a daughter to care for, and she's enough work as it is."

A sensation of relief was just settling over me, when the witch's smile grew in a way that made my stomach sink.

"I am referring to timewalking."

Timewalking? She wanted Morgan to give her timewalking? I'd never heard of such a thing. When I shot a glance at my mentor, I was sure she hadn't either.

Her ruby lips were pursed and her ginger eyebrows knitted together as if she wasn't sure what to say.

I cleared my throat. "You want Morgan to give you the powers of timewalking?" I asked in an effort to clarify, "or you want her to timewalk you somewhere?"

"I'm aware that she cannot just transfer the skill. However, an amulet or a pendant of some sort, imbued with the power to timewalk, should be achievable." The poisoner shrugged. "That is what I want."

Silence descended upon the room. Was that possible? My totem had allowed me to timewalk, but that was only because Morgan had been controlling it—and I possessed the inherent magic. We were connected by blood and a destiny that Merlin had foreseen before the pair split. Surely it wouldn't work for someone like La Voisin, who had never revealed such a talent.

After a prolonged pause, my ancestor spoke. "I'm not sure I can create such a thing. I can spell pendants for many reasons. However, timewalking is an innate skill and rather specific. How you alter time matters—a lot. I'm not sure that enchanting any sort of object would allow you to explore the eras as you wish."

La Voisin's lips pressed together until they turned white.

"Perhaps, I might be able to create one if you wanted to timewalk to a *specific* place and time," Morgan offered, clearly trying to come to a happy medium. "But many eras? I'm sure that's just not possible."

The black witch shot up from her seat. "You said I could have anything! Any magical favor! And now you tell me you will not give me what I want?"

"I'm not saying I won't give it to you," Morgan corrected. "I'm saying I *can't*. It's impossible."

La Voisin's hands drifted to her hips, and for a moment, I thought her eyes would start shooting daggers at Morgan.

After several long seconds, she dropped her hands, and sneered. "I'd hoped it wouldn't come to this, but as always, my master was right. Now I have no regrets whatsoever for telling him about you." She snapped her fingers.

The room grew stiflingly hot, and the rotten stench of sulfur hit my nostrils. I backed up, my skin tingling at the change in atmosphere.

A horned figure appeared in the salt circle.

In my periphery, I caught Eva's flinch, and knew what had caused it, as my scar had begun to burn dully too.

Morgan threw herself in front of us. "We had a deal."

"We did. And you couldn't give me what I wanted. You expect me to betray my master for a bit of coin, a cloak, and a slice of my future?" La Voisin snorted. "What good would that do? What good are you if you can't give the prince of darkness what he needs?"

I stifled a gasp as the black witch's plan became clear. She'd wanted the power of timewalking for her demon master, to help his ultimate cause, not to allow her the freedom of moving through the ages.

"No matter, my humble servant," Xaphan growled from where he stood in the salt circle, and expanded his impressive black wings. "If I kill them now, there will be no need for a timewalking amulet. It's either that, or they join us." The Prince of Hell's red eyes pinned me.

I sneered. "Never."

He shook his head, as if I'd just said the dumbest thing in the world. "Unleash me."

La Voisin darted across the room and kicked a bit of salt out of the perfect circular formation.

I groaned. What idiots we were. We'd missed our chance to rush out of the room while Xaphan had been bound in the circle.

Now, as he stepped over the broken ring of salt, there would be no simple escape. We had to fight him.

I lifted my hands, and pools of darkness sprang into my palms.

Xaphan was terrifying, with his glowing red eyes, black, scaly skin, and claws so sharp they could shred the bone over my heart. And yet, I knew instinctively that he was no match for the king and Queen of Hell. Which meant, perhaps, that Eva and I had the power to beat him.

Morgan caught sight of my magic and shook her head.

Fuchsia power bloomed in her hands. "Get back. What if—"

"Together, we won't fail." Eva stepped forward. I mimicked her boldness, flanking Morgan on the other side.

Xaphan boomed out a laugh. "We'll see about that." He thrust out his hands, and black spiderwebs spun out of them to crawl up the elaborately papered walls of the room.

Without hesitation, Eva and I flew into motion. Our black power surged, chasing Xaphan's magic. As it met the prince's power, the spiderwebs began to scream, to *wail*, as if his magic was alive, before they fizzled out entirely.

The demon prince loosed a roar, and, beating his wings, surged toward us.

A wave of fuchsia washed out of Morgan, hitting the demon in the chest, beating him back.

"Get out of this room," she ordered us. "Out of the house."

Eva and I took two steps back, but Xaphan's black spiderwebs shot around us, covering the door into the hallway.

La Voisin jumped into the mix. She began blasting off her own magic, a repulsive grayish-green mix of witch and demon power.

I caught Eva's eye. "Attack the web! I'll take her!"

My friend twisted and struck the web without hesitation. Both sunshine yellow magic and black demon power streamed out of her, as if she'd been born to wield them equally well.

For a moment, I stood transfixed, but when a beam of

light nearly sliced open my shoulder, I too whirled to face my adversary.

The poisoner witch smirked at me. "Come on, girl. Let's see if the light or dark shall prevail."

The room filled with fuchsia and yellow magic. Portraits flew off the walls and candles fell over as we battled. La Voisin was magically skilled but less fit and nimble than the rest of us. Using my endurance to my advantage, I danced around her and it didn't take long for me to land a blow to her leg. She dropped to her knees. Her hand pressed to her thigh, and with a wail, the witch pulled her skirts up.

I gaped. Rivers of blood gushed from her leg. I must have pierced her femoral artery.

And yet, the poisoner still had it in her to fight. She lifted her hand, a murky green light blooming in her palm.

"*Itoarazicus*," I murmured quietly so she wouldn't hear. The last thing we needed was a traitor like La Voisin knowing such a spell. Black tendrils soared from my fingertips and smothered the poisoner witch's power.

She tried to return my attack, but her magic fizzled right out of her fingertips. The witch gaped. "How—?"

The demon-touched witch thrust her hand out again, and a spell I didn't know slipped off her lips.

Nothing happened.

Victory bloomed inside me. The binding curse had worked!

"Master!" La Voisin screamed, cutting my inner celebration short by reminding me that a bigger baddie was in the room. "Master! Help!"

But Xaphan paid his follower no mind. He was locked in a battle with Morgan, streams of blackness fighting vibrant fuchsia light. The Prince of Hell never once took his eyes off my ancestor, which relieved me.

The prince knew I had demon power, but I didn't think he'd seen or heard me use the curse, which was something I'd like to keep in my back pocket. Anything to give me a leg up for the war to come. That is, if we made it to the war. Even as I watched Morgan, she started to flag, growing strained.

We had to get out of here. My mentor wouldn't last much longer.

To be safe, I wound up a net of black magic, and sent it flying over La Voisin, trapping her. She screamed for her master again, but once more, Xaphan didn't spare her a glance.

*That's what you get for making a deal with the devil, biatch.*

I twirled to see that Eva was making great headway with the black spiderweb. Whipping back around, I struck Xaphan, first with a witch spell, and then with demon magic pulled from the deepest recesses of my being.

When the black tendrils hit him in the heart, the Prince of Hell gasped and fell backward onto his ass.

I grabbed Morgan's wrist. "Run!"

With another blast of dark magic, I helped Eva make a hole in the web big enough for the three of us to squeeze through. We were in the hallway within seconds.

It took only a couple of heartbeats more for our lead to narrow. Heavy feet and beating wings sounded in the passageway behind us, telling us that Xaphan had recovered.

We only needed to get out of the house, past La Voisin's wards, to disappear.

My mentor loosed a scream as a torrent of shimmering black magic surged past her, the edge of it hitting her shoulder. She stumbled, but I was there, and caught her and pulled her forward with all my strength.

"Faster!" Eva screamed, throwing herself at the front door and wrenching it open.

She leapt outside and twisted to face the devil. Magic surged as she tried to fight him off, buying us time.

"Morgan! A warphole!" I shot a beam of black magic back behind us. Xaphan grunted as it hit him.

My ancestor cried out in pain as she extended her hand. I felt the essence of time shift milliseconds before a warphole opened and the strands of time materialized. Eva stood between them, her gaze swaying from the threads in front of her and the warphole behind her. I scoured the threads, but none popped out at me as the *right* one. So I plowed forth and trusted that Morgan would find it while I held her up.

Blasting another stream of demon magic at the Prince of Hell, I sprinted straight into Eva, felt Morgan reach for a strand of time, and saw her fingers graze one before we disappeared through the warphole.

# CHAPTER FIFTEEN

My breath billowed out of me, producing small, white clouds in the chilled morning air. Needing to feel the earth beneath me—needing the grounding—I slipped off my shoes. My bare feet pressed into the damp dirt, releasing the earthy scent into the air.

I studied my chipped polish and too long toenails. *Once this is over, a pedi will be a necessity.*

The thought surprised me. It was so positive, almost an assumption that we'd win. Despite my tendencies toward mantras to manifest what I desired, since we'd tumbled from 17th century France back to 7th century England the day before, my worry had escalated.

Xaphan had seen us and knew that we'd found Morgan. Thankfully, we'd been careful to use false names with La Voisin. Still, would this change anything? Everything? Hopefully, he wouldn't discover our true identities, and we hadn't inadvertently changed the future.

I huffed out a breath. Timewalking really confused a lot of things.

I glanced back down at my toes. But even the idea that a pedicure might be an option was kinda nice. A subconscious bright spot.

I loosed a sigh, allowing that hope to wash over me as I leaned back into the tree behind me.

A cheery hum cut through the silence I'd sought. Footsteps approached, and I twisted to glimpse the other side of the tree.

Morgan walked my way with two piping hot drinks in her hands. Her red hair gleamed in the sunlight, and contrasted starkly with the abundant green surrounding the cottage.

I smiled as she approached and handed me the mugs. They smelled of apples.

Using both hands, and more care than usual, to lower herself, she sat down next to me, her standard grace lacking.

Although Alex and Merlin had begun fixing up the injury Xaphan had inflicted, it was nowhere near healed. That would only come with time.

"Thought you might want something warm to drink. It's a nice day, but still chilly." She smiled and held out her hand. Now that she was settled, I returned one mug.

She was right. It was colder than I usually preferred, but I'd woken early and needed time outside the shack. Time to prepare for our journey home.

"Are you ready?" Morgan asked when I didn't reply.

I stared out over the waving grasses, breathing in the spring air of long-ago England. "I don't know. We've done a lot of timewalking, even with other people, but I've never done it without *you*." My free hand landed over my totem against my chest. "Or this."

Morgan nodded understandingly. "For what it's worth, I believe you're more than ready." Her eyes gestured down to the totem. "And you have no use for that anymore, love. It was your training wheels."

"Training wheels?" One corner of my lips lifted in a smile.

Morgan grinned. "I may not use modern words or sayings often, but I've timewalked across the centuries. I know a few things."

The question I'd been dying to ask burst out of me.

"Do you know if we'll be successful? Are we going to beat the demons?"

Morgan's hand landed on my arm. "I don't know, and even if I did, I wouldn't be able to tell you."

"That's so frustrating."

"Yes, but you understand why I can't. You're my blood. You can visit me in my time, but I *can't* visit you in your time. Hence why Merlin and I used the totems to speak with you before."

I would never forget that. Alex and I had been heavily making out when the illusions of Merlin and Morgan popped out of our totems. Thank the universe it wasn't the *actual* people.

She squeezed my hand, apparently taking my silence as

nerves. "It's just like how I can teach you things about others' pasts. And yet neither of us can reveal information about how the other might meet their end." She shrugged. "Timewalking has loopholes. That way, fate proceeds as it should."

I snorted. "Fate can suck it."

She laughed her musical laugh. I savored the sound, unsure if I'd hear it again.

We fell silent for a few moments. Then Morgan took a sip of her drink and looked at me once more. "The rest are awake and done eating, but I told them you needed a moment. Whenever you're ready, we'll be waiting for you." She squeezed my arm before rising and making her way back to the cottage.

I sipped my drink and listened to the birdsong. I felt the morning dew evaporate and fill the air with moisture as the sun rose higher. I smelled the flowers opening, lacing the day with their sweet scent.

Was I ready? I was almost positive I could timewalk back to the present, even with so many people in tow. Only a niggling doubt remained that they might arrive in the present injured or ill. But would I be ready for what I had to do when I got home? Had I squeezed every ounce of precious knowledge that I could from M&M, and even the traitorous La Voisin?

*Only time will tell.*

Once my cup was empty, I stood. When I stepped inside the cottage, everyone was sitting at the long table, waiting. Empty plates and bowls sat before them. There was a nervous tension in the air. A mix of excitement and fear, potent as any drug or dream.

"If everyone else is ready," I cleared my throat. "I think we should be going."

Diana shot up first. The others followed after a moment, putting away their dishes before filing out to our shack to get their things. We weren't taking much from our time with Morgan and Merlin: just the clothes we'd arrived in, and a couple of trinkets that Alex and Eva had wanted to keep. It was best that way. The more items someone brought back from the past, the harder it was for them to leave that time period. Morgan seemed to manage it fine, but she was the exception to the rule. I didn't want *anything* to hinder me from getting us home—particularly excess baubles.

After getting our things, we gathered in the same field that I'd passed the morning in, and faced our mentors and ancestors.

"It was a pleasure meeting all of you," Merlin said, fingering his beard. His eyes rested on Alex, his blood. "If you wish to visit again one day, our door is open."

I swallowed the lump rising in my throat. The emotion on everyone's face was plain. Even Hunter and Diana, who usually kept it together, looked like they might sniffle at any moment.

"Thank you. For everything," Alex replied, his voice cracking. "We owe our lives to you." He approached Merlin and slid his totem off his finger to put in the old witch's hand. "And if we get the chance to return, we will."

Merlin smiled, his eyes crinkling proudly at the corners into deeply grooved smile lines. "We hope that day comes."

A flurry of hugs and kisses ensued. Morgan grabbed me last, the sage she often burned in the cottage wrapping around her and clinging to me as protectively as her arms. When we broke apart, I unclasped my necklace, *her* necklace, and placed it in her hands.

"Thank you for everything. For teaching me, for showing me the past and how to act in it, for being *so* incredibly patient." My eyes darted down to the necklace. "And for saving my life more times than I can count. How can I ever repay you?"

Morgan shook her head. "You being here is enough repayment. Seeing my blood and knowing that she will do great things. To fight great evil is the biggest blessing of all."

Tears filled my eyes. "I'll try not to let you down."

"You never could, Odette." Morgan gave me another hug, and for what could be the last time, I took in her face, focusing on the freckles that I was fond of, trying to memorize their pattern.

My friends and I parted from the legendary witches. I'd just extended my hand to create the warphole when Morgan spoke again. "Be prepared for anything and everything. You're returning to a time unlike other magicals have ever seen." She clasped Merlin's hand. "We can't be sure, but we sense that you will be thrown into a crucible. Formed and tested in Hell's fire. Take care how you emerge."

"Crucible," Eva murmured, a little amusement in her voice.

I turned to face my ancestor and beamed at her. "It's funny you say that. Crucibles are exactly what we'll be soon."

The five of us waved goodbye again before I opened the warphole. Easy as you please, I called the strands of time, and grabbed the one I knew was right. I took one last look back at our mentors, unsure if I'd see them again, or if death would claim me first. They smiled encouragingly, and Morgan placed a hand over the moonstone necklace, the piece of jewelry that had saved my life and brought me to her.

My throat tightened and with a final nod, I turned and led my friends back into the future.

# CHAPTER SIXTEEN

*W*ith a gulp of air, I collapsed onto a soft rug as the warphole deposited me exactly where I'd envisioned

Home.

My heart rate slowed. I'd done it. I'd timewalked through centuries without Morgan or the totem. I lifted my head to take in my friends. To my great relief, I saw that they were all whole, no limbs lost. They appeared uninjured and awake. Joy burst through me, but I tempered it, needing to check on one more person to consider the timewalking a total success.

*Hello?* I asked in my head.

Louise moaned. *What happened? I feel funny—uncomfortable.*

*I timewalked. You're in the twenty-first century. You'll get used to it.*

She didn't reply. For once, I'd stunned Louise into

silence.

Fine with me. I needed a moment too.

Wondering if Claude still resided in Eva's head, I shot her a questioning look and tapped my skull. She nodded, a slight smile on her lips.

I exhaled fully for the first time since arriving in the present.

We were back—safe. Louise was still there, Claude too. No one would possess Eva and me as long as they stayed put. Everything we'd gone through with La Voisin had been worth it.

Tears sprang into my eyes as I took in the familiar living room. My mom's mid-century modern flair and love of plush throws and blankets shone through in the decor. Bits of Dad were present too, in the hints of red, his favorite color.

Where were they?

My pulse quickened as I listened for Mom and Dad. The house seemed quiet, hollow. It was also a little dirty. A fine layer of dust coated the side table, and now that I was noticing it, the air smelled stale.

Standing, I moved over to the alarm system in the hall. They'd set it to "stay," the setting my parents used when they were home but wanted to be alerted if anyone stepped onto their property.

On a whim, I moved over to the nearest oil diffuser and popped it open. It was bone dry inside, something Mom didn't permit unless they were away on vacation.

My stomach sank at the mixed messages the alarm and

the diffuser gave off.

"Mom?" I yelled. "Dad? Are you here?"

Hunter groaned. "Keep it down, will you? The room is rotating."

"Oh, sorry." I lowered my voice and pointed to the seat nearest him. "Don't worry, you'll be fine. Just sit down until the spins wear off."

Morgan had reminded us that if someone hadn't time-walked recently, which the guys and Diana hadn't, they might feel disoriented and nauseous for a brief spell.

"You sure? Hunter blinked rapidly. "I feel like I just slammed one too many beers or something. It wasn't this bad the first time."

I wasn't so sure he was remembering correctly. When we arrived in the past Alex had been a wreck, and Hunter had definitely been off for a few hours. The girls had reacted to timewalking a little better, but our magic had been wonky. Still, there was no point in reminding him of that now. "Positive. You should be okay in an hour tops."

My gaze traveled over the others. Eva had more experience timewalking and looked unruffled. Surprisingly, Diana looked fine too. That girl was tough as nails. Alex, however, looked out of sorts. The poor guy couldn't seem to catch a break.

"Babe, lie on the couch. Let me help—"

Alex shook his head and hauled himself on top of it. I supposed that after days of being bedbound, he wanted to do it himself.

"So glad we don't have to do that again soon." Hunter

gripped his head and allowed Eva to help him into a chair.

"Are they here, Odie?" Eva asked. "I can't hear anything."

"Me either, but the alarm tells me they should be here. If they left, they'd arm it 'away'. I don't understand."

I began searching the house. With each passing minute, my heart rate ratcheted up as a new troublesome possibility entered my mind. Had someone taken them? If so, how had they gotten past the wards my parents set? Were they still in the house?

I shuddered at the last thought, but found nothing to reinforce my worry. The house was tidy, not a dishcloth out of place.

"I have no idea where they are!" I walked into the living room and threw up my hands. "There's no sign of a struggle."

"Hmmm." Eva had been getting the guys water, but now she looked around the room.

"Maybe they had to flee after the Hellgate broke open," Diana suggested. "I wonder if they left a note? Mother used to do that when she went out."

Because the academy didn't allow them, my phone was still locked away at Spellcasters, probably long dead. I checked the spot where my parents charged their phones, and found nothing. They weren't on the tables and counters either.

We'd always been more of a call or text family, but Diana was right. It seemed that an old-fashioned note was my only hope.

*Where would Mom or Dad put one? Especially if they wanted only me to find it?*

Mentally, I moved from room to room. Right away, I disregarded my room. Too obvious. As was any place where leaving messages would be normal. If they didn't want someone to find them, which I had a hunch was the case, it had to be somewhere smart. Somewhere other people wouldn't consider.

I gasped. "I have an idea!"

I dashed out of the living room. Eva and Diana ditched the guys and followed, both their eyes widening as I led them into my dad's enormous study. I'd just crossed the threshold into the room, when the scent of leather from Dad's jacket, hanging on the wall, hit me. My throat constricted as the familiar aroma bolstered my need to find them.

Dad had a crazy big library. He devoted most of it to the film industry and history books on old wars. But there was also a section of magical books, if you knew where to look.

I went to the shelf, next to which, a statue of a woman stood. Placing my finger squarely on the tip of her nose, I pressed it inward. The hidden button receded into her face, and the shelf that appeared to house only historical war books began to turn. On the other side a new shelf appeared, this one full of magical books and artifacts.

"Just like in the movies. So cool," Eva breathed.

"Where do you think he got the idea?"

I waited until the shelf stopped moving before searching

for one specific book. The volume I sought sat tucked in the corner of the top shelf, as dingy and battered as the last time I'd asked to see it years ago.

I pulled the library ladder over and climbed the rungs to pluck the book from its place.

"Is that . . . a first edition of *Mastery of Potions and Elixirs*?" Diana asked. "Experts regard that text as one of the best instruction manuals on potions ever."

"It's also excellent at hiding love letters," I said, amused by Diana's awe over the book that my parents claimed began their courtship.

Eva tilted her head to the side. "Explain."

"My parents met at Spellcasters. They were in the same year, but I guess things were different back then. They didn't have every session together. Whenever they had to split, my dad would write a love note for Mom and put it in this book. She'd read it in class, and the instructor always thought she was just really into the text."

My chest warmed at the tale. "My mom told me about it when I was little. I thought it was so romantic and smart. And of course, I wanted to be in on the action. I asked them to leave notes in it for me too, and they used to do it all the time, before I got too busy to check. Hopefully, they remembered."

I flipped through the pages with bated breath. I was about halfway through the book when I found it, a regular piece of computer paper folded and shoved tight against the spine.

My heart thumped hard as I pulled it out, hoping that it

was a recent note. The paper still felt crisp as I unfolded it. The handwriting was undeniably Dad's, done in a hurry.

"Is that it, Odie?" Eva asked.

A lump rose in my throat. "Yes. They're safe. After we fought the demons in London, they had to hide. All our parents did."

"Where are they?" Diana's tone had gained urgency. I wondered if she'd even considered that her mother might be in trouble. I had to admit it was hard to envision battleaxe Priscilla Wake doing anything other than dominating. "Are they together?"

I nodded. "Andre and Sam alerted Headmistress Wake. She called our parents, and they banded together. They're all in the same place, somewhere the demons can't go." I shook my head, unable to believe this was happening.

"I swear, Dane, if you don't spit out where in two seconds, I'm going to hex you," Diana hissed.

"Faerie," I said. "They are currently guests of the Riverlands Court, thanks to the Torna twins."

Eva breathed out a sigh. "Going there should be easy enough."

I cocked my head at her. "Easy to get to Faerie? Why do you say that?"

"You and Diana already went there once. You know how to enter the realm. Even if we don't arrive in the same court, surely we have something we can leverage for someone to show us the way. Unless, of course, we land in the Dark Court. Then we're screwed."

"Yeah, about that . . . " Diana arched an eyebrow at me.

"The champions don't actually know where the entrance to Faerie is located."

"But . . . you said it was at their academy?"

"It is. But we warped there," Diana answered. "The location of the academy is kept secret from other magicals, except warpers who have been approved. Pretty sure Odette isn't on that list."

"No, I'm not." I set the book down on Dad's desk. "But we need to find a way there. Taking on a whole army of demons without help just can't happen. We need our parents and their friends."

Diana nodded. "Totally agree, especially considering we don't even know what's happening in the outside world. What if the demons have taken over the government entirely?"

"Well, shit," Eva muttered. "If it's not one stumbling block, it's another."

I was about to agree when a shrill sound cut me off.

My blood skittered in my veins, and I stampeded out of the room.

"What is that?" Eva squealed.

"An alarm!" Diana shot back. "Where the hell do you live that you've never heard a house alarm? Pleasantville?"

I ignored them and rushed into the living room. "Get up! Now!"

The guys, who were wide-eyed and already struggling to stand, swore.

I darted over to Alex and hauled him up. Eva did the same with Hunter. If someone broke in, we needed everyone on their feet, and all the magical power we could get.

"That's a human alarm, not a ward," Hunter said, his tone low.

"Yes, but my parents' alarm differs from others. The human alarm goes off when someone approaches the home. It's only when—"

Another sound, something similar to a cat yowling, pierced through the shrill beeping of the human alarm.

I stiffened. Someone had breached the front door.

"Everyone, conjure a weapon, and get ready to fight," I ordered.

A blade appeared in my hands. For a moment, I wished it was my demon dagger, the weapon I had given to my friends the night we disappeared into the past. If the intruder was a demon, the hell blade would supplement our black magic.

Hunter reached for his totem, an emerald encrusted dagger, which he'd had on him the night we first time-walked. My other friends conjured blades too, and everyone stood stock-still, waiting.

Footsteps sounded in the hall, coming closer. Listening through the blood rushing in my ears, I tilted my head. They sounded like normal human footsteps, not the tread of a large demon. There was no snarling or growling. No whiff of a noxious scent.

Still, not about to be caught off guard, I pulled my weapon back, prepared to strike as the shadow of a figure entered the room.

# CHAPTER SEVENTEEN

"Whoa, Dane! Back up!" Andre entered the living room, his hands raised in surrender.

Right behind him, Sam and Ayla Torna dropped the daggers they held out in front of them.

"Andre!" Diana ran to her boyfriend and flung herself into his arms.

They embraced and shared a kiss so thorough, it would normally make me avert my eyes. But this time, I couldn't. I was too shocked.

I lowered my weapon, blinking at the figures before me. Welcome friends, yes. But how had they gotten past my parents' wards? And more importantly, how did they know that we'd returned?

A smile blossomed on Sam's face as she approached me. "We'll explain everything. If you have food and booze, I'll even make the story good."

My eyes ran over her. She looked much thinner than the last time I'd seen her. Almost too thin. Andre and Ayla had lost weight too. Clearly, they'd missed a few meals.

"On it." I ran into the kitchen.

Eva followed a half-step behind me. "How did they—"

"No idea. Just get them what they asked for. I think they're starving."

As much as I wanted to hear about the events happening outside my home, Mom would keel over if she knew I didn't get our guests any food or drink. Particularly guests who were going hungry.

As it turned out, everything in the fridge had gone bad. Not a good omen. Luckily, there were lots of frozen pizzas in the freezer, all with a thick crust of ice on the boxes.

Pizza was not something my mom usually kept on hand. That made me think she'd anticipated this situation. When I realized that the pizzas were my favorite type, Hawaiian, tears pricked my eyes. Mom had suspected that I would be hungry.

With a found tube of slushy margarita mix and a bottle of tequila, I prepared drinks for our friends. Once the first pizza was ready, we popped another in the oven, and brought the food and cocktails out, alongside a pitcher of water.

Sam, Andre, and Ayla fell upon the pizza like a pack of hungry wolves. When all three of them had downed a drink and three pieces of pizza, Sam sat back in her chair, closed her eyes, and groaned.

"Even if it was sinfully topped with pineapple, I don't care. That was the best pizza ever."

"Okay, now you need to spill it." My heart was thumping so hard, I worried it might crack my ribs. "Or I'll take all this away," I added, trying to infuse some light-heartedness into the room.

Ayla threw her arms over what was left of the pizza. "If you even try, I'll aether-slap you."

A laugh, half nervous, half real, burst out of me, inciting chuckles from the others. The sound was strange, far too infrequent these past couple days.

Finally, after the laughter died down, Andre leaned forward and began telling us what we wanted to know.

"We've been on the run since London. Before we had to disappear for good, we spoke to your parents. They told us that when you returned, you'd most likely come here—your house is warded better than Fort Knox. It was a safe bet. They'd hoped that you'd find that book."

My eyebrows furrowed. "How did you know I found it?"

"They enchanted it. Once it opened, a spell would inform me that you had picked it up. A clever twist on a motion-detection spell."

"But . . . If you've been on the run, why didn't you stay here? You said it yourself, this house is protected. It always has been."

*Because Mom and Dad always rightfully suspected that someone was after me.*

Andre shook his head. "The house is being watched at

all times, and we needed to make sure it was still an option for when you returned. I had to warp us to a specific spot on the front porch so no one would see us. We set off the human alarm with our motion, but none of the more dangerous wards. Then I had to say a password your parents gave me to allow us inside."

I leaned back, stunned at all the workarounds my parents had implemented. "But then why haven't the baddies come inside and waited for me?"

"Some of your parents' wards are *real* doozies," Sam said. "Honestly, I'm impressed. Your mom and dad warded almost every inch of however many zillion square feet are in this place."

I huffed out a laugh. "Yeah, tell me about it. It's been like this since I was young."

Sam arched her eyebrows. "Well, the wards have already killed off dozens of demons. I bet our adversaries figure it's not worth it anymore. For now, as long as they don't see anyone coming in or out, they won't make a move."

"So why didn't you guys join the others in Faerie?" Diana twisted to face Andre, who sat at her side. "Demons can't go to Faerie. You would have been safe there."

"We wanted to," Ayla replied. "But the spell your parents placed on the book to inform us that you'd come back wouldn't cross realms. A fae had to stay behind to get you into the Fae Academy of Elemental and Arcane Arts, and from there, Faerie. I volunteered for the job—and to glamour everyone to make finding us more difficult. We needed Andre to warp us into the house, and Sam—"

Sam pulled a demon dagger from each of her hips. "To kill those bastards." She tossed one of the daggers so that it flipped through the air before she caught its hilt. "I've gotten *really* good at throwing these, by the way."

"Wow." I shook my head. "You guys must have some stories."

"We've had a few run-ins with dark witches, and one rogue pack looking for us. Just like you have stories too, I'm sure," Andre said. "Where have you been hiding these past few months?"

*"Months?!"* Hunter leaned forward and swayed a little because he still wasn't quite right after timewalking. "I'm sorry, what month is it? What year?"

"It's July," Sam replied. "You've been MIA since January."

July? We'd been gone nearly half a year. My stomach wound into tight knots.

*I missed a birthday,* I thought. Even though there were clearly much bigger things to worry about it still felt sad. I'd always liked celebrating my birthday. And my parents must have been so worried on that day.

I'd just gotten over my personal pity moment when I noticed that Alex, Hunter, and Eva all were staring at me.

"Months, Odie?" Eva squeaked, wanting an answer.

I lifted my palms in a defensive shrug. "Morgan said that time passed strangely. Sorry, but I'm still pretty new to this. I tried to get us back just a few days after we left, but clearly, I was off a little. Honestly, though, I'm happy to have gotten us here in one piece."

"Morgan?" Sam prompted.

"Morgan Le Fay," I offered, to which three mouths dropped open. "And Merlin. Yes, *the* Merlin. That's who we stayed with . . . and learned from."

Despite knowing that my black magic was powerful, and might be the difference between victory and defeat, I wasn't quite ready to admit to the others exactly what I'd learned. And from the way Eva was squirming, I could tell she felt the same way.

"We'll tell you all about it later," Alex said, coming to our rescue. "What's the plan for right now?" He was trying to appear pulled together, like the timewalking hadn't thrown him for a loop. "When can we leave?"

Andre gave him a once-over and arched a bushy eyebrow. "As soon as you and Hunter look like you can walk a few miles. Ayla tells me I won't be able to warp onto the fae academy grounds. Neither will Odette. Only specific warpers have that privilege, and Tittelbaum is . . ." He gulped loudly. "Still at Spellcasters."

"Why do you say it like that?" Diana asked, her tone high.

Andre and Sam shared a long, pointed look, until Sam turned to us.

"Spellcasters fell to the demons after the Hellgate broke open. The royals chose it as their new palace."

## CHAPTER EIGHTEEN

After Sam dropped the Spellcasters bomb, Alex and Hunter tried to insist that they were ready to journey to Faerie right away. However, since the guys fell over the moment they stood up, no one believed them. They tried to fight it, to insist that we leave, but ran out of steam after a half hour.

Honestly, it was just as well. As much as I wanted to see my parents and finish off the royal demons, a brief break was necessary.

Andre, Sam, and Ayla were still ravenous, and after they told us more about what they'd been through, I planned on feeding them until they passed out in a food coma. The rest of us needed a shower, a bed, and some quiet time to process what had happened in the months we'd been gone. Thankfully, my parents' house was large enough to shelter all of us.

After we'd devoured seven more pizzas, I showed everyone to the spare bedrooms.

Alex and I retreated to my old bedroom, where I called solo dibs on my en suite shower. I wanted to shave, and he did not need to be around for that mess.

Good-naturedly, my man took the separate bath down the hall. For the first time in living memory, my mom's insistence on too many bathrooms in our home proved reasonable.

I groaned as the water hit me and ran over my skin like silk. The fresh tingle of my rosemary-scented shampoo made me want to cry with joy. As I massaged my scalp, I breathed in the delicious scent, and mulled over the situation.

According to Sam, Andre, and Ayla, the demons hadn't made an overt play for world domination yet. Just small moves. Attacks and maneuvers that a layperson wouldn't see as too crazy or fiendish, unless they knew that thousands of demons had recently infiltrated the world.

I wondered if that was because they were waiting to use me and Alex to wrench the Hellgate back open. Or maybe they simply wanted to find us and make sure we watched the world burn.

*Damn demons.*

Twenty minutes later, I turned off the water and wrapped a buttery soft towel around my body with a pleased shiver. M&M's cottage had been nice enough, and I'd be forever grateful to them for housing us, but it had been too long since I'd been clean, warm, and swathed in comfortable fabric.

I primped a little more, and was still lost in thought and gratitude for modern luxuries when I emerged from the en suite bath. Alex was already sprawled on my bed. He was staring at the ceiling, clad only in a spare pair of my dad's sweats.

"You okay?" I asked.

The effects of timewalking had worn off by the time the group split to rest. But I wasn't sure if people could relapse or not. There wasn't a lot of data on that sort of thing.

"Fine. Just worshipping how soft this bed is—like a damn cloud after sleeping on hay for so long." He propped himself up on his elbows with a small grin. "And soaking everything in. Honestly, I just can't believe we're here—in our own time. You got us here in one shot, sweets."

"Why the tone of surprise," I deadpanned, and when his face tightened, a small smile broke on my face, and I threw a wave. "I understand what you mean. Morgan let me hold the reins after our first timewalking experience, but I'd never spanned so many centuries. Or timewalked without my totem." My hand went to my chest, where the necklace would've lain, had I been wearing it. "I miss it."

"Me too." Alex glanced down at his unadorned finger. "But it is reassuring that they don't think we need them anymore."

"I wonder if that means we'll get another one?" I smiled to let him know that I was being flippant. "Totems are kind of a status symbol."

Alex chuckled. "I'm sure that after we get rid of the demons, Headmistress Wake will give us another crack at Spellcasters' totem cache."

"I hope that if something chooses me again, I get earrings. I've always been more of an earrings person. Not that I didn't love the necklace," I added hurriedly, because that little necklace had saved my ass many times. "Particularly the moonstone. It looked good with all my outfits."

"You look good in anything, babe, even that towel."

I wiggled my hips suggestively. "White terrycloth doing it for you, Wardwell?"

"After living in that shack for weeks, you wearing a burlap sack would do it for me." He reached for me. "Come here."

I acquiesced, joining him on the bed and savoring the feel of his hands as they traveled from my exposed knees up my leg. It had been so long since we'd shared anything more than a kiss or a tight squeeze that my body hungered for him.

So much had changed. So many things we'd taken for granted had been wiped from our lives. Had I known how amazing I had it back then, I would've taken more care to be grateful for all the goodness in my life. Savored it more, which I intended to do right now.

Who knew when the good would come again?

My hands landed on Alex's cheek, freshly shaven and slightly red for it. "Smooth," I murmured and breathed in the smell of him, fresh for the first time in weeks.

"Although, I have to say, I was kind of digging the beard you grew."

"Ugh, not me. Food got caught in it. It was disgusting."

I chuckled. "How sexy." I leaned in for a kiss.

Our lips met, soft and tender at first, but growing more needy by the second. Heat rushed through my core.

I wanted him, badly.

"Do you have protection?" he asked.

I parted from him and arched an eyebrow. "Don't judge me. I never brought guys home when I lived here, but I always thought it was best to be prepared."

His lips twisted in adorable confusion.

*Oh, just wait.*

I pulled at the drawer to my nightstand with a flourish. Inside was an old Barbie jewelry box. I opened it, and packages of condoms glinted up at us in the lamplight.

Alex burst out laughing. "Who would guess that my classy lady would hide condoms in a Barbie jewelry box?"

I slapped his shoulder. "You should be happy that I even have any. If I didn't—"

He pressed a single finger to my lips. "Don't even end that sentence." He gestured down to his crotch.

I smiled. It seemed he was as ready for me as I was for him.

We started kissing again. Every touch, every breath along my skin, every soft growl and gasp from Alex made my heart thud harder in anticipation.

The towel disappeared, as did his sweats. Unable to

wait a moment longer, he grabbed for one of the condoms. "Sure they're not expired?"

"I am a responsible woman. I check that they're replaced every time I come home. That would have been just after Yule."

"Hopefully, you're not *too* responsible." He winked, and was about to rip open the package, when suddenly, my breath caught in my throat.

I slapped my hands to the mattress.

Alex's eyes widened. "Odie? Sweets, what's wrong?" He dropped the condom and reached out for me. "What's happening?"

But I couldn't answer. I was incapable of speech, because my scar had begun burning, and I could feel a vile influence spreading through me, trying to take me over.

Somewhere in my house, a scream—Eva's—rang out. I called back with one of my own.

Footsteps sounded down the hall, and though it should've been the least of my worries, I grabbed my towel and pulled it over my naked body, just as Alex ripped the blanket over both of us.

"Odette!" Sam yelled. "What's going on? We heard screaming."

"Come in!" Alex said.

The door swung open, and the girls barreled inside.

"What happened?" Ayla asked, her eyes scanning my face as I clenched my teeth, still gripping the bed sheets, unable to speak through the pain pummeling my head.

"Not sure. That first scream wasn't Odie." Alex's eyes were wild with fear. "I think it came from Eva."

As if in answer, Eva screamed again. A stream of curses in a deeper voice followed.

I drew in a sharp breath as another assault came at me.

"What's going on?!" Sam asked, the muscles in her neck sticking out. "She looks like she's in so much pain."

Holy universe, was I ever in pain.

A dark influence spread through me like wildfire, threatening to burn me from the inside out. My jaw was tight, and using everything I had, I commanded Louise to fight for me.

Lazy as ever, the mind witch moved at a snail's pace as she wrapped my head in a protective shield that dispelled the darkness. Each inch of ground we gained was like moving a mountain. Sweat slicked my body, and I trembled, but slowly and surely, the mind witch gave her full protection.

The inky blackness pulled back, like a slow tide, and I collapsed onto the bed with a sob.

Alex's hand found the back of my head. "Sweets, what happened? I tried to do a scan, but couldn't figure it out." His voice trembled as he spoke.

Alex was an excellent healer, and had been able to deduce practically everything that we'd ever encountered. But no one had taught him how to sense demonic magic from a royal floating in my body.

We hadn't even considered it.

Fast footsteps came charging toward our door. A second

later, Hunter appeared with Eva passed out in his arms. His breath was ragged, and green eyes wide with fear.

"She started yelling and grabbed her face and—"

"She's breathing now?" Alex asked.

"Check on her," I whispered, my voice raw.

After wriggling back into his sweats, Alex did as I asked and breathed a sigh of relief. "Everything seems okay."

"Yeah, except for the fact that both the girls are pale as ghosts and covered in sweat. What happened, Odie?" Hunter asked. "Do you know?"

I nodded. My worst nightmare had just come to life. "Ishtar and Lucifer just tried to possess us."

# CHAPTER NINETEEN

After Eva regained consciousness, she confirmed what I already knew to be true. Lucifer had been trying to possess her. While Claude had protected her, the pain had been too much for her to bear.

The question then became did the royals know we were here? That we'd defended ourselves? Or had they been routinely trying to possess us while we'd been gone, and the ghosts merely successfully stopped one of many attempts?

Things had just gotten way more real.

As much as I'd wanted to stay home, sleep for a night in my own bed, and feel secure with Alex's arms wrapped around me, that was no longer possible. After what had just happened, I wouldn't be able to sleep anyhow, not knowing that there were demon peons right outside my door—and they might try and break it down at any second.

Ishtar might not have succeeded in possessing me, but she had to have figured out that I could timewalk. During the battle in London she'd warded the entire area against regular warpholes, rightly figuring that I wouldn't be powerful enough to slip through time. At least, I wasn't powerful enough on my own. Not back then. With Morgan's help, my friends and I *had* escaped and traveled through time and Ishtar had seen it happen.

I wasn't positive, but that made me think that Ishtar routinely checked for my presence. If she knew that I was back, or even suspected it, she could probably guess where I'd hide out. And if she guessed correctly, my home was no longer safe.

Everyone else agreed, and we began packing. New clothes, dried goods for snacking in case our journey didn't go as planned, small toiletries, and flashlights because it was pitch dark outside. We threw all our supplies into backpacks and duffels, and once everyone was prepared, we met in the living room.

I turned to Ayla. "So we have to go to your academy to get to Faerie." I tried to infuse some pep into my tone, but truth be told, I felt exhausted all the way down to my bones. "Where is the academy? Can I warp into it if you tell me about it? Or do I just warp somewhere nearby?"

Ayla chewed on her bottom lip. "We won't be able to warp directly inside. We have aether wards up, and they'll deny any magical who hasn't been branded or approved. You'll only be able to get us nearby. Luckily, I brought a photo of a good spot, and think you might be semi-familiar with the area."

She showed me the photo, and I understood her assumption. I didn't know exactly where on a map the picture had been taken, but it was undeniably my home state of California, somewhere close to Highway 101.

"This is Bixby Creek Bridge." Ayla pointed to the bridge in the pic. "Do you think if you know the name and have a visual, that will be enough?"

Less than a year ago, I would've said hell no, but I'd progressed leaps and bounds in warping since then.

I nodded. "I got this. Just give me a couple minutes."

I studied the photo until I could practically hear the waves crashing along the shore and the seabirds calling out overhead. When the vision was firmly in my head, I turned to my friends.

"Andre, go through first," I said. "It's best to have a warper on the other side. Just in case there are demons around and we need to make a quick exit. I assume you can get anywhere now?"

He grinned proudly at me. "Have been able to for months."

*Months . . .* My poor parents.

"Good for you," I said, again shaking off the shock of how much time had passed. "Then I say we get right to it."

I inhaled a deep breath and worked the surrounding magical energies. The warphole opened easily, and grew to fill the room from floor to ceiling before it stopped.

I nodded to Andre. He passed through, then the others

followed one by one. When I was the only one remaining, I looked around my home and fought the lump rising in my throat.

Would it still be here if I returned later? Would I ever return?

*There's only one way to find out. Keep going.*

I spared the living room one last glance before stepping into the warphole.

The moment I exited, I noted the scent of salt and the sensation of sand pummeling the skin of my face. It was dark, but we were undoubtedly at the beach. I caught Ayla's eye.

"This is where we need to be." She pointed east, into the National Forest. "The academy is eight-ish miles that way. Everyone should stay close. There are traps along the way, but as long as you don't stray, we'll avoid them."

Everyone fell in line behind the faerie, their flashlights piercing the cover of darkness in front of them. After we'd trekked for ten minutes, I sidled up next to her, wanting to understand more about her magic.

"What in you, besides you being of the fae folk, allows you past the academy's safeguards?"

"Well, it is mostly that I'm fae. But also, all of us receive small tattoos when we enroll at the academy." She pulled up the sleeve of her shirt, exposing her forearm.

I glanced down at a nondescript circle bearing the five elements that fae could use. To a human eye, it might appear New Age, but not overtly so.

"Ingenious," I said, even though I wasn't sure I'd want a tattoo.

"Spellcasters should implement that," Alex muttered, clearly of a different mind. "Would've saved us a lot of trouble during the Culling and Grind."

"Will we arrive in the Snowcap Court again?" I asked Ayla.

She shook her head. "There's another portal to Faerie at the school. One made specifically for me and Sana in case we need to make a fast exit. It will take us directly to the Riverlands Court."

"Why only for you two?" Hunter asked, reminding me he didn't know much about the Spy Game champions from the fae academy.

"My sister and I are in line—far back in line, mind you—for the throne of the Riverlands. Distant cousins of Prince Halad, the heir. He has about two dozen cousins, so that's really nothing special, but our parents act like we're the actual heirs. They insisted upon a getaway portal if we were to attend a spy academy." Her cheeks reddened. Her lineage always seemed to make her uncomfortable. "We'll use that portal, and go to the Riverlands Court. To the castle, to be exact."

"Great plan," I said, thankful to not be visiting the Snowcap Court again. It had been nice, and the royals were kind, but the place was also freezing. The cold and I weren't friends.

We continued through the forest. Conversations popped up here and there, but fizzled out after a few minutes.

Mostly, we trudged forth in silence, listening for something approaching in the dark.

When the pleasant, distant sounds of a cascading waterfall became audible, Ayla held out a hand, stopping me.

"That's the signal. I have to remove the glamour I keep up—otherwise it sets off an alarm."

"Could anyone hear the alarm way out here?" I asked.

Ayla shrugged. "That depends on how close they are and who's around. The night we left London, Andre warped us as close as he could get to the shifter academy. Once we were there, we found the heads of the schools. Headmistress Cristala left immediately and began the evacuation of the fae students. The school has been empty since, except to transport people to Faerie. But who knows if magicals have been lurking in the area?"

"Has there been any sign of enemies?" Hunter prompted as his hand fell to his totem on his hip.

"The perimeter is heavily enchanted, so I doubt demons would have found it." Ayla bit her bottom lip. "But I guess you never know—especially if they have a fae ally who gives them a work around . . . "

She trailed off, clearly not liking the idea that a fae could betray their own kind.

A shiver spider walked down my spine. I didn't like the idea either.

"Should we have waited and found Headmistress Cristala?" Ayla asked, noting my unease. "She's assembling forces somewhere in this realm."

"No," I replied. "We don't have time to wait."

The fae ran her hand over her body, and inch by inch, the glamour she always maintained in the human world disappeared. She looked pretty much the same. She was still a petite, beautiful redhead with bright green eyes, but the glamour's removal revealed otherworldly attributes that had been hidden before. Like her pointy ears, and the diaphanous, ruby-veined wings that fanned out from her back.

Ayla sighed as she spread her wings wide. "You have no idea how good that feels. Like taking off a bra at the end of the day, but a million times better."

"Where do you hide them?" Diana asked.

"I use aether to bind them to my back. If you ever ran your hand down my back, you'd notice. But no one does that unless they're invited."

"Yeah, because that would be *awkward*," Sam sang the last word, and a few of us laughed.

"All right," Ayla said once the mirth had quieted. "The aether wards should be a hundred or so yards away. If you're too far from my body, you won't be let in, so huddle around me."

I claimed a spot right next to her, and we progressed forward as one tight-knit pack. The faerie warned us a few seconds before we walked through the enchantment to prepare us for the strange sensation of water flowing over our heads. I shivered as the aether ran over me, setting all my nerves on fire, but in a good way—almost familiar. Once we were on the other side, I blinked. Fae magic was palpable, making my head spin a little.

The Fae Academy of Elemental and Arcane Arts was right in front of us, white and glowing in the moonlight, which seemed mystically drawn to this spot. The sweet scent of flowers hung in the air, nearly intoxicating.

"Damn," Eva muttered. "This makes Spellcasters look like a prison."

"Yeah," Hunter agreed. "What's with that?"

Alex too looked impressed, but he said nothing. I suspected he just wanted to get into Faerie where we'd be safe.

I grabbed his hand and squeezed. "Lead the way, Ayla."

The faerie approached the castle gate, and opened it without issue or password. No one was on the other side, and from what we could see, no lights shone in the building.

"Looks dead inside," I said, my voice hopeful.

"Yeah, but demons aren't exactly fond of good lighting or hanging welcome signs," Andre said.

He was right. I needed to stay on my toes. Until we stepped foot in Faerie, we were in danger.

Ayla led us through the castle grounds, and into the courtyard that hid a portal to the Snowcap Court.

We marched deeper into the academy, past large halls and classrooms I hadn't seen before. Lounges filled with cushy furniture and relaxing plants dotted the surroundings.

Ayla led us up flights of stairs to the fifth floor, and then stopped before a door at the end of a hallway.

"You guys don't room in towers?" Diana asked.

Our guide's eyebrows scrunched together. "Why would we?"

"To separate the classes."

Ayla's hand twirled in the air dismissively. "Fae, even a lot of demi-fae, live extraordinarily long lives. Our time here is a blip on our radar. What would be the point of dividing us up when we'll run into other classes in the real world all the time, anyway?"

I agreed. I'd always thought that Spellcasters should be more co-mingled. Especially now, when so much relied on the bonds of friendship, love, and camaraderie to see us through the war to come.

"Anyway, this is our room." She turned to us, her cheeks pink. "Sana packed in a hurry, and then a bunch of people came through here retreating to the fae realm. It's . . . definitely going to be a mess. Sorry."

I choked out a laugh at the innocent and reassuringly normal worry. "I think we can all handle a messy bedroom. Lay it on us, Torna."

Ayla still looked like she was about to seriously regret letting us into her room, so I gave her a reassuring smile. With a small sigh, she pushed the door open.

I blinked. Damn, the girl hadn't been kidding. It looked like a tornado had been through here. Clothes everywhere, a lamp overturned, makeup lay scattered, and random items spilled out of the dressers and closets.

Ayla pressed her hands over her eyes. "By the aether, my sister is such a slob."

Behind me, Hunter let loose a laugh. A few others joined in, lightening the mood.

"When we get to Faerie, you can tell her how much she embarrassed you." I patted her on the shoulder. "But we should get moving."

I hadn't felt anything strange or demonic, but the hellborn could crop up at any second. The last thing we needed was for the demons to watch us retreating to another realm. *They* might not be able to enter, but they had other magical minions who could.

Ayla picked her way through the room, muttering and shaking her head every couple steps. She stopped when she reached a bed—presumably hers, because it was more well-made than the other—and ran her eyes over it. "I don't think anyone's been here since your parents left."

"Your bed is the portal?" Diana asked, a tone of incredulity in her voice.

In response, Ayla grinned and leaned over the queen-sized mattress to tap the headboard.

My eyes widened. What appeared to be a nondescript headboard, decorated with concentric circles from the middle all the way to the outside, was actually a well-disguised portal. In the dead center, a knob protruded ever so slightly, presumably the handle.

"Brilliant," I said. "How do we open it?"

The faerie's lips pulled up at the corners. "Easy. Be me, Sana, or our headmistress."

Her hand landed on the knob, and suddenly, it began to glow a brilliant white. When she pressed inward, the portal door swung away, and a stream of yellowish mist flew into her bedroom.

She turned back to us. "Shall I go first?"

I nodded and watched as the faerie crawled on her mattress and through the portal hole.

I went next, bracing myself for the strange sensation that had overwhelmed me the first time I visited the other realm. But as I traversed the ten or so feet of the portal, it didn't come. In fact, nothing about entering this realm felt strange, which both relieved and confused me.

I'd reached the other side, but was still on my hands and knees.

Ayla extended a hand to help me up. "You won't feel Faerie-drunk this time. You've acclimated."

I breathed a sigh of relief. My last visit, I'd been out of it for hours. But now, I didn't have time for that sort of nonsense.

"We'll have to have rooms prepared for Eva, Alex, and Hunter so they can sleep off the Faerie drunk," Ayla mused, as if it had just occurred to her.

"Rooms have been ready for you for ages," a familiar, yet pinched, voice shot through my heart.

I peered past Ayla, and found my mom at the door of the room we'd entered, her arms extended.

"Mom!" I ran to her and threw myself in her arms. "I've been so worried. When I didn't find you guys at the house, I—"

"I know, honey." Mom stroked my hair, and I noted that she smelled different. Still like vanilla and myrrh, but lacking the touch of her favorite perfume or oils. "It was so hard for us not to leave a more obvious message, but we just couldn't risk it. We had faith, though, that you would figure it out." She pulled away to look at me.

The months I'd been away had changed her, given her lines where there hadn't been any before. And she looked thinner . . . from anxiety, no doubt. Her brown hair even had a couple streaks of gray.

"I'm so glad you're here, and that you're safe, Odie." Her voice broke a little. "We've been so worried. All the parents have. We've been taking turns waiting here for word of our children." She gestured back to the single chair and table in the room. "I'd just gone to take my plate to the kitchens, and when I came back . . . you were here." A sob escaped her mouth, and tears began streaming down her face. "Finally here."

I pulled her tight again. "I'm here, Mom. And I have so many things to tell you. I—*Argh!*" My hand flew to my head as a pressure increased all the way around my skull, and then, just as suddenly, eased up.

I blinked, unsure what had happened.

"Odie?" Mom's eyebrows knitted together. "Are you okay? What happened?"

I was about to tell her that I wasn't sure, when Eva fell out of the portal from the human realm with a yelp, and pressed her hand to her forehead.

The truth crashed over me.

La Voisin had mentioned that timewalking and traveling between realms would loosen our ties to our ghosts.

Louise and Claude had stayed with us through two rounds of timewalking, already an extraordinary feat. Had the shift into Faerie been too much for them to remain bound to us?

*Louise? Are you there?*

There was no reply.

# CHAPTER TWENTY

Once I was sure Eva was okay—ghost-less and growing more Faerie-drunk by the second, but otherwise fine—we continued with the reunions.

Parents spilled into the room and clung to their kids. Mom and Dad fretted over a ghost having been in my head, even though Louise was long gone. Eva's parents exclaimed over every other story she shared. Both Wardwell units couldn't get over the timewalking.

Everyone cried, even Headmistress Wake.

After the initial reunions were over, Eva, Alex, and Hunter were shown to bedrooms to sleep off the Faerie-drunk sensation. Everyone else settled into a room Mom dubbed the "leisure room." Families congregated together, save Andre and Sam, who perched next to Headmistress Wake and Diana because their parents weren't present.

We'd been seated no more than a few seconds when two unfamiliar figures wearing long silk robes entered the room. Ayla, Sana, and their parents shot out of their seats and fell into deep bows. Mom and Dad did the same, as did the other witches who had been in Faerie for a while.

*Alrighty then . . .*

I rose and followed suit.

"Welcome to the Riverlands Court," the man, presumably the king, said with a warm smile. He was very tall, with long, brown hair that covered his pointed ears, but he had no wings—an elf, then.

His wife, on the other hand, greatly resembled the Tornas with her bright red hair, silver-veined wings, and pointed ears that marked her of the faerie race.

"Yes, welcome," the queen continued. "I do hope that everyone is well after the journey. I apologize that we're not more appropriately dressed to receive guests, but you arrived at such a late hour. Please sit."

Everyone did as she requested, and once we were settled, the queen spoke again.

"My name is Aquatia Vapos. This is my husband, and king consort, Elan Geysis from the Cove Court. I apologize that our son, Crown Prince Halad Vapos, is not here to greet you. It seems he has taken to a night out in the city." She pursed her lips, indicating that she didn't agree with her son's late nights out. "However, we're so pleased that you're all here and safe."

Her eyes landed on me. "You must be the one the demon queen is after. You look just like your mother, who has told me much about you."

I smiled at the compliment and nodded. "Thank you,

Queen Aquatia. It's a privilege to visit your kingdom, and even more of an honor to be given refuge."

"An enemy of the Dark Court is a friend to us," the king said. "I am from Cove Court, a cousin to the current king. As you probably have guessed, I have not seen my family in many years."

"Because of the Rift, right?" I asked, wanting to be clear.

The queen nodded and placed a sympathetic hand on her husband's arm. "The Rift spanning the inland boundary of the Dark Court is a terrible thing. It not only cuts those of the Dark Court off from the rest of Faerie, but the coastal kingdom of the Cove Court too. Although we realize that your battle is in the human world, there are parallels here. We're hopeful that if you defeat the demons, it will weaken their ally, the crown of the Dark Court."

"That would be wonderful," I said.

From the mountains of the Snowcap Court, I'd seen the Rift, the black swirling cloud on an otherwise pure emerald landscape along the border of the Riverlands Court. I'd heard tales of what happened to fae that tried to escape through it—and it was nothing good.

"That being said." Queen Aquatia smoothed the skirt of her robe. "We have been waiting for your return. To learn how we can be of assistance." Her eyes scanned Ayla, Diana, Andre, and Sam. "Besides providing a bed, of course."

After timewalking, reuniting with friends, walking miles through the forest, and arriving here, it was no surprise that our fatigue was noticeable. As much as I wanted to hear what was happening, the exhaustion was real.

Still, with Louise's and Claude's departure, I did need help. Since the queen was offering, I might as well ask a favor now.

"This might be a shot in the dark, but you wouldn't have a spirit walker and talker hanging around here, or the fae-equivalent, would you?"

"Actually, we do. I believe you're acquainted. The purple haired witch?" the queen offered.

My spine straightened. "Amethyst! She's here?" I cast a glance around, as if I could have somehow missed my sweet, loyal, purple-haired friend before that moment.

But instead of finding her, I saw looks of discomfort flit across many faces. An uneasy hush fell over the room.

Sana cleared her throat. "She's here, and a little . . . off."

"Faerie-drunk?" I asked, confused.

If she'd been here for even more than a few days, that should have worn off by now.

"Not quite," Sana replied, and gulped. "Her powers have amplified since coming to Faerie. She's talking to all sorts of ghosts."

"What Sana isn't saying," Ayla interjected, "is that Amethyst's parents perished trying to flee their home. She hasn't spoken to anyone but ghosts since coming here."

I exhaled. Hearing the news of Amethyst's parents made me feel like someone had punched me in the gut. After a moment, however, I latched on to the last bit of what Ayla had said. My brows knitted together in confusion. "You mean she's ignoring real life? Like, depressed?" My heart cracked for Amethyst. "That seems reasonable, considering her parents just died."

Hunter's parents shifted uncomfortably, the king dropped his gaze to the floor, and Sana began bouncing her leg up and down rapidly.

Ayla drew in a long breath. "Well, yes, but no. She's here, but not here."

"I'm sorry, *what*?"

Was I being dense? Why did everyone seem so scared?

"She's in the spirit world," Sana blurted out, all tact lost. "Mentally, not physically. And since she's arrived in Faerie, no one has been able to coax her out."

# CHAPTER TWENTY-ONE

When I woke the next morning, Eva, Hunter, and Alex were still sleeping, acclimating to Faerie, so I asked Diana to join me. We were silent as we followed Queen Aquatia and Ayla through the ivy-laced hallways of the castle. Occasionally, the queen would try to break the uncomfortable silence by pointing out a particular Faerie plant or decorative object of interest. Diana would reply, uncharacteristically engaging in small talk for the both of us.

I was grateful she realized that, at the moment, I just couldn't.

Although I'd been exhausted, after the meeting, I'd ended up tossing and turning most of the night. All my thoughts were on Amethyst. I felt so bad for her, but didn't know how to help. I hated that. Plus, selfishly, I knew that if Eva and I were going to be able to stand up against Lucifer and Ishtar, we needed Amethyst back.

I understood why she was in another plane of existence. She was trying to find her parents. I hoped that she hadn't gone so deep that she'd gotten lost.

When we reached Amethyst's room, I was astonished to see that her door was being guarded by none other than the vampire champions from the Spy Games.

"Francis, Simone, Magdalena." I cocked my head. One was missing. "Where's Anton? And what are you doing here?"

It was a polite way of asking how they had convinced the fae to let them into Faerie. The fae had *strict* requirements regarding other magicals entering their kingdoms. An event had to be underway, or their need for the creatures must be great. They extended the fewest number of invites to vamps. As far as the fae were concerned, vampires were the lowest on the magical totem pole.

"Anton died in London. A demon staked him as we retreated," Simone said, her tone typically chilly, although her eyes softened when she said her classmate's name. "He tried to fight. Claimed that he knew the city well enough to pick a few off. He was always too reckless."

"I'm so sorry," I said, and I meant it. I hadn't bonded with Anton, but he'd helped us the night we escaped from the demon horde. I'd be forever in his debt for that.

"The vampires insisted that they come to Faerie with the spirit worker," Queen Aquatia gestured to the vamps as she answered my second question. "Said that you put Amethyst in their care in London. They haven't wavered on their guard since she learned that her parents perished."

"Oh . . ." I tried hard to mask the shock in my voice. I *had* asked the vampires to get Amethyst out of there safely. Obviously, they'd taken that to the next level. Considering what she'd been through, it was pretty thoughtful. "Thank you, guys."

"We've all lost parents too," Francis said. "Even if it was long ago. And she might be a bit odd, but the spirit walker grew on me."

I nodded, knowing what he meant. Amethyst had that way about her. "How is she?"

"Awful," he sighed dramatically, reminding me what a showman he was. "There's been no improvement. I fear if she doesn't come back soon, she'll be lost for good."

Ice flew through my veins. That couldn't happen. We needed Amethyst—and more than that, I wanted my friend back, safe and healthy.

The vampires let us into the room. The moment I stepped foot inside, I was so transfixed by my friend that I barely noticed the door close softly behind us.

Amethyst sat by the window in a green, wing-backed chair, a blanket draped over her legs. Her shoulders were hunched as she stared out over the verdant rolling hills below. She didn't turn, didn't even blink her glassy brown eyes when I approached, confirming that the others were right. She was somewhere else—lost in a place that few witches could go.

"Amethyst? Hey, it's Odette."

Diana joined me as I knelt next to Amethyst and clasped

one of her thin, dry hands, hoping that my touch would get through to her.

"We heard about your parents. We're sorry." I swallowed a lump in my throat. "To be honest, I feel responsible. I shouldn't have brought you along that night. I should've gone alone. The demons would have broken through the Hellgate anyway, but none of the other stuff, the rest of the pain, would've happened."

"Don't think so highly of yourself, witch," Simone spat, and I twisted in shock. I hadn't realized that she'd followed us inside. The queen and Ayla, too. "If you went alone, you'd likely be dead. Then how would you stop them?" She arched an eyebrow. "Just wake the spirit walker, and quit making yourself feel bad over things that you can't control."

Damn. Vampires sure had a way with words.

I looked back at Amethyst. "Even if what Simone says is true, I'm so sorry about your parents." I fell into silence, not sure where to go from there.

"Amethyst," Diana piped up. "Do you think you could . . . return? We want to see you, to make sure you're okay. And if you're feeling up for it, Odette and Eva need you for something specific—and important." Her sharp, blue eyes roved over our friend. She'd grown thinner, and her purple hair was lank and oily. "Plus, I think you need to eat."

"We have been feeding her," the queen whispered, slightly defensively. "However, she's very particular about what she ingests. And honestly, it's only when she eats a few specific items that she seems to become more responsive." Her emerald eyes turned down. "I'm afraid we're unsuited for taking care of a spirit walker in this court."

My spine straightened. The queen's talk of food had sparked an idea. Alex had been ill after being pulled through the ghost plane. I suspected that the effects of that place were stronger on Amethyst because she, unlike Alex, resonated with ghostly energies. But still, Alex had gotten better. Why couldn't Amethyst?

"Diana, do you remember those potions you made for Alex at Morgan and Merlin's cottage?"

I had been present at the making of those potions too, but Diana was always the most serious about potions. At Spellcasters she'd memorized how to brew at least a hundred. In the past, she'd wake up nearly every morning at the crack of dawn, ready to brew a new batch.

"Of course I do," she replied.

"Good. We need to make those same potions for Amethyst. I think her grief has gotten her stuck in the ghost plane, paralyzed. Perhaps we even need to have her eat the most potent of the ingredients whole."

Diana cocked her head. "That's a very sensible plan, Dane," she said slowly. "For someone who's mediocre at potions, I'm impressed."

I rolled my eyes, but took the jab, because, well, compared to Diana, I *was* mediocre at potions. "Thanks. Ayla, will you show Diana to the kitchens so she can get started?"

The older Torna twin nodded and slipped out the door with Diana.

When they were gone, I twisted to look at the queen. "I don't think she'll be prepared to work magic any time soon, so I must ask, do the fae have anyone who can talk to ghosts?"

Queen Aquatia looked thoughtful. "There is one aether-blessed fae who claims she can speak with ghosts. She's the only one."

"Is she nearby?" I asked. "Maybe she can help us bring Amethyst back. Or even help us find two more ghosts of mind witches and bind the witches to Eva and me."

As much as I wanted Amethyst back, I had a feeling that leaving the spirit realm was not something that anyone could force her to do. She had to be ready, which hopefully Diana would help her with.

In the meantime, we needed to check out other options. Preferably before we returned to the human world, where Eva and I would be at risk.

"She lives on the outskirts of the Riverlands and the Dark Court," the queen answered. "Many years ago, we sent delegations to her aid. We begged that she move, so that if the Dark Court struck, she would not be in harm's way. After all, she is our citizen, and we felt responsible for her well-being." Aquatia shook her head. "But she refused."

I nodded. "I think I'll need to pay her a visit. Maybe after I speak with Eva, you can tell me more about her?"

"But of course," the queen said graciously.

I turned back to Amethyst and gripped her hand again.

"I know you're hurting, old friend, but hang in there. We'll help you out of there, safe and sound. You'll be in a place where you can grieve properly. And if you want, you can take revenge on those who killed your parents." I kissed her lightly on the cheek before leaving the room.

# CHAPTER TWENTY-TWO

hen I entered the corridor, the queen split from me, which I preferred. I needed some time alone to think. Unfortunately, I'd made it only a few steps out the door when Francis and Simone appeared at my sides.

So much for time to think.

"Where have you been all this time?" Francis asked.

Where hadn't I been? I might rattle off a dozen places and times, but I knew what he meant.

"My totem helped us timewalk to the era of Morgan Le Fay and Merlin."

Both vampires drew in sharp breaths. "That's before both our times. Wicked," Francis said, clearly impressed.

I spared him a small smile. "We stayed with them, Morgan is my ancestor, and Merlin is one of Alex's. They trained us in ways lost to witches over the centuries."

"Like?" Simone prompted.

"I learned how to use demon magic. And a few druid spells."

The vampires' eyebrows shot up.

"Demon magic?" Francis hissed. "Like the same magic the royals use?"

I nodded. Then, I remembered something I'd wanted to ask when I first saw the vampires. "Hey, where are the shifters? Are they—"

"Alive," Simone said. "Dasha wanted to come to Faerie too. We all figured this would be the first place you'd return to when you realized your parents had to abandon their house. But Alpha Conon pulled rank. He did it with all his students, and their families."

"Pulled rank?"

"Alpha rank. The shifter headmaster is what you would call an alpha's alpha. He's one of the top dogs, no pun intended, in their society. And he's using his influence to build an army of shifters," Francis explained. "That's what headmaster Ezra is doing, too, with vamps, of course. And the fae headmistress with her kind. They're reaching out to all of their most trusted acquaintances and best ex-students, telling them what happened, and seeing if they will fight with us." Francis' eyebrows arched. "Basically, we've been amassing people for your return. We figured that once you came back, you'd know how to finish this shit. Do you?"

I snorted, unable to help myself. That was the question of the century, wasn't it?

"Well, we're getting closer every day," I said noncommittally. "I think it's good that they're building armies, we'll need all the help we can get. We should also consider a base in the human world. The fae academy could be a good one. It seems more secure than most."

"More secure than Spellcasters," Francis jabbed. "I assume that you heard what happened there?"

"Yeah, the demons made it their palace."

He nodded. "Yeah. I'm not sentimental, but I feel for your peers there. Who knows what kind of torture the demons are subjecting them to."

I stopped dead in my tracks. "Wait. Students are still there? They didn't get them out in time?"

Francis and Simone shared a surprised look before she replied.

"No. Spellcasters was the first place the demons hit. A few parents tried to break their kids out later . . . it didn't go well."

"Why didn't anyone tell me that?" My voice was tight, laced with fury.

I thought back to when Sam had told us the school was under the demons' control, how the guys had blown up. We'd spent the next half-hour convincing them they couldn't just leave for Faerie. Which sort of explained why it hadn't come up then.

"I'm not sure," Francis said carefully. "For us, it happened months ago. And no one likes thinking about it much. Have you spoken with your headmistress yet?"

I shook my head. "Not one on one. That seems to be something I need to rectify."

After twenty minutes of searching, I found Headmistress Wake sitting with my parents in one of the three castle solariums. This one had an excellent view of the wide, raging river that ran right beside the castle and through the capital city of the Riverlands Court. Normally, I would have found the water and greenery calming, but I was wound too tight. Ready to burst. So many scenarios had been running through my mind while I searched for the headmistress that now the view was merely a blip on my radar.

I entered the room and stopped right in front of their table, which was covered in sheets of paper. "Was anyone ever going to tell me that the demons have taken over Spellcasters *and* are holding students hostage?!" My hands flew to my hips as my gaze traveled between my parents and landed on the headmistress.

She took in my body language with unimpressed, arched eyebrows. "I'm so sorry that we didn't get right on that when you showed up out of the blue after having gone missing for months, Miss Dane. I suppose it slipped my mind in between reconnecting with my *daughter* and the queen of the Riverlands calling a meeting in the dead of night." Headmistress Wake's tone dripped with sarcasm.

My cheeks heated as the truth of her words sank in. "Fine. I'm sorry that I'm being a bit of a ball-buster," I said, my tone much more level. "It's just that we've been talking about coming back and finishing this fight since we escaped London. It's practically all I can think about day and night.

I hated discovering that the demons took Spellcasters. And now I hear that my peers are hostages? How did it happen?"

"They arrived at Spellcasters the same night you went missing, and took the academy right away. Of course, many wished to fight, but we were too late to get the children out. Many who tried to liberate the students were injured or died."

She cleared her throat as unease flickered across her face. "As you well know, I was still at the shifter academy that evening—preparing for the third Spy Game event. I didn't even know my own school had fallen until Andre and Sam came running and shouting through the forest. I tried to contact Professor Tittelbaum . . . he didn't respond."

She stood up and paced the room. "No one did—not even my husband. After hours of trying to make contact, I called Miss Iris in Wandstown. She told me that a demon horde had flown overhead, blocking out the light of the moon. Screams tore through the darkness, and fires burned all around Spellcasters." Headmistress Wake wiped at her face hastily as if she'd shed a tear.

"But how did they move so fast?" I threw up my hands, no longer angry at her, but still not understanding. "The Hellgate opened in London. They'd have had to cross an ocean to get to the academy."

Mom gave me an understanding smile. "Demons have had hidden portals in our world for millennia. Some say new ones appear occasionally too. Witches close them whenever they find them. They teach you how to do that as a Crucible, but of course we'll never find all of the portals. Either that, or the royals have warpers at their beck and call." Mom drew in a long breath. "We're upset about the academy too, honey. It's the first place on our list to liberate once we build a large enough army."

I pressed my fingers to my temples. "Is the Hellgate still closed? Or did it rip open and we have more demons spewing in? Do the humans know?"

"You and Alex did a good job closing it up, pea," Dad said. "Although, we do think it's weakening. It will need to be permanently sealed again, after we force the demons back. And as for the humans . . ." He rolled his neck, telling that this next bit was a source of anxiety. "Many saw the demons fill the skies that night. Mind witches are currently scouring the globe to erase the memories of those the devils come into contact with. Thankfully, since that night, the demons haven't made their arrival public."

"But wouldn't they want to make themselves known? Don't they *want* to take over?"

"Of course," Dad replied. "For now, they're sowing a nice little environment of fear, and using the top echelons of world governments like puppets. They don't need to be in the limelight right now. They're preparing for war, just like us."

I flung myself onto the wicker couch between my parents. "I swear, it's just one thing after another."

Mom gripped my hand. "Yes, honey, it is. That's why we've been recruiting. Our army is building. And we have an idea as to where we'll get magicals willing to fight."

"Where?"

"Remember all those PIA agents who went missing?"

I nodded.

"We've found that they're being kept in a government facility in New Mexico. We're going to break them out. Alpha Conon is working to rally—"

"The vampires are helping too," Headmistress Wake interrupted, assumedly in case Mom forgot about them.

"Yes," Mom said. "All of those people will do their part. If we can coordinate an attack on Spellcasters when the royals are there, we'll have a good chance of success, don't you think?"

I mulled it over. It did sound like the start of a decent plan. Particularly the freeing the prisoners part. I was sure that none of the incarcerated magicals had done anything wrong, other than question a crooked wing of the PIA.

"Yes," I said. "And if the fae don't mind, using their academy as a base could be smart. It has really strong protections around it." I paused and steeled myself to add the bit I'd been dreading. "There's one other thing I need to do before we attack."

"What's that, pea?" Dad asked.

"I need to find another spirit worker to bind the ghost of a mind witch to me so I'll be protected from possession. Eva needs the same. If we can get this done, neither Ishtar nor Lucifer will be able to harm us from afar. We'll be able to fight them. I'd hoped that Amethyst's parents, or even Amethyst, could do it, but after seeing her . . ."

"Miss Rhines is not in shape to be helping anyone at the

moment," Headmistress Wake's voice was strained, making a lump rise in my throat.

Although she rarely showed her emotions, this had to be hard on her. The school she called home was under control of an enemy. Her husband was there, and the students she'd sworn to protect.

"Definitely not," I agreed. "Diana is working to help lure her back to this plane, though. Hopefully, it will work. In the meantime, Queen Aquatia tells me that there is an aether-blessed fae in her kingdom who might help. After Eva wakes up, we'll begin planning a journey to visit her."

"Does she live in the capital city? If so, why not invite her to the castle?" Mom asked, her face wary but curious.

I'd hoped this question would come up later, but should have known better. My parents always had liked to keep tabs on me.

"Not the city. She actually lives along the border."

"Which one?" Dad asked astutely.

I folded my hands tightly together and squeezed.

"The one the Riverlands shares with the Dark Court."

The room stilled. Dad's eyes latched on to Mom's, and they shared one of those moments that made me feel like they could read each other's minds.

When his gaze traveled back to me, I pressed my back into the couch.

They were clearly going to take some convincing.

# CHAPTER TWENTY-THREE

*I*t took the entire day to convince my parents that letting me seek out the aether-blessed fae was the best option. And honestly, I suspected that I only succeeded because Crown Prince Halad and three of his cousins wished to join in the quest.

Considering I still used GPS in my hometown, the escort was just as well. They'd keep us from getting lost, which would save time.

Of course, Alex, Eva, Hunter, Andre, and Sam wanted to come too. The only shocker was Francis, who brought our cohort up to twelve. Diana had wanted to come too, but understood that caring for Amethyst was a priority—especially if this aether-blessed fae couldn't do what I asked.

Thankfully, in the hours since Diana had started feeding Amethyst the right foods, our spirit walker friend had already shown slight signs of improvement.

As I entered the stables where the horses waited, Mom

grabbed my hand. "Please be careful. We just got you back."

"Don't worry, Mom." I mounted the mare I'd been introduced to earlier, Silverhoof. "You already have enough to think about. I'll be fine, I promise."

"I know you're capable, but you're still my baby."

I smiled, trying to ease her nerves. "From what I've heard, the fae we're seeking is an old biddy who lives alone. We should be fine." I gestured to the large contingent traveling with me. "And if she gives us trouble, Prince Halad will make it an order that she has to help." I didn't like the idea of forcing someone, but desperate times called for desperate measures.

And right now, I was so damn desperate.

"Still, honey, this is Faerie. The dangers are different here, and prevalent." Mom's gaze traveled to the prince, all done up in a royal uniform, and beaming jovially at all who passed by him. "The prince seems nice enough, but I'm not sure how capable he is. I don't want to nag, but please do be careful."

I snorted. Prince Halad seemed more the type to woo the court than slay a dragon or battle danger, but his cousins looked battle-worthy. However, I couldn't deny that the prince's position might help. And I wasn't about to turn down the assistance of someone familiar with Faerie. Mom was right that this realm was full of dangers.

"We'll be on alert for dangers, Mom. Tell Dad I said goodbye again. I love you guys."

"We love you too, honey."

Once everyone was astride their horse, we galloped out the castle gates and into the city that surrounded the fortress. As we rode, fae who recognized the prince cheered and waved. He waved back, grinning at all of them, and calling out the names of those he knew. The rest of us just took in the city and smiled at the crowds as if we were celebrities.

*Being royalty must be super weird.*

When we reached the city wall, the guards didn't hesitate to open the gates, and we rode through into the wild fields of the Riverlands Court. From the window of the room I'd slept in, I knew that the countryside around the castle was green and rolling, but until I was in it, I hadn't realized how all-encompassing the greenery would be.

Swaying grasslands stretched on both sides of the road dotted by the occasional tree or patch of shrubbery. There was nothing else in the wide expanse, no homes, no monuments or animals. Not even a stray gray boulder to break up the verdant scene of the fields.

I inhaled a full breath of fresh air. It smelled amazing, like grass, a sweet scent that mingled with Silverhoof's musty aroma.

For the first time in days, I felt as if I could take a moment to breathe, to think, to be in the moment. I planned on savoring the ride out to the aether-blessed fae's home. The day and night spent on the road would be the closest thing to a vacation that I'd had in a *long* time.

As we trotted down the road, my gaze roved over my friends. Most had ridden horses back home before applying to Spellcasters—because you never knew what they'd spring on us at the academy. The only one who was unsure about her skills on a horse was Eva.

Thankfully, Hunter was a natural horseman if I ever saw one, and his confidence was eroding her doubt. We'd only been trotting along for a few minutes, and already she looked more relaxed than when we'd settled her on her mare.

"You look like you were born on the back of a stallion," the Riverlands prince, who I'd met hours before, rode up next to me and beamed good-naturedly.

His cousins trotted in his wake, all grinning too.

"I've had a fair bit of practice," I admitted. "When I was young, Mom wanted me to be in horse shows. I think because she was terrified of horses growing up, and didn't want that for me. Anyway, I didn't like it so much. I preferred dancing. Still, I stuck with my riding classes long enough to pick up the basics and then some before she allowed me to quit."

"Riding is an excellent skill to have in one's arsenal." The prince nodded to Alex. "Your gentleman looks like he agrees."

There was no doubt about that. Alex looked nearly as comfortable as Hunter on the back of his stallion.

"He's good at most things he tries," I remarked.

"Ah, we have fae like that." Prince Halad arched an eyebrow. "Personally, I find them to be quite frustrating. It's such poor form to be good at *everything*."

"Yeah, none of us understand how that feels being

around you, Halad," a cousin teased. He was built like a linebacker, with black hair and vibrant blue eyes that rivaled Alex's. "I'm Lyon, by the way. My cousin has manners, but he sometimes forgets to use them."

"Good to meet you. What are your names?" I nodded to the other two.

"Grahn." The brunet with a crater-like dimple in his chin nodded at me.

"Flynn," the last one with long, flowing white tresses said. Unlike his cousins, he didn't have wings, but shared the pointed ears of the others, and towered over the rest. Probably an elf, then.

"Flynn's the baby of the group," Halad said. "Though you can't tell by looking at him."

The guys bantered, occasionally asking me questions until I broke off to ride solo for a bit.

Everyone fell into their own rhythm as we traveled across the countryside for hours, stopping only for food and water for the horses. By the time the sun began its descent, the prince had already diverted  toward a place to camp.

When we found it, I leaned forward and patted Silver-hoof's neck. "You did good today, girl." I dismounted, and my legs wobbled precariously. *That's not going to be good tomorrow.*

A squeal hit my ear, and I whipped around to find Eva had also gotten off of her horse, and fallen to the ground. Hunter assisted her in standing, and gave her a hand as she hobbled to the edge of the clearing. The poor thing would be in a world of hurt tomorrow.

Andre, Sam, and Francis were already pulling the tents from their mounts and tossing them on the grass.

"This semi-circle clearing looks like a good place to set up tents." Sam pointed to the indent in the thicket of trees we'd stopped by. "There's a little cover, but it's also open enough that we'll be able to see someone approaching."

The prince nodded. "We're a fair distance away from the border, but we should still rotate a watch throughout the night. Just in case."

"Vampires don't need as much sleep as other magicals do," Francis piped up. "Plus, my vision is far superior, so I'll take the whole night."

I smirked at his pride. My eyelids were already drooping, so as long as I got some sleep, he could keep his *superior vision*.

We took care of the horses, erected the tents, and made a fire. Dinner was simple, a few sandwiches, fruits, and a strange vegetable that reminded me of carrots, but with the spice of a weak pepper. I gobbled it all down and crawled into a tent.

I was lying on the mat inside the tent Alex, Hunter, and Eva and I shared, when Eva let out another squeal.

I shot up. "What is it?"

Before erecting the tent, we'd checked the area for anything strange. Leprechaun holes, or pooka dens. Most fae lived within the kingdom's town and cities, although there were still wild creatures that preferred to live in the old ways. We'd tried to be considerate and not encroach on their space.

"Dunno," Eva said, her brows furrowing as she palmed the ground under the tent. "What the hell? It feels like I'm lying on a tiny cooking pot."

"It's probably just a rock, sugar." Hunter rubbed her shoulders. "No one's about to disassemble this tent to find a strange little pebble. Do you want me to push it out of the way?"

I groaned at the idea. "Yeah, shove it to the side." I laid my head down, intent on ignoring my friend's grumbling as she shifted the rock out from underneath her.

In the next few moments, silence blanketed our tent and, eventually, the camp. My eyelids fluttered closed, and my body grew heavy as a haze of sleep dragged me under.

# CHAPTER TWENTY-FOUR

"*Aaaaaagh*! Something freaking bit me!"

I scrambled up and nearly bonked heads with Hunter in the pitch-black tent.

"What's going on?" Eva mumbled. She rustled under her blankets. "Guys," her tone became frantic. "I can't move my legs! They hurt! Help! I think I'm paralyzed!"

I rolled my eyes. "Dude, if you feel pain, you're fine. You're just sore. Stay there, I'll check out what the commotion is about."

I barreled out of our tent, Alex and Hunter following close behind.

"Do you guys see any—oh what in the world!"

"It's a dragon, isn't it?" Eva screamed from inside the tent. "I freaking knew we'd see a dragon!"

"Not a dragon, sugar!" Hunter called, sounding as baffled as I felt, staring at the swarm of teeny tiny pixies swirling around Andre.

Prince Halad was up, too, clearly trying to bargain with the pixies, which snarled and darted around him. A fair distance away, his cousins were sniggering and not even bothering to hide it.

"Maybe a dragon would be better?" I muttered as a pixie started yelling at the prince, who stepped back and cupped his hands around his mouth.

"Get up, everyone!" Halad called out. "We have to leave now, or the swarm will attack! They're only holding off out of respect to my mother!"

I blinked. Pixies attacking? A *swarm*? Was this a joke?

But instead of wasting time questioning things, we did as the harried Prince Halad said, hauling a whimpering Eva out of the tent, and taking it down in record time. As the guys rolled up the canvases, I glanced at the moon, high in the sky. It was probably near midnight.

"And don't think you can just move down the hill and camp there!" one of the larger pixies yelled as Prince Halad mounted his horse. "We own all the land until the next grove!"

The prince's lips flattened, but he didn't argue, merely nodded and told everyone else to saddle up.

I did so gingerly, my body still aching from earlier.

Once I was sure Eva was in her saddle, I rode up to the prince. "So, what happened back there?"

Prince Halad rolled his eyes. "Wild pixie swarms. They're *very* territorial, and this is their land. They weren't pleased when we made camp here, but decided against retaliating out of respect for my mother. Their resistance held out until the chief's mate couldn't find her favorite cooking pot. After that, he lost it, attacked Andre when he got up to relieve himself, and, as you've noticed, kicked us out."

Cooking pot? My mouth fell open, recalling Eva's description of the item she laid on. All that was for a cooking pot?!

"Okay, so they were upset, but why did you look so freaked?" I leaned close because I wasn't sure if pixies had sensitive hearing. "In case you didn't notice, they're tiny."

"Tiny and *deadly*," the prince said. "They have venomous fangs. With that number, we'd all have been dead in minutes."

"*Deadly?!* Did you just say 'deadly'?" Andre pulled his horse up next to us. He held up his arm, on which was a single, swollen, red lump.

"Not from *that*." The prince was unable to keep the exasperation from this tone. "One pixie bite is nothing. You'll be fine. But if the swarm had gotten to you . . . That would be a different story."

"It's not nothing," Andre muttered. "This shit stings."

I muffled a laugh and, as the prince cantered ahead, dug my heels into my horse's sides.

Between Andre's hysteria over his pixie bite and Eva's '*I knew it was a pot!*' ramblings, it was an hour or so before exhaustion took over our group once again. When everyone finally fell silent, it was still dark, and the prince estimated that we had at least three more hours until the sun rose. I wasn't sure if we'd reach the next thicket of trees that indicated the end of the swarm's land before then, but I sure hoped so. I was desperate for sleep.

As it happened, I was fated for disappointment. We came across the grove about a half hour after the sun inched over the horizon.

Prince Halad pulled his stallion up to the grouping of trees and squinted into it.

"Is it safe? None of those tiny devils?" Andre asked, his eyes narrowed.

"I see no signs of a pixie swarm living here. Of course, that doesn't mean it's not in another swarm's territory, but as long as they aren't nearby, we should take this chance to sleep for a couple of hours. The closer we get to the Rift, the more alert we need to be."

I blinked through blurred vision and nodded. A nap sounded glorious.

This time, when we dismounted, we didn't bother setting up tents, but simply lay in the grass and passed out.

Francis woke us all up three hours later, and we trucked onward. By the time the sun hung at its zenith, I was more than ready for another snoozefest, but knew that wouldn't happen.

According to Prince Halad, we would reach the aether-blessed fae's cottage at any moment. More importantly, we were approaching the border of the Riverlands and Dark Court—the Rift.

I'd noticed it an hour ago, a dark cloud on the horizon. As we'd journeyed closer, the inky stain had grown and expanded to encompass miles and miles. A cold emanated from it, one that made me shudder every few minutes.

"Wild, isn't it?" Alex said from his place at my side. "I feel like depression is washing over me, just seeing it."

I felt it too. "I can't imagine living so close by. Why would this aether-blessed fae want to subject herself to this? Even with aether power, it would have to affect her, right?"

"Most definitely," the prince replied from a few feet away. "I feel it. However, she has a strong motivation. Rumor has it that she lost a child to the Dark Court."

"They killed her kid?" Alex asked, horror-stricken.

"We're not sure. She claims that her son crossed the border right before the Rift appeared. He's either in the Dark Court, or the Rift sucked out his soul as he journeyed through the expanse. I doubt she'll ever learn the truth . . ." he trailed off.

"Why can't anyone get rid of it?" Eva piped up, eyeing the swirling inky storm up ahead. "And *what* is it?"

"No one knows, just as we know practically nothing about the Dark Court," the prince replied with a frown. "Personally, I believe that an aether-blessed fae—probably the most powerful in Faerie's history—created it."

I cocked my head. The Rift looked nothing like the bright aether power I'd seen, but the prince probably knew better.

"Not a demon?" Hunter asked.

Halad shook his head. "True demons cannot enter this

realm. Once, they were able, long before the Rift came into being, but not anymore."

I was about to ask what had changed to make this place immune to demon infestation when a hut came into view.

I pointed. "Is that her home?"

Prince Halad's mouth spread into a smile. "It must be. Anyone up for a gallop?"

Since we were all antsy to fulfill our quest, we kicked our horses into high gear. We were about halfway to the cottage, when I noticed that something was off.

The door was wide open. As was the gate door.

My gaze flickered from side to side. No one else seemed to have noticed. Or if they had, maybe they figured she kept her door open all the time. She did live in the middle of nowhere.

Despite that point, I couldn't shake off the inkling that something wasn't right.

Not wanting to worry them by shooting off a spell, I called up my demon magic, and bid it to slither through the lush grass like a snake.

*Glow red if adversaries are ahead.*

My magic flew forth, faster than our horses, and entered the cottage. When it didn't glow red right away, I released the breath that I hadn't realized I was holding.

And then the damn cottage lit up crimson.

"Stop!" I yelled as cries of surprise flew off the others' lips. "Everyone, stop! There's—"

My mouth snapped shut as two dozen armed fae resembling walking corpses burst from the home.

"Dark Court Shadows!" Prince Halad yelled. "Prepare to fight!" He darted a fearful glance at me. "If you can use your demon magic, it would be much appreciated."

An inky blast of magic soared from one of the Shadows.

My eyes popped open wide. *Oh shit.*

These fae weren't just soldiers from a crappy place. They had magic that most others didn't—magic that they'd gotten from their ruler, who answered to a royal demon.

"Eva!" I screamed.

"I saw!" she yelled back and rode up to my side. "Fight like with like?"

I nodded, and together, we kicked our mares forward.

The horses' hooves pounded against the dirt, as loud as thunder, as the Shadows sprinted ever closer. Prince Halad was at the forefront of our group, his other hand pressed out, bright white aether blooming from it. His cousins rode just behind him, all using their aether magic too.

I surged forward, maneuvering Silverhoof to fight by the prince's side, figuring the aether and shadows would be an unbeatable combination.

I was almost there, when a fae popped into existence literally out of nowhere and tackled the prince, throwing him off his horse. Before my eyes, the creature shifted forms into something more beastly, and sank fangs deep into the prince's chest.

The metallic tang of blood filled the air as Prince Halad loosed a scream, and the inky blackness inside me attacked. It soared around the Shadow shifter, encircling his neck and squeezing. Ice slithered across my nape as the fae thrashed and screeched, but I didn't let up. I pressed harder, and waved Alex over to care for the prince.

He was there a second later, falling to the prince's side, and shoving aside the body of the shifter who'd attacked him.

As if I had a target on my back, five more fae encircled us. While Alex assessed the wound, I took them down one by one. My lips trembled as the last Shadow fell. He had survived five witch spells before my demon magic sucked the life out of him.

*Too resilient . . . That's not good.*

A scream cut through my revelation, and I whirled to find that my friends were still battling ferociously.

Swirls of darkness floated around Eva as she struck down her opponent. Andre and Sam had made good use of their demon daggers, pausing in their attacks only to pull the blades from the fallen fae. Hunter had been struck and was bleeding from his arm, but he didn't stop fighting. He used his totem in conjunction with his magic to great effect, slaying three Shadows as I watched. Prince Halad's cousins had taken down their fair share too.

A growling voice came at my back, snapping me back into the moment, and I twirled to find a fae behind me. It lunged, and without even a second thought, I flicked my finger, and demon magic surged. It slammed the creature in the face and dragged the shadow fae to the ground, where my magic smothered the monster until its last breath.

When I looked up next, only our group remained standing. Though we'd been outnumbered two to one, we'd made fast work of the shadow fae.

Someone moaned, and Alex murmured something in reply. I twisted to find the prince still on the ground. Alex was pouring his energy into Halad to help stop the bleeding from his chest.

"Prognosis?" I asked as I fell to my knees next to my boyfriend.

"Not good," Alex replied, his gaze darting up to mine for only a moment. "We need to get him back to the castle, and fast."

"You can't fix him here?" Lyon asked, his blue eyes misty.

"I'm doing what I can, but I'm not as familiar with fae physiology. Particularly that of the aether-blessed. You guys have a whole different type of magical energy running through you. Aether magic changes things."

He chewed on his bottom lip, visibly upset by his limitations. "To be honest, the prince was lucky. Two inches higher, and that beast would have sliced through his carotid."

Alex's fingers fluttered over the gaping injury, at least eight inches long and four inches wide. Smaller tears spiraled off the main injury, turning the surrounding skin a sickly gray, nearly necrotic black, color.

"I can keep him alive, but I'm not sure that I'm capable of healing the wound," he finally admitted. "Fae healers will surely be able to help."

"There are many healers at the castle," Grahn said in affirmation. "What can we do to assist until we get there?"

Alex looked at me. "The aether-blessed fae we seek might not be able to help us any longer . . ." He trailed off, clearly not wanting to say that she might not be able to help because she was likely dead. "You should go check her home. Take one of the fae too, just in case."

My stomach sank. No doubt he was right. If the Shadows had infiltrated her cottage, it would be a miracle if they'd left her alive. Still, we hadn't traveled all this way for nothing.

Flynn volunteered to go with the rest of us, and we approached the cottage.

Absolutely no one was surprised when we found the home in shambles. There'd been a struggle—a massive one, if the singe marks and exploded furniture was any indication. The home smelled dirty, uncared for, with the telltale beginnings of rot hanging in the air.

We discovered a body curled up in the far back corner, covered by a tattered blanket. The fae we'd been looking for, dead. I pulled the blanket off to look at her face. Dried blood crusted her nose, and bruises bloomed beneath her eyes.

"The poor woman," I said. "I wonder why they attacked now? Do you think it was because they knew we were coming?"

Sam stepped forward. "No time for speculation. We need to bury her and get moving."

I nodded. She was right. We might never know why, but that didn't change what we needed to do next.

As a group, we lifted the fae and took her outside. Just off the cottage was a small, lovingly cared for garden. We found only two shovels, so everyone except Hunter, who was still bleeding a lot from his wound, took turns using them.

In less than an hour, the hole was dug. Once we nestled the fae inside, we covered her up and stood over her. A few people shuffled and darted unsure glances at their neighbor as unease mounted.

Feeling as if someone should say something, I bowed my head. "I'm sorry that this happened to you. I'm sorry that you waited for your son, and he never came back. I'm sorry that your life was hard, and we came too late to help."

I wiped away the tears beginning to form in the corner of my eyelids. My words could apply to so many people—particularly if we failed.

"We're going to do our best to beat the demons," I promised her. "If we do, maybe Faerie will change for the better too."

"May the aether light your way," Sam said, which made me lift my head to stare at her.

She shrugged. "It's kind of like 'amen' for humans, right?"

Flynn, the only fae present, nodded, looking surprised and a bit intrigued by her knowledge. "That's right. I like that many in your group have brains and bravery as well as beauty."

My lips curled up when Sam's cheeks flushed, but I bowed my head again in an attempt to finish the funeral rite as respectfully as possible.

"May the aether light your way," I echoed.

# CHAPTER TWENTY-FIVE

e rode the poor horses hard all day and through the night. Lyon, the best rider, pushed his stallion ahead to warn the castle to be ready. The other advanced riders, excluding Hunter because of his injured arm, took turns carrying the prince on their horses. When it was Alex's turn, he'd often try to infuse healing magic into Halad. Still, by the time we reached the capital city of the Riverlands Court early the next morning, the prince didn't look any better. He looked much worse.

As soon as we entered the castle, a group met us outside, among them, Queen Aquatia.

"Quick!" the queen yelled. "Healers, move!"

Within minutes, Prince Halad had disappeared into the bowels of the castle. Needing his own arm bandaged, Hunter followed, and Alex went with him, hoping to be of help.

I scanned the retreating crowd, and found my parents rushing through the fae to join me.

"We heard the news of what happened at the cottage, pea," Dad said. "Are you all right?"

"Fine," I replied. "We've barely slept since leaving, so I'm exhausted, but there isn't a scratch on me."

They embraced me, and I squeezed them tight in return.

When I pulled away, my gaze traveled from Dad to Mom and back again. "But we failed. The aether-blessed fae was dead, so I'm back to square one."

"Maybe not," a familiar, proud voice announced.

I craned my neck around Mom to find Diana walking my way. "Amethyst just spoke. She asked for you and Eva."

"Serious?" My lower lip trembled, partly out of joy for my friend, and partly because we still had a shot.

Diana nodded. "I heard people running through the halls. I glanced out the window to see your arrival, and she woke up. The first thing she said was to bring you two to her."

I nodded, and after calling Eva away from her mom and dad's grasp, we followed Diana to Amethyst's chambers. Our parents trailed behind, the Proctors asking questions every step of the way.

When we reached Amethyst's door, Simone and Magdalena were still there, standing guard. The door was open, and inside, Headmistress Wake was speaking with Amethyst.

I knocked on the doorframe before entering. Their heads turned simultaneously.

My friend's eyes lit up when she saw me, although her lips did not curl up in her familiar smile. "Odette, Eva, please come in." She waved us toward a few chairs settled around the one she'd sat motionless in for days.

We took the seats, and I leaned close to her. "Amethyst . . . I am so sorry about your parents. I should never have let you come. I would—"

She held up her hand. "I would've come, even if I'd known what would happen to my parents. I couldn't live with myself otherwise." Her words choked out of her, but she fought through the emotion. "They believe in what you're doing, you know. They've seen what has been happening to our world. Things that haven't even been set in motion yet—terrible things."

Her eyes drifted out of the window for so long that I thought she'd forgotten we were there.

Eva shifted in her seat, and Amethyst's attention snapped back to us.

"Thanks for helping me back, by the way. I needed the proper nourishment to become grounded. Not that I was *lost* while I searched for my parents, but I might have been."

"Of course. Diana did most of the hard work."

Amethyst nodded and cleared her throat. "They've seen so much where they are now. That's why they couldn't come back to me. It's why I searched for so long and never found them . . . until today." She folded her hands together as if that made perfect sense. Maybe it did to her, she was the spirit worker, after all.

"Did you talk to them?" Eva asked in a small voice.

"Yes. In the ghost plane. They told me everything. Where you've been, what you've accomplished." She bit her lip. "What you need me to do."

My breath hitched. I hadn't expected to show up and have my friend already understand what we needed.

"It will be difficult," I said carefully. "We had a very adept spirit worker do it for the first time in 17th century France. She had to have been at least seventy. Walked around the spirit worker block a few times, if you know what I mean."

Amethyst snorted.

"But I remember what she did," I said. "I can tell you. If you can do this, it'll be the key to us surviving the demons. And hopefully sending them back to Hell."

Amethyst gulped. "My parents said you'd say that. And as always, Mom and Dad were right."

"Maybe the fae have books on how to do it too," Eva offered. "Then you can study up for a day before you try."

Amethyst shook her head. "I don't need that. My parents will help me. They're actually already on the hunt for the perfect ghosts. They said you'd need strong, trust-worthy mind witches, right?"

"Right," Eva replied.

Amethyst's gaze trailed out the window once again. "Well, then they're on it. So now, all we have to do is wait."

We left Amethyst in her room, awaiting the return of her parents. I hoped they would find the ghosts of mind witches quickly. The sooner Eva and I were protected, the sooner we could all return to the human realm, free the prisoners that the U.S. government had locked up, and build an army.

Eva and I had made it halfway down the hall when Alex and Hunter turned in to our corridor. They were both coated in dirt, and dried blood caked Hunter's dark blond hair. I pressed my lips together hard as my gaze landed finally on Hunter's bandaged arm.

"You okay, honey bunch?" Eva asked as she picked up her pace to meet the guys.

Usually, when they came together, she would throw herself into her man's arms, but not this time. This time, Eva stopped carefully before him, caressed his arm, and kissed him softly on the lips.

Alex slid his arm around my shoulder and squeezed me close to his body. I cuddled in, savoring his familiar, comforting aroma, mingled with the scent of horses, sweat, and dirt that we all carried, and the herbal concoction that was seeping from beneath Hunter's bandage.

"Fine," Hunter said. "Those fae, whatever they were, are apparently more dangerous if they bite you. I only got slashed by a blade."

"So, Prince Halad?" I prompted.

Alex let out a long, slow breath. "He'll be fine. The

healer said that if we had been even two hours later, the story might be different." My boyfriend frowned. "Still, there'll be scarring."

"You did your best," I said, not about to let him feel bad about being unable to heal someone when he didn't know how. "He's a prince—a leader. Halad is sure to earn a few more scars in his lifetime."

"How's Amethyst?" Hunter asked, gesturing down the hallway.

"Well enough, all things considered." I shook my head. "Her parents' spirits told her everything. They're already on the hunt for the ghosts of trustworthy mind witches. Now, we just wait."

"Well, we have a few more things to do." Alex pivoted and brought me with him. "Queen Aquatia requested to see us in the Poppy Lounge as soon as possible."

My spine straightened, and a trickle of fear washed through me. Was she mad? Halad had gotten injured on the quest? I'd tried to warn her that it was a possibility—that perhaps someone else would be better suited than the future king of the Riverlands Court.

"She didn't seem mad," Hunter said, clearly reading the worry on my face. "Sam and Andre are already waiting."

"Oh, you mean Andre's not still at the infirmary for his pixie bite?" I teased, trying to lighten the mood a little.

Alex snorted. "Because of Halad's condition, Andre wasn't so dramatic about his own when we all arrived at the infirmary. But you could tell he wanted to be." He rolled his eyes. "He *so* wanted to be."

Everyone chuckled, and we made our way through the halls, trying to keep the conversation light.

When we reached the designated lounge, we knocked on the door. Surprisingly, the queen herself opened the double doors. Behind her, the room appeared empty, save for the king, two servants, Sam, and Andre.

"Won't you please come in?" she asked.

We acquiesced, and when she gestured to a circle of chairs surrounding a heavy table made of blue-gray stone, we made our way over there. I stifled a groan as I fell into the chair. After hours of riding, sitting in a regular seat with cushions had never felt so good.

The queen took us in. "I know that you have slept little, and would probably like to wash up after such a long journey. I'll make this quick, I promise."

She snapped her fingers, and the servants stepped forward and placed two boxes on the table. Gracefully, the queen leaned over and opened one of them.

In the box, a dozen blades glinted up at us from a bed of green crushed velvet. I sucked in a breath, recognizing the wavy ornamentation of the metal.

"Demon daggers," Andre whispered, and pulled his own blade that the prince of the Snowcap Court had given us from his scabbard. His was smaller than the ones in front of us, although no less deadly.

Demon daggers, also known as hell blades, were weapons made of metal forged in Hell. They were powerful equalizers, able to kill all levels of demons, and could be wielded by magicals and humans alike.

"Yes, demon daggers, made from the same supply of metal as yours I believe."

I blinked in confusion. "But Queen Tially told us that one of their citizens journeyed to Hell and brought the hell blades back."

Queen Aquatia nodded. "That's true. But he didn't go alone. Many of the neighboring Faerie courts sent one or two citizens. It was a coordinated effort. Not all returned, but the blades that they brought back were split evenly amongst the participating courts."

She gestured to the box and the closed one next to it. "There's an equal number of blades in that box. They're yours, if you so wish."

We all stared at her.

"What if you need them?" Eva asked after a few moments of stunned silence. "What if we fail, and you end up needing these to protect your people?"

What she wasn't saying was obvious. We witches could use spells, albeit very difficult spells, to kill demons. But unless they were aether-blessed, and there weren't many of those, the fae had no such talent. Their only saving grace was that demons couldn't cross over into Faerie.

Then again, if we failed, if the demons grew in power, even that might change. And then all the fae courts would be in peril, just as our world was at that very moment.

"I'd still like for you to take them. If you fail, and I hadn't given them to you, I would always wish that I had." She paused and swallowed. "Plus, you saved Halad. You saved my son's life. Nothing can repay that, but I hope that these blades might come close."

The room stilled as her words sank in, true and heavy. And just when I thought none of us might ever speak again, Alex leaned forward and plucked a dagger from the box.

"Thank you for this gift." His blue eyes seared into the queen's green ones. "I promise we'll put them to good use."

# CHAPTER TWENTY-SIX

wo days later, we were still waiting for Amethyst's parents to return with ghostly tributes. During that time, I slept a lot. My friends took their fill of much needed rest too, and when we were awake we made it a priority to teach others the druid spells.

A handful had actually mastered the freezing spell, and when I learned that they'd never used the killing curse for greater demons, I was happy we'd taught them. Personally, I would fall back on demon magic, but they didn't have that option. And the more tools people had, the better.

Once they tired from practicing the new spells, we insisted that those who would fight with us work with the demon daggers. There might only be twenty-four hell blades, but as far as I was concerned, as many people as possible needed to know how to wield one.

Despite keeping busy, by lunchtime on the second day, the minutes dragged like hours.

"When do you think they'll come back?" I asked as we lunched in one of the castle's three solariums.

Dad chuckled. Patience had never been my strong suit.

"There's no telling, honey." Mom picked the cucumbers from her salad and placed them on my plate. "The ghost plane is different from our world. Obviously, I don't know firsthand, but I've heard stories. It's large and easy to get lost there, even if you belong."

"We can't wait long. I wonder if we could have found a more experienced spirit walker faster in the human world?"

"Faster isn't always better, pea." Dad set down his fork. "I'd like to kick those devils out of our world as much as you, but we have to do it right. Our sources say that they're still manipulating world governments left and right, preparing to make a big move."

"What do the humans think?" I couldn't imagine being on the other side of this—oblivious and unsure as to why the world was changing for the worse.

Mom heaved a sigh. "Lots of them are raising questions. Others are just going with the flow. Or even cheering for the changes the demons want to make. There's always division when it comes to how people want to lead or be led."

"Or lose all of their free will," I muttered.

Once the royals wrested power from the government, the humans wouldn't be leading at all.

"That's one way to look at it," Mom agreed, and began picking at her salad again.

I took a couple bites of my own food, a sandwich with some unidentifiable meat. I didn't dare ask what animal it came from, lest it be a unicorn or some other mythical creature. Especially because I couldn't deny that I liked it.

"How are you getting your information?" I asked.

"Headmistress Wake made contact with Ezra Darklight and Alpha Conon not long after you arrived," Dad replied. "They've been building an army, and she urged them to do so faster. Since then, they've been sending messages using the older students—well, the shifters have, at least. Vampires can't get past the fae wards without another fae, but shifters are allowed through if they take certain precautions. Headmistress Wake meets them at the academy and takes the brief."

"Was one of them named Dasha?"

I considered my friend's mates. The outgoing and nerdy Howley, quiet Heath, and gruff mountain wolf Gregor.

"Or maybe Gregor, Howley, or Heath?"

Mom tilted her head. "Dasha sounds familiar. Do you know her?"

I nodded. "She's alpha blood. Although she said she wouldn't become an alpha until her parents step down from their leadership roles. She was a champion of the Spy Games—along with her three mates."

My parents blinked simultaneously.

"*Three* mates?" Mom asked.

I bit back a laugh. She looked horror-stricken, much like I had always felt when considering having to deal with three dudes all the time. Particularly three possessive wolves who were all so different.

"Yup. Her alpha blood calls to all of them, and apparently, that's okay."

"Universe have mercy on that girl," Mom muttered, and Dad broke out into laughter.

"Anyway," I said, trying to bring the subject back around to what I was really interested in. "If you guys are getting word from messengers, have they figured out where the prison is?"

Dad's face hardened. "We're still working on that."

Mom patted his shoulder. "Your father's upset. We think we've located the prison, but it seems that breaking in will be harder than we could have imagined. It's well guarded by humans and technology. But there are signs of magical protections too."

A second later, I was about to ask another question pertaining to the prison, when Hunter burst into the solarium. All three of us jumped and spilled some of our lunch on the floor. He had some sort of condiment smeared across one side of his face, telling that he had been mid meal when he came to find us.

"Hunter! What happened?" I asked, my voice high from the shock.

"They're back!" he cried out. "Amethyst's parents are back!"

I leapt out of my seat and dashed down the hall, Hunter a half-step in front of me.

We were both out of breath when we arrived at Amethyst's room. We found her sitting in the same wing-back chair she had so often occupied. But this time, two ghosts perched opposite her.

*Her parents.*

Tears threatened to flood my eyes, but I wiped them away when a smile appeared on Mrs. Rhine's diaphanous face.

"Odette Dane, is it?" Her smile brightened as her eyes darted behind me to take in my parents, who had just burst into the room. "Lauren, she looks just like you, but with your height, Joseph. What a beautiful girl."

A sob choked out of Mom's throat.

I was no mind witch, but I knew my mom. From how her wide eyes took in Amethyst's mother, it was obvious to me that she was envisioning how easily she and Dad could have been in the Rhines' position.

Dad wrapped his arm around her shoulder comfortingly.

"Thank you," Mom sniffled. "Amethyst is lovely too."

Mrs. Rhines nodded. "Thank you."

For the first time, I noticed that she smelled cold—like menthol. I'd never experienced that with another ghost. Or maybe I just hadn't noticed it.

Mr. Rhines floated over. "We're here at the request of our daughter, although we cannot stay for too long. We haven't been ghosts long enough to tolerate this plane for extended periods. But Amethyst tells us you need something done and she'll require our help. However, I must ask, are you ready to bind yourself again?"

His ghostly white gaze pierced me, and although I'd been waiting for this moment for days, I hesitated.

"Yes," I said after a moment of silence. "Have you found someone who Eva and I can trust?"

Louise had done a fine enough job back in the 17th century, although I couldn't say that I had liked having her in my head. She'd been too lazy for me to totally trust her.

Mr. Rhines nodded. "We conducted a thorough search and asked for many opinions. The witches we found will suit your needs. You might even recognize their names."

My gaze shot to Amethyst, and her lips quirked up.

*Recognize their names? Are they famous?*

"Who are they?" I asked, electricity dancing across my skin.

"If you can believe it, they were both in our year," Amethyst interjected, her tone wobbly, as if she were nervous. "Their mind powers aren't as strong as some witches who lived full lives and practiced, but my parents *assured* me they were keen for the job."

"They're also naturally talented, and have an excellent reason to want to be in your head," Mrs. Rhines said. "Both will work harder than those other ghosts you bonded with. That matters quite a lot."

I cut a glance back to my parents. They looked intrigued, but from how Mom was biting her lip, I knew worry was simmering in her gut, just like in mine.

My eyebrows arched, and I turned back to the ghosts. "Go on . . ."

# CHAPTER TWENTY-SEVEN

"**No** way," Hunter said, sounding like a high surfer dude.

"*Efraim and Tabitha*?" I gaped. "But . . . even if they had a natural proclivity toward mind magic, there *must* be better choices."

I was so confused. La Voisin had made sure to choose mind witches who were renowned. The spirit worker who had planted them in our heads had even mentioned that both mind witches had been powerful. So why would Amethyst's parents think it would be okay to choose such young witches?

"And by 'better,' I mean more experienced," I clarified, because no one had answered me yet.

Amethyst glanced at the ghosts of her parents. "Mom? Dad?"

Mrs. Rhines glided forward. "It's an unconventional choice, I admit. But part of the reason we were gone so long is that we were researching. The ghost plane has a wealth of knowledge. Many powerful witches of the past agreed that a mind witch's power is less important than their connection to the cause. Louise, who we met and were not impressed with, by the way, only wanted to live again. So she was not a good choice. And Claude, while a better option, missed his wife too much to separate across realms, straining his connection with Eva to breaking when you entered Faerie. You need ghosts who will stick it out."

Mr. Rhines approached me. "You have to admit that, as Efraim and Tabitha have living family and friends, they have a lot to lose."

Amethyst nodded. "Yeah, plus, revenge. I'm certain they want revenge."

"But . . . are you sure? Wouldn't it be better to have someone with a little mind witch training? I mean, did they *ever* train in it?"

Amethyst's mother clapped her hands. "We forgot to mention that both of their parents had been training them up a bit before they came to Spellcasters. Parents often do that, you know. To give their child a leg up." She glanced to the side of the room.

Headmistress Wake and Diana had entered the room without my notice. Diana looked unsurprised by the information about Tabitha, but was throwing her mother nervous glances. No doubt she had known about her best friend's illegal practices and hadn't told her mother.

"Not too much, mind you." Mrs. Rhines added. "Seeing as witch law forbids mind magic until a witch reaches the age of twenty. They only taught them little bits here and there, enough to get the juices moving."

Headmistress Wake shrugged. "There's nothing to do about it now. They're no longer with us. And if their abilities will help us win this war, I'm all for it."

Diana mock-scoffed. "I can't believe that came out of your mouth."

"So they learned a little bit," I clarified. "Like enough to make it not hurt when one of them enters my head . . . and they mind their manners."

Memories of Louise picking through my brain resurfaced, making me cringe. But surely, someone I'd met in real life wouldn't do that. I hoped.

Mr. Rhines nodded. "They learned the basics. And since they've volunteered for this, other mind witches in the ghost plane have been giving them tips." He paused, and his gaze grew solemn. "I realize it's asking a lot for you to trust us on this, Odette. My wife and I might not know much about being mind witches, but we're experts when it comes to spirits. Believe me, the most powerful ghosts are the ones with a driving purpose."

Silence fell, and blood rushed in my ears. Everyone was waiting for my word. It was strange to be the one hesitating and questioning, after I'd been so determined to find a solution.

All three of the Rhineses knew more about the world beyond than I ever would. Probably more about mind witches, too, considering their recent investigations. If they thought this would work, I needed to trust them, no matter how scared I was. Or how strange it would be to have someone I'd actually known inside my head.

I drew in a long breath. "I have to talk to Eva and make sure she's cool with this, but if she's down, I say we do it."

Eva shared my concerns, but in the end, she decided the Rhines family had probably done their due diligence in figuring out who would be the best candidate to keep our minds safe. After all, it wasn't just our lives on the line. Amethyst had already said she wanted to fight alongside us again, as would many of her family's friends.

"You still want Tabitha?" Eva shot a glance at the door just beyond which Amethyst was preparing her circle. My bestie was clearly not convinced that I wasn't just letting her have the more easygoing of our classmates out of the goodness of my heart.

"Yeah," I said. Tabitha and I had a spotty past, and some making up to do. For some reason, it felt right to claim her.

"Okay, just double-checking. We all know you two had . . . history."

"Well, so did you guys." Hunter had messed around with Tabitha before he started dating Eva. For that reason and because of how Tabitha treated me, Eva had never liked her much.

"Both Tabitha and Efraim will do well for you girls," Alex said, squeezing my hand. "They have loved ones who are still alive. People to protect."

Amethyst poked her head out of the room we'd been waiting to enter. Her expression was equal parts excited and nervous.

I understood that mix all too well.

"I'm ready," Amethyst said.

After giving Alex a kiss, I strode toward Amethyst, trying to project confidence. My parents were waiting just down the corridor with Eva's family, talking in low voices. "Us and our parents, right?"

She nodded. "Mom and Dad say these sorts of things work best if only blood relatives witness it. It has something to do with the blood you'll shed to bind the ghost to you. I don't really get it, but I trust them." She extended something to me.

I looked down to see a dagger in her hand. I chuckled, though none of this was funny. "You know, Amethyst, I like things that aren't daggers too."

"I promise, I'll never give you one ever again." She bit her lip, obviously conflicted.

I knew where she was coming from. The deed itself was positive and would bring a lot of good for our side. But a ghost had possessed her against her will. I doubted she relished the thought of implanting a ghost inside someone else.

"Hey," I whispered. "I was teasing. You're doing the right thing. This gives us a *real* chance."

She gave me a wobbly smile. "Thanks, Odette. You want to go first?"

I nodded and blew Alex a kiss before disappearing into

the room Amethyst had prepared.

Besides being a brighter space than La Voisin's sitting area, the setup for the binding was identical—a salt circle surrounded by candles giving off smoke, a silver bowl, though this one was larger than Mélanie's, and of course, the dagger in my hand. Everyone filed in behind me, necessitating that I moved out of the way. I looked at Amethyst, wanting direction.

"Stand in the middle of the circle and cut your hand. Drip the blood into the bowl, and when I tell you to, lift it high," Amethyst instructed. "Tabitha is nearby, waiting. But she's too new as a ghost to cross over by herself. She still needs an actual invitation."

I sucked in a breath, preparing to meet a mean girl from my past. As I got into position, I dug the blade into my palm. A metallic tang filled the air as red blood welled against my skin, a feature that was becoming all too common in my life. I allowed a good amount to drip into the bowl.

From the sides, others watched. My parents looked worried, but I wasn't. And neither was Eva. We'd done this before, and though she'd hated me in life, I trusted Tabitha more than Louise. She had skin in the game, whereas Louise had only wanted a shot to feel alive again.

"Tabitha Goode, I call you to this plane. I call upon your powers and request your help. I call out on behalf of an entire realm, hear my request."

Amethyst nodded to me, and I lifted the bowl above my head.

The air next to me shimmered for a blink, and Tabitha appeared. Like the Rhineses, Tabitha smelled cold, and faintly like menthol. Her eyes, eerily white, took me in, as if unbelieving that she was here.

"Hey, Dane," she said, her tone kinder than it ever had been in life. "Who would have guessed this would happen, eh?"

I couldn't help myself, I snorted out a laugh. "That I'd invite you into my head to protect me from the Queen of Hell? I can't believe you didn't realize that was my master plan all along."

Tabitha's lips curled up in the first real smile she'd ever given me. "Well, then you're a hell of a lot smarter than I gave you credit for. Sorry about how I treated you, by the way. It was shallow and unearned." She shook her head. "I'm glad you and Di became friends."

"I'm sorry you had to die. And I'm also glad Diana and I have become friends. If you'd like, you two can talk later —through me, of course."

When Tabitha's eyes lit up, I knew that was a date I'd have to set up.

"For now, though," I held out the bowl of blood, "what do you say we work together to finish off the royals?"

Tabitha's smile grew so big that all of her teeth showed. "I'm so down with that." She took the bowl from my hands and drank deep. Once done, she set the bowl on the floor, and we waited for Amethyst.

"Tabitha Goode, do you promise to bind yourself to

Odette Dane's mind? To protect her from possession by the Queen of Hell, Ishtar, with all your might?"

"I will," Tabitha said.

"And Odette Dane, do you promise to house Tabitha within you, and make her comfortable until such a time that she must leave?"

"Yes," I said.

Amethyst inclined her head. "Join hands."

Tabitha's ghostly hand clasped mine, and a strange sensation rolled through me, as if I were being lifted from the earth ever so slightly—it was accompanied by cold, almost freezing temperatures.

"It will go away once she's finished," Tabitha whispered.

"Thanks," I whispered back, grateful the sensation would be fleeting.

Amethyst extended her hands to us, and a ball of purple light bloomed there. It struck me in that instant that her magic was the same color as Mélanie's power.

*Huh, maybe purple magic is a spirit worker thing?*

I didn't have time to ruminate on it long, because Amethyst began to chant.

"May two join as one until the living's work is done. May two join as one until the living's work is done. May two join as one until the living's work is done."

Amethyst stretched the purple ball of light toward me, and I prepared myself for the binding.

"*Capistrum.*"

Tabitha disappeared with a wink, and a strange weight

appeared in my head. Unlike when Louise moved in, Tabitha didn't shuffle around much—or pry. She simply checked out a couple of spots and stilled.

I blinked. That was easy—much easier than in the past.

"Are you okay?" Amethyst rushed forward.

"Yeah." My eyebrows pulled together. "Fine. I barely notice her there. Which is weird. The other ghost was nosy."

*We're from the same time period, and I don't care about any of your boring secrets. Only revenge on those damned demons.*

I caught a strange flash of Tabitha rubbing her hands together like an evil villain from a movie, and laughed out loud.

Amethyst startled. "Are you sure you're okay?" she pressed, not convinced.

"Yeah, fine. You did great," I promised. "What do you say you do Eva? Then we can make a plan to return to our realm."

# CHAPTER TWENTY-EIGHT

The moment Amethyst bound Efraim inside Eva's head, I wanted to leave Faerie. But Headmistress Wake and my parents insisted that Eva and I wait a few hours to let the ghosts settle in.

Although we both argued that Efraim and Tabitha were more suited to being bonded to us than the other ghosts we had harbored, they weren't having it.

"A few more hours won't hurt anything, pea," Dad asserted calmly.

*So not true. The demons are probably roasting people over spits right now.*

"To put plans in motion, we have to send word to our associates in the human world," Mom added. "Unless you want to return to an empty fae academy and wait there all alone, you might as well remain here."

I didn't want to wait *at all*. Especially not once we got to the human realm. I wanted to act.

*Me too*, Tabitha said inside my mind.

It was crazy to think she was there, someone I'd known and fought with nearly two years ago. At least she was less intrusive than Louise. And I had a feeling that when push came to shove, she would be more prepared to act too.

It was unfortunate that Tabitha and I had only found a way to bond *after* she died.

"Fine," I told my parents grudgingly. "I'm going to go find Alex."

He was still waiting outside the door to the room where we'd performed the rite, so I didn't have to look far.

His face spread into a grin when he saw me. "How'd it go?"

I snapped my fingers. "Piece of cake."

"Good to hear," Alex replied. "Because we have to be in top form tonight."

I cocked my head to the side.

Eva squealed, catching my attention, and then she and Hunter, who had been just down the hallway, darted over to meet us.

"Did you tell, Odie?" Hunter asked, his tanned face flushed with excitement.

"I was getting to it," Alex replied and turned to me. "The queen knows we're leaving soon. She's holding a feast tonight in our honor. Apparently, she has a surprise for us."

A surprise? She'd already gifted us with demon daggers. What more could she want to give us?

He read the question in my eyes. "I'm not sure what she has in mind, but I am curious to find out."

He extended his hand to me, and I took it, delighting in the familiar feel of him and the rush that shot through me as his blue eyes bored into my own.

*Ugh, get a room. Actually, don't. I'm here, remember that,* Tabitha said in my head.

*You'll have to get over that real fast. May I suggest taking a nap when we get busy?* I smirked.

*Gross...*

"Odie?" Alex asked. "You okay?"

"Huh . . . oh! Yeah, sorry."

"It takes some getting used to," Eva explained. "Having someone in your head. They want to have conversations for a little bit. At least, Claude did." She closed her eyes and breathed out a sigh. "And Efraim doesn't seem any different."

The guys exchanged a look. "Weird," Hunter muttered.

"Very weird," I agreed.

"Well, if you can manage two conversations at once, I was hoping that we could all go for a walk on the grounds before the feast starts," Alex suggested.

My hand squeezed his. "I'd love that."

We spent three hours walking the castle grounds. Although I'd wanted to get out of Faerie before, I had to admit that downtime was necessary.

Diana stopped by for a bit and asked to speak with Tabitha. As I had to act as the conduit, it was awkward, but that was okay. The headmistress' daughter needed closure, and now that we were friends, I was happy to be the one to give it to her. Plus, it was nice being around friends who loved each other, and witnessing that love.

I wanted to soak in the pleasantness of the day. The moments of stillness, of laughter between my friends and me, had become far too rare. And as we sat on the grass and talked about everything we'd seen the last few days, every-thing we'd learned, everything we wanted to do, it refilled my well with hope.

While I would treasure forever those few hours that we bonded and laughed on the castle lawn in Faerie, I was also a little relieved when the feast began. The act of moving on, of driving toward our goal, was something I'd become familiar with. Sometimes, I even craved it.

Finally, after tonight, we would leave this realm to return to our world.

With that in mind, I entered Wild Rapids Hall with open eyes, trying to take it all in. Alex's arm looped through mine, and already, though the feast had just started, people were dancing.

"Is this normal?" I gestured to the dance floor.

Alex shrugged. "I thought it was just a meal, but clearly, I was wrong."

Sana swept up beside us, her arm wrapped through Volwin's, her guard.

*And now possibly more,* I eyed the closeness of the pair.

"A feast is never *just* a feast in the Riverlands," her hand twirled through the air. "Don't think either of you are getting out of here tonight without stepping on the dance floor. The queen will insist."

"We can do that." I turned my attention to Volwin. "It's good to see you again. When did you return?"

He bowed, to which I returned a poor curtsy that made Sana break out in giggles.

"Today," Volwin replied. "We returned to the academy this morning with Headmistress Cristala. She's been conferring with the queen ever since."

He gestured to the opposite side of the room, where the queen and the fae headmistress hovered over something at the queen's table, their heads close together.

"Did you gather a lot of fae?" I asked, because I couldn't help myself.

"Not as many as we wished," Volwin's smile turned to a frown. "It seems that many of the most powerful fae in the human realm believe that, because they have Faerie to retreat to, they are safe. It's cowardly, but also difficult to blame them. They know that their monarchs would not refuse them refuge. Nor could the kings or queens really demand that they fight. That being said, unless they attended one of the fae-specific academies, many have never trained to fight anyway."

"A lot of fae and demi-fae use their talents to be models and singers and such," Sana agreed, placing a soft hand on Volwin's bicep, probably to call him down.

"We'll figure it out," I said, though the hope inside me had deflated a little at his admission. "Have fun, you two. For now, I'd like to sit."

The pair waved as they returned to the dance floor.

Alex wove us through an ocean of mingling fae. When I spotted the table at which Hunter and Eva sat with a waving Ayla and her less excitable guard Luvon, I pointed it out.

"Is there space at this table?" Alex asked as we approached the group.

"Duh," Ayla said. "I've been trying to catch your attention for five minutes! Do you know how many people we had to turn away?"

"Uh . . . no?" Alex answered seriously, making me twist away to hide my smile.

"Well let me tell you! There were more people than wanted to sit at the royal table!" Ayla exclaimed as if she could barely believe it. "And that's *with* Prince Halad released from the infirmary."

I glanced up and saw that she was right. The prince was just settling in at the head table. His mother had stopped chatting with the headmistress, and turned her attention to the prince, obviously checking up on him.

When he caught my eye, he waved, beckoning me over.

"Speaking of His Highness," I gestured to him. "I think he wants to talk to us."

We made our way to the head table, waving and chatting with those we knew as we passed. When we finally stood opposite Prince Halad, he was chuckling.

"You two are like those people in your world who are on those strange screens with moving people," he said.

"Celebrities?" I offered, trying to keep in a laugh.

"Yes!" Halad held up a single finger. "That's the word."

Alex chuckled. "Maybe here, but not back home."

The prince shrugged. "The closest thing we have to that is royalty, but with you two around, no one cares that I'm here." His eyes danced as he watched the crowd spin and twirl in front of him. "To be honest, it's a pleasant change, not being the center of attention."

"How are you feeling? Are you all healed up?" I studied the spot where the Shadows had attacked, but could discern no injury through his regal attire.

"Not quite," he admitted. "I'll need a few more days before I'm good as new."

"Makes sense. You were hurt pretty bad."

The prince nodded. "I was lucky that you killed the beast who attacked me, and everyone worked to return me quickly to the castle. Thank you for what you did—for saving my life."

"You don't need to thank us." I gave him a small smile. "To be honest, I feel a little guilty."

Halad cocked his head, and I explained.

"There was no need for us to go to that fae cottage. The aether-blessed fae we sought was dead when we arrived. You got injured for nothing and could have died too."

Alex ran his hand softly along my back, but didn't deny my words.

The prince, however, shook his head. "I don't look at it that way. That woman was a subject of my kingdom, and no one knew that she had died." He heaved a sigh. "If anything, the journey brought me to a stark realization."

"What's that?" Alex asked.

"We need to be more involved outside the cities and villages. Even in your world. And while I can't come with you, since Mother would have a fit, and I'll be the first to admit that I'm not battle ready," he gestured down to his wound, "my cousins would like to go."

"Like the Torna twins?"

Prince Halad nodded. "Well, yes, but also those who joined us on our journey to the border. Flynn, Grahn, and Lyon have more aether magic than Ayla or Sana. If the Shadows are any indication, spells and brute force are effective against them, but aether—like your dark magic—will work too."

"You know . . . you don't have to send them," I said. "It's not your realm to protect."

"It might not be my realm they invade today, but tomorrow, who knows? If our journey made anything clear to me, it's that the Shadows have infiltrated the Riverlands. If they continue to do so and grow stronger then my kingdom is at risk. Not to mention," he grinned and gestured to the right, "it seems to me that some of your kind might like that my cousins join you."

I followed the gesture to find Sam and Flynn dancing closely together. Flynn's long, white mane practically obscured their faces as their lips inched closer together. Not far away, Amethyst appeared caught up in talking with Lyon, whose blue-veined wings seemed to shimmer with excitement over what they were discussing.

The idea that a romance or two could blossom during this time made me smile.

"I see what you mean. Well, thank you. We appreciate you sending people you can trust."

The prince smiled. "The Riverlands Court will do whatever we can to assist. Mother and Headmistress Cristala have been discussing all day exactly how many trained soldiers to send."

I blinked, and my heart rate sped up. "Seriously?"

"As the aether that runs through me," Halad replied, which I took to mean 'very seriously'.

"Wow," I breathed. "That would really help. Even if they don't possess aether magic, as long as they can fight, we can use them."

"They can, and they will. Just like we need to take better care with our borders, we must do so with our allies' lands too," Halad said. "We will assist you as much as we are able. You have my word."

"Thank you," I said. "Tonight is turning out so much better than I expected."

Alex pulled me closer. "And on that note, I'm going to whisk my lady away for a celebratory dance."

# CHAPTER TWENTY-NINE

The next morning, Ayla poked her head through the portal and then led the way back to our world. I was right behind her, hell blade in hand, ready to strike any demons that might have somehow found their way into the Fae Academy of Elemental and Arcane Arts.

Because I was so close, I could feel Ayla's aether streaming from her, putting out feelers for darkness that didn't belong. It tingled across my skin like bubbles popping. Aside from when the twins had glamoured me, which had made me uncomfortable because for some reason it had reminded me of when I'd nearly died, I'd never felt the aether so up close and personal. When it wasn't directed right at me, and perhaps because months had passed, the aether was strangely pleasant. It warmed my insides, invigorating me in a strange way I'd never experienced before.

*So strange,* I thought and pushed the sensation away.

Given that we might run into trouble at any moment, I needed to be on alert in case Ayla needed me.

After a few minutes, she released a lengthy breath. "All clear."

Tension unraveled in my chest. I twisted to look at Eva and nodded.

"All clear," Eva echoed, passing the message on.

One by one, my cohorts sent the message down the line until a clamor broke out behind me; a raucous cheer, because Prince Halad had been correct. At the end of the feast the night before, the queen had promised to send us home with one hundred elite fae soldiers.

The thought of them fighting with us when they didn't have to still made my throat constrict.

As soon as Ayla bounced off her dorm room bed, I exited the tunnel, and blinked as spots swam in my vision.

"Whoa. Why do I feel so weird?" I gripped the side of my head and made sure Tabitha was still there. She was, and my racing heart slowed.

"Same. I'm so dizzy!" Eva scooted off Ayla's bed to stand by me.

Ayla laughed. "You've been in Faerie for a bit too long. You've gotten used to being steeped in the most pure fae magic around. During the Spy Games, we were only in Faerie for a night and a day. Long enough for you to feel normal, but not for the magic to become your new normal. Don't worry, it's not like being Faerie drunk. The sensation will pass in a few minutes."

"It had better, I—"

A sound from the hallway hit my ear.

I stiffened and grabbed Eva's wrist. Telling that he'd heard it too, Alex leapt out of the portal next, his knees bent as he lowered into a crouch, preparing to attack.

"What is that?" I asked, my eyes locked on the dorm room door.

Simone emerged from the portal next. Right away, she tilted her head just as a dog would, and snorted. "Chill out, witches. It's Headmaster Ezra and a bunch of wolfies."

Not a second later, she was proven right when the vampire headmaster entered the room, followed by the statuesque and glowing, blonde, alpha-to-be Dasha and her three handsome mates.

Dasha's face broke into a smile. "Odette! You have no idea how relieved I am to see you. You were gone so long!" She ran to me, and wrapped her powerful arms around my torso, enveloping me in the pleasant aroma of apple-scented shampoo.

I gripped the shifter champion tight. "I missed you too," I said, then added, "Although, where I was, only weeks had passed. Not months."

Dasha pulled away from me, her golden eyes wide. "Weeks! How? Where did you go?"

I told her the story as others entered the room from the hallway, Alpha Conon among them. More people poured out of the portal, and soon enough, the dorm room became cramped.

"Since we have so many coming, I'll take people to a larger space," Ayla said to Amethyst, who had just appeared. "Wait here for me, and tell them to chill? I'll be back."

The spirit walker nodded, blinking away the disorientation.

Ayla gestured to everyone else. "Come with me."

She led us to the same courtyard that I'd been in before. The one that hid the entrance to the Snowcap Court. It looked identical to the last time I was here, but more flowers were in bloom. The air was warm, and despite being located miles inland, I swore I could smell the salty sea air of the Pacific.

I shivered, pleased to be home.

"Good to be back, isn't it, sweets?"

"Amazing," I smiled at him. "Even with war on the horizon, I don't want to leave this era or realm anytime soon."

"And we won't let you leave!" Howley, Dasha's bespectacled and outgoing beau, called out, pulling a smile from me.

We waited while Ayla conferred with the headmasters, relishing being home, and listening to Dasha talk about what had been happening while we were away. Finally, what felt like years later, everyone had come through the portal and joined us in the courtyard.

"Let's regroup," Sana said, standing on the bench that Headmistress Cristala had once announced my first visit to Faerie from. "Clearly, you all got past the school wards with the directions given."

"And a bit of help," Headmaster Ezra admitted from

where he stood with his students. "One of the alumni, an old friend, was our guide."

Headmistress Cristala moved toward the center of the courtyard and sidled up to the vampire headmaster. "Of course, a vampire cannot get in without a fae. I'm pleased you found an escort."

For the millionth time, I thought Spellcasters should consider taking a few pointers from the fae academy where security was concerned. If they had, perhaps the demons wouldn't currently be using the school as a home base.

My jaw tightened just thinking about it. Now that we were back, I couldn't help but want to run to Spellcasters. To help liberate the people I called friends and peers from the clutches of those monsters. But that would be a foolish move.

The demons would expect us to want to reclaim Spellcasters. If we were going to take it back at all, we would need fighters. Even more than we'd already recruited. That meant first freeing the prisoners that the crooked PIA members had locked up.

"More recruits will join later today and throughout the weekend." Dasha took the stage. "At least two hundred shifters have volunteered to fight, and I'm sure that more will join as they hear of the cause." She paused for a couple breaths. "However, I'll admit that, lately, we've had to be more careful in our recruiting efforts."

Headmaster Ezra nodded. "We have, too. The demons have been finding and killing recruiters. Only three vampires have died so far, but it's made everyone else wary of seeking magical kin." His lips twisted into a frown. "There's a rumor going around that this could be because there are demon supporters within our ranks, assessing those who are weak or acting alone."

"Is there evidence to support that theory?" my dad asked from the back of the room, his arms crossed over his chest in an appraising manner.

"No," Ezra replied. "But there's no denying that people are dying. I only mention this so that, if you do bring people into the fold, you're careful." His eyes shifted to me, and then to Eva. "Not all of us can sense when demons, or demon supporters, are around, but if you know the person, and they're acting strange, think twice before telling them of our cause."

People in the crowd squirmed, and murmurs flew around the room. It was not a welcome idea, to believe that someone you knew, potentially someone you'd trusted, might not be a good person after all. I'd already experienced it when I learned that David Chena was a mole and demon peon, enacting their plans for them, and using the PIA's resources to do so.

"So what would you say our forces are up to now?" Headmistress Wake began striding down the aisle toward the front of the room.

"Five hundred, give or take those who chicken out, which is inevitable," Headmaster Ezra replied. He nodded to the fae who had congregated on one side of the courtyard. "Of course, that's not including the many Riverlands soldiers I see before me. Most of the others we've recruited are waiting for a call to action. In the meantime, they've been working in the shadows to keep their communities safe."

"So around six hundred . . ." Headmistress Wake closed her eyes as if the number pained her. When she spoke next, her tone was tighter, more strained. "By all accounts, hundreds, potentially thousands of demons were let into our world the night that the Hellgate broke open. And that's not counting the ones that were already here, biding their time. If Ishtar and Lucifer call them to battle, they *will* come. And Spellcasters defenses are already down." Her cheeks darkened. "As everyone knows."

The vampire headmaster nodded. "Don't feel poorly about the loss of your school, Priscilla. If anything, I've come to consider it an advantage."

"An *advantage* that my student body is at the mercy of devils? That some of them have already died!" the witch snarled at the vampire. "What an idiotic claim."

The vampire flashed a bit of fang before he caught himself and muscled his expression into a mask of calm. "I apologize. That came out wrong. I did not mean that we are at an advantage because your students are captives."

The headmaster moved to meet her, his cape billowing behind him. When he stood before her, he lifted his palms to the sky and gestured to the many witches in the crowd. "I meant to say that the royals are in a place with which you're intimately familiar. Your academy drew them in, corralled them, which makes it easier for us to fight them.

We have the advantage because Spellcasters alumni and students know the academy well."

His eyes drifted from Alex and me, back to Eva with interest. He obviously knew about me and Alex, and suspected something was different about Eva too. "Two of those students, perhaps three, if I'm not mistaken, are of particular interest to the devils. Your students and alumni are uniquely positioned to lead us into battle. And if you so wish it, the vampires will follow your every command."

Headmistress Wake blinked at the claim that the vamps would follow us. After a prolonged silence, she gave a tight nod. "We'd appreciate that assistance, Headmaster Ezra. I apologize for my outburst." Her cheeks grew even redder.

I'd never seen the headmistress embarrassed, and when my gaze slithered over to Diana, I noticed her mouth was hanging open. Apparently, it was uncommon.

"As you might imagine," Headmistress Wake continued, "I am embarrassed over my profound failure as a head of school."

My heart went out to the woman. She was a force to be reckoned with. At times, I'd despised her. But if anything was true in this world, it was that in spite of many obstacles, most of which she could never have foreseen, she worked to keep the academy safe.

"No one could blame you, Priscilla. We need to look forward, not dwell on the past." Dad piped up again. "Now that we know we're steadily building an army, the next question becomes what about the ex-spies the corrupt portion of the PIA took prisoner?" He folded his hands together. "Does anyone know the location of the prison?"

"And if you do, what state are the prisoners in?" Alex added. "I can't imagine they're healthy."

I bit the inside of my cheek, feeling foolish. I hadn't even considered such a thing. To me, we would liberate the jail, and then march on to Spellcasters.

Dasha let out a low whistle. "Bird shifters have located the prison. As they flew over, they noticed a few people moving outside. They looked to be on some sort of magical leashes and were weak—one collapsed and died on the spot. It will take time to heal them, but some might be strong enough to fight." She scanned the crowd. "How many here consider themselves experts in the healing arts?"

Out of just over one hundred and thirty people, four hands shot up. Three of them belonged to Alex and his parents.

"I can call my mentor, Tiberius Thorn," Alex said, his eyes wide at the shortage of healers. "If I can reach him, I'm sure he'll help."

Headmistress Wake nodded. "I would guess that Tiberius is still home. I happen to know that he has a bunker of sorts filled with medical supplies. It's an extension of his home, well hidden and fortified. He knows of the impending war, of that I'm sure. If I had to wager his location, I would say it is there, and he's in hiding."

"Sounds about right," Alex muttered. "I volunteer to go find him," he declared louder.

I gripped his hand. "We can't separate."

He squeezed my hand. "We have to."

My tone lowered. "But Morgan and Merlin said we should never do so." There had been exceptions, of course, but none of those times had been when war was on our doorstep.

"We're well past that restriction," Alex said, his eyes soft and understanding. "I think we might have been since the night you died. Something tells me that bringing you back, might have been my major purpose in all this. At least, from M&M's standpoint. The demons wanted my blood, *our blood*, of course. But they already got that." He leaned over and kissed me on the cheek. "After all that we've been through, we'd never betray each other."

A lump rose in my throat. I'd not considered that one of Alex's primary roles in this was to bring me back to life, but it struck me as reasonable. After the demons opened the Hellgate, Ishtar had become much less obsessed with him. But her focus on me had *never* wavered. "True, but—"

"We don't have time, sweets. Thorn has a network of healers who would jump if he called. I have a feeling we're going to liberate a lot of spies from the prison, and they won't be well. We're going to need the extra hands, which means I have to find him and convince him to join us." His tone softened. "You, Eva, and Hunter should go to the prison, help there."

I looked into his blue eyes and, although I didn't want to, I nodded. "If that's really what you think is best."

He twisted to face Dasha again, who looked sad for me.

"So, where is this prison? What sort of structure could keep assorted magicals inside and garner no notice?"

She forced out a laugh. "You're never going to believe this. I barely did when the other shifters told me, but now that I've considered it, the location makes so much sense."

My heart began pounding as the room stilled, and everyone waited.

"Who here is familiar with the old gods?"

# CHAPTER THIRTY

I gripped Dasha's fur as the massive white wolf bounded away from where we'd parked the cars, over the arid desert plains of New Mexico. Surrounding the alpha were her mates, Heath, Howley, and Gregor, all in white wolf form. On their backs rode Eva, Diana, and Hunter.

Each of my friends looked as weirded out and nervous as I felt.

Above us, fae wings beat the air: the Tornas, Prince Halad's male, winged cousins, and five other fae. Diaphanous wings and the daggers hanging off their hips caught the light of the full moon as they flew.

At our sides, vampires sprinted, each carrying on their backs a witch or flightless fae. Other shifters were behind us, and those large enough to carry other magicals did so.

When we'd formed the squads, we'd made them vampire and shifter heavy, specifically because we'd suspected that we'd have to drive as close as possible to the base, which was impossible to warp to as there were no photos of the secretive area. Nor had Andre or I ever been there. From the nearest rest stop we'd have to approach the base on foot so as not to give away our arrival. As we got closer, it seemed as though our precautions had been wise.

The barbed wire fencing circled the perimeter about a mile away from the facility. Vampires and agile shifters like Dasha and her mates leapt over it, their tagalongs clutching them with all their might. The winged fae lifted the witches who had been riding on heavier, less agile shifters over the fence. When Eva and I were on the other side, we used our black magic to lift the massive bear shifters and the remaining wolves.

So far, we'd done well. And yet, I could already sense that stronger, magical, protections would crop up soon. Maybe it was the aether in the area, but for some reason, I felt hyper sensitive to it. My gut bubbled as I climbed back on Dasha's back. As we ran ever closer, I stole glances at the magicals around us, so strong physically and magically.

*What if it's not enough?*

I bit the inside of my cheek and closed my eyes, determined to wipe the negative thought from my mind as we approached Dulce Base in northern New Mexico desert.

*You can do this. You can do this. You can do this.*

The mantra ran through my mind until I'd almost convinced myself that infiltrating an über secretive and dangerous government base was actually possible. Because that was totally what we were about to do.

The shifters had discovered the militarized base about a week ago, and had been rotating watch on the area, each team trying to discover a way inside. As far as they could tell, there was only one; the site was largely underground and as secure as the Pentagon.

Hours of research on the internet told me even less than what Dasha had relayed. There was speculation that it went down ten levels. The various floors held genetically engineered animals, others housed secret labs, and then there were those that confined people.

*Magicals.*

Everyone was confused as to why the crooked government officials had put the prisoner spies there. Why not just a regular prison? Hire a strong enough witch, and it would be easy to ward it against them.

Our confusion had evaporated when Dasha explained that the government built Dulce Base on what used to be an ancient godswood. A site that Native American magicals had once called sacred ground. The land was positively brimming with the power of aether. We were sure that the government had employed an aether-blessed fae to secure the area.

After the retreat of the old gods from our world, and the devastating hunting of their half-human offspring, the godlings, only the fae remained as aether wielders. The fae the government hired would likely have used the fifth element to create external wards that were sensitive to magic. And because they were made of aether, they would be impenetrable by magicals other than aether-blessed fae. Magicals of that type were rare in this realm.

Thank the universe that Prince Halad's cousins had joined us. We now had five such fae.

Still, we all knew what we were about to do was freaking crazy. Especially considering we had only one healer. Alex had gone to recruit Tiberius Thorn, while his parents had stayed at the fae academy to prepare for an onslaught of patients. If anything happened, and a handful of people needed a healer before we returned to the fae academy, we'd be screwed.

Dasha ground to stop. The wolves and shifters behind her fell in line, and the vampires skidded to stand motionless, waiting. A flutter of wings told me that the fae were descending.

Dasha glanced around at her mates. I got the sense that they were having a conversation mind-to-mind in the way that packs could.

Howley nodded, and with Hunter on his back, prowled forward.

Hunter shot us a terrified look. I pressed my finger to my lips before the darkness swallowed him up.

The seconds ticked on. My heart pounded so hard, I thought it might fly up my throat. It seemed like an eternity had passed when finally, Howley's bright white fur glinted in the full moon's light, and the wolf prowled out of the darkness.

Howley motioned with his paw for Hunter to get off. Once Hunter's feet were on the ground, the air around the white wolf began to shimmer as he shifted. A few seconds later, where a wolf had been, Dasha's bespectacled mate appeared.

"We're close to the aether barrier," Howley said. "My nose says it's not even thirty yards away. Once the fae break the aether enchantment, we need to move right away, quietly. There are guards nearby. I could smell them."

"Perfect." I scanned the vampires. "You know your roles, right?"

"We're ready," Francis responded for the group of fifteen vamps.

"Once the aether ward is down and you take care of the external guards, Eva and I will be in the first wave to enter. I'm not sure if I'll be able to warp when we get inside, or if that would even be useful. There's too much mystery surrounding this facility. We'll have to wait and see. Diana and Hunter, stay with us, okay?"

Hunter scoffed. "As if you could get rid of us. If I'm going into some secret government base, I'm *definitely* taking a warper and my black magic sugar-mama with me." He winked at Eva who playfully slapped his arm as she shook her head.

"Black magic sugar-mama? Where do you come up with this shit? And why do the girls seem to love it?" Diana teased Hunter before directing her attention to me. "Yeah, you know I'm with you."

I chuckled and slipped off Dasha's back. The Tornas and Halad's cousins crept forward with a wolf escort. A minute later, flashes of light, aether magic, caught my attention.

Someone, a guard, yelled for help, but the fae's work brought the forcefield-like shield down quickly.

The man cried out in the darkness again, and the vampires hissed as they shot forward.

I clenched my jaw as everybody listened for the sounds of snapping necks. It came a second later, six of them, then Simone and Magdalena dashed back our way.

"The outside guards are dead," Simone said, her face covered in blood. "Francis is disabling the electronic surveillance. But we won't have long until the inside guards realize they're flying blind, if they haven't already." The raven-haired vampire relayed the information succinctly, as if she'd done this before.

She probably *had* done something like this before. The government used vampires as spies more liberally than other magicals, precisely for their speed, viciousness, and strength.

Everyone advanced. I tried my best to ignore the bodies on the ground, and focused on Francis, hanging off a steep pole and messing around with wires and pressing buttons. One knob glowed green just as we joined him, and a door eased open.

He pumped a fist in the air. "Hacker-life! Still got it!"

I couldn't help but roll my eyes as we assembled before the door of the facility.

The vampires streamed in first, taking care of the five human guards who patrolled the upper level, while Eva and I scanned for magical opponents. There were none, so we called in the rest of our rescue squad.

There was no indication of which way to go. Luckily, there weren't many options. Two long hallways stretched to the left and right. Directly in front of our fifty-person infiltration squad was an industrial looking elevator.

"Any ideas?" I asked as people piled into the complex.

Magdalena stepped forward and sniffed the air delicately. "I don't think there's anything on this level. It smells like microwaved food. There might be a few offices or a break room up here, but nothing magical."

I nodded. That made sense. Why keep the most dangerous prisoners so close to the exit?

"Still, we can't leave any stone unturned." I gestured to the wolf-shifters, who'd transformed back to their four-legged forms. "Why don't you quickly run through this level. Take care of anyone who's here."

The wolves ran off.

"I think we should be on the front line." Francis stepped forward to stand by Magdalena. "We're the most difficult to kill."

No arguing with that.

"Does anyone feel comfortable using that elevator?" I eyed the metal box skeptically.

"Nope and no need. There's a stairwell right here." Simone had wandered a ways down the hallway. "And an emergency evacuation sign that confirms there are nine levels below, not including this one. Whatever wacko website you found was right."

Nine levels, and fifty of us. I heaved a breath. That meant we would have to split up to search thoroughly.

I shot a glance to Hunter, who had always been better at strategizing than me. He stepped forward, scanning the crowd that we'd arrived with.

He began pointing out people, ten at a time. Once he identified the groups, he gave them levels. The non-aether-blessed fae, all of whom just so happened to be wingless, got the top levels. Shifters earned the next two levels closer to the surface, while the witches, vampires, and aether-blessed fae were given deeper levels.

Once he finished, I arched my eyebrows. "So we're hitting the bottom?" He'd given us levels eight and nine.

Hunter nodded. "I have a feeling they'll have put the spies deepest down. And that magic will be necessary to get through barriers."

"Shouldn't we bring a fae in our group?" Eva countered reasonably. "What if we need aether magic?"

Hunter gestured to Francis, who was also on our team. "That's why we have vampires. If we need help, we'll send him to find the aether-blessed. But we can't take all the most versatile people just because I have a hunch."

He was right.

Having set out squads, everyone made their way to the stairwell and descended. We were passing the third floor, when I knew that whatever we found down here would be unpleasant. Screams and moans came from some hallways, and the cries of animals from others. The air around me seemed to tingle as my senses heightened.

"What the hell kind of place is this?"

"Testing site," Diana said, her voice tight. "Some nutjob

website swore it was true, and now I'm fairly sure they're right."

When we reached the eighth floor, Francis held out his arm. "Guards. They probably don't know we're coming, since the walls are so thick. They're even hard for me to hear through. Let me go first and disarm them. I think there are only four on this level."

He disappeared through the door. Before it closed, scuffling ensued, followed by two yells and the sounds of snapping bones.

I winced each time there was a *thunk*, imagining blood seeping from the neck of a man lying dead on the floor.

Ten seconds later, the vampire poked his head back into the stairwell. "When you enter,  keep to the middle. I tried to push them to the side so you wouldn't trip, but the lighting sucks down here."

I took a big breath and exited the stairwell. It was as dark as the rest of the facility, with fluorescent lights interspersed every ten feet providing an eerie, weak glow. The hall smelled sterile and metallic, like the steel walls were routinely cleaned with bleach. Twenty doors lined the hallway on each side in both directions.

My stomach twisted. *Eighty rooms to check. Well, crap.*

I turned to the group. "Split up. Five go left, and five go right. Make the groups as magically even as possible."

Everyone nodded, and we split up naturally. Hunter went with Eva, Simone, and two older witches that Headmistress Wake had recruited. Diana, Andre, Sam, and Francis joined me.

We tiptoed down the hallway. Francis listened at every door, shaking his head at the empty ones. We were about halfway down the passage when he stopped suddenly. His spine straightened in a way that lifted the hairs on the nape of my neck.

"Something is in there. It's alive, but it doesn't sound human."

My jaw tightened. "Should we check? Maybe it's a shifter in their animal aspect."

"Of course we should check," Diana proclaimed, not bothering to lower her voice. "We need to find the prisoners. But what if something else is down here that we need to know about? What if they're harboring demons down here? The experimental kind." She gave me a pointed look. "You know, like in the book Merlin showed us. What if that's what they're doing down here?"

My mind reeled back to the illustration of the witch-turned-demon. I hadn't even considered such a thing, but clearly, Diana had.

My muscles tensed at the idea that the government wasn't just imprisoning these magicals, but performing tests on them. Maybe even letting the demons get the first shot.

*They're in an alliance with the devils. It's not off the table.*

Slowly, I extended my hands. "I say we blast this door with everything we have. The moment we create an opening, stop. We'll see what's on the other side, and go from there."

Everyone nodded their assent, and all except Francis, who prepared to fight, held out their hands.

Our magic flew from us. The door burned red-hot, soaking up the energy.

"More," I grunted.

We pushed, and the metal warped and began to weep slightly.

After a full minute of pummeling the door, I realized that witch power wouldn't be enough. It could make a dent, but nothing more, which made perfect sense.

Given enough time and energy, any imprisoned witch could blast themselves out. We needed something more destructive.

I closed my eyes and, midflow, switched to demon magic.

The inky tendrils replaced my bright fuchsia glow, gracefully swirling through my friends' colorful magic. The second the demon magic hit the metal door, it shuddered.

"Hit harder, Odette!" Diana urged.

I did. The door groaned, and the metal shook, threatening to burst inward. Sweat dripped down my brow as I gave it another violent push.

And that was all it took. The door flew open, slamming against the metal siding.

I lowered my hands and expelled a breath, peering into the room. "I don't see—"

The words died in my mouth as a growl tumbled out of the darkness.

# CHAPTER THIRTY-ONE

The stench of urine and rotted meat slammed into me, making me gag, before I could take in the totality of the monster.

"Werewolf!" Diana pitched her magic forward.

Man in body, wolf in face and claws, the eight-foot-tall beast hurled itself against her purple shield, and let out a roar of fury as its fur caught fire.

Diana's hand wrapped around my arm and yanked me backward. Everyone darted away, trying to put space between us and the monster as it recovered from the magic and prowled closer.

We stopped a good distance away, Diana and I in the front.

"Of freaking *course* we would plan this rescue on the night of a full moon," Diana muttered.

"Stay back. I'm going in." Francis sidestepped around us, his muscles hard.

"Do you think a vampire is strong enough to take on a werewolf?" I whispered, truly not having any idea. I'd never seen a transformed werewolf before—and if I never saw one again, it would be too soon.

"We're about to find out." Diana glared at the werewolf, which towered over the vampire as they began to duke it out. "Francis said no magic, but if we get a shot—"

"Take it," Andre finished.

From down the hall, a scream emanated, setting my nerves alight.

I twisted away from the werewolf, and my mouth fell open.

Eva had loosed her demon magic, and the black tendrils were wrapping around the neck of a manticore.

*A manticore! A werewolf!*

"This level won't have spies," I said, certain of it. "Only dangerous magical creatures." I gestured behind us. "Look."

"I'll be damned," Andre murmured, his eyes locked on the manticore that Eva had wrestled to the ground with her black magic. "I've never seen a creature like that in my life! Where did they get them all?"

"I don't know," Diana replied. "But look!"

Francis and the werewolf were still battling, fangs against claws. They'd both gotten in a few good swipes. Thankfully, so far, Francis had steered clear of the were-wolf's teeth, the part of the beast that carried the Lycan curse.

And he'd also presented us with the werewolf's furry back.

I lifted my hands, and without hesitation, flung my demon magic at the monster. It hit him square in the back, and slithered up to tighten around his neck. The beast struggled, but couldn't fight off the magic, and soon enough, it dropped to the ground with a whine. His body twitched, and I cinched the dark tendrils tighter, not stopping until he moved no longer.

"I told you not to use your magic!" Francis threw his hands in the air, strangely annoyed that I'd just helped him out. "What if I'd just jumped on his head and you hit me? What then?!"

"Well, you didn't, and he's dead now. We don't have time to waste. We're on the wrong floor." Andre's tone was defensive on my behalf. "There's no reason to open any more of these doors and discover more monsters. Let's gather the rest of the crew and descend."

I shuddered. This whole complex was creepy as hell, but that they put the spies on the ninth subfloor, spoke to one of my greatest fears: being trapped deep underground. It also worried me that they considered the spies more dangerous than the violent magical creatures.

*We don't actually know that they're on the bottom,* I reminded myself.

It was still possible that the spies were on the upper floors. Possible, but not likely.

We called to our friends, who rushed down the hallway.

"Did you see that?!" Hunter cried out. "Eva just demolished a manticore!"

"We saw," Sam said, clearly ready to move on. "We have to go down a level."

Simone shook her head. "I was afraid of that." She shot a glance at Francis. "One of us should run upstairs and alert the other floors."

So she thought the spies would be at the deepest level too.

Francis nodded. "Why don't you go? If they've already found them, come get us. If not, bring the others to the bottom. Considering how many doors are in these halls, we might need help with extraction."

We reached the stairwell, and while the rest of us traveled downward, Simone zoomed up. We hadn't even made it to the door at the bottom level when a door above us slammed shut.

*Damn, she's fast.*

By the time we reached the bottom of the stairwell, Francis was already in front of our group, prepared to attack the guards on the other side.

He cracked open the heavy door and slid through the few inches of opening. A gunshot rang through the air. The snap of a neck followed, then another. The door slid closed, and for four nerve-wracking breaths, we all stood in silence, poised to fight.

The door finally swung open, and I tensed, only to relax when Francis' head appeared in the stairwell.

"All clear. Those guys were more prepared. These halls

seem pretty secure and soundproof, but the guards have comms in their jackets. Someone could have gotten a message out when the other squads attacked. We need to be fast."

We flew into motion, dividing into the same teams as before and taking sides. My crew ran down the right side of the hall, and we hadn't even made it ten feet when I knew, I just *knew*, this was the correct floor.

"Do you feel that?" I asked, darting a glance back at Sam, Diana, Francis, and Andre.

The witches nodded.

"There's . . . something, but I can't place it . . ." Francis trailed off, his lips pursed.

No doubt Francis could sense the magic swirling in the air, the wards. But as someone who didn't actually *wield* magic, he wouldn't be as in tune with it as the rest of us.

"Will the wards hinder us from using our powers?" Diana asked. "Or just those inside the cells?"

"If I had to bet, I'd say we're in the right spot, and that they ward these cells even more strongly against witches than those above," Andre said. "They'll probably stifle a shifter's power too."

"And if they keep vamps down here, the cells will be extra strong," Francis added.

The door to the hallway flung against the back wall before we'd chosen a cell to open. I twirled, prepared to strike, only to find the Tornas' groups filing in. I exhaled in relief. Simone was working fast.

"We think the spies are down here," I yelled, in case

Simone hadn't explained. "We'll go farther down the hall. You try to open one of the cells closer to the stairs."

The faeries' teams began trying to use aether magic against the doors. Despite being in a hurry, I couldn't help but watch.

Their efforts didn't make a dent.

*This is bad.*

"Odette," Andre said. "I think these cells are more resistant to magic. You and Eva might be the only chance. If the demons had a hand in this facility, I doubt they would have warded it against their own magic. The rest of us should probably just save our energy."

The door to the stairwell slammed open, and the shifters appeared.

"Only labs on our levels!" Dasha called out.

*They have to be down here.*

I nodded. "Everyone, stand back." I thrust out my hands. "The moment whatever is behind this door appears, be prepared to either help it or attack."

With that, I let my demon magic fly. It hit the cell door and began eating away at it as if it were nothing. The hallway filled with the reek of burnt metal as my power easily burst through the wards placed on the cell door.

I shook my head, unable to believe this shit. That all the protections placed down here were only meant to keep out magicals commonly found in this realm—the magicals who called it *home.* Not demons. If anything, demons would probably be welcome here.

*Total BS.*

It took a few moments before a hole large enough for us to peer through appeared. The instant it did, a strangled scream hit my ear, and I stopped.

"Were you with the PIA?" I asked, throwing up a shield of demon magic between us and the door.

"Yes," a weak voice croaked. "Fae division in the U.S."

"Will you harm us if we let you out?" Andre asked.

"No! Just get me out of here." She released a sob. "Please!"

"Move to the back right corner," I instructed. "I need to blast the lock off, and I don't want to hit you."

There was a shuffling, slow and heavy. "I'm there," the imprisoned fae said.

I directed my dark power at the lock, shattering it. The door stayed put, so I flung it open and found a faerie, huddled and shaking in the back of the cell.

With her wings and pointed ears, she looked like most faeries I'd seen, save for some key differences. Her skin didn't glow, she was thin, so very thin, and trembling like a leaf in the wind.

"Help her," I instructed, ignoring the smell of the cell and the buckets piled in the corner. This place was beyond vile. "I'll move on to next door."

I dashed out of the cell and waved down the hall. "Eva!"

My best friend looked up from the door she'd been examining.

"This is the right floor, and only black magic will work," I informed her.

She nodded, completely unsurprised.

Eva and I worked our way down the hallways, blasting doors open while others retrieved the imprisoned. There were about ten doors left when a high piercing wail cut through the corridor.

My heart slammed into my throat. Someone had sounded the alarm.

# CHAPTER THIRTY-TWO

"Help the prisoners!"

Just as I gave the instruction, at least half of our rescue party burst into the hallway, their chests heaving.

Dasha, now in her human form, stiffened as she sniffed the air, and then barreled toward me, her gold eyes wide.

"Guards?" I asked.

She nodded. "Lots, from what I can hear and smell. They're coming from the top. I think some people are fighting them in the stairwell, but I smell gunpowder, so the guards came armed."

I gulped down a lump rising in my throat. "Hopefully our friends can keep them at bay long enough for us to get the prisoners out. Then we can help as we fight our way up."

"Here, wolf, take this shifter." Francis stormed over and handed an inmate to Dasha.

She took the man's weight and offered her other arm. "I'm strong enough for two."

Her mates did the same, and I left the others to sort out who would carry who.

I continued blasting down doors, glancing over every few seconds to find that the vampires had followed the shifters' lead, taking a prisoner under each arm. Since they were less physically inclined, the fae supported one inmate each.

My heart hammering with each step, I hurried to open the last five doors on my side. Two more held prisoners, shaking and sobbing in the back of their cell. The last three held corpses.

Tears pricked my eyes as I stared down at the last woman. She was young, no more than four years my senior, and probably still an emissary spy, if she'd followed the usual climb up the PIA ladder. And here she was, dead. All because she was working to make the world better.

Although intellectually I understood that there was no point in saving her, I couldn't help myself. She was small, smaller than Eva even, so I bent over and picked up her thin body. In death, she weighed nothing.

When Francis noticed that the prisoner I carried was dead, he shook his head. "You can't. We have to fight our way up the stairs, and we need your hands free. Not to mention, once we get outside, you'll need to run on your own. The wolves are already carrying two people each."

"I left two," I said, my voice wobbly. "But I *can't* leave

her. She deserves more. A burial—or whatever her kind prefers."

Distantly, because I was very distracted, I heard Tabitha moan in my head. She clearly didn't approve of my decision either.

But I didn't care. I wasn't sure what sort of magical this girl had been, but it didn't matter. I wasn't leaving her. She deserved a death ceremony.

The person on Francis' back whimpered, and the other in his arms let out a moan. Francis shifted his gaze from me to the people he carried.

"You," he said to the one in his arms. "We want to take this girl's body back. Normally I wouldn't ask this, but—"

The man gave the smallest nod. "Bring her," he croaked, likely seconds from death himself. "I'll hold on if I can."

Francis took the corpse out of my arms and crushed her up against the man just as the sound of gunshots ripped through the air.

"We have to go!" Diana yelled. "Eva and Odette, up front."

I scrambled to the door. Eva arrived at the same moment I did, and we paused only long enough to give each other a nod before pulling the heavy door open.

Two bear shifters, one grizzly, one polar, were in the stairwell. With dinner-plate sized paws and claws at least five-inches long, they lashed out at armored guards trying to charge down the steps. Behind them, Lyon and Grahn shot aether at the soldiers.

The fae parted when they noticed me, but the bears didn't budge.

"We have to move!" I screamed loud enough to get the bears' attention.

One shot a look back at me and released a roar. The other's paws swiped faster, more viciously, and the guards scrambled back.

"Make space!" Eva yelled, and the bears squished their massive bodies to the side.

Once there was an opening, we attacked with witch power. When one of my spells bounced off the guards' armor, I groaned.

"Switch to black magic," Eva said.

Black tendrils unfurled from my hands and shot up the stairwell. They twisted like vines around each of the soldiers' necks, cinching tighter and tighter until their bodies fell.

As we climbed higher, stragglers from our rescue team burst from their levels, shaken, and joined our ranks. The number of fallen guards grew so that they clogged the stairs. The bear shifters helped make a path, their enormous heads nuzzling the guards to the sides, piling the unconscious humans atop each other.

We progressed upward, getting closer to the surface. Every few steps, more guards descended, and Eva and I pummeled them with demon magic.

It wasn't until we neared the top that we faced the largest obstacle. A wall of a dozen guards pointing guns straight at us. Behind them, red eyes glowed maliciously.

"I see you have embraced the darkness within yourself," the cambion said. "That's wonderful news. In fact, if you turn sides now, there will be no retaliation for your attacks on the royals' property tonight."

I seethed at his insinuation that the royals controlled this facility completely, and perhaps even the prisoners inside it.

"We'll never join you," Eva screamed, and released a barrage of dark power.

I attacked with her, black magic swirling from me. Others accompanied us, and witch magic and aether mixed in, soaring past our shoulders. Our friends had our backs, and while their power deflected off the guards' uniforms, when the cocktail of magics hit the cambion, they were effective.

The human-demon hybrid fell with a moan.

For good measure, I shot off the demon-binding curse, preventing him from using his power if he woke before we got far enough away. Black magic did the rest, and our group tromped up the last few stairs and out the door.

Cool night air filled my lungs as I emerged into the desert. Not able to relax just yet, I spun around, scanning the area.

No one was there.

The cars that the extra guards had arrived in sat a ways away, all turned off, not even a driver waiting inside.

I took a full breath and turned to face my people, still spilling out of the doors of the facility like salmon swimming upstream.

Though guards had been sent to annihilate us, I didn't

believe that was the end of our troubles. This facility had too much to hide. The alarm system had to be linked somewhere else—another base or armed facility. If it didn't get turned off, more humans, and perhaps even demons, would arrive soon.

*We need to get out of here.*

When the string of people petered out, Eva and I divided the group in half and began to count.

"Twenty-one on my side," I said.

"Twenty-seven on mine," she replied.

I did the math. Two people were missing.

"Who's not here?" I asked.

"Magdalena's missing," Simone announced.

One wolf transformed into a human.

"She's gone," said Gregor, Dasha's burly, ginger mate. "She was one of the first to go after the guards when they infiltrated. He must've known exactly what she was, because he didn't hesitate to stake her."

I noticed Francis and Simone both stiffen, though that was the only outward emotion they exhibited. They were trying to be brave, to lead. I'd have to give them my condolences later, in private.

"Okay, well, we're not going to go get her ashes, right?" Eva asked tentatively, clearly not wanting to upset the vampires.

"Not for ash." Francis shot me a look because he clearly thought I was about to go sprinting back in there and look for ash on the ground. "Vampires rarely get to use the ash in our final death ceremony, so it's not necessary. We'll mourn without it."

"Who's the other missing person?" Diana asked, looking around.

Sana gasped and hands flew over her mouth.

"Flynn! Prince Halad's cousin!"

I groaned. As great as having the additional aether-blessed fae on our side, I felt an extra responsibility to return those three to the prince.

Sam stepped forward. "I'll find him."

Her chin wobbled, and I recalled seeing her and Flynn the night of the feast, close together, flirting.

"No. I'll do it," Simone said. "You might find him, and even perhaps escape. But if he's injured you'll never be able to carry him while you run or scale that fence." She nodded to the people she was carrying. "Someone take these spies in case I have to fight off the guards."

The bear shifters who had been on the front line as we fought our way up the stairwell each took a trembling prisoner on their backs.

Simone approached the door. "Don't wait for me. I'm fast. I'll meet you at the cars."

"What if you're not fast enough?" Francis' voice cracked.

"Then leave me. I'll be fine."

With that, Simone slipped through the facility door and disappeared.

"You heard her," I said, trying to sound braver than I felt. "Let's go."

We started running over the dry, desert plain. Although I wasn't carrying anyone so that I could remain alert and fight, my lungs burned after only a few minutes.

Next to me, Eva grabbed her scar and yelped.

I tensed. "Don't even tell me . . ."

She shot me a look. "The royals know we're here. What we did."

I was afraid she'd say that.

# CHAPTER THIRTY-THREE

By the time we reached the cars, my breath was thin, and my legs burned so badly that I thought I might collapse. I leaned on the hood of the car I'd ridden in earlier and pulled air into my lungs. At my side, Eva was sucking wind too—but unlike me, she seemed more alert, her eyes scanning the air.

"What's up?" I asked. "Do you feel something else?"

I hadn't felt a thing, but Eva was proving to be more sensitive in the burning-scars department.

"No. That's the problem. I think what I felt was Lucifer's anger. He knows what we did, where we are, but then the burning . . . dimmed." Her blue eyes caught mine, full of fear. "That's never happened before. I think he's masking our connection."

*Holy shit.* I brought my hand to my mouth in a half-assed attempt to cover up the anxiety mounting within me.

Eva was right. She had to be. There was no way Lucifer

was just going to let us traipse away with powerful magicals who could fight his army.

That my scar hadn't burned now seemed less strange. Perhaps Lucifer was the first to learn of our break-in, and had only told Ishtar after warning her to keep her anger under control.

*They're hiding their emotions from us.*

I hauled myself off the car and scanned the desert. The wolves and other shifters had transformed back into their human form. Everyone who had carried an injured and starved magical was helping settle them into the cars. Witches who weren't catching their breath, like Andre and Hunter, were helping too.

Because the base was in the middle of nowhere, we'd driven in on one road; that meant we would drive out on one road. And if Eva was right, the royals knew what we'd done, and where we were.

We were sitting ducks.

Memories of the hundreds of demons swirling out of the Hellgate filled my mind. There'd been so many. Now they'd bring their army here and demolish us in the middle of the New Mexico desert.

The hair on the nape of my neck lifted. "They're coming, and we'll be completely exposed," I murmured, my voice thin, laden with fear. "There's not even traffic to hide in."

"Get us out of here, Odie," Eva choked out.

"Andre!" I pushed past my rising terror, and yelled for the other warper. "Andre! I need you!"

"Just a sec!" my friend called back as his head poked out of a car he'd just settled someone into.

"What's up?" he asked after dashing our way.

"The demons," I whispered, trying not to incite panic. "They're coming. Right now. We need to warp these people out of here."

Andre stepped back and scanned the skies. "How do you—?"

"Our scars," Eva spat out. "Mine burned right after we broke the prisoners out, but now, Lucifer and Ishtar are muting their response."

"Craaaaap," Andre breathed. "How fast can they be here?"

"Not sure," I answered. "But probably faster than we think."

I didn't know of a type of demon that could transport others, like warpers, but I wouldn't be surprised if they existed.

Even as I mulled that over, another possibility—one that could easily come to fruition—filled me with cold dread.

The demons held Spellcasters hostage. Professor Tittelbaum was trapped there, no doubt bound to the demons' will with black magic, and he was a powerful warper, one of the best. They could just use *him*.

That was definitely what they'd do.

"Actually, they have Tittelbaum, so expect them at any second," I amended, making Andre swear. "We have to get the others out of here."

"Right," Andre said, twisting to face the group. All the

prisoners were almost in the cars by now. "I'll get them out—"

Eva shrieked and pointed up. "Look!"

My head snapped upward, and my heart stopped.

Red lights, thousands of gleaming, crimson *eyes*, blinked in the sky.

"There's no time to get them out of the car!" I yelled. "Eva, tell everyone to get in the cars and aim for the warpholes. Andre, come with me!" I grabbed his hand.

In the crowd, Diana yelled his name. Hunter shot me a confused look. In reply, I pointed up as we dashed past him.

A stream of expletives left my friend's mouth as he caught up with me.

"We can't go back to the fae academy. You're not an approved warper," he reminded me.

"Shit! Where can we go?"

Not Spellcasters either, but we needed a large building just like it. A fortress, somewhere secluded.

I released Andre's arm. "Run in front of the car line. I'll be right there. I need to find a shifter or a vampire."

Unable to help myself, my eyes snapped to the sky. The lights had crept closer, so much closer. I could even see flashes of fire, and the neon green glow of either a succubus or daeva.

I sprinted over to the first vampire I saw—Francis. "Was your school taken over by the demons? And is it warded to keep away outsiders?"

His eyebrows furrowed. "Why—"

"Answer the question!" I gestured above.

He followed the motion and hissed. "It's only warded to be invisible to humans and their planes. You've been there, so you should be able to get in. But I'm not sure it's safe."

"What about the shifter school?"

He shook his head. "There are rumors that some turned packs attacked it, but I'm not sure."

I whirled around, seeking Dasha or her mates or any shifter I knew.

A roar rang through the night, much too loud, and my blood skittered in my veins.

Ditching my quest for the shifters, I dashed back to Andre. "Open a warphole to Nightdwellers! I'll make one right next to you!"

"I'll fend them off for as long as I can!" yelled Hunter.

"Me too!" Eva screamed as she ran up to us.

I pushed them both behind me, and faster than I ever had before, I flung open a warphole. As this one had to be large enough for cars to fit through, it took a bit more effort than normal, but after a few seconds, I got there. Andre was working to expand his too, just a few steps behind.

"Drive through!" I screamed at the closest car.

The poor person behind the wheel, a shifter whose name I couldn't remember, stared back at me wild-eyed, his hands gripping the wheel.

Hunter shot a blast of green magic that bounced off the car's hood to get the driver's attention. The shifter revved the engine, and drove into the warphole.

Car after car passed through, and with each one, I

breathed a little easier. A sense of relief flooded me when I noticed Dasha and the Tornas driving by and waving.

When the last vehicle disappeared, I allowed myself to glance up again. The demons were still flying towards us, and were now close enough to be identifiable.

Ishtar and Lucifer flew in the front, their wings beating, their eyes blazing red in the dark night sky. The queen of darkness curled her lips up at the sight of me.

"Wait!" someone screamed in the distance.

I broke my stare from Ishtar, and whipped around. Simone sprinted toward us, Flynn's massive body hanging limp in her arms.

I sucked in a breath as my attention darted between her and the demon horde. She was fast, but was she fast enough?

"Andre! Keep your warphole open!" I screamed, releasing mine and twirling to face the demons. I nodded to Eva and Hunter. "Fight them back."

Dark magic rose within me and, taking aim, I let it fly. In the black of night, my trajectory was difficult to track, but Lucifer roared as my power pushed him backward.

Shocked, Ishtar stopped flying, and every single little devil behind her halted too.

"*Itoarazicus!*" Eva cried, aiming for a daeva complete with a cloud of swirling, green, noxious gas around it.

A moment later, the gas disappeared. Eva had bound the demon's magic, rendering it powerless.

The daeva let out a screech and nosedived straight for her, but Hunter stepped in front of her.

"*Morsultimus!*" he yelled, pulling out the big guns, the killing curse for royals and greater demons.

His spell hit, and seconds later, the daeva splattered to the ground.

Everyone seemed to still.

"You dare use our magic against us?" Ishtar boomed. "You dare use magic born of darkness, girl?"

My mouth dried up as she turned the full power of her horrible gaze upon me, and a ball of fire bloomed in her palms. I raised my hands, calling my black magic to defend me.

And then, unexpectedly, a squeezing sensation engulfed my skull.

I gasped. The fire had only been a diversion to what she really wanted to do—possess me.

*Tabitha! Help!*

*On it!* the ghost called back, and although I hadn't noticed before, I could tell that she was.

If Tabitha wasn't already fighting, would Ishtar have possessed me by now?

I dared to meet the queen's stare again, and saw that I was right. Smoke literally spewed from her nostrils, and her eyes gleamed a brighter red. She was furious.

But unlike when I'd used black magic against her, she didn't scream her indignation. In fact, as I watched, she inched backward a little. The reason why materialized immediately.

Ishtar didn't want to rage and storm because others

would know that I had a means of fighting off her possession.

*There! I got her off you. Now get out of here, I'm not ready for round two!*

Not wasting a moment, I twisted.

Simone was almost to us.

I waved. "Faster!"

The raven-haired vampire's eyes narrowed, but she didn't shoot back any snark as she bore down, zooming toward us at unbelievable speed. My hair blew back a little as she flew through the warphole and disappeared.

"Hunter! Eva! Go!" I pushed my friends through the hole.

"Odie, your turn. *Now.*" Andre pointed up, and I noticed that, while the demon queen and king hadn't moved, they had retaliated.

Balls of flames, each the size of a smart car, were headed straight for us.

I'd apparently become crazy, because the sight made me grin and wink. *Too slow.*

Ishtar let out a shriek, and I stepped safely through Andre's portal.

# CHAPTER THIRTY-FOUR

"Oh my god! Odie!" Eva threw herself at me the moment I appeared in the mountain valley that surrounded Nightdwellers, Andre right on my tail. "Are you okay?" Her eyes ran over me, searching for any sign of injury.

I grinned. "I'm fine. Tabitha protected me from possession. It scared Ishtar! I—"

The words died on my lips.

Although I'd felt proud just moments before, cocky even, now I realized that I'd made a terrible mistake.

Before this, the royals might not have known that Eva and I could use black magic. They also might never have realized that they'd almost possessed us our first night back in this world. In fact, if they had, surely they would have tried again before now, right?

A pit formed in my stomach.

But tonight, the royals had seen with their own eyes

what we could do. They learned we could keep them from our heads. And then, to rub it in, I'd winked.

No matter how slight or dubious, we'd lost both advantages—and I was to blame.

"Shit!" I clenched my fists. "If I hadn't been so damn proud and just *left*, I—"

Eva gripped my arm. "What! What happened?"

"Eva, I'm so sorry. Ishtar and Lucifer know I'm protected against possession." I threw my hand over my eyes and squeezed hard, as if by doing so, I could will the truth away. "They don't know the same about you, but I'm sure they'll guess. I lost us our advantage."

"But I'm here. So is the fae." Simone appeared at our side and gestured to Flynn, passed out on the ground only a few feet away. "You made a tradeoff, witch. One I appreciate."

The vampire closed her eyes, and shuddered. "They would have fried me alive with those balls of fire. I couldn't run fast enough."

When her eyes snapped back open, they landed on me. "If I wasn't already dedicated to keeping you alive, I would be now. I'm in your debt. As we used to say centuries ago, *a life for a life.*"

My heartbeat slowed. "Thank you."

She was right. I had revealed both powers for a reason, to save her and Flynn. At least something good had come out of it.

I gestured to the fae she'd recovered. "He's alive?"

She nodded. "I think he got bit by something in one of those cells. But he's breathing."

As if Flynn knew we were talking about him, his eyes opened. A second later, he scrambled up off the ground, and swayed on the spot, disorientated and fearful.

"Hey, it's okay. We're safe." I reached out to steady him.

When he recognized me, his shoulders loosened. "That place was a nightmare," Flynn wiped his long, white hair away from his face. "We don't have to go back, right?"

I shook my head. "No, we got the prisoners out."

At the mention of the prisoners, I took in my surroundings for the first time. The cars' headlights had been left on to illuminate our new surroundings after the others had driven through the warphole. The vehicles themselves were parked every which way on Nightdwellers' lawn. Our healthy magicals were checking that the injured and starved were in no worse condition than when we'd retrieved them.

As we were in a mountain valley at night, it was cold, even in summer, and many of them were shivering. We needed to get them into beds, hydrated, and fed.

My eyes sought Alex before I remembered that he wasn't there. Hopefully, he'd found Tiberius Thorn and other healers, because we'd need them.

"Simone, can you round up any other vamps who know the school well, and have them lead the way to the healing wing?"

"We don't have an infirmary, but I have a better idea." She darted off to confer with Francis.

My lips parted in surprise, but after a moment's thought, her words made sense. Why would a vampire school have an infirmary? They were indestructible as long as no one decapitated them, stuck a stake in their hearts, or lit them on fire.

I lifted my hands and waved to catch everyone's attention. "Where's our healer?"

The woman who had identified herself as such at the fae academy stepped forward.

"Remind me of your name again," I said wearily.

"Theodora. I've been a healer for decades."

"Theodora, please follow Simone to a place where the injured can recover. Take a few able-bodied people to gather beds too."

I paused. "Hey, Simone! One more thing?"

She was at my side in an instant.

"Does your school have a phone?" I asked, aware of how dumb my request sounded. But I honestly wouldn't be able to locate one at Spellcasters, though I was sure the academy must have one.

Simone's eyebrows pulled together. "The headmaster has one in his office. After I take the healer and ex-prisoners to Dracula Hall, I can show you."

Alex had left me the number to Tiberius Thorn's home, in case something terrible happened, or we needed specific supplies. As it was the dead of night, I had hope that the famed healer was there.

"That would be great." I looked around at all the magicals being carried into the relative warmth of the academy.

"I'll come with you right now."

Two hours later, it was going on three a.m., and I was blinking back tears.

How did healers do this every day?

We'd lost two prisoners already, and one was barely holding on. It didn't help that we had no way to get them fluids, other than hold cups up to their lips. But most of them had been starved for days, and keeping water down proved difficult.

Theodora was doing her best, but she was only one knowledgeable person, and had over seventy patients, all in critical need of care.

More than anything, I hoped that the other healers would arrive soon, although I knew it wasn't likely. When I'd gotten off the phone with Alex, he was just about to run out the door to meet with another of Thorn's students. And of course, Tiberius Thorn didn't carry a cellphone—the stodgy old fuddy-duddy.

I'd told Alex to call my parents to arrange the quickest transport, as I'd be busy trying to keep the patients alive.

Although they needed me here, I regretted not warping to Seattle and helping round up healers. At least there, I'd be gathering people and transporting them back. I could do that, but this? Oh, no. My training from basic and intermediate healing courses was not enough to help these people.

"Miss! Miss!" a raspy voice called out.

I scanned the beds we'd brought down and laid on the ground. A hand waved weakly, the palm hovering only a couple of inches in the air.

I knelt by the patient, an older man of perhaps forty, and read the name tag placed next to him. William. I wondered if he knew my parents. If not, he'd probably heard of them when he'd joined the PIA.

"What can I get you, William?" I asked softly.

I'd learned that a lot of the patients had been kept in silence for weeks or months. As a result, their hearing was sensitive.

"More water," he croaked. "And maybe a painkiller? My head hurts."

I nodded.

The vampires at Nightdwellers didn't use painkillers, but we had found a bottle in the outbuilding that they used for bloodletting. The painkiller was about the only thing in there, because the building hadn't been restocked after the last round of humans had been led into the academy and drained for sustenance.

Francis claimed that after the process, before the humans left—alive, thank goodness—the vampire handlers pumped them full of IV-fluids and drugged them up so they didn't hurt or recall a thing.

I got the patient what he wanted, and knelt down beside his mattress to hold his cup.

"Thank you," William said, once he'd drunk his fill and forced down the pill. He leaned his head back on the pillow.

"It might turn my stomach for a while, but after two years of pain, I can't wait for that pill to kick in."

"Two years?!"

Most of the other ex-prisoners I'd spoken to had been in the cells for only months. They said most didn't last longer than three. The guards starved them, and if they were shifters, the inability to shift often drove them mad before they tried to kill themselves.

"That's eternity," I whispered.

"Yup."

I shook my head, unable to believe how tough the man before me must be.

Two years . . . I thought back to my life then. I'd been in my internship, so confused, and a baby warper. At that point, I hadn't even suspected that the PIA, or a portion of it, could do something so terrible to its employees.

An image of David Chena, the man I'd respected and later killed after he sent Alex to Hell, arose in my mind. He'd lied to me about so many things, and specifically, these people.

When we'd first gotten the patients settled in here, I'd done a lap and searched for the witch I'd seen "taken in for questioning" during a PIA field trip in Culling-year. A witch who, as it turned out, had been spying on the demon-lovers at the PIA. I assumed she'd been brought to the government facility, but she wasn't among the ones we rescued.

In all likelihood, she was dead, just as Chena claimed. At least he hadn't lied about everything.

My stomach tightened in anger that only subsided when the soft snores of the man on the mattress caught my ear.

I glanced at William and smiled. He still looked awful, too thin, and with a mouth full of rotted teeth, but at rest, he looked peaceful.

Knowing it wouldn't last, I lay on the ground next to him, and soaked up that moment while I still could.

# CHAPTER THIRTY-FIVE

It took over ten hours—an endless stretch of time when you're watching over people who might die at any moment—but finally, the vampires who'd run across the mountains to retrieve the newcomers returned right after lunch, carrying seven more healers.

The moment I glanced out the window and caught sight of Francis hauling butt down the mountain, I sprinted out of Dracula Hall. Rapid footsteps followed behind me, but I was the first to burst through the front door of the castle.

"It took you longer than I thought," I said.

Francis ground to a stop right in front of me, kicking loose rocks onto my shins. Even carrying Tiberius Thorn on his back and a full rucksack in his arms, the vampire wasn't half as out of breath as I was from running through the castle.

"The wards around the academy confused the choppers'

navigation," the vampire replied. "The helicopters landed in the wrong spot. Miles off."

Well, that was annoying, but I couldn't be *too* mad. The enchantments ensured no humans came close to this place, making it more secure. And if my parents hadn't called in a couple of favors to their rich friends and borrowed helicopters, it would have taken even longer.

"One person is barely holding on," I reported.

Tiberius hopped off Francis' back, nimble for such an old man, and stretched before holding out his hand for the sack the vampire carried. "Show me to them."

"Please, take him," I said to a fae who had been helping me tend to the ex-prisoners.

Before Tiberius had even entered the doors to the castle, Simone screeched to a stop beside me and grinned mischievously.

A windswept Alex blinked, and then, seeing that I was right there, hurled himself off Simone's back.

"Odie! You're safe! Simone told me everything about that terrible place." He crushed me against his broad chest.

"And the demon horde at the end," she added, setting the leather bag she carried on the ground. Inside, glass tinkled. I hoped that the old-fashion doctor's bag was full of vials of antibiotics and other meds. The patients needed all the help they could get.

"It was horrific, but we're here now, safe," I assured my boyfriend, who was holding me so tightly, I could barely breathe.

I squirmed a little, and he let up just enough to look me in the eye.

"There are so many people who need you," I told him. "We tried to help. The one real healer on site is doing all she can, but—"

"Lead the way," he insisted.

When we entered Dracula Hall, Alex drew in a breath. "All these people were there?"

"Locked up tight in the bottom of the secret government facility." I cleared my throat, trying not to cry. "There were other things there too. Magical creatures . . . one of the vampires claims she saw an alien."

"*An alien*?" Alex echoed.

"Wardwell! Get your ass over here!" Tiberius Thorn's voice boomed over the hush of the room.

Alex's blue eyes widened, and he leaned over to kiss me on the cheek. "I've been summoned. We're triaging first. That will probably last a few hours, but then we'll rotate nine-hour shifts. Mine starts early tomorrow, so I'll see you later?"

"If you aren't already off, I'll come get you for dinner. We're sharing a room right next to Hunter and Eva."

Alex smiled. "Kinda like old times."

I returned his sweet smile because I knew what he meant—that he was trying to be optimistic—even though in reality everything had changed.

*If only it were like old times.*

After checking to see if the healers and those assisting

them needed anything, I left the hall. I hadn't gotten far when Francis and Simone joined me.

"The helicopter pilot said he'd return as soon as he could. Apparently, your parents and a few others from the fae academy want to join us." Francis took a drink out of a glass. His lips stained crimson, and a wash of blood coated his white teeth.

I repressed a shudder, because he couldn't help it if what he ate was repulsive. Plus, we needed the vampires in top form. If that meant they had to drink every bit of blood from the supply their academy had on hand, then so be it.

"Okay," I said, relieved that older adults would be arriving and taking charge. "We could use more people, although I'm not sure it's safe." I gestured out the front door.

Nightdwellers was located in the middle of the valley, surrounded by mountains. Tall, craggy mountains without roads leading in. It was fine for the vampires, since most of them could scale the peaks within minutes, and run through the forest to the nearest town with little effort. But we all had to leave at some point, and although Nightdwellers had been a great choice at the moment, now I sort of wish we had chosen somewhere more level.

"What if we need to make a fast exit? The school is hidden from humans, but magicals can find it—specifically, flying demons. With the number of injured and sick we have, getting out in time will be impossible."

Simone heaved a sigh. "You're right. We're too isolated and in a bad battle position. Not that the fae academy isn't in the middle of nowhere, but at least they're better warded." She clicked her tongue in thought. "Sooner or later, we will have to leave and reconvene in one spot. And then coordinate an attack."

An attack . . . on Spellcasters. It was the only reasonable solution.

The demons had made my academy their seat of power in the human world. I was sure that they'd chosen it to frustrate and infuriate us. Spellcasters was isolated, in the middle of the Maine wilderness. Only one long road went past it, and the nearest small town was miles away. Really, the academy's location was terrible, a poor choice for a seat of power.

Unless it had been selected to hurt specific people—or lure them in.

I sighed. "We can cover that when the others get here."

Subconsciously, we had been walking toward the library. I hadn't been inside it the first time I'd visited Nightdwellers, but while we'd been waiting for the healers, I had needed to retrieve a few books. Tomes on how to help those who were dying. Books that showed me how to heal wounds, or taught me how to reintroduce foods to someone who had been starved for weeks on end. I'd even had to read up on how to deal with an aether-blessed fae, because their power over the fifth element could make healing tricky—and painful if done incorrectly.

The magicals who hadn't been helping to heal the ex-prisoners or keeping lookout for enemies had congregated in the library. After what we'd witnessed at the Dulce Base prison most of them wanted to be together. That, and many wished to avoid wandering the castle alone. The questionable decor, heavy on blood reverence, meant Nightdwellers was creepy as hell.

The moment we entered the massive gothic-inspired library with floor-to-ceiling bookshelves, I caught sight of Dasha waving.

"Hey," I greeted her. "Have you seen Hunter and Eva? Or Diana?"

Dasha shook her head, but Gregor, the burliest of her mates, pointed to the right corner of the room. "I saw them when I was looking for a book. They're in the very back, looked to be settled in too."

"Thanks. I really need to talk to them, but let's chat later," I said, and went to find my friends.

At my approach, Eva's gaze shot up from the book she'd been reading. Her eyes widened. "Are they back?"

"Yeah," I replied. "Thank goodness."

I'd been up since yesterday, performing tasks that I wasn't great at, and fearing failure every step of the way. To say I was exhausted was the understatement of the year. Once they brought me up to speed on the happenings around the castle, I was going to take a nap.

"What are you guys researching?" I gestured to the books.

"Battle tactics," Diana answered, her lips curled up smugly.

"So what did you find? I can tell it's good."

It seemed that, whatever it was, she had just found it, because both Hunter and Eva shut their books to listen.

Diana's proud expression only grew as she twisted the book around to face us. "Who knows if it's true, I haven't encountered it in any of the other books, but that doesn't mean anything. It only has to be correct—"

"Can you *please* just spit it out, Wake?" Hunter said, his tone tight. Clearly, someone else needed a nap too.

Diana shot him an annoyed glare before continuing. "*Anyway*, this book claims that if someone can kill a royal demon," her intense gaze lifted to latch with mine, sending a shiver down my spine, "those sworn to that specific royal will also perish."

# CHAPTER THIRTY-SIX

"How's everyone getting to Wandstown?" I asked as I led Hunter, Eva, and Diana outside, into the fresh mountain air that would help me stay awake. I still wanted a nap, but after Diana dropped the bomb that we might only need to kill the six royal demons rather than a thousand peons, my brain was abuzz.

"The recruits that Headmaster Ezra and Headmistress Cristala gathered are already flying into Maine," Hunter replied. Since we'd turned up at Nightdwellers Academy, he had been largely in charge of developing a battle strategy—a task that suited his skill set. "They're arriving in small batches so as not to attract unwanted attention. The airport isn't that large. From there, they'll trickle into the town."

"Through the woods, not via the road," Eva clarified for me.

"Yup." Hunter slid his arm around his lady. "Towns-people are waiting at checkpoints with ATVs to transport them."

I nodded. If they used the road, they would drive straight past Spellcasters. And if they tried that, who knew if they'd even make it to Wandstown?

"Great. Numbers?"

"Six-fifty when we returned from Faerie." Hunter shrugged. "More people join every hour. We'll only know the exact numbers when we get there."

"Wandstown is so small . . ." I trailed off. "Was there resistance to this plan? Have the people who live there been safe? Any demon visitors to the town since they took the academy?"

"They're good with the plan," Diana said. "Mother made calls to the residents and they wanted to help. Many fled already, because a few demons *have* popped by, wreaking havoc. Not as many or as often as you'd guess, but often enough to spook some people. Actually, to hear Miss Iris tell it, the stronger greater demons and royals have been completely absent."

"I wonder why they haven't attacked the town?" Eva mused. "It clearly has a relationship with Spellcasters. Miss Iris' father was even a headmaster."

It was true, and Miss Iris' café was a favorite pit stop for PIA agents—crooked or not.

Diana shrugged. "Apparently, the demons have been largely confined to the academy. Whatever the reason, we need to take advantage of that." Her arms swung, hands clenched into tight fists, hinting that while the headmistress' daughter was trying to play it cool, inside she was really pissed. "Word has it that at least half the town stayed behind."

"If our fighters get there early will they be okay with people invading their town?" Hunter asked.

Diana nodded. "Mother has already mentioned that people will be arriving and will need spots to stay. Luckily, it's such a tight-knit community that a lot of Wandstown residents have keys to their neighbors' homes. If a home is empty, those who arrive early will use it until we join."

I let out a long breath. Things were coming together, and my parents and other leaders were scheduled to arrive in early evening. I hoped they'd bring more good news. In the meantime, we'd spar, practice magic, and care for the ex-prisoners.

"You all saw the demons," I began to broach the question that had been on my mind since the night in London. The one I hated considering, but couldn't avoid any longer. "How many would you estimate there were?"

Hunter cleared his throat. "I can't remember much of that night, aside from the fact I was nearly shitting myself the entire time." His emerald gaze dropped to the ground, indicating that he didn't like what he was about to say. "But if I had to guess, I would say a thousand demons flew out of the Hellgate. Maybe more."

I closed my eyes briefly. It was more than I wanted to believe, but either way, we were outnumbered. *So* outnumbered.

"Okay," I said, trying to sound stronger than I felt, while also changing the subject to something that didn't make ice flow through my veins. "And we've been making sure everyone who joins knows the druid spells too, right? Even since we've been here?"

Diana nodded. "We haven't kept any of that information secret. Witches practiced them in Faerie, and have been doing so here too. The information has been passed along to those we haven't met too. The recruits joining us in Wandstown. Although, rumor has it that few people have had success with them."

It figured. The druids were powerful; it made sense that not everyone could make their spells work. Still, disseminating the information was worth a shot.

We were about to turn onto a trail that led up the mountain a ways and then jogged parallel to the valley floor, when I caught a flash of movement in the woods.

"Hey there!" I called out, not wanting to startle the person when we appeared on the trail.

No one answered, although I thought I saw a flash of stark white run deeper into the forest, away from us.

My eyebrows furrowed as my hand fell to my demon dagger, nowadays always on my hip. "Did I just hallucinate, or did I really see someone?"

"I wasn't really paying attention to the scenery," Eva admitted.

"I didn't see anything either," Hunter said.

Diana gave me a concerned look. "When was the last

time you slept, Dane? Did you get to nap at all when you were taking care of the prisoners?"

I shook my head. "I haven't really rested since we arrived. I'll try to squeeze in a nap so I'm fresh when Mom and Dad arrive. They'll want a thorough debrief, and I need to be on my game."

After three more claims that I'd spotted someone in the empty forest, Eva insisted that we cut our nature walk short and return to Nightdwellers so that I could lie down.

Since I felt like I was going a touch crazy, I didn't argue.

Hours later, as the summer afternoon slipped gradually into evening, Eva woke me and told me that a runner had spotted choppers. It seemed that my parents had pulled a few *more* strings to get additional rides into the mountains. This time there were ten aircraft, swelling our numbers greatly. The new arrivals should be here at any minute.

I rolled out of bed and stretched. My spine popped, all the way up to my neck. I sighed, feeling like a new woman. Eva had washed my clothes while I slept, and they were still warm from the dryer as I put them on. I glanced down at my all black outfit, chosen specifically for our prison infiltration, and loosed a breath. There was no longer any remnant of blood from the prison break or my caring for patients.

"Thanks for doing the wash," I said. There had been so

much going on that I hadn't even thought about my appearance.

"I got you girl. Now come on. Let's go meet the new arrivals." She grabbed my hand, and I followed her through the castle.

When we made it to the front entrance, a small group had already gathered, including Diana, Alex, Hunter, and the Torna twins.

I sidled up to Alex, who gave me a squeeze. "Sleep well, sweets?"

"I feel much better. Ready to take on the world again."

"That's my babe."

Next to us, the Torna sisters whispered to one another and started giggling.

I arched an eyebrow. "What's going on?"

Sana responded to my question with a sly smile.

"Headmistress Cristala should be coming in today too," Ayla replied, more serious than Sana. "She was trying to recruit more fae, a last-minute push."

"Luvon and Volwin are with her," Sana added, nudging her sister's side, causing telling patches of pink to bloom on Ayla's cheeks.

I cocked my head to the side. I'd seen Volwin dancing with Sana in Faerie, but other than that, the guys had been notably absent. "About that . . . I thought they had sworn allegiance to you or something. Where have they been?"

"They are sworn to us," Sana said. "We insisted that they travel with Headmistress Cristala. Our parents hated that, but too bad, so sad."

"Before you returned from the past, our headmistress was putting herself at the most risk," Ayla explained further. "Sana was safe in Faerie. I was with Andre and Sam. Andre could get us anywhere at a second's notice. But the headmistress was approaching powerful fae and demi-fae in this realm, sometimes daily. Even after Queen Aquatia gave us soldiers, Headmistress Cristala continued to contact high-powered families. Since she began her mission we knew that if one of them turned out to be in league with the demons, she would need help."

"So the guys went with her. They provided muscle so others would think twice before messing with her," Sana finished. "But, man, have we missed them."

Ayla's cheeks turned a deeper red, and my lips curled up in a smile. "Yeah, I bet."

"There they are!" someone cried out and pointed to the top of the mountain.

I craned my neck to find three dozen vampires stampeding over the mountain ridges. Although they were too far away for me to make out their features, I knew that others clung to their backs. Headmistress Wake, my parents, and my friends' parents among them.

My heart began pounding faster as the sprinting vampires neared.

When they were close enough that I could make out the faces of each vampire and the person they carried, I tilted my head in confusion. "Is my dad carrying somebody?"

Eva squinted. "It looks like it. Maybe the person passed out, and he had to save them?"

It wasn't until the vampire carrying my dad ground to a stop in front of us that I realized something was wrong. Dad's face was red with anger and he handled the person he carried roughly as he leapt off of the vampire's back.

"Dad!" I cried. "What's happening?"

He pulled the limp body of the other person behind him, still taking no care at all for their well-being even though they were clearly passed out. "The helicopters had just landed, and we were dividing up the supplies we'd brought for easier transport, when your mom saw someone sneaking out of the woods and into a chopper."

My stomach dropped.

"This vampire had been lying in wait for us to land."

Dad held up the unconscious woman he was dragging behind him. Her skin was pale and her shirt stark white, like I'd seen on our hike.

"She said that she came with the first round of healers. As a spy. Who invited her?" he snarled.

The group fell silent as everyone exchanged nervous glances. When it was clear no one was going to fess up, my eyes darted down to the vampire's face. I recognized her from that morning, and recalled thinking how strange it was that a vampire would be a healer. But Alex had mentioned that a few extra people had wanted to help and I'd been *so* desperate for the real healers to take over that I'd forgotten all about her. It was especially easy to forget as I hadn't seen the vampire much since. Probably because she'd been hiding in the woods—listening to my friends and me discuss our numbers and the state of the army.

"This is only a fraction of our people. The rest are inside," I said. "We should ask the others."

Dad's eyes bored into me. "That's exactly what we'll do, pea. In the meantime, everyone else, gather your things. This vamp had already used the helicopter's radio by the time she got caught. I'm fairly certain she's given away our location."

He drew in a long, hard breath. "Our enemies might arrive at any minute."

# CHAPTER THIRTY-SEVEN

The spy had tagged along with the healers after one of Tiberius' crew asked her to lend a helping hand. Little did the healer know the vampire wouldn't help at all. She would only screw us over.

The poor, distraught healer had no idea that their old friend had gone to the dark side. But once we found the small demon stone in the vampire's pocket, there was no denying we had been compromised.

Dad was right. It was only a matter of time until our enemies showed up. Hours, if we were lucky, minutes if they forced Professor Tittelbaum to warp.

We had to leave. Fast.

Hunter slammed his fist on one of the many tables dotting the room. "People are already assembling in Wandstown. What's stopping us from joining them?"

"It's true," Headmistress Cristala said. "I sent the fae

army there yesterday. Already, more fae and other magicals have been arriving too."

"Do they have room for the patients?" Alex asked. "A lot of them can't move, and we can't transport them more than once. They might not survive it."

Hunter rubbed at his neck, clearly having forgotten about all the people in Dracula Hall. "I doubt it. Some homes are empty, but Wandstown is small. And if something major happens, we won't be able to get them to a hospital in time. Driving past Spellcasters is out of the question."

"It's not an ideal location anyway," Dad said, and all eyes in the room snapped to him.

He might have left the spy community years ago, but every time he spoke up, people listened right away.

"I agree that we have to leave, but I think that means splitting up." Dad's gaze scanned the crowd. "Is Tiberius here?"

Alex shook his head. "He's still with the patients. What do you need?"

"The healers won't be able to come with us. We'll need them, but those freed prisoners should take priority. They need to go with Thorn. How much room does he have in his home office?"

Alex furrowed his eyebrows. "Ten beds. Not enough for how many people need help."

Mom moved next to Dad. "Perhaps the other healers can take some prisoners to their homes?"

Alex mulled this over and finally nodded. "It'll stretch

the healers, but it could work." His eyes drifted to me. "One warper, preferably Odie, can focus on getting our fighters to Wandstown. From there, we can start gathering the army and making a plan. Andre can deal with healer logistics."

I gulped. "Minus you. You're not going with them."

Alex looked torn. Healing was his life's calling. He'd always excelled at it, he was the best in our year. I had no doubt that one day, he'd be one of the best in the world. Still, I couldn't let him leave my side. Not now.

"Alex, you have to go with Odette." Alex's father grabbed his son by the shoulder. Although he was trying to be strong, his voice was thick with emotion. "The royals want you both, which means you two have a lot of power and leverage. Use it wisely."

"We'll take care of your patients, baby." Alex's mother laid a hand on her son's arm. "We've never been great fighters, anyway."

At that, my boyfriend's shoulders lowered in relief. "Thank you. That means a lot, knowing that you'll watch over them. And that you'll be safe—"

"*Safer*," Hunter said. "I doubt any of us are safe. No matter where we are. Particularly if we fail."

A hush fell over the room. Hunter was spot on.

When Dad began speaking again, giving orders and sending people to fetch items, Alex left to help prepare the patients for extraction.

I stood back to let my parents and Headmistress Wake take care of the details. I didn't have anything of value besides my hell blade, and I kept that on my person at all times, so I was all set. It was a relief to let those with more experience lead.

Once Dad finished giving commands, we moved to the entryway. It was closer to Dracula Hall, which allowed us to move the patients a shorter distance. It also offered the beneficial view of the surrounding mountains. We'd know right away if our enemies arrived.

"You're not going to be able to warp straight into Wandstown, honey," Mom said. "The town has wards. Due to its proximity to the school it always has, but there are woods outside the town that we can land in."

Diana stepped forward. "There's a cottage not too far out of the village that would be a solid landmark for you to warp to. Butcher Cottage."

"Do you have a photo?" I asked. Considering we had little room for error, I wanted to be precise.

"No, but Tabitha has been there with me before. You should ask her to show it to you."

My spine straightened. *Freaking brilliant!* "I'll try it."

*Hey, Tabitha. Did you hear that?*

*Course I did. I hear everything you do. See everything you see.* Her tone was short, as it had been so often in life.

*Feel . . .?*

The ghost in my head snorted. *I don't feel everything you feel. It's muted, like touching skin through fabric. I can show you better than I can explain it.*

I tilted my head to the side. "Okay," I said out loud,

despite the fact we'd been speaking telepathically the entire time. "Show me."

A sensation like a cloud rolling through my mind overtook me. I gasped as the haze encompassed everything—my thoughts, how I saw the world around me, my inner senses. And then, I saw Wandstown.

I'd visited the cozy little settlement many times before. Through Tabitha's eyes, the village didn't look much different: smallish, quaint, charming. A rare town that didn't have to hide its magical nature. But as Tabitha walked me through it, she took a route I had never seen.

We wound through the cemetery and into the woods surrounding the area. We kept going, down a trail that was so faint, one might miss it even if they were trying to follow it. She sped up, and the memory fast-forwarded. Although it gave me a bit of motion sickness, I just placed my hand on my stomach and let it ride, allowing Tabitha to drive.

Moments later the cabin came into view. It was decrepit, with the front door busted off its hinges and the windows smashed.

"*That's* where they want to go?" I asked incredulously.

*It's a shithole, for sure,* Tabitha said. *But it's also outside of the town's wards. And no one goes there. Unless they were somehow forced to tell the demons, I'm sure the residents wouldn't mention Butcher Cottage.*

I allowed my mind to shift into Tabitha's vision once again, taking in the cabin and the surrounding area, peaceful and empty.

*Then it's perfect,* I replied.

Andre had already been hard at work for a few minutes, asking healers where they needed to go and making a reference list of who was going where. Alex was already back and rapidly prepping bags of supplies for the healers to take.

The patients were trickling into the entryway, and Andre opened a warphole to the first healer's home. Once the healer confirmed he'd gotten it right, the shuttling of ex-prisoners began.

It was then that I noticed others were watching me, waiting. I scanned the crowd. It had grown while Tabitha showed me her memory. Most everyone was present.

"People know to hurry, pea," Dad said. "Best to get the show on the road."

I rubbed my hands together and inhaled deeply. "All right, is everyone ready? I'm going to open a warphole to Butcher Cottage, outside of Wandstown."

The crowd nodded in unison.

Using Tabitha's image to guide me, I opened a warphole.

No one moved.

I cleared my throat. "You just walk through."

Still, no one came even an inch closer.

It hit me then that they were scared. Not by the warphole, but by what could be on the other side. Demons were rife around the academy, and walking into the wrong place at the wrong time was a distinct possibility. *Saying* they were ready was much easier than acting. Wasn't that always the truth? Words were always easier than action.

My gaze cut to my close friends, and understanding my intention, Alex handed the packing task off to another healer and they all approached.

One by one, Eva, Hunter, Diana, and Alex disappeared through the portal. I watched the cautious faces of others, those who I didn't know very well, as they watched them.

When no screams came from the other side of the portal, people relaxed, and the stream of fighters quickened. Fifteen minutes later, only the Danes remained.

"That took more energy than I thought it would," I admitted, wiping a stream of sweat from my brow. Though this warphole had been much smaller than the one I'd created in New Mexico, because there were more people here I'd had to maintain it for longer. "I've never held a warphole open for so long."

"You did a wonderful job, pea," Dad replied, his voice proud. "You've been doing so well throughout all of this."

Warmth spread through me. "Thanks, Dad."

I let them go first, and then stepped through behind them.

My feet had just touched down on dirt, the scent of pine in the early evening flooding my nostrils, when a scream cut through the chatter.

My heart rate ratcheted up, and my eyes darted over the crowd in time to catch a middle-aged witch fall, followed by a fae. And then I saw a winged woman with glowing, red eyes set in a human face. A cambion.

I flew into motion, calling my shadows, and sprayed a spider web of blackness over the crowd. My aim was true, and it wrapped around the demon's neck and cinched tight. Once I had her locked down, another net flew from me, and I bundled her up.

"You bitch!" someone screamed, and green acid soared toward me.

"Oh, hell no!" Eva's voice filled my ears, then she sent a wave of darkness to gobble up the succubus' poison right before it slammed into my stomach. Pivoting, she sent her own net of darkness at the greater demon.

The succubus growled, but when Eva's demon magic hit her, she crumpled to the ground with a screech.

Two demons down. Were there more hiding nearby?

"Everyone, spread out!" Hunter gripped Eva's wrist, studying her as he took charge. "Look for anyone with red eyes."

"Why were they here?" Eva asked. "This was supposed to be safe ground."

After realizing that one was wearing thick tights, and no skirt, it took only a few minutes of searching the cottage to deduce why the demons were in the area.

"We found a skirt, a cardigan, and two pairs of shoes in the cottage. Please don't tell me you use this disgusting cabin to get your jollies?" I approached the demons with a sneer on my face.

"We use it for *privacy*," the succubus snapped. "There are so many of us at that dreadful school that alone time is hard to find."

*'So many of us,' freaking wonderful.*

"How many more are there in the area? In Wandstown?" Hunter was holding his totem to the succubus' neck.

I couldn't help but notice that he despised the succubus in particular. Probably because that was the exact race of demon that had scarred Eva.

"*So* many," the demoness said with a smirk. "They'll be here any minute now."

A pit formed in my stomach, only to vanish a moment later when Eva spoke.

"She's lying."

I twisted to face my best friend. "How do you know?"

"Efraim told me. He can hear what's in her mind."

The succubus growled, and Hunter's blade pressed tighter against the skin of her neck.

"For instance, she's thinking right now that she would like nothing more than to pour her acid all over me. Finish the job that the other succubus started." Eva's voice got tighter as she spoke.

"Oh, hell no," Hunter said, and without further preamble, he sliced the demon's neck open. She fell to the ground, blood spilling on the dirt around her.

The room quieted. We were here for a war, but no one had expected that.

A heartbeat later, Hunter dragged his eyes up from the body of the demon. "I'm sorry. It's just that she threatened Eva, and—"

Alex placed a hand on his cousin's forearm. "We get it. It was a little startling, but we understand."

It was only then that I became aware of the cambion growling low in her throat.

"You're going to let him do that? Kill somebody and not get reprimanded?" Her burning red eyes flashed up at me with pure loathing. "It seems that you're not as different from us as you think."

"Don't try to screw with my head," I said. "It won't work."

"If you want to live more than the next minute, you'll leave my daughter alone and answer my questions." Dad's magic, a burning ball of silver, swirled in his hand. "Believe me, I know all the sacred incantations, and I'm not afraid to use them."

The cambion sneered.

"Are there demons in Wandstown right now?" Dad asked.

Murmurs ran through the crowd.

The cambion didn't answer, merely smirked and crossed her arms over her chest, the gesture awkward in the net of black magic.

A few seconds later, Eva piped up. "No demons in Wandstown. There's some sort of ritual ceremony happening at the school tonight. A celebration that requires every demons' presence. So they're all there, preparing for a party, but these two idiots decided to sneak away."

"Okay, then maybe we can get in without notice," I reasoned, unable to hide my tone of shock at Eva's, or perhaps Efraim's, ability to read the demon's mind. That could be very useful.

"Not bloody likely," the cambion said, earning my attention once more. "We're going to smash you. We—"

My dad, apparently done with his questioning, allowed the ball of magic to ignite the demon.

Her screams rang through the woods for only a moment before quieting. Then her body fell limp.

"That's all we need to know," Dad said. "Let's move."

# CHAPTER THIRTY-EIGHT

*W*e had to work quickly to gather those who were waiting for us in Wandstown. Thankfully, Diana and Headmistress Wake knew just who to ask to coordinate things.

Miss Iris, the owner of Potions and Pastries, a sweet little café in the heart of town, led the charge. Less than an hour later, her business was packed with fae warriors and others preparing for battle. Most from this realm where dressed in casual dark clothes that didn't hinder movement, or black athletic attire and tennis shoes, myself included. The fae warriors wore lightweight metal and leather armor. When juxtaposed with the floral curtains, bright little nosegays on the tables, and dainty French country decor of the café, we looked very out of place.

Since fitting eight hundred people into Potions and Pastries was out of the question, a spell had been placed on the surrounding businesses. It was like one big video call, where the speaker in the designated speaking area would be amplified to the other businesses.

*Magic is so cool,* I thought, sitting  at the edge of the staging area Miss Iris had created.

"We have to approach from the woods," Headmistress Wake addressed the room and all those beyond it.

"Should we drive up the road to be a little closer? Then we can enter the woods at that point?" Howley asked. "I've never been here, but I heard the academy is a few miles away."

The headmistress shook her head. "No driving. For those of you who are not familiar with the academy, there's one road that bypasses the main gates. The gate itself is enchanted. Only those of witch blood who know the password, or those who have already been approved, may enter. Clearly, the demons either have insider knowledge from the PIA, or they've bypassed my precautions. Either way, I believe that the front gate is off-limits. We need to be stealthier."

"Also, the road has been teeming with demons these past few weeks," Miss Iris added. "They haven't come into town *too* often, though when they do, they always wreak havoc."

"None of us have had the guts to stand up to them," an elderly Wandstown resident piped up. He wouldn't be fighting, but he still wanted in on the action. "Not with the royals so nearby."

I cocked my head. "I wonder why they simply haven't demolished the town?"

"That approach would make sense." Eva chewed on the inside of her cheek. "Particularly if they're trying to lure us in."

"I suspect that's the point. They don't need to lure us in," Headmistress Wake offered. "They *know* we'll come. Maybe they don't suspect us tonight. Or tomorrow. Maybe not even next week. But they know that *someday*, we will show up to take back the school. And if they believe that, they'd do well to always be prepared."

Goosebumps pebbled my arms. "So if they know we're coming, and they want us to show up, what's the point of attempting to sneak up on them?"

A hush fell over the room. I hadn't wanted to bring everybody down, but if the demons were already expecting us, the road would be faster.

Headmistress Wake's chocolate brown eyes took me in, seemingly understanding what was going through my mind. "Miss Dane, I know the best way to enter my academy. I understand that you have a key role in this war, but I need you to trust me on this one."

My lips pressed together, and a moment later, I nodded. "Okay. Where should we go?"

Once again, I was riding astride a massive white wolf. This time, I didn't fear falling off of Dasha's back as she sprinted through the forest. In fact, I kind of enjoyed it.

Was it because death was so close? Or at least, the threat

of it? We would be arriving at Spellcasters with a contingent of eight hundred people, give or take a handful. No one was foolish enough to think that we would all make it out alive.

I banished the thought, gripped Dasha's fur tightly, and closed my eyes.

*Everyone that came here with you will leave alive.*

Of course, I was lying to myself, coming up with a mantra that would never manifest. But if I'd learned one thing over the years, it was that if I didn't put it out there, I didn't stand a chance of it coming true. So I would think positively, up until the moment I couldn't any longer.

At the head of our group, just a few yards in front of Dasha and her mates, Headmaster Ezra slowed. Begrudgingly riding on his back, Headmistress Wake pointed to the right, and he diverted a few feet before coming to a stop.

The wolves changed course and joined them. When we arrived, Headmistress Wake was already standing on her own two feet, and brushing herself off to look more dignified. Not like somebody who had just piggybacked through the woods.

"Is this it, Mother?" asked Diana curiously, as she dismounted from Simone's back.

It had come as a shock to me that Diana had known nothing of the magical back gate that prevented entrance from the woods and contained students on the property. Then again, it probably shouldn't have surprised me. Her mother always tried to keep Diana on a level playing field with the rest of the students so as not to incite claims of nepotism. So the secret gate had come as a surprise to everyone, Headmistress Wake excluded.

The leader of Spellcasters assured us that the secret gate was only to be opened in the most dire of circumstances. Of course, the gate and the fence that extended from it kept students inside academy grounds, but it had primarily been created in case those inside the school ever needed a hidden escape route. According to Headmistress Wake this would be the first time it was ever used. And we would be using it for the opposite reason.

Not to escape a school under siege, but to infiltrate Spellcasters.

Headmistress Wake nodded in answer to her daughter's question. "It's somewhere very close by, I can feel it."

She closed her eyes and reached her hand out, feeling along an invisible line. "Miss Iris' father showed it to me the day before I took over his position. It's been many years, but this area hasn't changed that much. The enchantment around it assures this, so the head of Spellcasters might always find it easily."

It took her a few more moments of searching before she stopped suddenly. "Here we are."

Headmistress Wake's eyes drifted away from the invisible fence that no one else could see, scanning the large crowd behind it. Almost everyone had arrived—or at least it seemed that way, because I couldn't see any more streaks of shifters or vampires running through the woods. Nor could I hear the fluttering wings of fae overhead.

Headmistress Wake's gaze cut to me. "Are you ready,

Odette? Alex? Eva?" Although she did not say his name, she looked at Hunter too.

Simultaneously, we nodded, as the weight of what was about to happen crashed down around us.

Without another word, the headmistress turned her back to us, and pressed her hands forward. Blue magic, the same color that guarded the gate at the front of the school, poured from her, illuminating an invisible fence set a few feet back from the real, iron fence that we would have to scale in just moments.

The headmistress began muttering words, pausing for only a breath before issuing a spell.

"*Dominum princeps!*"

There was a *click* like a latch unlocking, a shimmering of the air. Then a gate glowing blue with magic swung toward us.

Headmistress Wake twisted to face the crowd behind her. "If you've never been here before, welcome to Spellcasters Spy Academy."

# CHAPTER THIRTY-NINE

Our army advanced through the thick, dark woods, until the leaders motioned for them to split. We'd divided into six large battalions, intent on attacking Spellcasters from all four tower entrances as well as the front and back doors. Diana was in charge of leading our team to the back left corner of the school—the staff wing—while the more seasoned spies, like Headmistress Wake and my parents, took the primary entrances alongside a large contingent of fae soldiers.

As the night was relatively young, the older spies assumed the demons would still be celebrating their demonic holiday in one of the larger gathering halls, which were more accessible through the primary doors. Our parents had chosen their attack points in an effort to protect us, but I wished that they hadn't.

The thought was nice, but I wasn't getting out of battle tonight without facing Ishtar. Trying to protect me wasn't really doing me any favors. It was just drawing out the inevitable.

"How many people mastered the druid spells?" I asked Hunter, who had been in charge of teaching them to as many people as he could in Faerie, then later at Nightdwellers, and for a few minutes in Wandstown.

He shook his head. "Maybe three dozen? All generally older witches."

Alex swore under his breath.

"Guys, just because a spell is more potent doesn't mean it's the be-all and end-all," Eva reasoned correctly. "We still have *nex* for lesser demons, and *morsultimus* for greater and royal demons."

Her voice trailed off; she knew the last spell was the most difficult of all.

"And we have us, too," I said, feeling the need for positivity.

"Shhh!" Diana shushed us and pressed her finger to her lips. "We're almost there."

I would take her word for it. Spellcasters was eerily dark, and the wilds of Maine were thick as molasses, making it difficult to see.

We'd gone a dozen more yards when Diana twisted back around to check that we were still following close behind. I watched as her blue eyes tried to count and then stopped, probably realizing it was pointless. We'd divided up, but the groups were still large as there were only so many entry points into the academy. And unlike our usual missions, in which staying together was paramount, we all knew that once we were inside, it would be a free-for-all.

And as long as I stayed with my best friends and Diana, I was fine with that.

"We should've formed even smaller groups," Diana muttered, twisting to catch my eyes before she let out a yelp and tripped over something. She fell to the ground, her hands catching her just before she face-planted.

I scurried forward to help her up, and caught sight of the thing she'd fallen over.

No, not a thing—*a person*. Registering the blood, my gaze shot up. I focused on the face and bile climbed up my throat. Trying to be strong, I swallowed, forcing it back down as I yanked Diana to her feet.

People gathered around, all staring in horror at the body laying sprawled out before us. Even Diana, usually stoic, trembled with emotion. The corpse's torso was split open from neck to navel, innards spilling out. The vision would've been disgusting and horrific enough, but to make it worse, I recognized the girl.

"Jasmine," my voice wobbled. "No!"

A hand clamped down on my shoulder. "Were you close to her?" Sana's voice was calming, trying to bring me back down from what could easily turn into a total meltdown.

I shook my head. "No. Not really. But she was in my year."

Jasmine Sahni had been among the many students who had disliked me for the majority of last year. But near the end of term, before I'd traveled back in time, she'd apologized. I wondered if she was dead because she stood up for us.

*Hopefully, she had just tried to escape.*

I couldn't bear the idea that someone had died to stand up for me.

"I'm sorry." Ayla came up along my other side. "But be prepared. We will see more death tonight."

My throat closed up, but I nodded as stoically as possible. Of course we would see death. I'd known that. I just hadn't expected the first body to be someone I knew. Or that it would happen out here, in the peaceful woods.

*The demons left her out here on purpose.*

The thought struck me cruelly, but I knew deep in my soul I was right.

We pulled ourselves together and continued to trudge toward the academy. Soon enough, I realized that finding Jasmine's body was just the beginning of what would turn out to be a horror-filled walk in the woods. The closer we got to the academy, the more corpses littered the forest. Each one seemed relatively fresh, as if put there just for us. They were from every class, and the demons didn't seem to discriminate by any measure I could determine. They hated all Spellcasters students.

By the time a few flickering lights from inside the school came into view, we could no longer walk without checking the ground every few feet so we didn't step on a corpse.

When we reached the stone walls of the academy, Diana pulled back a curtain of lush ivy to expose the door.

"Here we are," she announced, her tone tight with rage that I understood all too well.

I was shaking, ready to murder the first demon I came across.

She spoke a few words, which I barely heard through the blood pounding in my ears, and a hidden door swung open.

She twisted to face the rest of us, her expression grave. "This part of Spellcasters is where the professors live. My mother and father lived—*live* here too." She looked uncomfortable at her slip, the assumption that they didn't live there any longer, that her father might not be among the living at *all*.

I prayed that assumption was wrong.

"That being said, it's the nicer part of the academy. This might be where the royals have claimed their rooms . . . it's where I would live, if I were them."

Diana's eyes blazed. I could tell she was imagining one of the royals in her family home.

"The staircase will lead you to various levels of staff. At the bottom are the housekeepers and kitchen workers. The farther up you go, the more senior the professors."

She swallowed heavily. "My family suite is at the top. If anyone wants to go up there and check it out, I'd appreciate it."

"I will!" a fae called out near the back. "I'm not aether-blessed, but I am a good soldier."

My throat closed up. If he wasn't an aether-blessed fae,

he would have no way at all to fight off the royals if they were lounging in the headmistress' suite.

"I'll go with him," Flynn volunteered. "I'm aether-blessed."

Sam raised her hand too, clearly not wanting to part with the white-haired elf who she'd taken a shine to. I was relieved by her offer. Flynn had insisted that he join the battle, and Alex had cleared his injuries, but I still wasn't so sure he should be here.

"Thank you," Diana said and then turned to face the door.

We filed inside, where people began to split into groups. Some immediately marched up the stairs to check out the upper levels.

Once everyone was inside, Diana shut the door and spoke the password again. The door disappeared before my eyes.

"Well, that's handy." Hunter shook his head as a look of amusement flashed across his handsome face.

"All the employees know about it," Diana assured him. "Spellcasters has never been breached like this, but failsafe entrances and exits were created when they first converted the building into an academy. You know, in case of emergencies. Although we never imagined an attack would come from our own government, or that they'd be working with the devils."

"Who could?" Eva asked seriously.

"We should get going," Alex prompted.

He took the lead, and I fell into step beside him. Diana,

Eva, and Hunter were right behind us, their steps light. We had done this many times before.

*Too many times. It's like we're seasoned professionals, not students.*

I banished the thought from my mind. It really didn't matter what we were. Culling-year. Grind-year. Crucible-year. Witches with no affiliation to Spellcasters whatsoever. Tonight, we would throw everything we had into defeating the demons of Hell.

I would do *anything* to see them cast out.

A lump rose in my throat, and emotion clouded my thoughts so thickly that I missed the ball of fire shot at me.

Hunter deflected it with a beam of magic, and we all twisted to find a tall, thin cambion, a human-demon hybrid, standing in the middle of the corridor. The tapestry next to him moved, hinting he'd been hiding behind it.

"About time you showed up," the cambion growled as he pulled a blade from a scabbard he wore on his hip, and slit his own throat.

# CHAPTER FORTY

*I* gasped as the demon fell to the floor. His blood dripped on the stone tiles, staining the ground red.

And sounding the alarm.

"Move!" Hunter yelled.

"Damn blood!" Eva yelled as we sprinted down the corridor, trying to place ourselves in a better position to fight, should more demons stray in our path. "Why is it always blood? They're obsessed! Demons! Ghosts!"

"And vampires!" Francis flashed a bright, fangy smile as he and Simone sprinted around the corner to run next to me. "For a witch with such a strong scent, you're difficult to find in this school. Is there a scent-cloaking spell in Spellcasters or something?"

"Why are you here?" I asked, blinking. They were supposed to be with their headmaster and the shifters.

"I need to be with you—" Francis trailed off, eyebrows

knitting together as he worked through a thought. "I think that's why we met. You don't live as long as I have without realizing that fate is real. I believe that I'm meant to help you specifically. And I'm not the only one who feels that way." He gestured behind him.

I shot a glance back just in time to see an attacking demon fling itself out of a room, straight into Dasha's wolfish jaws. The massive alpha tore the creature in half, and loosed a howl that made my skin crawl.

"But your teams!"

Francis shook his head. Annoyingly, he wasn't breathing hard at all, unlike me. "Headmaster Ezra agreed that we should find you. As did Alpha Conon."

"But Headmistress Wake—!"

"As much as I respect your headmistress—" Francis paused to swipe at a door that was opening as we passed, slamming it shut and forcing whoever had been trying to come out, back inside. "I also respect her wishes for each side of the academy to be covered in our attack plan, but I *don't* answer to her."

"Like I said before, witch, I owe you a life debt." Simone scanned the hall before us as we ran at breakneck speed. "And I plan on honoring it."

"Fine." My emotions rolled through me, a mix of exasperation and swelling gratitude that I couldn't express because we were running so fast. What could I say anyway? The vamps and shifters were loyal to me. Although I worried for their teams, I had to admit, that felt good.

I inhaled sharply as we intersected another hallway, and

Alex shot off the *nex* incantation at a gray, wrinkled wraith lying in wait.

"Watch our backs," I told the vamps. "*All* our backs. Shifters' too."

Francis rolled his eyes, clearly not as concerned about the shifters as he was about me. "Obviously. Now let me guess, you're trying to find their supposed celebration. Well, let me tell you, I don't think—"

A door that I recognized as belonging to the Demonology classroom burst open in front of us, and thirty demons streamed into the hall.

"Spread out!" I yelled. "Hold them back!"

There wasn't anyone behind us, but I wanted the demons to *think* we had backup.

The witches and vampires took the front. At our backs, the four white wolves growled, ready to rip open the throats of demons.

An ifrit moved first, turning incorporeal and zinging towards us in a blaze of fire and spark. I threw up a web of black magic, trapping it. I was about to issue the killing curse when Hunter swung his arm out to stop me, and leapt forward, his totem extended.

"*Relligio!*"

The spell hit the lesser demon, and the ifrit screamed as its body was ripped from my web of magic, and soared toward Hunter's blade. Once the demon hit the metal, it disappeared.

I gaped as Hunter's blade began to glow red-hot. Only the hilt seemed unaffected.

There was no time to ask how the hell he'd known to do that, because the rest of the demons, mostly wraiths and shapeshifting fenrirs, charged.

"Let's get ready to *rumble!*" Francis struck a pose like he was about to face off in the ring, before crouching and leaping phenomenally high and landing on top of a snarling fenrir demon.

The vampire sank his fangs into skin, and the beast screamed, twisting and turning. Francis hung on like he was a rodeo cowboy.

I was about to shoot off an incantation to help the vamp when a ball of fire from another demon came flying at me.

*Oh hells no.*

I leapt out of the way and began firing off demon-killing curses at any devil unlucky enough to be in my sight. My friends did the same and we hit our marks more often than not, eliminating the opposition quickly. There were only two left when the wolves, probably attracted to the blood, pushed past the witch line and began tearing the stragglers limb from limb.

"Nice work, team," I said as the last demon fell to the ground. "Anyone injured?"

Heath's fur had briefly caught fire, but it was extinguished, so we continued running down the hallways.

It was clear to everyone that either there had never been a demon ceremony, or our arrival had broken it up. Still, I couldn't help but think the royals might be waiting for us in one of the academy's larger, grander rooms. They were theatrical like that.

My heart was pounding and my legs burning when we arrived in the entryway. I skidded to a stop and gasped at the state of the room.

The beautiful stained glass windows that portrayed the elements had been smashed to pieces. Flecks of green, blue, red, and orange were scattered on the ground. Next to the glittering glass, pools of blood dotted the floor.

"Who do you think that's from?" Eva asked, her eyes locked on one of the many pools.

"We thought you would never ask," a snide voice came from above, and we whirled around to see that demons lined the double staircases and the three levels leading to smaller classrooms and dormitory towers.

The demons gazed down upon us, eyes blazing, and in the middle of them all was Xaphan. The prince of darkness' black wings were spread as wide as his glittering, hateful smile.

My hands balled up as he pinned his eyes on me.

"Good to see you again, Dane."

"Yes, so, so, *so* good!" a feminine voice added. My attention snapped right, and my eyes widened.

The Furies were present too. They were just as I'd seen them before, as beautiful as they were horrible. Their long, blonde tresses fell in perfect curls, and their ruby red lips curled up seductively.

"I can't say it's good to see you," I retorted.

The demons around the royals growled.

I inched closer to Eva as Xaphan lifted his arms for the crowd to quiet.

"Do you remember that I once offered you the chance to side with us?" he asked casually.

When I didn't answer, he continued. "It was foolish to deny me, even if you were able to evade us longer than I would've expected."

Although we were more than likely screwed, a sense of satisfaction that the prince of darkness hadn't known who we were or been able to locate us throughout the centuries filled me.

"So I ask again." His eyes shifted slightly, to Eva. "Both of you."

"No!" one of the Furies screamed. "No more chances! We kill them all, except the girl!"

My eyes cut to Eva. *The girl? Which one?*

Did they mean me? Or had they decided that my friend would be more valuable? And if so, for what?

It struck me they hadn't mentioned Alex at all. Had he been right when he suggested that they no longer needed him? Had using his blood to open the Hellgate in London been all that they needed? Was his purpose in this fulfilled as far as they were concerned?

"Yes! Yes! Dead! We want them all dead!" another of the Furies yelled out, and began dancing around as if she were slightly mad.

The other demons, a mishmash of races, roared, and my group scooted closer together.

"Deady! Dead! Dead!" Another Fury began clapping her hands and shimmying her hips.

All the while, the prince of darkness' eyes narrowed and

began to glow a deeper red. His stance stiffened in annoyance.

"Get ready," Hunter said, his eyes latched onto the prince.

"It's not for you to decide," Xaphan whipped around and screamed at the Furies, clearly at the end of his rope.

With his back turned, we attacked as one. Black magic streamed from me and Eva. Spells flew from the other witch's hands. The vampires leapt upon opposing staircases and began snapping necks. The wolves positioned themselves in front of us, our protectors, shields of muscle and might that the demons would have to get through to get to us.

"*Itoarazicus!*" I screamed, and my black magic hurtled toward Xaphan, hitting him square in the back.

The prince of darkness twisted and pulled his arm back, ready to retaliate. But when he released, nothing flew from his palm.

No fire. No magic. *Nothing.*

I lowered my palms and smiled. Victory soared through me, so vibrant and hot that it made my skin tingle. "You should really sort your shit out in private." Snapping my fingers a bloom of fuchsia magic flooded around my friends to get their attention. "Xaphan is fair game, guys."

Alex acted first. "*Morsultimus,*" he muttered, and before the prince of darkness could move again, the killing spell slammed into his chest.

All around, demons froze. The Furies released simultaneous, deafening howls. But my team only watched, and waited. My heart began to thump harder and blood buzzed through me, seemingly electrified with joy.

The death of a royal demon was unlike anything I'd ever seen. Xaphan's black, glistening skin dissolved, and flames ignited as if he was made of them. When the fire burned out, only ash remained, fluttering to the ground.

And then, more cries flew to the heavens, and twenty demons disintegrated into nothing.

# CHAPTER FORTY-ONE

"I can't believe that worked!" Alex exclaimed as we sprinted toward the door of Spellcasters, away from the demons we'd just pissed off.

We flung the massive doors open, and fresh, clear air, so unlike the demon-stench I'd acclimatized to, filled my nose.

And then I gasped.

It wasn't a full-out war outside, but there were dozens of groups fighting on the Spellcasters front lawn, their figures illuminated by the light of the moon reflecting off the lake. Some with glowing red eyes were recognizably demon, while others, like the two massive trolls who were trying to pound an aether-wielding fae into the ground, were their allies.

As I watched the troll's fist nearly pummel the fae. I wished they were closer and that I could help, but it was better to remain incognito while I could. My range wasn't that far, anyhow.

I even thought I saw a few shifters—felines of some type—prowling around Merlin Amphitheater. A shudder dashed down my spine as memories of the Colosseum came rushing back.

"Odie! Come on!" Eva grasped my wrist and pulled, informing me that I'd actually stopped dead in my tracks on the threshold between the school and the outdoors.

I surged and joined my friends.

"Let's go for the Furies next," Hunter said, his tone determined. "I don't know if we have to kill all of them, or just one. They're a triple goddess, so who knows if they can survive alone or not?"

I was about to reply that any of the royals would do, when a sharp, stinging pain cut across my arm.

"Crap!" I glanced down. My arm had been sliced open by some type of blade.

Blood welled up and poured down my bicep onto the ground. I glanced around, but only saw friends in my immediate vicinity. Twisting my neck slightly, I noticed that a few demons were dive-bombing from the dormitory tower windows.

*Perhaps the attack came from there?*

But still, what the heck? If someone was trying to attack me, why not be serious about it? Why not just end me, instead of giving me an annoying flesh wound and disappearing like a coward?

A dangerous shriek, identifiable as belonging to one of the Furies, hit my ear, erasing my questions.

As one, everyone in my group glanced over their shoulders. The demons were just now exiting Spellcasters.

Well, *exiting* would be too mundane of a term. Breaking down the doors and stampeding toward us with fire blazing in their wake was more like it.

However, they weren't unopposed. To my great relief, I saw Francis and Simone, still alive and in the midst of the demon mob, snapping necks as they ran.

It seemed that although the demons were powerful and could use vampire-killing fire, the vampires had a knack for outmaneuvering them. Thank the universe.

"I love those goddamn vampires," I whispered.

"Let's help them out," Eva said. "We're in the open, away from other fights. Here is as good a spot to mow them down as anywhere. We don't want them to go after anyone else." She gestured to the smaller groups of warriors.

I couldn't agree more.

Being inside the school was fine when we believed that breaking up a celebration was the key to our success. But it had obviously been a ruse, and then finding ourselves in the entryway, poised below the demons, in a position of danger, had been less than ideal.

Now we were on even ground, albeit still vastly outnumbered.

At least, so far, no one had broken away from their own fight to attack us on other sides. Perhaps we'd get lucky, and land a fatal spell on one of the Furies. That might help hundreds of fighters on our side.

We began shooting off spells. The wolves, who had been shielding us, rushed forward and took care of a few demons, mostly wraiths and fenrirs, who had muscled their way to the forefront. They sank their jaws into the demons, ripping open their flesh and spilling blood across their own snow white fur. Once the wolves left the creatures on the ground, one of the witches would finish them off with a spell—just in case.

The Furies flitted among the opposing press of darkness, clearly trying to stay out of the witches' line of fire. I suspected that, for the first time in their millennia-long lives, they feared death.

I had just downed another demon, leaving the force that followed us outside greatly reduced, when a familiar voice sounded behind us. I darted a glance behind me, and saw Headmistress Wake emerging from the woods.

A giant, orc-like demon chased her, too slow to keep up, but determined enough to keep chugging along. A girl with moon-white hair down to her navel was at the head-mistress' side, shooting flames and gusts of wind from from her hands—a fae, then.

The headmistress was running backward, her hands extended and shooting beams of blue magic at the giant demon. Her magic hit the beast, and he fell with a defeated whine. The white-blonde girl sent a blaze of fire at the crea-ture, and though it twitched a few times, I knew it wouldn't be long before it burned to death.

Internally, I cheered. The headmistress was in the same squad as my parents, and she was kicking major ass.

Twisting back around, I joined my friends, shooting off two more killing curses at one of the Furies, who managed to wriggle her hourglass frame away from both.

*Damn her,* I thought as the Princess of Hell flitted further away, out of my range of fire.

A monstrous bellow rang through the night, yanking my attention away from the frustrating Fury. I cast about wildly, and my heart leapt when my gaze landed on the creature that the sound had to have originated from.

One of the trolls was on the ground, kicking and screaming as fae soldiers attacked. At their sides were Professor Tittelbaum, Professor De Spina, and Ms. Seeley. All three looked haggard—far too thin and in rags—but they were fighting. Their presence gave me hope that somewhere, other professors, and perhaps students, were battling too.

Unfurling my dark magic, I bid it to go after my enemies, and took the time to really study the area around us. But when my gaze landed on Headmistress Wake again, I stopped.

Mom and Dad still weren't fighting with her, or even out of the woods. *No one* else had emerged from the woods, save the headmistress and the girl with white hair.

My heart began to thunder like a racehorse speeding down the track, and I knew, I just *knew*—something had happened in the woods.

My parents were still in there.

I chanced a glance back to the army my best friends and I were fighting. With every second, fewer opponents remained. I didn't want to leave my friends, but the pull to find my family was strong, and intensifying by the second. I had to listen to my intuition; I trusted that my group would be able to overcome.

"I have to go!"

Without providing an explanation, I broke away. My friends' cries sounded after me, but I didn't turn around, and soon enough, they were lost in the melee.

They'd be fine, they could easily take on what was left, and then move on to assist others. But I had a terrible feeling that Mom and Dad needed *my* help.

"Miss Dane!" Headmistress Wake called out as I ran up to her and began firing black magic from my hands at the glowing eyes within the woods.

"Where are my parents?" I shouted.

The girl with white-blonde hair twisted to look at me. Her eyes widened. She was younger than I'd thought, and from our world, judging by her tight, black leggings and modern top. "Are you Lauren's daughter?"

I nodded, and turned my attention back to Headmistress Wake, who looked supremely uncomfortable with my question. My eyes shot to the woods, and I caught dozens of pairs of eyes gleaming back at me. The pit in my gut deepened into a bottomless hole.

*Oh no. No, no, no . . .*

"Are they," I gulped, "in the woods?"

"I'm afraid so, Miss Dane. My squad got split up. Alice and I are the only ones who made it out of the forest. We—"

I broke into a sprint toward the tree line, right for the demons who seemed to be hiding within its darkness.

"Miss Dane! Stop this second!"

I didn't turn around, and when a spray of blue magic hurtled past me, to stop me no doubt, I began zig-zagging.

I was about halfway to the forest, blasting my power with every step, and mowing down demons  as I went, when the girl, Alice, sprinted up next to me.

"I was with them for a while. I can help you find them." She hurled a ball of fire at a wraith who dared to step out of the cover of the trees.

"No thanks," I said, not wanting to be responsible for anyone's death. Least of all, some girl who couldn't be older than seventeen.

"I'm fae, I can fly you above all this. I undid the clasps around my wings earlier, when I was fighting, but the fabric is restricting them." Alice twisted ever so slightly. "Rip open the back of my shirt."

My eyes widened. "Serious?"

I glanced at the demons in front of us. We'd be upon them in seconds. Behind me, I could still hear Headmistress Wake yelling my name. My friends' voices had joined in.

"Do it!" Alice yelled as she thrust her hands out, and a powerful gale of wind surged from her.

I blinked.

Damn. She was strong. Clearly not aether-blessed, else

she'd be using it, but still, strong. And seeing as I was about to run into a line of dozens of demons, I needed her help.

I unleashed my black magic, and bid it to rip the back of her shirt. It did just as I said, and the moment her gold-veined wings were free, the girl leapt into the air, swung back behind me, and grabbed me under my armpits.

We were airborne a second later, and I gasped.

I was so wrong about being up against 'dozens' of demons. Behind the front line, the forest was filled with *hundreds* of glowing eyes.

*My friends . . .*

I twisted to look back. Had I just made a huge mistake?

"Don't do that," Alice grunted. "My wings are bound most of the time, so, while I *can* fly, I'm not great at it. Don't squirm and make it harder."

"Why are you helping me?"

She glanced down, and I noticed just how blue her eyes were. They were practically teal and glowing —mesmerizing.

"When I met my squad, my boss, an asshole of a vampire, said something shitty. But your mom overheard and was kind to me." Her eyes blazed at the memory.

"You're trying to save your parents. I don't have mine anymore, and my job leaves me with a lot to make up for. If I can help you find your family and save them, that'll make a dent."

"A dent in what?"

"I just need to make reparations—big ones. Plus, once I

get out of my contract, I sure as shit don't want demons running the world."

*Her job? Contract? She's so young, too young to be a spy. She—*

My train of thought derailed, and my eyes widened as we soared above a clearing, and I found my parents.

Right next to Ishtar.

# CHAPTER FORTY-TWO

"There!" I pointed down at the small clearing, where the queen of darkness, wearing a long, glittering, black gown, was sitting on a stump like it was her throne, and looking like she was waiting for someone to show up.

Judging by the fact that she had a ring of fire around my parents, who, at that particular moment, she seemed to be mocking, that someone could only be one person.

"She's waiting for me."

"Obviously," Alice muttered. "Do you see all those Shadows, though?" She pointed at a ring of fae on the edge of the clearing. Dark Court Shadows that I hadn't noticed before. I'd been too focused on Ishtar. "Are you sure you want to go down there? I'm the first to admit that I'm a badass, but we're pretty outnumbered."

"*I'm* going down there. Not *you*," I shot back.

"Says who? You're not my boss."

Universe help me. I needed to take a different tack with this girl.

"Clearly. What I meant was, I need you to go back to the school grounds. I left my friends, and they'll want to know what's happening. Particularly the black-haired guy with glasses, and the redhead girl." My voice cracked at the thought of my love and my best friend. "They have . . . specific powers. Magic that can help us win."

"You want me to guide them here?"

"No!"

My stomach twisted. Oh my god, what was I thinking? That was the last thing I wanted. I couldn't bear to see Ishtar hurt them.

"Tell them to go after Lucifer and . . . *the item*," I said in an inspired lie. "They'll know what it is."

The girl studied me, her bright blue eyes narrowed skeptically.

"Please," I begged. "It's very important that you help them find what we need. Make sure they're safe."

*And don't bring them here.*

If I was going to die, which suddenly seemed like the only possible scenario, I didn't want my friends to die too. I wanted them to kill the other royals and live.

I'd do my best with Ishtar, even if I had to go down with her.

"Fine," Alice said. "But I'm not dropping you off right in front of her. You can sneak up on her and snipe a couple of those Shadows on the way in."

"Er, cool." I shook my head at the girl's use of 'snipe'. She was something else.

Alice landed twenty yards into the brush and released me. I dusted myself off, noting that the forest smelled more earthy here. My senses were heightened, prepared for battle.

"Are you sure you don't want help? I'm great with a dagger." As if to prove it, Alice pulled a blade out of its sheath, tossed it in the air, and caught it behind her back. "Not too bad at magic, either."

"No," I said, but her little performance had given me an idea.

I handed over the demon dagger that I hadn't even touched during the fight. Black magic was just more effective.

"Take this as thanks. It will kill any sort of demon."

Alice looked over the blade. "It's been in Faerie. I can sense the fae on it."

I furrowed my brows. "Are you aether-blessed?"

If she was, I didn't know why she hadn't been using aether magic the whole time.

She shook her head, and then, to my utter astonishment, twisted and hurled the hell blade into the woods.

Someone moaned, and I peered around her to see a daeva who had been sneaking up on us fall, its noxious gas cloud still streaming from its lips, but dissipating as it died.

I exhaled. That demon could have given me away before I was ready.

"You weren't joking about being good with a blade."

"Nope," she said, walking over lightly and pulling the blade from the daeva's sickly gray skin. "And you weren't joking about it being deadly. Thanks for the piece, I'll put it to good use."

With that, she expanded her gold-veined wings, and lifted into the air. "Good luck. I'll relay the message to your friends."

The next moment, she was off, leaving me alone in the woods.

My stomach began to churn. *What the hell am I doing here?*

I'd *always* worked with my friends. Everything we'd accomplished had been as a team. And now, I was approaching Ishtar alone? Why?

*You're not really alone,* Tabitha reminded me. *And I can tell you exactly why. You love your friends. Just like you love your parents. You've always taken great risks for those you love. I may not have liked you in life, but even I could tell that. And now, being in your head, I know it for sure.*

I bit my lip, knowing she was right.

And now that I was here, nothing would change my mind about moving forward.

I sighed. "Guard my mind, okay? I need to be clear-headed when I fight her. All I need is one good shot, and who knows how many demons will die with her death."

*That's what I'm here for,* Tabitha said. It sounded like she wanted to say more. Probably to tell me that I was being an idiot and to turn around and gather reinforcements. But no matter what she wanted to say, Tabitha held her tongue.

I started walking toward the clearing, slowly, so as not to alert any of the Shadows. When I finally glimpsed a Dark Court fae soldier scouting the area, I unleashed a little demon magic.

It slithered through the underbrush, silent until the moment that it struck.

The fae, who hadn't even seen it coming, fell.

"You're mastering the darkness better than I imagined," Ishtar's voice boomed through the trees.

She was so loud, it was as if she was right next to me. And while I should have been much more scared, her words made me bristle.

"Come, Odette, face me. My soldiers will let you pass."
*So much for being stealthy.*

I drew in a huge breath and walked forward, stepping over the fae I'd just killed. Though he'd been dead only seconds, he stank like rot and blood. Bile rose in my throat.

There were more Shadows surrounding Ishtar, but none so much as twitched a muscle as I approached. I watched them carefully as I entered the clearing and stood before her.

The Queen of Hell.

"Honey!"

"Pea!"

My parents' cries cut through me like a knife.

I turned to see their eyes, large and wet, their hands wringing. Surprisingly, they didn't seem injured. My eyes locked with Dad's. There was no fury in them over being captured, like I would expect, only worry for me. And strangely, neither of my parents were fighting back—which was not their style.

*She probably said she'd kill me on sight if they resisted—the monster.*

"Pea! Get out of here—"

"*Silence!*" Ishtar commanded, and as if she controlled their bodies, both my parents' mouths snapped shut.

"Don't hurt them!" I yelled, taking a step closer.

Ishtar chuckled. "Your line always was brave."

Her red eyes glowed brighter, and as she took a step forward, I noticed that there were two slits in her gown, all the way up to her hips.

"Never could I have guessed that you—a mere girl— would grow into bravery that surpassed your predecessors. Though perhaps I should have. All queens grow powerful, if tested thoroughly enough."

*Queen.*

She'd used that exact term to describe me before, though I didn't know why. Truly, at that moment, I didn't care. I only wanted my parents released.

"Your fight is with me," I said. "Let them go."

The queen laughed. "And what? You'll do as I say?" She shook her head, and tutted. "I know better than to believe that line. I've used it a *thousand* times, never once following through. And you—the woman who is embracing her darkness—would do the exact same."

"I'm not embracing it," I retorted. "You gave this to me. I didn't *want* it."

"You've used it. Sometimes you've even enjoyed it, haven't you?"

I wanted to reject that claim, but couldn't deny that joy had buzzed through me when my black magic had bound Xaphan so that Alex could make the kill shot.

"Only when it helped to kill the prince of darkness," I replied smugly.

A ripple of something . . . was it fear? . . . crossed her face, but the queen pulled it together quickly.

"Others believe it's the Furies who are vain and silly. They give off that *air*, always prancing about, seducing people." She rolled her eyes. "But then again, few know Xaphan. He's much more vain and absurd, but better at hiding it."

Ishtar snorted and began to pace around the clearing as if I was no threat to her.

Which, considering she had my parents in a literal ring of fire, I guess I wasn't. Who knew if my spell would hit her before she could kill them.

She had me right where she wanted me, and she knew it.

The Queen of Hell stopped pacing and shook her head. "He was always so showy. So *ostentatious*. How did he approach you? With spectacle, I'm sure."

An image of Xaphan and hundreds of demons looking down upon us like we were beasts to watch die in the Colosseum flitted through my mind. She was dead-on, but I would never admit it.

I didn't need to.

Ishtar's lips curled up knowingly. "Yes, of course he did." She threw her head back, and roared with laughter.

The hair on my arms lifted. She was having fun with me —making a damn game of terrifying me. Of threatening the lives of those I loved.

Unable to help it, I darted a glance to my parents. Their eyes were locked on me.

Dad mouthed, "Run!"

I couldn't. Just like I couldn't watch them stay trapped for a second longer.

Throwing caution to the wind, I shot off the binding spell Merlin had taught me.

The demon queen seemed to anticipate it, and leapt out of the way, pivoting smoothly to face me.

"Poor choice, Dane. Now you'll have to live with it." She ripped a blade from a sheath strapped to her thigh. "Or come to my court and fight for what you hold dear."

The blade in her hand glinted in the moonlight, stealing my breath. It was a dagger that I knew well, and seeing it covered in blood made my skin prickle.

My hand went to the injury on my arm. Whoever had made it had done so with the Realm Slicer.

*Those damn sneaks*, Tabitha growled inside my head.

The Queen of Hell grinned. "Thanks for the key home, girl."

With that, she flung the powerful blade into the dirt. When the ground beneath her cracked open, my heart stopped.

Walls of fire twenty feet high flew up between us. I leapt

backward, closer to the Shadows, who snarled. Instinctively, I twisted and hurled black magic at them. Dark tendrils wrapped around three necks, snuffing out their lives in a second.

When I turned back around, I was just in time to watch Ishtar descend into a pit of fire and darkness.

As she disappeared, the Realm Slicer glinted in one of her hands, and in the other, she held a tendril of dark magic, lassoing my parents together.

# CHAPTER FORTY-THREE

*M*y parents were gone. Dragged into the pits of Hell.

And as the Shadows from the Dark Court began creeping closer to me, sensing that their master wasn't coming back, and they could do with me what they would, I knew I had only one choice.

I jumped.

Heat blasted over my skin, and the stench of sulfur choked me. The finest downy hair on my face seared away as I fell. I'd made a terrible mistake.

I mean, *obviously*. Who in the world jumps into Hell willingly?

As I fell, the heat grew more intense, like the sun was feet away instead of hundreds of thousands of miles. The fabric of my clothes began to melt.

Panicking, I called black magic to swath me in cold. It

worked, and, while I was still falling, at least now I could concentrate.

Below me was illuminated, probably by the eternal flames that plagued the underworld. The floor, covered with jagged obsidian rocks, came at me faster and faster. If I hit those, I was a dead woman. A short ways away, maybe twenty feet to my left, I spotted a flat area and acted.

Calling a warphole to appear right under me, I fell into it. I was there for only a second before the warphole deposited me on the flat platform of black rock that I'd been picturing. I landed with an *oomph* on the rock.

"Ouch!" I moaned, and gently cradling the arm that I'd landed on. Slowly, I bent and straightened it to ensure it was still usable.

"Pea!"

My head snapped up at the sound of my parents' voices. I scanned the area, which resembled a dried-up lava flow rather than the inside of a building, despite there being a door. No one was present.

*She wouldn't fight you here*, Tabitha said in my head. *She's too full of herself. Look for grandeur and that's where Ishtar will be.*

For the first time, she sounded a little off—funny.

*You okay?*

*I think so, but that fall rocked me. I feel unsettled.*

I gulped, and my stomach tightened as understanding washed over me. *We've traveled through two realms since you've been in my head. The last ghost who was bound to me timewalked twice, and then traveled through one realm portal. Maybe our connection is fraying?*

Universe help me, I hoped not. Without Tabitha to protect me from possession, I didn't stand a chance against Ishtar.

Tabitha was quiet for a moment too long, so I prodded.

*Hey? Are you still there?*

*Yeah.* She coughed, clearly uncomfortable. *I guess I didn't think of Hell as a different realm, but you're right.*

I looked around at the strange surroundings. *Definitely a different realm.*

I jumped as a spray of acrid green smoke shot up from the ground a mere two feet from where I stood. I wrinkled my nose at the rotten scent that infiltrated my nostrils. Scraped my tongue with my teeth because a gross acid seemed to have coated it. Hell was disgusting.

*Do I need to do something to bind us more tightly? I really need you, Tabitha. If I'm going to get my parents out of here and kill Ishtar, you're the key.*

I didn't bother to think *I* would be leaving. Ishtar wanted me more than them. If I had to, I'd bargain myself. Then I'd fight her, and hopefully bring her down with me.

*I'm with you no matter what,* Tabitha replied. *I'll hang on. Let's find them.*

I crept forward, closer to the door, on alert for any movement that might come from within. Random sprays of green gas from  below made me jump, but no bodily adversaries appeared.

When I reached the door, I edged around and peeked

beyond the other side, my hands extended and ready to fight.

No one was there.

I exhaled and walked through the door to find myself in an opulent room with gothic undertones—possibly the palace. I thought back to the visual that our Demonology professor had shown us the year before. The thrones had been in the dead center of Hell. I'd taken that image literally when I'd landed in the throne room the first time, having had no reason to question it.

But what if the thrones actually just represented the palace? If so, why bring me here? Weren't there way more deadly sectors? Places where she could bury me headfirst in the sand and light my feet on fire, or where a vulture could constantly pick at my flesh? Unless Tabitha was right and this was all about putting on a show.

As if in response, a laugh rang through the empty, black-and-gold-drenched room.

My spine straightened and, forgetting all caution, I sprinted into the connecting hallway. Choosing a direction, I didn't stop running.

The laughter continued and grew louder, becoming more maniacal by the second. Strangely—or perhaps not, considering the army of demons in my world—I passed no demons as I ran.

The palace of Hell, for I was sure that was where I was now, was deserted. Save for me, my parents, and the queen of darkness.

My lungs began to burn from the patches of thick, black

smoke that I ran through as I followed the sound of Ishtar's cackle, growing ever louder. I was close, so close. And when a glimmer of bright red fire and gleaming gold metal came into sight up ahead, I sucked in a breath.

The air reeked of sulfur even more than before. I was nearly there.

The throne room.

It was like returning to a bad dream—or, more accurately, the day Alex had been kidnapped. When I'd allowed the Realm Slicer to be stolen by the Furies and, subsequently, the Hellgate to be ripped open.

I supposed that was why she came here. Because why *wouldn't* Ishtar want to battle me where I'd already been humiliated once? Before her throne of bones, so I knew exactly who I was dealing with.

As if I'd ever forget I was up against a fallen goddess—one of the most powerful magicals to have ever lived, gone bad.

*Sure. That could totally slip my mind.*

When I entered the throne room, I saw that I'd been onto something. Ishtar stood before her throne, but there were hundreds of other demons ringing the room, watching me with snarls on their lips.

I repressed a shudder, and pointedly ignored them, which wasn't as hard as it could have been, considering my parents were lying on the ground, just a few feet away.

Dissolving.

"Noooo!" I screamed and rushed forward, to Ishtar's great delight.

Her laughter rang through the cavernous room, echoing off the stone walls.

When I reached my parents, I dropped to my knees. "Whatever you're doing to them, stop it! Let them go!"

I went to grab Dad's shoulder, and my hand went through his flesh, like he wasn't even there. Like he wasn't real.

"What the—"

Cold dread gripped me.

*Oh shit, girl,* Tabitha said. *They were just an illusion. That bitch tricked you.*

The dread intensified, rushing through me like a wave. Tabitha was right. Ishtar had tricked me. I'd leapt willingly into Hell for *nothing*.

"Honestly, I thought it wouldn't work on you," Ishtar's voice was sultry, like velvet—so unlike I'd ever heard it when she'd been attacking me. If she used that tone on others, it didn't surprise me in the slightest that people followed her.

"I thought you'd realize that your parents were smarter than that." She arched an eyebrow. "They'd never take on me and so many dark fae alone. The Danes I've heard so much about were *excellent* spies, but never too prideful to ask for help. It's part of the reason they got so far—at least, until they left the spy community."

She tilted her head and studied me for a few moments. "Before tonight, I would have said that you understood the value of teamwork too, but apparently not."

She gestured at me. "Where are your friends? As you

can see, I've brought mine." Her slender-fingered hand made a slow circle, encompassing the room and the other demons.

I had no words. She was right. I'd faced her before, but never alone—not truly. My friends had always been there to back me up, or Morgan had, via my totem.

Now I had no one. Nothing.

My stomach clenched. *Universe help me. Why am I such an idiot?*

Ishtar was studying me, waiting for my answer, but I didn't plan on giving her one. There was no way I would admit just how alone I was.

Slowly, she took a seat in one of the larger, middle thrones, and crossed her legs, exposing a mile of bare blue skin, punctuated only by dagger sheaths. All the while, she never took her eyes off of me.

*Tabitha? Can you hear what she's thinking?*

*Ugh, no. I've been trying. I don't know how Efraim did that!*

Subconsciously, I nodded.

Ishtar caught the motion, and her brow quirked. "You know, the ghost bit is really quite clever. Few black witches know the trick—and none that I'm aware of today."

My lips pressed together.

The Queen of Hell chuckled. "It appears I will be doing all the talking today." She leaned back in the throne, as if she were just fine getting comfortable. "I only brought up the ghost because that's what gave me the idea for the illusion." Her eyes darted to the spot on the ground where I'd started to mourn my parents' bodies.

"That and, while it's clever, to use a departed witch's skills is unnecessary for the likes of you. The blood of a fellow queen."

Goddamn this devil, she knew just what to say to get me to break down.

"Why do you keep calling me that? I'm a lot of things, but I'm no queen."

"But of course you are. Why else do you think I've sought you for so long?"

"Because my ancestor sealed the Hellgate, and you needed my blood, and Alex's, to open it. Since that's long passed, now you just need us out of the way. And you probably want revenge, since I've made you look stupid once or twice."

Annoyance flashed across her features. "While all that's true, my motives have shifted. I do not need you now because *Morgan* is your ancestor—but because someone *far* more powerful is."

Far more powerful than Morgan Le Fay? Besides Merlin, I couldn't think of a single witch in history, and they were basically equals who excelled at different things. And there was only one other strong witch throughout history in my family bloodline.

"If you're talking Deliverance Dane, I hardly think she's more powerful than—"

"Not the Salem witch!" Ishtar spat. "That side of your lineage is *nothing* to the other branch. Don't you remember what I told you so long ago? How the world has always judged women more harshly? Even now, you default to your father's line, when your mother's blood is that of royalty. The blood that carries that of Isis herself."

"Isis?"

"Isis! Hekate! Freya! Many more goddesses, all the same, all the progenitor of magic."

I froze. What Ishtar said was so similar to what Merlin had preached back in his English cottage. And while I might not have known who Isis was off the top of my head, Hekate was a name I could not mistake.

"The . . . goddess of magic? You're saying I'm her descendant?"

Ishtar nodded. "In blood, as well as magic, which few witches can claim. It took me a while to understand, but now that I've seen it, I would recognize her power within you anywhere. It, just as much as the ghost in your head, is keeping me from entering—from possessing you. You don't need the mind witch, just like you never truly needed the little trinket you wore for protection."

"But you almost possessed me before," I argued.

"Almost. With anyone else, it would have been instantaneous, but something in you always stopped me. It's why you've been able to evade me more than any other, though your skills were *lacking*."

My lips pursed. She wasn't making any sense.

"But Morgan—"

"She didn't know. Her birth was already shrouded in so much mystery. Was she the daughter of a fae king as they said? Or perhaps just the offspring of a common witch? No, your ancestor never delved into her past as she should have. Perhaps she was too preoccupied with others' pasts and lives. It was one of her few mistakes."

"But . . . I . . ." I fell silent, unsure what that meant for me. "Does that mean I'm a godling? If so, how come I'm not more powerful?"

The demon queen smirked. "Technically, yes, you are a godling. As for your abilities, you *could* be more powerful if you learned the ways of the old gods. Ways that I know."

She patted the throne of bones next to her. The one I suspected had been Xaphan's seat of power. "We've had an opening in the underworld. Join us, and I'll show you the way to unlock all the power within you. I'll show you how truly great you could become."

My lips trembled. No way did I want to join her, but I did want to know. Dammit, I wanted to know *so bad*.

"I can't. I—"

A roar flew from the demon soldiers around us who had been standing by quietly, and suddenly, half of them fell to the ground and dissolved into nothing.

My breath hitched, realizing that could only mean one thing.

Another royal had fallen.

# CHAPTER FORTY-FOUR

he Queen of Hell's intense crimson gaze scanned the room, her blue lips parting slightly as she took in the fallen all around us.

*If I move now, I can strike while she's unprepared. This will be the easiest shot I'll get.*

I leaned forward just enough that my heel separated from the ground, and Ishtar's eyes snapped back to me.

My moment of easy victory vanished.

"What did you do?" Her sultry, velvet tone was harder, like gravel rubbed into a wound. "Who did you kill?"

I gulped.

Was it Lucifer? Was it one Fury, or all three at once? Would it matter to her?

"Was it the king?" she pressed.

There was my answer. She might respect the Furies more than she did Xaphan, but Lucifer, her partner in ruling the underworld, was the one she cared about.

"Yes." I pretended it was a fact. "They targeted him, and now he's gone." I gestured to the fallen demons, now just bits of ash spread on the glittering black ground. "I bet there are many more like this in our world. *Dead.*"

"How dare you strike down the king!"

Ishtar shot out of her throne. From her hands, fire blazed like lava spewing out of a volcano, flying high and licking the edges of the black ceiling. The temperature climbed, and sweat beaded my skin.

"How dare you think you can strike *any* of us down?" she stormed. "Mere mortals dictating the lives of gods."

"Fallen gods," I declared, not sure where I was getting the strength from when I should be running from her rage. "You're *fallen* gods. And you said yourself that I'm a godling. Why would you find it so impossible that we can beat you? I must have *some* ability like yours. Others might too."

The queen's chest heaved up and down as her jaw clenched, and the fire in her hands died. "Most likely, yes. Too bad you, at least, won't live to find out."

Black snakes, a dozen of them, each ten feet long, burst out of her hands. "But I'll show you what *I* can do. The ability you will never have."

The snakes slithered toward me, urged on by their master's laughter and the cheering and jeering of the surviving demons around us.

I darted backward, away from the creatures, my throat tight.

They didn't look like any snake I'd ever seen. They were too long, too glittering, too focused on *me*.

Well over one hundred demons, too many snakes for comfort, and the Queen of Hell versus me. Things weren't looking good.

*But you only need one good shot,* Tabitha reminded me. *Don't falter now. Everyone is counting on you.*

The tears that had been pricking my eyes trailed down my cheeks. She was right. Succumbing to my terror was unacceptable.

I thrust my hands out, and black tendrils of magic flew toward the snakes. My power looked so similar to the creatures slithering across the floor—almost as if they were the same thing.

But when my magic met the snakes and tried to wrap around them, to strangle the life from their streamline bodies, the creatures hissed and gulped down the blackness. To them, my demon magic was nothing more than a harmless mouse. A snack.

Ishtar laughed.

*Oh shit.* My hands trembled. *What now?*

Tabitha moved inside my head. I sensed her insecurity, reflecting my own thoughts.

What was I supposed to do? What did I have that Ishtar didn't?

*That's it!* Tabitha said. *Do what you do best. Make them disappear.*

*What? I—*

*The warphole, idiot!* the ghost snapped, reminding me of the flesh-and-bone Tabitha.

I blinked, understanding immediately, and followed through.

I conjured a warphole and directed it over the band of snakes. They disappeared as suddenly as they had arrived, banished to the room that I'd landed in.

Ishtar's insane laughter ceased the moment her snakes vanished. She placed a hand on her hip. "Clever. Let's see how you wriggle out of this, then."

She struck, unleashing black gas that plumed toward me, encompassing me before I could even take a step back.

I screamed as my skin began to burn and bubble and blister. After only seconds, I could no longer stand, and collapsed to the ground, gripping the floor with trembling fingers.

With each inhale, breathing became more of a chore, and air only came in thin, unsatisfying streams. My vision clouded, but right before I blacked out, the queen let up, just enough for me to draw in a full breath.

"No clever rebuttal, Dane?" My adversary's lips spread wide. She shook her head and tutted. "I'd expected more. That's no fun."

Even though the last thing I wanted to do was give Ishtar what she desired, I couldn't help it. I went on the attack.

Separating my fingers from the ground as much as I could, I directed a killing spell at her. But it seemed that the gas had zapped my magic too. Fuchsia power flew only a foot or two before it died out with a fizzle.

"Huh, it really is all you had. Maybe I was wrong about your ancestry." Ishtar laughed again. "No daughter of Isis would be defeated so quickly. They would fight with the strength of an entire army until they were—"

"And here's her army now!" a voice I recognized blasted across the throne room.

It took everything I had to twist my neck to confirm that I wasn't dreaming. When my eyes ran over Alex, Eva, Hunter, Diana, the Torna twins, and the girl, Alice, who must have led them here, I whimpered.

As I did so, blood flew out of my mouth, its metallic taste coating my tongue before the liquid dripped down my chin.

For the first time, I realized how close death was— hovering just over my shoulder.

"Run!" I whisper-screamed. "*Run!*"

"An army? All I see are humans who are little more than children. Weaklings who are nothing compared to my power." Ishtar pointed to me. "If she cannot beat me, neither can you."

"We'll see about that," Hunter replied as he brought his fingers to his lips and blew out a loud whistle. "Infiltrate!"

The fae soldiers we'd brought from the Riverlands Court spilled into the room. White wolves bounded in behind them, and two vampires streaked by.

*How did everyone get down here?*

*Who cares? Just get up! Fight with them,* Tabitha yelled. *This is your chance!*

I pressed my palms to the ground and tried to lift my torso, only to crumple to the floor again.

I heard metal hitting metal, spells being fired, the snarls and roars of demons, and wolves growling as others fought. But I didn't have fight left in me, not any longer. My side might win, but Ishtar had defeated me.

I rolled over and blinked up at the black ceiling.

Suddenly, Alex appeared in my vision with a small contingent of fae soldiers from the Riverlands.

"Watch my back," he instructed them as he fell to his knees next to me. "Odie! What happened?" He crushed my hand to his chest, popping blisters on my fingers with his grip.

I groaned and tried to pull away, but it came out as a twitch. "Sh—She poisoned," I forced out.

It was the only thing that made sense. The smoke that the devil queen had shrouded me in must have been poisonous. And whatever toxicity the gas had brought into my system only seemed to be strengthening. With each passing second, I weakened.

Alex's blue eyes widened, and he wiped away the blood that had dribbled out of my mouth. "I see what you mean. Here, let me help." He placed a hand on my stomach, making me wince. "Sorry, sweets. I'll try to be gentle, but I need to touch you."

"No. I'm done."

Alex shook his head. "I can't accept that. And neither

can the world. If we're going to have any chance at beating her, we need you."

I was sure he was too late. Death was coming for me. Her velvet hands were wrapping around me now, cradling me.

But Alex either didn't notice, or he was determined to beat death. He worked, pouring his life-force into me—just as he had done when I'd died before.

It was strange to be cognizant of it this time, the gentle pull from dark to light.

And the snap backward as the darkness reclaimed me.

No matter how hard he pulled me toward the light, the rebound happened time and time again. Alex was failing.

"No, no, no," I heard him murmur as the blackness closed in around me once again. "How can this be happening?"

Somewhere in the surrounding battle, Ishtar released a scream of fury, and a dozen cries of pain flew up.

My heart rate reacted, beginning to race for those who had come to help.

*You can do it,* I cheered them on weakly.

*So can you! Don't give up!* Tabitha screamed, though even her tone sounded lame—injured, like she was dying again, right alongside me.

*But I'm so . . . just so tired.*

And I was. I'd spent years fighting Ishtar, a much more powerful being. Who was I to survive when she'd so clearly bested me?

*A mother effing godling! That's who!* Tabitha argued.

*I don't even know what she means by that.* I was already exhausted by the conversation. *It means nothing if I don't know how to use it.*

*Aether, it must have something to do with aether,* Tabitha replied coolly. *The old gods were made of it. Get a fae—those twins!*

When I didn't move, I felt a sensation like she was kicking something inside my head. *GET THEM!*

"Ow," I mumbled.

Alex ceased trying to pour magic into me. "I'm so sorry, sweets." His voice was thick with anger and worry. "I don't know why it isn't working. I—"

"The Tornas," I gasped. "I need them. Aether-blessed fae."

"But why?"

"Please . . ." I coughed up blood, and Alex's eyes widened as he cast a wild glance around.

"Hunter!" he bellowed.

His cousin was at his side in a second, his ifrit-possessed sword glowing red with fire. Even through the haze of death coming for me, I could still register that my friend looked terrible, covered in blood and black ash.

"What's up?" Hunter's green eyes flashed down to me, and he swore. "Dude. Why haven't you healed her yet?!"

"Something has changed inside her—maybe the release of her black magic is affecting her physiology." Alex sounded frantic, as if he were seconds from breaking down. "Or Ishtar is blocking my ability. My magic isn't working like it did before. She requested aether-blessed fae. Get the Tornas for me. Or Halad's cousins. Both if you can."

Hunter dashed off.

Why was the fight still happening? My friends outnumbered the demons. But even through my dulled senses, I heard cries coming from not only the monsters of Hell, but people.

Ishtar had to be pulling out all the stops.

As if in confirmation, a rampage of fire flooded the ceiling like before, and a dozen cries of pain filled the air.

*When will it end? Someone has to get a kill shot in soon . . .*

"Odie. Open your eyes, sweets. Please, open your eyes," Alex urged. "Stay with me."

*Open them?* With significant effort, I lifted my eyelids. I hadn't even known that they'd closed.

"I love—"

"No! Don't say that!" Alex sounded panicky, a tone alien to his deep baritone. "You're going to be fine. Look! The Tornas are here! Lyon too!"

Ayla and Sana fell to their knees next to me. A second later Lyon knelt next to Alex.

"What can we do?" Ayla asked.

"Odie said she needs you. Something about the aether."

"You didn't try healing her?" Sana's eyes scanned my face, which had to look horrible.

"I did, but it's not working, and I don't understand why. I've healed her before, this same way. I think Ishtar's magic is stopping me."

"Aether won't heal her either," Ayla said. "Unless she's

one of us—aether-blessed—it won't do a thing. It—"

I lifted my fingers.

Catching the motion, Ayla slammed her lips shut.

As best I could, I pointed to myself. "Not fae, godling."

"Godling?!" Sana's eyes widened. "Wait a minute, Odie, are you—" She twisted mid-sentence and shot a blast of fire at something. "Sorry about that, the bastards keep trying to attack you. Are you saying *you're* a godling?"

I nodded once.

My friends stared down at me, stunned and silent, until a piercing wail pulled them out of their stupor.

"That can't be right," Lyon said.

"And if it is . . . how?" Ayla asked. "They're supposed to all be dead! How did you find out?"

"Ishtar." As soon as I said the queen's name, my stomach began twisting into deep and vicious knots. I moaned, low and soft.

"She's fading!" Alex said. Only then did I become aware that one of his hands remained on my stomach. He'd been scanning me the whole time. "What can you do for her?"

"I'm not sure . . ." Ayla said, her tone hesitant. "I think she believes that if we fill her with aether, like we would an aether-blessed fae who was mortally wounded, she can come back."

"Yes," I croaked, my eyelids drifting closed again.

"Then do it!" Alex cried out.

"Okay, okay! Stand back, and take your hands off of her," Ayla replied. "Lyon help me. Sana keep guard." The older twin's green eyes locked with mine, and she lowered her voice. "Odette, this might hurt. Especially if you're *not* what you say you are. Aether is healing for those of us who can handle it, but at first, it's always . . . unpleasant. And there might be side effects."

My eyes closed, but I managed a faint hum of acceptance.

Another pair of hands, smaller and more fine-boned than Alex's, landed on me. Then another pair belonging to Lyon.

"Together," Ayla said, presumably to Lyon. "Sana, you'll have to take over if one of us can't give any more."

"Hurry," her sister urged. "She looks terrible."

Without so much as a warning, the magic I'd felt when walking through wards or just by being too close to Ayla when she was using aether, filled me. At first it was nice, pleasant as it had been before.

And then the burn set in.

I whimpered. Inside my head, Tabitha screamed, and I caught a vision of her curling into a ball.

Ayla responded to my cries by pressing her hands down harder. "We're so sorry! It'll hurt, but if you're sure of what you said," she sounded like she didn't quite believe me, "this could be the only way."

"Hold tight, Odette," Lyon urged. He hadn't let up in filling me with aether for a second.

Someone else, Alex, began stroking my hair. I focused on his hand on my head, needing a grounding point.

The aether that Ayla and Lyon sent through me burned hotter and more intense by the second. My nerve endings fried, and the heat burst the blisters that Ishtar's magic had seared onto my skin.

I released a yowl of pain, and my entire body tensed.

Alex stopped stroking my hair. "What's going on?"

"She's reacting to the aether," Sana answered.

"That, and," Ayla panted, and though I couldn't see her, I sensed the effort rolling off of her in waves. "There's something inside her that I've never seen before. I think you might be right that Ishtar's black magic was blocking your healing. I can feel Odette's witch power, but it's weak."

"Very weak," Lyon agreed. "And an oily, corrosive blackness is surrounding it."

"Trying to snuff it out . . ." Alex said as if he finally understood. "But if she's truly a godling, would that be enough to kill her?"

There was a pause in which I willed someone to speak, to take my mind off the pain flying through my veins, burning me up from the inside out.

"Perhaps," Ayla said. "Ishtar is a fallen goddess, so she might know how to kill godlings. But aether is the power of the old gods. Those that never fell. If anything will save her, it's aether."

My jaw clenched, and I gnashed my teeth, trying to piece together Ayla's words and what I'd learned from Ishtar.

After a few moments, I understood that only one thing was certain.

There was a part of me I didn't understand. And if I didn't understand it, then Ishtar sure as shit didn't either.

Pushing away the pain so I could concentrate, I searched the crevices of my body, of my soul, for the missing piece.

To my utmost surprise, it made itself known right away, like it had been waiting for me to turn inward and find it. I marveled at the bright ball of white light within my heart, watched as it bloomed open through the darkness of Ishtar's toxic power.

Ayla gasped, and I knew that by seeking the magic, I was onto something.

I looked deeper, through the thick, black gas, and in response, the light pulsed.

*Help?*

A sense of déjà vu crashed over me. How many times had I asked the bright glowing light of Morgan's necklace for help? Was this the same? Had I been talking to an aspect of aether magic all along?

*Accept the aether*, a voice, ancient and all-knowing, called to me. *Let it fill you. And use it.*

*That's it? I only need to relax and let Ayla's aether in?*

Even as I considered it, the act seemed impossible. The sensation of aether running through me wasn't as horrible as Ishtar's attack, but dammit, it still hurt.

*Release and live. Fight and die*, the voice said, and the light pulsed again, beating back Ishtar's swaths of black.

Her power moved faster now, perhaps knowing that I was seeking help. That I was close to understanding.

Not about to waste any more time, I took a deep, shuddering breath, and relaxed every muscle, bone, and tendon in my body so that the aether might take me over.

# CHAPTER FORTY-FIVE

The moment I gave myself over to what could be, aether flooded through me like water raging down a river.

It quenched the fires burning inside me.

The pain lifted slowly, like a sunrise.

Light beat back the dark.

Ishtar's poisonous gas dissolved, and the parts of me it tried to kill, throbbed with life.

And a pulse of something I didn't understand yanked me back from the brink of death.

# CHAPTER FORTY-SIX

I lurched up with a gasp. Ayla fell backward, and her twin caught her.

"Odie!" Alex sounded frantic. "Are you . . . okay?" The last word fell from his lips hesitantly, as if he sincerely doubted it.

But why? I'd never felt better, more alive.

"I'm good. I—"

A vibrant light caught my attention. I looked down to see that my hands were glowing white.

"Oh my god! What is this?"

Sana's lips trembled as if she couldn't believe what she was seeing. "It's aether. Maybe Ayla's or Lyon's . . . Maybe yours to command? We won't know unless it dissipates. *If it dissipates.* Either way, I think the aether is allowing you to use it."

*Use it . . .*

"Help me up."

Three pairs of hands helped me to stand. I prepared to wobble, but found that I was fine. Strong. Brimming with magic.

Ready.

I scanned the room. I wasn't sure how long I'd been out, but judging by the bodies on the ground, it was too long. Most of the casualties were fae soldiers. Diana was still fighting, but with a terrible limp. Andre had found her, and was at her side. Sam and the white-haired elf Flynn fought together too, and they seemed to be kicking some ass.

Then, I saw something that made my heart stop.

Stark against the obsidian ground were the bodies of two white wolves. There was no way I could tell who they were, or if they were even dead, from here.

But when Ishtar loosed a high-pitched scream, I knew I didn't have time to find out.

I needed to end her. Now.

My gaze snapped to the Queen of Hell, still near her throne. It seemed that a few demons had joined from topside, and were assisting her in beating back the swarms of magicals. Fae soldiers, the remaining two white wolves, the vampires, and Alice were all lashing out every chance they got.

But it was my best friend and Hunter, positioned closest to the queen, who made my mouth dry up. Eva was fighting back with all her might, black tendrils soaring from her, only to be punctuated occasionally by sunshine yellow magic that stood out against black stone. Hunter struck down any demon that dared come close to his woman. He alternated between using his totem, which glowed with fire from the ifrit he'd trapped inside the weapon, and green magic. Watching them, how Ishtar was targeting them with great intensity because she knew they loved me, made my heart stutter.

*You ready, Tabitha?* I asked, drawing in a breath.

There was no answer.

*Tabitha?*

Still nothing.

A pit formed in my stomach as I recalled how she'd curled in on herself when the aether filled me. Had it forced her out? It seemed that way. A ghost couldn't be killed . . .

"Odette? Are you okay?" Sana asked

My worry for the resident in my head must have shown on my face. I cleared my throat. "I'm fine."

And I was. Sad, scared, and countless other emotions, yes. But I was also ready and prepared to do what I must.

Before, I would have been worried that, without Tabitha, Ishtar could possess me, but not anymore. The Queen of Hell had proclaimed that I hadn't needed the ghost. After what had just happened with the aether, I believed that I could keep myself safe.

I was a godling, brimming with aether.

I lifted my hand and summoned my demon magic.

Black tendrils curled from my fingertips, teasing, warning.

Aether. Demon magic. And . . . I directed my palm at Ishtar.

"*Morsultimus.*"

A blindingly bright stream of fuchsia magic, my witch power, soared toward the queen.

Perhaps sensing it, her gaze darted toward me, and at the last second, her wings snapped out, and she lifted into the air. Her crimson eyes bore down on me, gleaming with hate, although I thought I saw something else there too.

Fear.

Rightfully so. I'd survived her lethal attack and returned for more. I was just as she'd said, a godling, one possessing three magics. I was the closest thing she had to an equal in this room.

My lips curled up slightly. "What do you say, Ishtar? Up for round two?"

The queen flew at me, claws extended. Unthinkingly, I levitated into the air.

Those below us gasped, shocked by my new power. I caught sight of Eva's red hair barreling down the dais steps toward me.

Before she made it, Ishtar and I were locked in battle. I alternated between using black magic, my natural-born power, and aether. The last of which flowed from me as if I'd been using it all my life.

"Odie!" Eva screamed, and I glanced down to find her holding up her demon dagger, offering it to me.

Using black magic, I ripped it from her hands and sent it soaring at Ishtar.

The queen deflected and sneered. "A little knife won't bring me down, witch."

I gestured at my floating form. "Obviously not just a

witch. Not anymore. Thanks for letting me in on that secret."

Fury flitted across the demoness' face, and she hurled a wall of fire at me. I threw up a shield, sending the flames up toward the ceiling, and retaliated with a binding spell.

Others were below us, still trying to land spells or shoot aether at the queen when they could, but she always seemed to feel them coming.

*She senses the power. We need a non-magical attack to get her off her game. We need—*

A blur of motion sidetracked my thought, and my eyes snapped to a spot just behind the queen. Simone was barreling through the fray, her black hair flying as she sprinted straight for Ishtar's back.

"Simone! No!" I screamed as the vampire leapt up and hurled herself at Ishtar.

Since the demoness' back was turned, she didn't see the vampire coming, didn't even notice her, until Simone's fangs were latched onto her neck.

Ishtar roared and, so quickly one might disregard it, Simone's eyes flashed to me.

*A life for a life.*

Her words rang through my mind. This was how she was repaying her life debt, by giving me an unguarded moment against the demon queen.

So, despite my natural inclination, I didn't try to pry her off Ishtar, or throw a shield over her body. Instead, as the demon goddess lit herself on fire to burn the vampire to a crisp, I seized the advantage.

"*Morsultimus*," I said, defaulting to my natural-born magic—the only one that felt right for such a moment.

The spell soared out of me, and slammed into the middle of Queen Ishtar's chest. A moan as loud as thunder rang through the throne room.

The fighting around us stopped. Although just seconds before, we'd all been going a mile a minute, now, no one seemed to even breathe.

Slowly, the fire encompassing the demoness fizzled out, and Ishtar's gleaming red eyes locked with mine.

I held her stare as her body caved in on itself. Piece by piece, Ishtar flaked away, sent off by the cries of every other demon in the room as they followed their queen into eternal darkness.

# CHAPTER FORTY-SEVEN

The throne room of Hell was quiet.

Everyone stood still, staring at where the demon queen had disintegrated before their eyes.

I gulped, unable to believe it was over. That my greatest adversary had been defeated.

And then the room began to shake.

My heart launched into my throat as rocks fell from the ceiling. "Quick! Grab the injured! Get everyone out of here!"

I soared down to where Ishtar and Simone's ashes mixed on the black floor. It was easy enough to tell the vampire's ashes from the Queen of Hell's; there were less of them and they were a lighter gray.

I scooped a little into my pocket, placing a barrier of aether around it so it would still be there when I wanted to transfer it to a better container. As I did so, a hint of metal glinted through the black ash on the ground.

The Realm Slicer. It hadn't dissolved with Ishtar.

I snapped it up. Who knew if we'd need it again, but I sure didn't want any other demons getting their hands on it. Whether they were in Hell or my realm I wanted them trapped. That way, they'd be easier to hunt.

I levitated again to get a better view and scanned the room. Thankfully, many of the fae soldiers that Queen Aquatia had sent us had wings. All the flying fae had already grabbed an injured person and taken off down the hall, to the hole leading to the surface. But then I spotted the two wolves on the ground, and the other two hovering around their bodies. The prone shifters were so large that no fae could move them alone.

I pressed my hand out in front of me and bid the aether to take them to the surface. The living wolves growled as the lifeless bodies swooped out of the room, but when they saw it was me controlling the movement, they stopped, understanding.

It was always difficult for me to tell the guys apart in wolf form, but without a doubt, one of the living shifters was Dasha.

The alpha loosed a mournful howl, and my heart cried in response as she ran from the room. I hoped that the other two were only injured, not gone forever.

A chorus of familiar voices called my name, and I looked down to see Eva, Alex, and Hunter waiting for me. Alex extended his hand, and as I lowered to the ground, I gripped it tight.

"That's everyone," I said.

"Good," Alex said, "because we need to leave before this room caves in."

As if to make a point, a massive boulder fell right on top of the throne that used to be Ishtar's.

We dashed from the room, the last ones to leave. As we ran down the dark hallway, I noticed the bodies of the snakes that Ishtar had attacked me with stuck to the wall.

"How—?"

"They were coming down the hall when we arrived," Hunter said, his eyes darting to the snakes. "The Tornas and Grahn zapped them with aether. Another fae used earth magic to create nails from their armor ornamentation to nail them down."

"Good," I said.

A part of the hallway wall collapsed inward, and we put on a burst of speed. We sprinted into the room that served as a conduit between realms, and skidded to a stop to stare up at the gaping crevice into our world.

"How are we going to—oh my god, Odie!" Eva yelped as I used the aether to lift her into the air.

Hunter and Alex were next, and only when I knew I had them under control did I follow, soaring upward.

When we emerged from the portal Ishtar had made, cheering met my ears. For the first time in what felt like hours, my lips lifted into a smile as I set us down on the ground. The moment my feet touched the grass, my knees buckled. Alex caught me, steadying me like he so often did.

I waved my hands, trying to get others' attention.

Quickly, the cheering died down, leaving behind a telling silence.

I strained to hear fighting in the distance, but my ears picked up nothing. No screams, roars, or crashes. Was the fighting over?

At that very moment, Alice descended out of the sky to land right in front of me. Her long white-blonde hair was tangled and matted with ash and blood. Cuts marred her slender arms, the blood a stark red against her skin. "Fae flew overhead to check out the academy grounds. No one is fighting. It seems like the remaining demons have retreated."

My heart swelled. We'd done it. We'd pushed the demons from Spellcasters and won. Although that was amazing a groan from someone nearby made me rein in my internal celebration.

"We think the demons have retreated," I repeated what Alice said. "Get the injured and dead back to the academy. Treat them, and help whoever you find in need of assistance. Of course, be on the lookout for any enemies who might still be on the grounds. Just in case."

The surrounding crowd sprang into motion. I was about to do the same, but Hunter laid a gentle hand on my arm.

"Odie, you're not glowing anymore." His eyebrows knitted together. "What happened? Are you okay?"

Sana appeared in front of us. "She's probably fine. The aether transfer just wore off. Odette used it, but she doesn't *own* it." She paused and gave me a pointed look. "Unless you can use your own aether magic. And I'd love to learn more about how you acquired that . . ."

"Yeah, same," Eva said. "I mean, come on, girl. If you're going to just level up like that, and get another type of magic, I'd appreciate a heads up so I can try too." She nudged me playfully to lighten the mood.

I chuckled. "I would have loved a heads up myself." My gaze went to Sana. "Thank you so much for helping me. Your sister and Lyon too. Where are they?"

Sana's face fell. "Luvon was injured in Hell. We're not sure he's going to make it. Ayla and Lyon are flying him inside the academy now."

I hadn't seen Luvon or Volwin, but of course they were both there, defending their ladies.

"And Volwin?"

"He's with them. I should be, too, but I wanted to make sure you got out of there. And that you didn't need a lift." She fluttered her wings.

"Go. I'll tell you everything I know later. I have a few things to take care of first."

Sana disappeared, and the first thing I did was bring the Realm Slicer to my palm and cut across it so blood welled. I transferred it to the blade, approached the crevice in the earth, and stabbed the enchanted weapon into the ground.

Before my eyes, the fissure closed. When it sealed all the way, I turned to my friends.

"I need to check on some people." I'd already spotted the wolves, just inside the trees. "Wait here for me?"

"We'll be here," Eva assured me. "Let us know if you

need anything. Or they do." Her blue eyes traveled over the wolves, full of empathy for them, but knowing Eva she didn't want to intrude.

"I will. Thanks." Turning, I steeled myself for what was sure to be an emotional conversation and approached Dasha, now in her human form.

Howley was at her side, gripping her hand as they huddled over Heath and Gregor. When neither wolf glanced up at my approach, I knew the worst had happened.

I knelt down next to the alpha, careful not to place a hand on her fallen mates, because I knew shifters could be protective.

"This is in no way adequate, but I'm sorry, Dasha."

"They were all so good, so brave, I don't understand why this happened."

Howley's face was screwed up so tight, I could tell he was just trying to keep it together for her.

The whole situation was unfair and wrong and horrible. While I hadn't known Heath and Gregor as well as the alpha herself, I knew they had been good guys. And they'd given their lives to make our world safer, to rid it of the devils who'd wanted to rule.

"This might not mean much right now," I said. "And I agree with you that this wasn't fair, and you two don't deserve it, and neither did they. But I want to thank you and them for joining us. Gregor and Heath died heroes' deaths."

Dasha's eyes welled with tears, and her chin began to

tremble. I wrapped my arm around her shoulder, and she leaned into me, allowing me to offer her strength and condolences.

We were still holding on to one another when footsteps approached behind me.

I twisted to find the other person I wanted to speak with —Francis.

I squeezed Dasha. "I'm so sorry, again."

She gave a single nod, her eyes darting between each of the white wolves' bodies. "Thanks for getting them out of there. I'll see that they get respectable sendoffs."

"I'd love to attend," I said. "But for now, I think Francis needs to speak to me."

The alpha turned, and shock flitted across her face. In her grief, she must not have heard the vampire approach.

"Go ahead," she said.

I stood and gestured for Francis to walk a ways away.

When we were far enough from Dasha and Howley that we would not intrude on their mourning, I turned to him. "I'm sorry. I know you and Simone were an item during the Games. I'm not sure if you were recently, but—"

"No." Francis cut me off. "That ended a few weeks after London, but we were still friends. And we still cared for each other. She was one of the few people who really knew me."

I swallowed down a lump rising in my throat. "I owe my life to her. Actually, we all do. If Simone hadn't sacrificed herself, Ishtar would have won."

Francis sniffled, a strange sound coming from a vampire who didn't even need to breathe. "Maybe."

"I retrieved some of her ashes before I left. Would you like them?" I had been intending to keep them for myself, a memory of a life-debt cycle that now could never be repaid. But Francis, Simone's once love and true friend, needed her ashes more.

His gaze lifted to latch onto mine. Only then did I realize that he was impossibly paler than normal. His albino skin seemed to have lost all the blood that had run through it. "It would honor me to take her ashes. I'll create a necklace, and wear it at all times."

"Once I find a suitable container to put them in, they're yours," I promised. I gestured toward the academy. "We need to get back to the school. We should see what damage has been done, and I'll need to find people strong enough to carry the wolves, if Dasha will let them. Would you help?"

Francis nodded as he shot a glance to the mourning alpha. "Give her time. Wolves' emotions run deep. I don't know how she had that bond with three shifters. Something about her is special." He pinned me with his gaze. "Like you. This whole godling business is something I want to hear about another time."

"You will. I promise you will."

The walk through the woods back to the academy nearly ripped my heart out.

Bodies littered the school grounds. I felt sure that, although we did our best to find everyone we could and bring them inside, we would be discovering corpses for days.

The destruction to the school's property was also great. Craters the size of kiddie pools littered the lawn. Portions of the building had collapsed, and the rubble was strewn across the drive and into the grasses. One tower had been hit, and the top had fallen off. The front doors were broken down, leaving the school wide open.

No one had assessed the outbuildings yet, but we expected to find them similarly damaged.

When we entered the academy, I finally found my parents. They were standing on the third level, overlooking the entryway, searching for me.

"Mom! Dad!"

They sprinted down the stairs, and I ran up. We met in the middle, and they crushed me between them.

"Where were you?" Mom asked, her face streaked with tears. "We looked for you *everywhere*."

There was no way I would tell them that Ishtar had lured me into Hell by using their likenesses. Not now, probably not ever.

They'd only feel undeserved guilt over it.

"I fought Ishtar." I paused, and my gaze went from Mom's brown eyes to Dad's hazel ones. "I have so many things to tell you, incredible things, but first, we have work to do."

Dad nodded. "Are your friends safe?"

I gestured down to the entryway, where my friends streamed inside, some with bodies in their hands, some without.

"Eva, Alex, and Hunter are all good. Eva was the one to kill Lucifer," I reported what my friend had told me on the walk through the woods. "Only Diana got injured. The rest are fine—mostly."

My throat closed up thinking about Dasha, still in the woods, and Ayla, worrying over Luvon. And poor Francis, who was with his headmaster, getting business done, even though I was sure he couldn't stop thinking about Simone. I certainly couldn't. She'd made the ultimate sacrifice, so that I had a chance to kill Ishtar.

"They will be okay, one day," I murmured.

My dad studied me as if he were trying to see into my soul, until finally, he nodded. "I think that'll be the case for most people."

A shuddering sigh left me. "Where are the students?"

During the battle, I hadn't seen a single living student. Of those I knew were at the academy, I'd only witnessed three professors fighting. I didn't believe the demons would have killed them all, or at least, I hope they wouldn't. They would've been smart to keep some students alive to lure us in.

"They're locked in the Battle Magic classroom," a voice from behind spoke up, startling me.

I turned around to find Professor Tittelbaum, my warping mentor. He'd always been a thin man, academic and nerdy, but he looked even thinner now. Almost sickly.

"I hear that you leveled up in your warping, Dane. And perhaps a few other things, too?" He looked at me pointedly.

I nodded. "Timewalking, and . . . yeah, a few other things."

"A tale for another day," he said. "For now, I'll show you where the students are." He turned and descended the stairs.

I trailed behind, and my parents followed.

"Professor De Spina and I should have been down there with them," he continued. "They kept the students and teachers locked up in the Battle Magic room most of the time, but a group of demons needed our assistance with something. Ms. Seeley, too. So when you arrived, we were free to fight."

"I saw you," I said. "Thank you for your help."

"I don't deserve your thanks," Professor Tittelbaum said sadly.

I suspected he was experiencing a great sense of remorse for working with the demons. Even if he was possessed part of the time, or they would've killed him had he not done what they wanted, it would be hard to swallow.

He would have to come to terms with his guilt on his own, though, so I refrained from commenting.

When we got to the door of the classroom, the professor turned and looked at me.

"It's sealed. But Headmistress Wake tells me you might be able to open it."

The tone of his voice left me with little doubt about what he meant.

I allowed my demon magic to pour from my hands, over the knob, and bade it to open. It did so easily, and when the door swung wide, my hands flew to my mouth in horror.

Far fewer students and professors stood before me than I had hoped. Those who remained were almost too thin and filthy to recognize.

"I'll make sure the infirmary is prepared," Mom said, and dashed back up the stairs.

As soon as she was gone a voice I hadn't heard in a long time piped up. "Once a few of us get some water, we can help with whatever is going on upstairs."

I turned to find Phoebe, Diana's best friend, shifting through the crowd. She looked slightly better off than most, but still covered in a layer of dirt.

"You don't have to help at all. You guys have clearly been through a lot."

Phoebe's chin jutted out. "I'll do what I can."

Recognizing that this was personal for her, I nodded. Professor Tittelbaum said he'd wait for my mom to return, and I helped those few who could walk upstairs to get them food and water. After that the hours passed in a blur, and night turned into day before I stopped moving.

We had designated a spot for the bodies, and for the living, we created a temporary sleeping area in Agnes Sampson Hall. While many of the dorm towers were still habitable, no one wanted to sleep in them, as the demons had been living there for weeks. I couldn't argue with that.

When I finally fell asleep early the next day, it was in Agnes Sampson Hall, surrounded by loved ones, and wrapped in a sense of surety that finally, we were safe.

# CHAPTER FORTY-EIGHT

For the next two days, we worked tirelessly, cleaning up rubble, caring for the injured, searching the woods for bodies, and most importantly, contacting the families of the dead. It was a sensitive task that we gave to only the most empathetic.

Most of those we contacted planned to pick up their fallen kin as soon as possible, although some proved more difficult.

"Does Joseph's mom still believe you're a demon calling to lure her here?" I asked Amethyst, who had been one of the few charged with the tough task of calling the deceased's kin.

She was also the most dedicated, perhaps because she could speak to the ghosts, and understood how much they wished to be with their families.

I didn't ask, because that thought was just too sad.

She nodded, her brown eyes resigned. "She's sure that I'm trying to trick her, but I'll keep trying."

I placed a hand on my friend's shoulder. "You're doing your best. Don't forget to eat." I gestured to the plate I'd brought her because she hadn't made it to the cafeteria yet, and it was already two in the afternoon.

"Thanks, Odette." She gave me a wobbly smile.

As I left the Demonology classroom and shut the door behind me, I sighed. Although we'd made a lot of progress, it seemed that the pain streaming through Spellcasters would never end.

Spellcasters wouldn't reopen in time for the next academic year, which was two weeks away. Too much of the school was in shambles for that to be feasible. And honestly, it was just as well. The students and staff who had lived under the demons' reign of terror needed time to heal. They needed to go home and return on their own terms. For those who wished to reenroll and continue their education and the fight against the dark, when classes eventually resumed, it wouldn't be here. At least not right away. We hadn't completely succeeded the night of the Battle of Spellcasters.

The Furies still lived. First hand sources claimed that they'd fled the academy grounds, and taken a large contingent of demons with them. That they remained walking the Earth meant the school was at risk.

That, and Headmistress Wake suspected that the royals had enchanted the academy. If that was true, they could force their way in again. She was building a team of powerful witches who would inspect the school after the students and staff had left, no later than tomorrow.

My parents had volunteered to be a part of that team, and knowing of their skills with wards, Headmistress Wake had accepted their offer of help right away.

Until a team of witches had inspected every inch of the school, they would allow only select people back inside. It might take months for them to give the school a clean bill of health. Until then, if a student wished to continue their education, witch professors would hold classes at the Fae Academy of Elemental and Arcane Arts.

I wasn't sure I'd be attending.

My hesitation didn't stem from fear of another attack. Or even from suspicion that parts of the PIA were still crooked. In fact, after hearing of the battle, the PIA was launching *another* investigation of their institution.

The organization assured us that this one would be more thorough than the first investigation that helped suss out traitor agents. The agency claimed that if there were additional secret prisons, they'd discover them and liberate people wrongfully imprisoned. I believed them because this time, they'd called in unaffiliated mind witches to help.

And yet, despite the PIA's commitment to weed out corrupt officers, I'd come to terms with the fact that espionage might not be my dream any longer. I suspected that no professor at the academy, or possibly anywhere, could teach me what I needed to know.

I'd already asked the most senior professors—all except Professor Adyto, who had perished at the hands of the royals—what they knew about the godlings. It wasn't much. The library hadn't quenched my thirst for knowledge either.

Still, the possibility that I wasn't the only one in existence burned inside me. There had to be more godlings out there. Perhaps they were also seeking information. Or perhaps they were just binge-watching TV shows like a normal person. Oblivious to their true nature.

"Wherever they are, I'll find them," I muttered under my breath.

"Talking to yourself, Dane?"

I turned to find Diana hobbling up behind me. "Hey. Where did you come from?"

She laughed. "You passed me as I was coming out of the bathroom. Didn't even see me, you were so lost in thought. And then you started talking to yourself." She arched an eyebrow. "Want a sounding board?"

I heaved a breath. "Nah, just considering my future."

Diana knew what Ishtar had told me. I'd informed all my closest friends, my parents, and Headmistress Wake, hoping they'd have answers. Of course, they had none.

"There's a lot of that happening now," Diana replied. "I never thought I'd see the day when Spellcasters would be empty."

At that very moment, we passed a downed statue of Alice Kyteler. Her arm had been broken off in a scuffle.

Diana eyed the statue and shook her head. "Or that an epic battle would be fought here. Are you planning on going to the fae academy when we have to clear out?"

"For a bit. At least to see the soldiers off. Mom and Dad will be busy here for a while, and I don't want to go home without them."

"And after?" Diana asked.

"Tiberius asked Alex to return to Seattle. I guess a few of the people we rescued from Dulce Base aren't recovering as well as they'd hoped. Tiberius told Alex he might learn a few novel things if he went to help. Obviously, Alex was all about that. I'm going with him, and so are Eva and Hunter."

"The dream team."

I smiled. "We're only missing you."

She stopped walking, and I had to turn to face her.

"Thank you for saying that," Diana said, and her lips twisted in a strange way that I'd never seen on her face. "It's been really hard since Tabitha left. I know I have Phoebe, but she was here . . ." She huffed out a breath. "Thank the goddess and all the other old gods she wasn't an idiot, and kept her head down while the demons ruled."

"You're one of us now, Wake," I said seriously. "You have been for a while. We wouldn't have made it so far without you."

She gave me a wobbly, very un-Diana-like smile. "You know, I'm going to miss you when you don't return. Are you sure that's what you want to do?"

"Pretty sure," I shrugged. "It just feels right, you know? Everything has changed for me. I need a new beginning."

"I get that," she replied, and we fell into silence as we walked.

When we reached the entryway, it was filled with people coming and going, fixing things, leaving the academy, picking someone up.

"Honey! Odette!"

I cast a glance around, recognizing Mom's voice, but couldn't find her.

"Up here!"

I twisted, and spotted her beaming at me from an upper floor.

"Honey, would you come up here please?"

"Catch you later," I said to Diana.

She went to join Andre. He was trying to help repair the front door hinges.

I climbed the stairs. When I reached the right floor, my parents moved to stand against the wall, right in front of a line of paintings.

For the first time in days, they were all alone, which was strange enough, but it was the wide grins on their faces that told me something else was up.

"Hey, what's happening?" I asked. "You guys look happy."

Dad put his arm around Mom's shoulders. "We have something to show you, pea. We'd hoped to unveil it when the academy resumed sessions, but after hearing about your plans last night, we figured now was the time."

"Okay—what is it?"

They broke apart to reveal a blank canvas on the wall, right between the portraits of Merlin and Morgan.

"Wait a minute . . . why separate them?" I moved closer to the gold plaque that gleamed back at me, and read:

*Odette Dane, Eva Proctor, Diana Wake, Alex Wardwell, and Hunter Wardwell. Students who led the charge against the royal demons at the Battle of Spellcasters, and helped ensure victory.*

My throat closed up. Not knowing what to say, I looked to my parents.

"Obviously, there's nothing there yet. You'll have to sit for a portrait with your friends," Dad said. "And the others haven't seen it yet, so don't tell them. Headmistress Wake would like their parents to show them. She'll show Alex herself, since his parents are still helping with the rescued spies. But soon enough, there will be a painting there, and you'll stand alongside all the other great witches of history."

Tears filled my eyes, and I dragged my gaze from the plaque bearing my name to the paintings of Merlin on the left and Morgan on the right.

It astonished me how true to life their paintings were, although they were missing some key characteristics. Like the freckles across Morgan's nose, and the premature fine lines at the corners of Merlin's eyes, the result of his constant smiles.

"They had to relocate the one of Nicolas Flamel," Mom said, her lips twisting in an amused grin. "Personally, I think it was the right choice. He looks like such a sourpuss. You five will brighten the hallway up much more."

I laughed. Long ago, when I'd stumbled across these

paintings in my Culling-year, I'd thought the same thing about the famed alchemist

I turned my head again, glancing at the paintings of M&M, and shook my head. "I can't wait for the others to see this."

Dad wrapped his arm around me, pulling me close to him. "You all deserve it, and so much more."

I appreciated the sentiment, although, in that moment, I couldn't say that I needed a single other thing to make me happy.

# CHAPTER FORTY-NINE

Headmistress Cristala handed me a champagne flute filled with bubbling gold that smelled faintly of pears. "For the soldiers' sendoff."

*As if I need a reason to accept champs.* I took the glass with a soft smile. "Thank you."

My friends accepted their own flutes, and as soon as the fae headmistress disappeared, Hunter arched his eyebrows. "Different from Spellcasters, huh?"

"Night and day," Eva replied.

"We just needed to get out. To breathe a little," Alex said. "Hell, maybe after we leave, we should try something fun and normal just to remember what it feels like. See a movie?"

There was no denying that everything felt different about the fae academy. Although there had still been a lot to do when we'd left Spellcasters an hour before, my parents had insisted that we leave.

They too wanted us to 'go have fun.' While I hadn't been sure I would be able to do that, particularly after saying goodbye to Dasha, and committing to attend her mates' funerals, I was pleasantly surprised that a little lightness had been able to seep into my soul.

It wasn't that I'd forgotten about all the terrible things we'd seen or been through, but there was something about the fae academy that made me feel lighter. More free and less worried.

I hoped that when the next year of Spellcasters students arrived here, they'd feel the same way. That no one would experience terror or pain at coming back to school.

"Pardon my interruption," a soft, regal voice came from behind me. "I've been wanting to speak with you four since I noticed you arrive, but the headmistress kept me occupied."

I turned to find Queen Aquatia standing before me, dressed in an exquisite sea green gown.

"Hi," I said, and paused for my friends to greet the queen. "I wasn't expecting to see you at all."

It wasn't often that fae royalty came to our realm.

The queen smiled. "I'm grateful for everything that everyone in this world has done, but I wanted to thank you four, and Miss Wake, who I've already spoken to, in person. I know the threat isn't completely over, but you've minimized it considerably."

"People are already searching for the Furies," Alex said, as if trying to soothe the queen. "All sorts of magicals. Headmaster Ezra and Francis, included."

"So I've heard." She smiled at him before her eyes turned to me. "Forgive me if this is stepping over the line, but the Tornas told me what you discovered about yourself."

I stiffened. I didn't mind that the twins knew, they were my friends. But why would they tell a Faerie queen?

"Please don't be angry with them. I understand things are different here, but I am their monarch. I asked for updates on anything important, and they felt like they had to tell me. However, your secret is safe with me. I have no intention of spreading the word," Queen Aquatia assured me. "I only wanted to extend my assistance, should you need it."

"Do the fae have information on the old gods?"

I'd asked Ms. Seeley, but she hadn't seemed to think so. Then again, the Spellcasters Faeology professor didn't live in Faerie. Surely, Aquatia had access to information that Ms. Seeley would know nothing about?

"Not that I'm aware of," the queen said, dashing my hopes. "However, there are rumors of lost libraries in Faerie. If you're interested, I could look into them? Additionally, there are a few exceptional historians in my kingdom."

"I'd appreciate that," I replied.

"And if you decide to pursue this power and learn to unlock your aether magic, please know we'd be happy to teach you what we know of the aether. If you need the help, that is."

I drew in a breath. "If I get that far, I'm sure I'll need your help. I really don't know what to expect."

If I searched for knowledge about the godlings and how to unlock those powers within me, what would happen? *Could* it even happen? Or had the old gods hidden it for a reason?

"Few do," the queen replied. "Particularly when they are called on to complete unprecedented tasks."

At that moment, Headmistress Cristala called attention to the Faerie portal and the soldiers who would be returning home.

Holding the queen's eye for a moment longer, I nodded before twisting to face her soldiers. With the crowd, I raised my glass, honoring the fae who'd helped us, and toasting to peace in all the realms.

And the new possibilities to come.

# CHAPTER FIFTY

"Hey, babe. How are things looking today?" I asked Alex as I entered Tiberius Thorn's healing sanctuary.

The facility was a bunker in that it was underground, but unlike most bunkers I envisioned, it was actually kind of nice. Thorn had brought in lamps that mimicked the light of the sun, and tons of plants, most of them medicinal.

"Not bad," he said, glancing up from a medical chart, and beaming at me.

"I'm such a slug. Hunter and Eva are out jogging around Seattle, and you've been in here for hours. And here I am, just now getting up at noon." With the cup of coffee in my hand, I gestured down to my silk polka dot pajamas.

"You needed the rest, sweets," Alex assured me, taking a seat at his desk. "Especially if you're going to stay awake for me to take you out on the town tonight." He winked.

My heart leapt. I couldn't wait for our long-overdue date.

"The PJs don't matter, anyway," Amelia, the patient in the bed closest to where I stood, spoke softly so as not to wake those who were sleeping. "We haven't been out of our pajamas in days!"

"You wear them better than me." I smiled at her. "How are you?"

"Better by the day. Thorn gave me a can of soup to use as a weight to start building up my muscles again. I'm up to five reps!" She beamed at the accomplishment, which was a huge one.

When we'd assessed her at Nightdwellers a little over a week before, Amelia couldn't even stand. Lifting a soup can? You might as well have asked her to bench a car.

"You're killin' it, girl," I congratulated as I moved over to where Alex sat, his eyebrows knitted together in concentration as he mixed up a tincture for a patient.

After we made a quick stop in London to seal up the Hellgate as tight as we could, a relatively painless task now that we weren't being threatened by a horde of demons, Hunter, Eva, Alex and I had traveled to Seattle. Tiberius Thorn had requested Alex's help, and the rest of us weren't ready to split yet. Seeing as most of the royals were dead, it was probably silly, but we'd come to rely on each other a lot. We were each other's safety blankets.

And the ex-prisoners needed as much help as they could get. Most had been experimented on, or enchanted in such a way that normal remedies hadn't worked. Since we arrived three days ago, Tiberius and his favorite protégé had been brainstorming up new cures for whatever ailed each patient.

To be honest, it was kind of ironic that Alex claimed *I* needed my rest. Lately, my man had been surviving on less than five hours of sleep a night.

No thanks. I would take being a slug over that.

"Whatcha working on?" I perched on the edge of the desk, and leaned over for a kiss.

"Will has an infection—magically-induced, we're sure— that we can't quite pin down. He's better, but not as far along as we hoped. I'm mixing up a new treatment to see if it will help."

I glanced at the vial, which held a liquid the same color as a bright blue sky. "You and Thorn are amazing."

Alex cocked his head.

I gestured to the sanctuary. "Most of your patients have improved so much."

My boyfriend gave me a sweet smile. "It's just what we do."

There was a loud sigh from somewhere in the room, and Alex's joy fell from his face.

He glanced past me, at the beds. "Do me a favor?"

I nodded, ready to do whatever he needed.

"Chat with a few of the patients? They're getting bored, and we need to keep their spirits up. They're probably sick of talking to just each other, or maybe just me. We need new blood."

I slapped his shoulder; I didn't like him making digs at himself.

Alex chuckled. "Seriously, though. I need an hour or so to concentrate. Do you mind?"

"Not at all," I said. I needed something to do besides sleep, eat, and scour Thorn's massive library for information on the godlings—the final task I was failing at spectacularly.

I left him to work his magic, and scanned the room.

Of the eleven patients remaining, nine were sleeping. Amelia looked fairly engrossed in a thriller novel. But William was just staring out the window.

I approached the man I'd met at Nightdwellers, the spy who had lasted two long years in the underground prison. After being there so long, it was no wonder that his healing progress would be slow.

"Hey, Will. How's it going?" I lowered myself into the seat next to his bed.

"Better every day." He turned to face me, a smile on his thin face. "But I might be even better if you'd give me some of that coffee. I haven't had coffee in *years*."

"Don't give him any!" Alex called out, clearly having heard.

I laughed. "Sorry, healer's orders. But I promise once Alex or Thorn gives you the all-clear on caffeine, I'll buy you a venti."

We chatted for a few minutes about the book he'd been reading and the shows he'd watched since breaking out of prison.

When the conversation dwindled, I could feel him wanting to ask about the battle and everything leading up to it. Truthfully, it was the last thing I wanted to discuss. I'd rehashed it a million times and it was so emotionally draining. But I did want to know something in particular and Will seemed to have enough energy to handle it.

"Can I ask you something personal?" I asked.

Will looked taken aback. Although we'd spoken at Nightdwellers, and occasionally since my friends and I had come here, we'd kept things very superficial.

After a few seconds, he nodded. "Sure."

I inhaled deeply, preparing to ask the question I'd wondered about every single prisoner we'd found at Base Dulce. "Why were you imprisoned? Did you discover the PIA's connection to the demons? Or something else?"

Will chuckled. "I'm surprised it took you all so long to ask. You're so polite."

"We didn't want to cause extra strain on anyone while they were still weak, but you seem to be doing pretty well. And knowing how long you lasted in there makes me think that whatever you found drove you to survive."

"Fair point." Will nodded. "Your guess is correct. I discovered that a sector of the PIA was working with demons. They'd been doing so for years before I figured it out. But that wasn't the only reason they threw me in a cell."

I leaned forward, interested.

"I'd been doing research, and stumbled across a finding

that stunned me. Had I shared it, my discovery would have rocked the entire supernatural world."

"What was it?" I asked, unable to help myself.

I might not follow my childhood dream and become a spy, but I still loved learning secrets. It was in my blood.

"There's a race of magicals that didn't die out, like we thought."

My spine straightened, but Will continued on, not noticing.

"I found an old book explaining that they are simply hidden, protected from the demons. And when the time is right, they'll rise and bring justice to the world."

My mouth went dry, and my heart thumped hard. "What race?"

Will shook his head as if he still couldn't believe what he'd discovered. "The *godlings*. They exist. For centuries, we've thought they were dead, but their lines have just been hidden. Hidden in plain sight! Crazy, right?"

I sucked in a breath, meeting the man's stare.

I knew without a doubt that he had been put in my path for a reason.

"Actually, I can believe that." I scooted closer. "And if you wouldn't mind, I'd love for you to tell me everything you know about the godlings."

*I* gripped Alex's hand tightly as we left the sweet little restaurant he'd taken me to for our date. We were about to join Eva and Hunter for a nightcap, but I wanted to savor every moment of alone time I had with him.

"I had a lot of fun tonight," I said pressing up against my man. Despite being summer the winds coming in off the Puget Sound chilled me.

"Me too," Alex rubbed my arm, warming it. "It was nice to get out of Thorn's place. Away from business, adventure, and you know, saving the world."

"Us and our little hobbies," I joked. We walked a ways more before I broached the question I figured we were both thinking. "So what are we going to do with ourselves now?"

Alex stopped before a door, barely noticeable in the side of a warehouse-type building. Hunter had discovered the hidden speakeasy earlier that week and had been dying to go ever since. "Don't you mean what are Hunter, Eva, and I going to do with ourselves now?" Alex asked lightly. "I have a feeling that after you spoke with Will, you're brewing a plan in that beautiful brain of yours."

He wasn't wrong.

"You know me well, babe," I said, helping him to push the door open. "But first, drinks and good company."

I stepped inside the clandestine bar. Jazz played, making me tap my feet. The speakeasy was decorated as if they'd plopped it straight out of the 1920s. Art deco accents sparkled from every nook and cranny. There was a gleaming golden gramophone in one corner, raised so that everyone could admire it. Dark green and black colorings dominated. Adorable fringe lamps topped every circular table.

I spotted Eva in the far back corner waving, and we went to join her and Hunter. We'd just sat down and barely had a moment to greet them when the server arrived to take our drink order. Alex and I scanned the sparse menu, and chose a cocktail each.

When we were alone, I turned to Eva. "How was the restaurant? Did you find it?"

Hunter had claimed that the restaurant he'd booked was one of the best hidden gems in Seattle.

She threw a wave. "Please! It's tucked away, but its little pink door beckons people like a siren. There's a line down the alley because the place is so popular." Her eyes shone as she glanced at Hunter. "It was great though. Amazing food.

You guys should try it. Apparently, their reservations book out months in advance, but I bet Tiberius could pull some strings."

"How do you think I got us in?" Hunter said. "He'd get you a spot for sure, cuz." Hunter punched Alex on the shoulder, and the guys exchanged boyish grins.

The server arrived with our drinks, setting down the artisan cocktails with a flourish before disappearing back into the crowded bar.

"One thing's for sure." I glanced around at the amazing decor again. "You Wardwell guys definitely have a gift for wining and dining your ladies." I lifted my glass to my friends. "To many more nights like this, where we're together, happy, and healthy."

They echoed my toast and our glasses clinked. We took a sip and set the drinks down. There was a brief silence before Eva turned to face me once more.

"So, Alex mentioned that Will told you something about the godlings." Eva gave me a pointed look. "We said tonight was all about fun, but I'm *dying* to hear all about it. And your plans."

I snorted out a laugh. My friends were as bad as me. They were always thinking about the next big thing, never able to truly relax.

My eyes cut over to Alex. He was trying to hide a smile and failing. "Do you mind? We said fun and easy . . . "

"Of course not," Alex said. "Hunter's been wanting to hear about it too."

"Damn right." Hunter's green eyes gleamed in the light

from the fringed lamp on our table. "So spill it, Odie. What did Will say?"

I leaned over the table, ready to divulge all that I knew. "They imprisoned him because he discovered that godlings do exist. More than just me. He actually found a book, leading to some sort of enchanted object. It will allow the descendants of the gods to access their powers."

"You mean someone else can't just fill them with aether?" Hunter countered. "Like Ayla and Lyon did?"

I shook my head. "That was only temporary, anyway—a workaround of sorts. I haven't been able to access my own aether magic, although I sense it churning inside me now." When I focused on it, the sensation was actually almost overwhelming. It made me wonder how it had stayed muted for so long. "Apparently, the hidden objects will unlock the powers of the godlings and usher in a new age of magicals. One that will turn the supernatural world on its head, and the darkness will disappear."

"That must be why Ishtar wanted to kill you or have you join her," Eva said, her blue eyes wide. "Keep your enemies close."

"Yep," I said. "Godlings and royal demons are equally powerful. And even though hundreds of people are on the hunt for the Furies right now, that doesn't mean this is over. They could create more demons and probably will."

"Not to mention now they're *pissed*," Alex said. "We halved the royal's numbers." He stirred his drink with the decorative stick speared with crystallized ginger. "I hate to say it, but I don't think anyone will find the Furies. The godlings will be the ones to take them out."

I agreed with him. The only reason we beat the demons at Spellcasters was because Eva and I had leveraged our dark magic against them. Now, however, the Furies knew all our tricks. They understood what they were up against, and Ishtar herself had said that everyone underestimated them.

I couldn't make the same mistake.

"So these objects," Eva said. "Any idea where they are? Or what they are?"

I heaved a heavy sigh. "No. When the crooked PIA agents discovered that Will had learned about godlings, they not only imprisoned him, they burned the book he found referencing the godlings. He claims that it was a small book of clues leading to one of the objects, but he thinks that there are more. One for every major god."

"So dozens." Alex rubbed thoughtfully at the stubble growing on his chin. "I'll have to study up on the lore of the old gods."

"You and me both, babe," I said. "Actually, I wanted to talk to you guys about something related to studying." I fingered the base of my stemmed glass, nervous for what I was about to say. "Term starts soon and I know I mentioned possibly not going, but I'm positive that I'm not returning to Spellcasters. I'm going to try to find one of the books."

The table was silent for a moment, and then suddenly, Eva clapped. "Hell yes! This is what I've been waiting for my whole life. I am so in!" She fist pumped the air.

I chuckled. "Waiting for what? You should go back to Spellcasters, finish your education."

Eva shook her head. "No way, girl! You know that I've never really wanted to be a spy. That was my parents' plan for me. I've wanted to be an archaeologist my *whole* life. Well, since I knew what they were, anyway. Before that I wanted to be a balloon seller, but that's beside the point." Hunter and Alex snorted out laughs, but Eva ignored them and pointed to me. "You're basically going on an archaeological hunt. I'm going with you."

My heart swelled at the idea that I wouldn't be alone, that my best friend would be by my side.

"I'd love that." I turned to the guys. "But neither of you can make the same claims. I've never once heard you say you wanted to be Indiana Jones."

Hunter cleared his throat. "You girls have exceptional powers. Alex has a speciality that he's dedicated to, but I don't have either yet. I need to work a little harder to figure out my purpose." His eyes cut to Eva. "I was planning to finish out my year at the academy. Are you okay with that sugar?"

Eva gave him a small, sad smile. "Of course. A long distance relationship might be coming a little sooner than I'd like, but it was always likely to happen. After graduation, if we entered the PIA, they'd have split us up. At least for a little while, until we built up clout and could request to be stationed together."

"And we don't have to be separated all the time," Alex said. "We hold sway now. Hunter and I will negotiate terms with Headmistress Wake. We'll advocate for more freedom so we can come see you girls whenever you need us." His hand landed on top of mine. "Or if you just *want* to see us."

My heart rate kicked up. He was right. After winning the demon war, Headmistress Wake would probably allow them a greater degree of freedom. While I'd been prepared to go at it alone, it was reassuring that I wouldn't have to be flying solo the whole time.

"It looks like we all have a discussion with the headmistress in our futures," I said. "I have to say, I appreciate all of your support so so *so* much. You guys are the best friends I ever could've asked for."

A smile bloomed on Hunter's face. He wrapped his arm around Eva and then gestured for Alex and me to lean in. We shared an awkward, but sweet over-the-table-hug. When we pulled back, everyone's eyes were shimmering with unshed tears.

We dropped the subject, moving on to discuss more mundane things, like the outfit a hipster across the bar wore. Then what we'd like to see and do before we left Seattle.

All the while my heart was overflowing with happiness. Although this moment might be short and sweet, I would enjoy the hell out of it. Relishing every second with my friends, until we moved on to our next chapters.

# ALICE THE DAGGER EXCERPT

*A curse on my hips!*

I shifted to the right, hoping the dagger on my left hip would slide over the window frame and allow me to shimmy inside with greater ease. I probably should have taken the blasted thing off before trying to shove myself through a tiny window, but you know . . . hindsight and all.

*Why does this have to be the only way into this stupid home?*

The mark, a shifter mafia leader, must have thought no one would come after him while he was on the toilet. And honestly, it was a good assumption.

How many people could scale four stories, and squeeze themselves through a window barely bigger than a chihuahua-sized doggie door?

I was among the few, and I'd only chosen this route because Xavier wanted this job done fast. What that dang vampire wanted, he usually got.

My fingers gripped the windowpane, and I pushed.

Inch by inch I wiggled my way forward, until the next thing I knew, I was flying over the toilet and headed straight for the floor. Thankfully, my hands had remained in front of me. Air flew from them, cushioning my fall so I didn't break my face.

Still, I hadn't acted quickly enough to eliminate *all* the evidence of breaking and entering. The sound of my landing rang through the bathroom, loud and telling.

I leapt up and froze, waiting to see if anyone in the mansion had heard. Shifter ears were particularly sensitive. When no footsteps or voices came closer, I breathed a sigh of relief. I'd gotten lucky.

Taking a moment to readjust my dagger, I caught my reflection in the mirror. My long, white-blonde braid had gone *seriously* astray in my struggle with the window.

I huffed out a breath and deftly fixed it. Even the most despicable marks—and they were all pretty nasty individuals—deserved more respect than being done in by someone who looked like hell.

Once I was presentable, I moved to the door and twisted the knob slowly. Entering the hallway, I scanned left and then right before turning in the direction of the master suite. Quick glances inside every room I passed confirmed that they were empty of people. Actually, they weren't just empty. Most reminded me of staged rooms in a furniture store, cold and un-lived in.

I'd taken a right turn when confirmation that I was closing in on the mark hit my ear. Music, identifiable as a song from the first Godfather movie, trilled through the hallway, punctuated by bursts of male laughter.

*The Godfather, how typical. He's probably taking pointers.*

I rolled my eyes and pulled my dagger from its scabbard, careful to keep the tip away from my skin.

Shifters were formidable foes, their senses unparalleled. They were also strong and could outlast most of their opponents. Especially when the shifter was a 250-pound alpha wolf, and his opponent was a 140-pound demi-fae.

But not even shifters could survive the batrachotoxin my employer purchased from South America for jobs like this one. Still, even with the aid of poison, I had to be silent as the night to succeed.

I called air again, and bid it to create a buffer along my skin, holding in my scent. Only when I was sure that defense was secure did I begin walking, dagger poised in my striking hand.

Once I reached the door to the theater room, I peeked inside.

An exhale left me. The alpha wolf was alone. This job would be much less messy than I'd expected.

I pressed the air buffer as far out as possible, bidding it to muffle my sound as well as my scent. Then, with bated breath, I tiptoed toward the brown leather sectional.

I had the good luck of arriving right in the middle of a scene riddled with gunfire. The sound system was on point, loud and crisp and perfect for covering my tracks. And, unsurprisingly, the alpha wolf was cheering and howling with laughter at every grizzly death.

*Geez, this guy's a disgusting asshole.*

As I got closer, the scent of popcorn, buttery and delicious, filled my nostrils. I approached the couch and was close enough to distinguish the alpha's gray hairs from the brown when the wolf-shifter turned slowly and stared me dead in the eyes.

"You're a little young, aren't you?" He spoke without a trace of fear in his well-lined face.

"I've been around the block a time or two," I replied coolly.

A corner of his lips lifted. "We'll see about that. Get her, boys."

My stomach dropped as the air shimmered with magic and suddenly, two figures appeared at the edges of the couch. Hulking wolf-shifters with pistols aimed straight at me.

I flew into motion, rebounding off the couch and into a roundhouse kick that clocked the closest wolf straight in the temple. As he fell, I swiped him with the dagger before twisting and hurling it at the other attacker. The blade landed on target—between his eyes—and he fell too. I yanked the dagger out of his skull, and was about to burst out of my crouch when the *click* of a gun cocking stopped me.

"Who sent you?" the alpha demanded.

I turned my neck ever so slightly to look at him, and he growled.

"Don't move an inch, faerie. Now, answer me. Who sent you?"

"My boss. I don't know who wants you killed, but they hired us for the job."

I gave him a longer explanation than was necessary. It bought me time to figure out what to do. At this range, he wouldn't miss me if he pulled the trigger.

"You aren't around when he takes the jobs?" the alpha pressed. His need to learn who'd betrayed him was written all over his face.

"No. My boss called me today." I tilted my head to the side as if I was thinking something over, hoping to deflect from my slight repositioning my dagger. "Maybe around five. So whoever wants you dead must have come in before that. It's usually someone close to the mark. Who wasn't around you today?"

His brows furrowed, unable to resist the urge to recall his day.

Knowing that I wouldn't get another chance, I pushed a gust of air at him—straight in his eyes.

The gun went off, but I was already out of the line of fire, ducking and then hurtling over the couch. The alpha opened his eyes milliseconds before my blade sank into the side of his neck.

Blood spurted everywhere, splattering the rich brown leather of the couch, and my clothes. I pressed my lips together. I hated the thought of someone's blood on my clothes.

A heartbeat later, the alpha fell. When he stopped breathing, my shoulders relaxed.

*One more bad guy down.*

Knowing that the alpha was no longer roaming the streets of L.A., doing shady criminal stuff to innocents, made what I had to do a *little* easier.

At least, that's what I told myself so I could look in the mirror.

The door to my apartment whined open.

"I'm home!" I sang out, aware that no one would be there to welcome me. It was just a habit from the days when there had been someone here, someone to love and call mine. And though those days were gone, for some sick reason or another, I still felt comfort in the ritual.

Moving into the kitchen, I laid my scabbard on the counter, pulled a jug of OJ out of the fridge, and drank straight from the carton. After a brief examination of my meager rations, I settled on making mac and cheese with frozen peas tossed in for nutritional value.

Once the water was on the stovetop, I went to change. As soon as I stepped foot into my bedroom, my shoulders lowered and my heart rate slowed.

Despite Xavier's warnings, I liked to keep a window cracked open to feel the fresh air on my face and watch the way my veil-like white curtains fluttered in a breeze. My bed was a massive canopy, also surrounded by gauzy linen. Sheepskin rugs littered the floor, and a teal pod chair, perfect for reading in, sat in the corner.

Unlike the shell I presented to the outer world, which

included an all-black attire and hard attitude, this place was all softness and light and air. I loved it and hoped that when my contract with Xavier was complete, I could bring a bit of this feeling out into the world with me.

I stripped, releasing my wings from the bindings that allowed me to pass as human. I hated wearing the straps, but visiting an aether-blessed fae, the only type of fae with the ability to construct glamours to conceal such features, cost time and *a lot* of money. So much money that organizations like the government and fae academies often had an aether-blessed fae on retainer—but not Xavier Doru. When the vampire did hire one, he thought the money the fae demanded was better spent hiding my pointy ears.

His reasoning was sound. If my wings were rendered invisible, and therefore freed from their bindings, I'd still have to be careful that they didn't hit anyone in crowds. The bindings were more practical than a glamour, even if they were annoying and stifling.

Immediately, my clothes got tossed into the trash. I couldn't wear them again without thinking of the shifters I'd killed.

After a hot shower to rinse the blood off my body, I wrapped myself in a loose, soft robe that gave my diaphanous gold-veined wings a little room to breathe, and padded barefoot to the kitchen.

The water was boiling, so I poured in the noodles. I'd just finished stirring them when a knock came at the door.

My spine straightened, and I dashed to the counter where I'd set down my dagger.

As soon as I unsheathed the cold metal, a chuckle came from the other side of the door. "It's me."

I exhaled in annoyance. Xavier.

I flung the door open to find the ice-blond vampire leaning against the entryway, looking as cool as a cucumber.

"How did you know I was home already?" I asked, unable to shake the idea that despite all our talks of trust and being a family, he'd bugged my place. After all, there was precedent.

Jax, my ex-boyfriend, knew that Xavier had been spying on him, but he'd never done anything about it. Well, nothing except live at my apartment until the day his contract was up, and then skip town without so much as a goodbye.

*Asshole.*

My heart clenched. It still hurt to think about Jax, the one person I'd thought I could trust. He'd been the first guy I'd given myself to and thought I loved. My best friend . . .

But I should have known better. No one wanted this life. Everyone who aged out of their contracts left as soon as they could. Why would Jax be any different?

I should have guarded my heart. Over the years, I'd learned many times that the ones closest to us had the power to hurt us most. And yet, in the face of my first love, I'd forgotten. Like a prize idiot.

"Our client called," Xavier said, ripping from my own misery. "They wanted to thank you for a job well done. I did the math. Your place isn't far so I figured you'd already be home."

I blinked. That was fast. Too fast.

"They already know he's dead? But it's only been—" I glanced at the clock above the stove. "Forty-five minutes since I left."

"The mate was in the next room." Xavier's lips curled up as shock flitted across my face. "I see you didn't realize she was present. You're losing your touch, Queenly."

I rolled my eyes and stirred the noodles again. "Please. I'm the best assassin you have. Just because I didn't check all ten-thousand square feet of that monstrosity doesn't mean I'm losing anything. It means that I was more direct— more lethal—than usual."

Xavier chuckled. "I've always appreciated your inclination to get down to business."

"In that case, why are you here?"

The vampire flopped onto my hard gray couch and planted his feet on the coffee table adorned with various sci-fi romance novels that I was halfway through. "What? We've known each other for so long! We can't be pals? Paint each other's nails?"

Pals? That was a laugh, coming from a vampire who I'd once called Father, only to receive a long lecture about how Xavier was better than both of my parents because he would never leave me—as long as I stayed in line.

Not long after that, the lonely child I'd been had signed away her freedom. My desperation had cost me greatly, and I'd been paying the price ever since.

"I don't do pals, Xavier. You know that."

"I've been meaning to bring that up. It's something you should consider. In the real world, people appreciate being smiled at now and then." He shook his head. "Maybe I should have let you get that cat. It might have softened you up a bit."

My teeth ground together. His refusal to let me buy a kitten was a major sore spot. "This may not be made of silver but I'm sure I can do some damage with it." I picked up my dagger and waved it at him. "Tell me what you want or get out. I've had a long day."

He leaned forward and placed his elbows on his knees. "New job came in, and you've been requested. No details yet, but they'll come in soon enough. Swing by my apartment at eight in the morning. I'll have travel arrangements sorted out by then."

I arched an eyebrow. "But I just finished a job."

Xavier shrugged. "Money is money. Surely you understand?" He gestured to the empty room as if he was trying to make a point that he didn't need to make.

I wasn't yet a legal adult, so I lived in an apartment Xavier rented for me. Each month, I paid him rent. After that sum was gone, I survived on the difference between the money my jobs brought in and what it took to pay back my other debts to the vampire. Debts I had to repay or risk being hunted down by a team of fellow assassins or a vampire clan. I'd seen both groups hired for those who broke their contracts, and they always found their mark. As a result, I understood the value of money well. It bought freedom.

I also understood that Xavier was a cheapskate, and I couldn't wait to age out of my contract. When that day came, and I could legally get an apartment on my own, I'd pay off the last of whatever I owed Doru and walk away. And I'd *never* look back.

I exhaled a long breath. "Why didn't you text me?" The noodles were almost done, and I moved on autopilot, adding the frozen peas for thirty seconds before transferring the mix to a colander then back into the pan. I added an obscene amount of butter, followed by the nuclear orange cheese powder, and stirred.

"I need you at my place early, and you would sleep through a bomb, Queenly. I couldn't risk you missing the text."

*Touché.*

"Fine. I'll be by tomorrow. Now, if you'll excuse me." I began pulverizing the cheese clumps. "I'd like some personal time."

Xavier stood, a shit-eating grin on his face. "Until tomorrow, blondie."

I scowled at the hated nickname, and was about to retort something cutting when the sound of the front door shutting hit my ear.

Looking up from the pan of mac and cheese, I found myself alone yet again.

# ALSO BY ASHLEY MCLEO

## Coven of Shadows and Secrets

Seeker of Secrets

Hunted by Darkness

History of Witches

Marked by Fate

## Spellcasters Spy Academy Series (Magic of Arcana Universe)

A Legacy Witch: Year One

A Marked Witch: Internship

A Rebel Witch: Year Two

A Crucible Witch: Year Three

The Spellcasters Spy Academy Boxset

## The Wonderland Court Series (Magic of Arcana Universe)

Alice the Dagger

Alice the Torch

### Standalone Novels

The Alchemist of Silver Hollow (Magic of Arcana Universe)

### Fanged Fae Series - A Bonegates sister series

Blood Moon Magic

Faerie Blood

### The Bonegate Series - A Fanged Fae sister series

Hawk Witch

Assassin Witch

Traitor Witch

Illuminator Witch

**The Royal Quest Series**

Dragon Prince

Dragon Magic

Dragon Mate

Dragon Betrayal

Dragon Crown

Dragon War

**The Starseed Universe**

Prophecy of Three

Souls of Three

Rising of Three

The Starseed Universe (five-book boxset)

Ashley lives in the lush and green Pacific Northwest with her husband, Kurt and their dog, Flicka.

When she's not writing she enjoys traveling the world, reading, practicing or teaching yoga, kicking butt at board games (she recommends Splendor and Dominion), and connecting with family and friends.

For most direct access to Ashley sign up for her reader group, The Coven, at ashleymcleo.com. You can also find Ashley in her Facebook group.

# ACKNOWLEDGMENTS

Thank you to my husband for being so very patient during the writing of this book, and assisting me in every way that you could. You're a freaking saint (like seriously, halo and everything).

Special thanks to my editor, Jen McDonnell for helping me whip this baby into shape. I love working with you.

Strangely, I'd like to thank 2020. It was a rough year, but not without blessings. My quiet time has increased this year, which has given me time to focus on what's really important. For that, I'm thankful. And finally, thank you to all my readers. Without you, I couldn't do what I love.

All the magic,

Ashley